THE BLUE PILLOW CASE

Roger Lawrence Quay

ONE IRON PRESS
Jacksonville, Florida

Publisher's note:
This book is a work of fiction. Names, characters, places, and incidents are the product of the author's imagination or are used fictitiously. Any resemblance to actual events, locales, or persons, living or dead, is coincidental.

Book and cover design by Sagaponack Books & Design
Illustrations by Hannah Amidon

ISBNs
978-1-7355640-0-5 (softcover)
978-1-7355640-1-2 (hardcover)
978-1-7355640-2-9 (e-book)

Library of Congress Catalog Number: 2021906025

Summary: Dylan, a confused and curious teen, transports to a parallel universe—determined to find his missing grandmother and return home with her.

YAF019010 YA Fiction / Fantasy / Contemporary
YAF001020 YA Fiction / Action & Adventure / Survival Stories
YAF038000 YA Fiction / Magical Realism
YAF027000 YA Fiction / Humorous

One Iron Press
Jacksonville, FL

Printed and bound in USA
First Edition

ACKNOWLEDGMENTS

First, I owe a debt of gratitude to Clifford Martin. Although he is no longer with us, I can still hear him saying, "Keep writing!"

I cannot express enough thanks to my dedicated and overworked editor, Deborrah Hoag, and I was lucky to have found Hannah Amidon, a talented and accomplished artist, for her whimsically appropriate illustrations. Hats off to Ann Pace Sutton, for her persistent and creative copywriting flair, and to Frances Keiser for her excellent publishing guidance. My sincere appreciation to numerous friends and family for their enthusiastic support.

Most of all, my deepest appreciation goes to my wife, Carol, whose boundless encouragement and patience made my vision a reality

Contents

If we find ourselves with a desire that nothing in this world can satisfy, the most probable explanation is that we were made for another world.

—C.S. Lewis

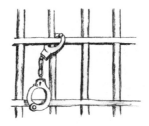

Chapter 1

PRISON

Today I promised Mom that I would not get into any additional trouble for the entire day, not that I usually do, but today her dad, my grandpa, was being released from prison and she did not need any additional stress in her life, least of all from me. Not that I'm a bad kid, but being a fifteen-year-old, almost sixteen, and living near the beach in Key West, Florida, it's kind of hard not to find trouble. It's usually fun and games—no major crimes that ring a bell.

My name is Dylan Michael Cabrella, and my story should intrigue anyone willing to listen. Mom never worries about my little sister, Chloe. She's ten years old. She has always been a goody two-shoes, and she is a clone of our mother. Her nickname is "CC," Cloned Chloe. She is always shadowing Mom at work or home. Just about anywhere Mom is, Chloe is nearby. She doesn't like school because she misses time with Mom at work. Oh, by the way, my mom, Isabella, is an animal and marine biologist veterinarian. She has so many designations behind her name, I'll try to name a few. She's a member of WAVMA (World Aquatic Veterinary Medical Association), ARAV (Association of Reptilian and Amphibian Veterinaries), AVMA (American Veterinary Medical Association), AAV (Association of Avian Veterinaries), and VECCS (Veterinary Emergency and Critical Care Society). If that's not enough, I have more. So, as you can see, she's very accomplished and well respected in her field. Supposedly the best in the country. What do I know? She's just Mom to me. I left out that she's also a martial arts expert.

I have another sister, but she's older. Her name is Alessandra, nickname "Alex," and I think she's twenty-one. She is a novel all by herself. She is in college, located in Missouri, studying criminology and rarely comes back home to visit since the devastation brought on by our grandpa's adventure. According to her, he had caused her emotional stress, meaning little dating while in high school.

She is a red belt master Kung Fu martial arts expert freak. Whatever the highest-ranking color belt there is, that's what she is. I am not sure, but I do know not to mess with her. Needless to say, many of her dates ended up in casts or with bloody noses, especially the ones that mentioned Grandpa.

Alessandra left her freshman year of college to practice martial arts. She studied with some Kung Fu expert for about a year, lived in Hong Kong, and after a year, returned back to college. I guess she couldn't handle the BS from students harassing her about Grandpa. She is very talented. She started fighting in the boy's division until they rewrote the handbook which said, women were no longer allowed to compete.

Mom has one brother, my Uncle Tony. He's fun, but we never get to see him since he is always on some type of archeological hunt or something like that. He's like a modern-day Indiana Jones-type. Most of my immediate friends have stopped harassing me about my grandpa, but plenty of the other kids still enjoy picking on me. Not many kids I know have a convicted felon as a member of their family. I may have left out the minor detail that Grandpa possibly murdered my Grandmother, though I am pretty sure he's completely innocent. Sure, he's innocent. He can't explain rationally where the body is, how she died or disappeared, and where she may have wandered off to, but we all believe him—at least most of us in the family do. He often told us she was in another dimension just waiting to return when the time was right.

Sounds like aliens to me.

She was not the wandering-off type, even though Mom's stories say differently. I never met Grandmother since she disappeared right after I was born, which is about sixteen years. But I have heard a multitude of stories, about Grandpa and Grandmother. Grandpa got twenty years, which is better than life, and his sentence got reduced due to good behavior, plus they never did find Grandmother's body. Today he is a free man.

So, this morning, I decided to be good. You have to make a conscious commitment and tell yourself to be good because before you know it, you and your friends are in trouble. And I need to stay grounded-free with the big end of school semester party coming up. It's my big chance to get a date with Violet.

I love and hate school. It is one of my many escapes. The only reason I love it is because of Violet. She is the most beautiful girl on the planet and probably on all the planets. The bonus is I sit behind her in a few classes. I am trying to get up enough nerve to ask her out on a date. That, my friend, has been a struggle. Other than that, my life sucks. I am the middle child between two sisters, and not one brother. All I wanted was one brother, but no—I have two sisters.

"Good morning, kids. Did you all sleep okay?" Mom asks.

I growled a few times.

Chloe burst out, "I can't wait to see Grandpa. I like all the funny stories, he would tell me, when we would visit him."

I continued to growl.

"Do not forget," Mom says as she stares right at me, "be at the house by two p.m. sharp. It's a long drive, and I want to be on the road before rush hour."

"Dylan, do you want more pancakes?"

I growled again, and wolfed down a few more plus a mound of bacon.

"Dylan, did you hear me? I need you home by two p.m. today, so no dawdling. Come straight home after school," Mom added.

"I know, Mom. You told me five thousand times."

"Okay, finish up. The bus will be here any minute. Chloe, do not forget to brush."

"Jonny is taking me to school today." I remark.

"Oh, hell no. When did he get his license? I don't think you should be riding with him. He's probably a bad driver and is always finding ways for mischievous activities," Mom remarks.

Chloe screamed, "Mom, you said hell!"

I growled again and left the table.

Well, one thing is for sure—Jonny is always getting into trouble. But we grew up together and have been friends for years. His dad is a big-time lawyer in town. My mom calls him an ambulance chaser. I have never seen his dad chasing any ambulances, but mom says, 'it's just a saying'. They live in a giant mansion with a huge swimming pool and a lap pool. It is awesome, and his folks are always going out. Since I am on the swim team, practicing at his house is very convenient.

We have a nice pool, but now Mom uses it for work. It's full of sea critters. Not that we are poor. We live in nice house, but I think most of Mom's money goes to the animals. Mom runs a veterinarian clinic in town and at home. She is always taking in any stray animal, large or small. She especially loves the sea animals. We all learned how to scuba dive at an early age. Most of my life I was in the water either swimming or scuba diving.

Mom and Dad split up a long time ago. Mom said Dad never grew up and was always looking for new candy. Now, I know what that meant and figured if Mom said it, I'd let it be. It seems Alex had caught Dad in our pool, skinny-dipping with a young lady. Alex kicked Dad in the head. She was thirteen at the time. That was that, and Dad was tossed out. Mom was so upset, she had our name changed after their divorce. It was hyphenated to Cabrella-Bland, and she took the hyphen out. I guess she didn't like the name Bland anymore. We never see my dad's parents. My grandmother is missing, my grandpa just got released from prison, and my dad's folks despise Mom.

Mom always keeps in good shape. She works out daily, does yoga, pilates, runs, plus we have our own gym. She is one sexy lady, even if she is my mom. She has many trophies, plenty of awards in martial arts, saber, and epee, which are all fencing styles. We have one room dedicated to everyone's trophies and awards.

Yes, I have contributed a few swim and archery awards. But the majority of the trophies in the room are Mom's and Alex's.

Dad still lives in the area, and he is also my swim coach, but they never got back together, so Mom basically raised us. So, let's see, we lost Dad, then Grandpa, then Grandmother. We always seem to be losing someone, but today we get one back.

We're driving to Homestead, Florida to pick up Grandpa and bring him back home. He had been transferred to the Homestead Correctional Institution, which was approximately three hours from home. Mom has been keeping his house cleaned and ready just in case he would get let out early. Well, it happened, so this should be interesting. If I remember correctly, Grandpa had some strange habits and his stories were quite peculiar. But I did enjoy his tales, all of which he claims are real. Let's just say if they are real, there should be some fascinating times ahead.

School was quite a bore today, but summer is coming, so all I can think about is the end of the year party bash, plus our family summer vacation. Mom has made plans to take us to the Cayman Islands. Rumor has it that Alex will be joining us this year. I'll believe that when I see it.

I arrived home at one fifty-nine p.m. with Mom and Chloe looking at me as if I was late. I knew Mom was wound up, so I wasn't about to mention the fact that I was one minute early. I let it be as we all jumped in the car. Of course, Chloe wanted to bring Brandi—she's our big old black Lab. Brandi is getting so old she can barely walk, but Mom says she is in no pain and wants to keep on living. She always talks to the animals as if they understand. I guess Mom is also a dog whisperer.

But Mom wouldn't allow Brandi on this trip. She still loves the car rides and will hang her head out the window for the entire trip while drooling and slobbering on every car that passes. Most of it comes back into the car mainly on the back seat, which is where I will sit.

"How was school today, kids?" Mom asks.

Chloe blurts out, "We learned about insects today, Mom. I wanted to dissect a small lizard, but all the other kids starting screaming, so maybe next week."

Mom always reminds us that when she was young, she was constantly dissecting things. At four, she stabbed her first lizard and loved every minute of it. Grandpa said Isabella knew what she wanted to be the day she was born. Always dissecting and taking temperatures of every pet in town. Guess who is following in Mom's footsteps? Miss Goody Two-Shoes, alias CC, Cloned Chloe. I almost puked the last time I took my temperature since Chloe forgets to clean the thermometer after testing every animal on our block. Whatever, it's like living in a real animal house but with real animals. Everyone in town knows Mom, and whenever any animal large or small is ill or lost, they call her. She is busy twenty-four seven.

"Now remember, kids, what I told you about Grandpa. I don't want anyone to mention Grandma. It's best if we just welcome Dad home and help him get acclimated back to the real world. It will not be easy for anyone, so please be a little forgiving at the beginning. And please, please be nice, Dylan," Mom stares at me again.

"What did I do?"

"Nothing yet."

"What about Chloe? She's the devil in disguise."

Chloe screamed, "Dylan said devil!"

"Whatever," I exclaim. Cuss in front of Chloe and she will call you out. Whoever you are, young, old doesn't matter. She will call you out.

I am always tired throughout the day so I walk through school in a daze. My schedule is full. I go to school and swim after for one to two hours, that's if we don't have a swim meet. Then I joined the archery club, that became my second favorite sport. I have medals for both archery and swimming. Now you know why I'm not a straight-A student. I don't have time to study.

I pleaded with Mom to let me drive for a while.

"I have my learner's permit."

"Not with Chloe in the car," was her answer.

"Oh, you mean the devil."

Chloe screams again, "Dylan said devil!"

As soon as I closed my eyes, I was asleep for the rest of the ride.

**

This water is perfectly clear. I wonder how much air is left in my tank. How long have I been down here? I usually know that information, but no harm, I can still see the surface. I must not be too deep. Even if the air runs out, I can just slowly swim to the surface. I cannot believe how clear the water is. Where are we again? Why am I so puzzled? I am way too young to be losing my memory. Wow, a huge seahorse just swam by. Holy cow! I've never seen a seahorse that large. I follow the seahorse. You can't miss it. It's giant—must be over nine feet tall. I wonder if I could ride this puppy. I'll try to catch it if I can. Come on, where is everybody? Oh well, I am not missing this for those losers. Where is everybody? Where's my underwater camera? I need a picture of this.

Was that a scorpion fish? Never seen one that large in these waters. Where did that seahorse go? What was that? A giant shadow just swam above me. Must have been a big ship for it to be that large. I can see for miles in this water, unbelievably clear. Never seen it this clear before, and of course no one else around to share this beautiful scenery. Maybe they went back up for lunch, but I'm not hungry. I need to find that seahorse.

There is a plethora of sea life right before my eyes. Almost every exotic fish I can name is in full view. There are flame angels, golden puffers, clown triggers, starfish, hog fish, sting rays, barracudas, coral everywhere, anemone, and many more. I could not remember their names, but it was beautiful. Where's my camera? I always bring my camera. Not only is it the most beautiful array of fish life, but they all look ten times larger than normal. I may have found an undiscovered reef. I have never seen or read anything like this before.

Where are Mom and Chloe? My goodness, can't they miss one meal? Wait until I tell them about the phenomenon they missed. I may not tell them. I might just keep it my secret place since they would never believe me anyway. Where is that darn seahorse? Do I have enough air in my tanks? They feel so light it's as if I didn't need the air tanks. I was just swimming on my own. How long can I hold my breath? Probably not a good time to test my limitations. I think I've got about twenty minutes left. My gauge still shows full, but I've been down for quite a while now.

What am I worrying about if my tank is running low? Mom would come get me or I could just swim to the surface. Holy cow, there is the giant seahorse again. It looks as if it is just floating, and did it just nod at me? I must be losing my mind—still, I nodded back. It looks like it motioned for me to hop on its back. I must be seeing things. Is my mask fogged or what? I am losing it big time. Did that seahorse just ask me if I wanted a ride? Did a trigger fish just say hello?

Okay, that's it. I must be running out of air and getting delirious. Mom's going to think I've been smoking marijuana or something. I tried cigarettes once, but I felt nauseous and then I puked. I must be allergic, so I decided that cigarettes aren't for me. Probably shouldn't smoke anyway being a swimmer and all, and anyway Mom would kill me. She is Miss Health Nut. Of course, Chloe would tell on me in less than a second or quicker, that Miss Goody-Two shoes. Where are those two? There is no way I can explain talking fish, so this story is going nowhere fast.

That's it, I'm getting on that seahorse. It bowed in front of me at least three times, so here goes. How many people have ridden a seahorse? Not sure. I'll have to research that. Probably not many, but what have I got to lose? It seems friendly enough. How mean can a seahorse be? I am such a baby, scared of my own shadow. Get on the thing before it changes its mind.

Well, it didn't move so I got on. Slowly at first, then it turned to me and said, "Hold onto my neck and kick my side when you're ready to go." Sure thing, I thought. No reason to answer out loud since I am positively sure I've already lost my mind.

I kicked and it bucked like the wind. Took off like a rocket through the water so fast that I almost lost my face mask. I'm flying at such a fast pace I can hardly see anything, but it finally slowed down after I kept kicking and kicking its side until it eventually came to a complete stop.

Holy Toledo, that was fantastic! Scary and fun all at the same time. Just like the roller coaster but much wilder since I was under water, which reminded me to look at my air tank meter. As I reached to read the meter, my body suddenly stopped in shock. There was no tank. What is going on? How in the world am I breathing? But that's soon the least of my concerns as I turn around and hear the seahorse snickering. I'm looking into this giant mouth, of some monstrous fish, filled with razor sharp teeth. Whale sharks are not known to be in these waters. It seems to be grinning as if I am dinner. The seahorse bucked and threw me right into the giant fish's mouth. I started screaming—

**

"Okay kids, you ready? Dylan, are you awake? You were screaming. We're almost there and I want to stop and hit the restroom. I certainly don't want to use the facilities at the prison." Mom remarks.

"What, where are we? What happened? Where's the seahorse?"

"I don't know, dear. You must have been daydreaming. You were jumping around a little, plus screaming, and I thought it best if you got some rest before Grandpa comes home. Are you okay, son? You look like you just saw a ghost," Mom comments.

I've always daydreamed, but my dreams are getting more frequent and they feel so realistic.

"He always looks like that, Mom," Chloe remarks.

"I'm stopping for some gas, and you guys should use the restroom here. Not sure which is cleaner, the gas station or prison, so go now. Only one piece of candy and a drink for each of you. Here's a ten, you guys split it." Mom hands me the money.

"Don't give Dylan the money. He won't share with me," Chloe blurts.

"Okay Chloe, come with me to the restroom. I don't want you in there by yourself. See you inside, Dylan."

"Oh, it's okay if someone attacks me in the bathroom. Sure, I know who your favorite is."

"Not now, Dylan. See you inside. You want to come with us into the ladies room?" Mom grins.

Once inside the mens' room, I watched the water come out of the faucet before splashing some on my face. Not sure if I wanted to get wet anytime soon.

"You want some Nerds or Sour Skittles?" Chloe asks.

"I feel like Cheetos and a Red Bull. Should we get some Budweiser for Grandpa?" I ask. "I could have a few with him."

"Real funny. You better not be drinking any beer. You can have some in about six years," Mom replies.

"Great, if I live that long."

"We don't need any beer. I have his favorite Scotch at home. I'm sure Dad will be hungry, so we will stop off for dinner once we get on the road. Tomorrow he will probably want a home-cooked meal," Mom remarks.

"I'm going to buy Grandpa some candy," Chloe screeched.

"Okay, let's get going. We need to be there before six."

I was afraid to close my eyes again since I didn't want to start another dream or nightmare to see where I left off the last time. I kept my eyes wide open and gulped down my Red Bull. As I slug the Red Bull, Mom just rolls her eyes.

"Not sure why kids your age need Red Bull or its equivalent."

Mom's GPS, Valentino, said: *"Giri prego a destra 500 yarde* (turn right 500 yards)."

Well, it was no surprise that Mom changed the GPS system to speak Italian. I think Mom named her GPS system Valentino after her future lover.

Chloe screams, "I see the sign, Mom!"

**

HOMESTEAD CORRECTIONAL INSTITUTE.
PREPARE TO STOP.
ALL VEHICLES SUBJECT TO SEARCH

**

"Siete arrivato alla vostra destinazione finale,ciao bella (you have arrived at your final destination, beautiful)."

"We should have brought a machine gun and busted him out years ago."

"Don't start, young man. Just do what they say and let's get Grandpa out with the correct procedure. No need to have both my men in prison," Mom quips.

As we roll up to the gate, an armed guard comes outside the guard house and asks, "What are you doing in a place like this?" I guess it was a joke, but Mom just said, "We are here to pick up—."

"Grandpa!'" screeches Chloe.

"Sorry, Mr. Vincenzo Cabrella, my father, is supposed to be released today."

"Let's see, oh here it is. You're correct, today at six p.m. Not sure if his paperwork is ready. Wait here. And if you would, I need everyone to depart the vehicle and stand over by the painted box."

Two additional men and one large German Shepherd suddenly appeared from the guard house. This dog looked like it was going to eat something or someone. I slowly moved closer to Mom. Chloe wanted to pet it.

"This is Ginger. Don't let her name fool you. She does not like to be touched, so give her some space and do not try to pet her."

The guards start opening car doors and letting this huge German Shepherd, Ginger, sniff and sniff inside and out.

"She better not eat my Cheetos," I tell Mom.

"Shush," Mom says. "Be quiet."

They finally finished searching the car for whatever.

The guard says, "You have passed our vehicle inspection. You may get back in and head straight down the driveway."

Then out of nowhere, Ginger breaks away from her trainer's leash and runs straight towards Mom.

Now the guards are going crazy since the dog never allows anyone to pet or touch her or anything else for that matter, other than her trainer. And even when he pets her, he's a bit hesitant.

I thought we were dead, and I closed my eyes since she looked hungry, mean, and as if we were soon to be her dinner. Chloe and Mom didn't budge as this huge dog jumped up and was much taller than Mom, and started to lick her face. I told you that my mom was loved by every animal, big and small.

The guards were taken aback but Mom just said, "It's okay. I work with animals every day, and they know when someone is looking out for their best interest."

The guard yelled out, "Ginger get back here, *NOW.*"

As Ginger turned, she growled at the first guard and ran back to her trainer. Not sure what her trainer was saying to her, but it wasn't very nice.

Mom turned to the first guard whose mouth was open wide and said, "She's such a nice sweet puppy."

"Whatever," he said, "I've seen her tear apart a——"

"Okay, you can enter now. Drive to the second gate, give them this pass, and they will direct you where to park. Good evening, ma'am." As the guard mumbles "witch" under his breath.

"Well, that was easy enough. Let's see what's next," Mom remarks smiling.

I was still shaking.

Then Chloe says, "Ginger was so sweet. We need another pet."

I replied, "Like a hole in the head."

"Not now, kids. Let's stay focused and get out of here with Grandpa."

The second gate was no easier than the first. This clown reminded me of Barney Fife. A real Jonnie by-the-book. He came out of the guard house and had one hand on his pistol. Looking back and forth expecting danger, I guess.

"Okay ma'am, let's see. You're here to see Vincenzo Cabrella. Not sure if he's been officially released. I will call the warden's office and get the details. I know the warden personally. We chat a lot, have coffee, hang out—I will be promoted any day. Just waiting for my promotion. Been doing this for the experience, I want to learn all the ins and outs of the prison system."

"Dammit Wally, open the gate and let her through."

"Yep all set, ma'am. You're all set. Ready to go. Now go straight ahead and park up on the right. Says 'visitors parking.' Good day, ma'am."

"Mom, are you sure they're going to let us back out of this place? I'm ready to go already. This place always gives me the creeps. Hope Grandpa hasn't freaked out and goes crazy at our house."

"Dylan, I told you to keep your comments to yourself. Dad is fine and we will be out of here very soon."

"How you doing, Chloe?"

"I'm fine, Mom. Let's get Grandpa."

"Hello, Ms. Cabrella."

"It's Doctor, if you must know," Mom informs guard.

"Sorry, Miss. I mean Doctor. Let me see your paperwork, please."

As the guard looks over the papers, I hear this loud buzzer as a gate opens and we walk through. Then the gate closes behind us. Oh crap, we're in for sure now. Chloe grabbed onto Mom as we proceeded further down the hall.

Then I say in a whisper, "Is this like the airport and you can't say bomb?"

Now Mom was a little tense herself, and if I get the one-more-time look, I'm dead. So that was all I said since being punished now would be a disaster with the big party coming up. She puts you in lockdown, kind of like this prison. No TV, no computer, no cell phone. It's just like death—no probably worse than death.

They put us in a glass cage, and we wait. Chloe was sitting on Mom's lap. I was on the other side of the room acting tough but slowly moving towards Mom, just in case. Then out of nowhere, a siren went off. It was so loud I almost jumped on top of Chloe. Chloe looked as if someone stabbed her with a knife. But when the siren stopped, I look up and there was Grandpa. Grinning like there was no tomorrow. Chloe ran into his arms and gave him a big kiss. Mom started to cry, and I held out my hand to shake. He put Chloe down and then hugged Mom and me.

"Well, let's blow this joint," Grandpa said.

Grandpa, always a kidder, turns to the guard and says, "Paul, I'm ready to get out of this rat hole, push the buzzer and open the gates."

That was all it took—a buzzer and siren rang and then the door opened, and out we went.

Grandpa was saying goodbye to all the guards and wishing them well, saying he hopes he never sees their lowly asses again. Mom didn't say a word, nor did Chloe scream when he said ass. All we wanted to do was get out of there, quickly.

As we approached the final gate, the guards did a minor inspection and that was all she wrote. Mom drove like a race car driver out of the entrance, and we never looked back. I wish I could say that we'll never see another prison again, but I may be getting ahead of myself.

"Well, that sure was a fun place. Too bad they kicked me out. I was just getting used to the luxury lodgings. If I don't eat some homemade pasta in the next twenty-four hours, I cannot account for my actions," Grandpa announces.

"*Ciao, giri a sinistra in 500 yarde* (turn left in 500 yards)."

"What in the world was that?" Grandpa asks. "My God, how long have I been locked up? We're no longer speaking English. Hell, I thought we'd be speaking Spanish before Italian."

And we all laughed out loud.

Chloe screams, "Grandpa said hell!"

Times will be a changing.

I have never seen Mom so happy, crying tears of joy. Grandpa reached over and kissed his daughter's face. This prompted more tears, and Mom almost ran off the road. Not sure how she could see out the window, but soon the tears stopped.

"I'm hungry, how about you Grandpa?" I asked.

"You kidding? I could eat this leather seat if you had any ketchup."

Chloe said, "How about McDonalds's, Grandpa?"

"Sure, whatever you like, sweetie," Grandpa replies.

"Now Dad, I am not going to feed you that crap your first night out. Let's try a steakhouse. I think there's an Outback Steakhouse nearby. I'm going to make you some homemade pasta and meatballs this weekend," Mom remarks.

We pulled in and got lucky. It's usually a long wait, but a table opened up since we were much later than the usual early crowd. We missed the four p.m. Florida blue-haired crowd. Everyone eats early in Florida. Not sure why.

Not much was said at dinner. It was getting crowded and noisy, so we all just ate and didn't have a lot to say. Grandpa was looking tired after he had a scotch and water. We finished and headed home. Grandpa slept the rest of the trip. We get home around midnight and Chloe was sound asleep. I picked her up and carried her per Mom's request. Grandpa wanted to carry her, but he looked weak, and I wasn't sure he could lift more than five pounds just now.

After we all got settled in, I went in to see how Grandpa was doing. Mom was with him and they were talking about something. I couldn't hear for sure, so I just stopped by the door and listened as best I could. Until Brandi gave me up. She was at Mom's door, whining.

"Dad, this is not the time to talk about it. Get some sleep and we will talk more later. I will get Liz. You're too weak. We don't even know .... Yes, is that you Dylan? Do you need something?" Mom asks.

"Oh, hi guys, just came in to say goodnight."

"Hey sport, are you still swimming? I'd like to see one of your swim meets," Grandpa comments.

"Okay great, night all."

"Come here and kiss your mother."

"Oh Mom, why do I always have to kiss you?"

"Because I say so."

I was little hesitant to fall asleep, but I was out as soon as my head hit the pillow. Didn't think about my seahorse dream, but what was Mom talking about, going to get Grandmother Liz? Why don't we all go get her? Where is she? Why the big secret? Why didn't she get her before Grandpa went to prison? I must be hearing things.

Chapter 2

DETENTION

"Good morning," I said, bright and cheery. Grandpa was already up and drinking coffee.

"May I take anyone to school today?" Grandpa asks.

Of course, I heard a screech from Chloe in the affirmative.

"Now Dad, when was the last time you drove a car, and are you still licensed? I need you around today to get organized, and the kids can take the bus as usual. Sorry kids, overruled," Mom announces.

"Maybe next time after I crash a few cars down at the motor vehicle department, I'll be legal again," Grandpa laughs.

"Kids, I've got to run, so Dad will you make sure they finish breakfast and get on their buses? And please, without any issues."

Chloe exclaims, "I want to go with you!"

"Not this time, I'll be back soon," Mom smiles.

"Love you all," as she kisses Dad and Chloe and tries to get one on me before I ducked.

"Paybacks are hell," she whispered to me. Luckily Chloe didn't hear her say hell.

Jonny had planned to pick me up this morning and since Mom was gone, Grandpa wouldn't care. So, I kind of left that out of the equation before Mom left the house.

"Hurry up, Chloe. The bus will be here any minute."

"Okay, bye, Grandpa. Will you play with me when I get home?" Chloe asks.

"Sure kiddo, whatever thy princess wants thy princess shall get," Grandpa replies.

Giggling, Chloe runs out to catch the bus.

"How about you, sport? What time is your bus arriving? What happened to your bike?"

"Oh, I've upgraded to a new Fuji, but today Jonny's coming to pick me up. I have a swim meet after school, so it's much easier on my muscles if I catch a ride."

"Sounds like a load of crap to me, sport. Why not ride your Fuji and get the muscles warmed up?"

"Not today. Bye, Grandpa."

"Have fun. Maybe I'll come by the swim meet."

"Oh suuure, great."

I think to myself, I'm sure my friends and neighbors will be so pleased to see that the convict is back in town—start locking the doors again.

"Hey dude, did you get Gramps? Is anyone missing? Did you check your fingers and toes?" Jonny wisecracks.

"Real funny, crackhead. I told you not to mention it anymore."

"Alright, calm down. I'm just kidding."

"Let's get going before I miss first class. You know who sits right in front of me, and today, I'm going to ask her to the big party."

"Are you nuts? Conan the Barbarian, her boyfriend, will crush you," Jonny remarks.

"They broke up!" I exclaim.

"They never really break up, man. You're going to die. Don't do it. Wait until Conan croaks, or moves to another country."

"Mark is still having the school blow-out party, right?" I ask.

"It's going to be rave, dude. Mom and Dad are leaving Thursday morning and will not be back until Sunday. They asked Uncle Charlie to watch over things. He'll probably buy the booze. Let the games begin," Jonny smiles.

"Maybe I'll wait until after lunch to ask her."

"You're crazy. Ask no one and find the girls that are passed out."

"You're sick, dude."

"No way, it's safer that way. You'll be dead by lunch if you ask Violet. Hey, I got it—violence before Violet."

"You're brilliant, Jonny."

"That's me, brilliant and lovable."

"You forgot a mentally challenged moron."

"I'm still trying to figure out how to stay over at your place the party weekend. Mom will be hovering around the house now that Grandpa's back home."

"You haven't asked yet? What are you waiting for, man? Oh crap, you're going to blow it."

"I'll ask tonight. She's been really distraught lately and the time hasn't been right. We're supposed to move Grandpa back to his house this weekend, I think."

"Dude, I think you ran every light in town. Later, I've got to get to class its almost—"

Briiiinnnnggggg.

"Crap, the bell. Later"

"Glad you decided to join us, Mr. Cabrella."

As I look around, I see no Violet, though I sit right behind her in this class. *Oh no, not today.*

"Take your seat, please."

"Now, Ms. Taylor, would you take roll."

"Yes, Ms. Bleeker."

"Akins, Belmont, Bowden, Dance, Davidson, Edg—"

I started to tune her out. She is such a teacher's pet. Where in world is Violet? She's never sick. Probably an early vacation. Maybe she moved out of town. Heard about my Grandpa's return, and packed up and moved. Sure, genius, they packed and moved within twenty-four hours after hearing about Gramp's return to the Island. Get realistic, she's running late. Well, she's never, ever been late. No, something's happened and I know it. Oh no, she eloped with Conan and they are on their honeymoon. Probably in the Canary Islands getting a golden tan.

"Mr. Cabrella, would like to participate with the rest of the class and start reading where Ms. Bowden stopped."

"Yes ma'am. What page was that again? I was taking notes and the page turned."

"Notes, sure Mr. Cabrella. Page nine six, second paragraph."

I start: "In the tenth year of the Trojan War, the Greeks tricked the enemy into bringing a colossal wooden horse within the walls of Troy. The Trojans had no idea that Greek soldiers were hidden inside, under the command of Odysseus. That night they emerged and opened the city gates to the Greek army. Troy was destroyed. Now it was time for Odysseus and the other Greeks to return to their kingdoms across the sea. Here begins the tale of the Odyssey, as sung by the blind minstrel Homer."

"I'm sure everyone read chapters ten and eleven last night, so here's a pop quiz. Ms. Taylor, would you hand these out, please? You have until the next bell to finish. We will discuss the answers to the test tomorrow."

Are you kidding me? A test? I didn't open a book last night. And it's not like I have a lot of friends in this class since it's Greek mythology, and I only took it because of Violet. Who by the way is not here!

I whispered, "Mark, can I copy off you? I didn't study last night."

"Quiet back there. Heads down and forward."

I'm dead. Oh well.

First question: Which armies fought in the Trojan War and how long did it last?

Hah, Trojans, named after rubbers. Better not write that. And Greeks, ten years.

Second question: Describe the Bronze Age.

Bronze, the color of Violet's skin. It's definitely natural and not the spray type. I've seen some orange-looking spray paint on some folks. Looks like crap, but not Violet. Hers is just right, all natural.

Then I did the worst thing possible. I nodded off.

**

"Hey babe, can I rub anymore lotion on your back? It's getting red."

"Not yet. I'm going for a swim and I'm burning up."

"I'll race you to the bottom."

We both turn and run to the side of the boat and jump off into the clear, blue water.

Now this is a real vacation, swimming in the Caribbean with the prettiest girl in town. As we swim towards the bottom, she stops and points at what looks like a wrecked ship with a ton of fish swimming in and about the sunken ship. Cool stuff. We both head back up towards our boat.

"Hey, let's get our scuba gear on and check it out."

"Great idea—last one on the sunken ship pays for dinner."

One by one, we roll backward off the stern into clear eighty-four-degree water, and then we let the air out of our vests and gently sink downward to the reef. Next thing I know we're heading for the shipwreck. What a display of colors. As if a rainbow was floating around the ship.

Wow, this is awesome stuff and I'm seeing all this with my girlfriend. Must have been a nice-size deck about a hundred foot or so. Not a big cruise liner or anything, but it makes a great reef for the fish and a great diving experience with all those colors swimming around.

My goodness, mandarinfish, flowerhorn, discus, clown triggerfish, rainbow parrotfish, and cichlid are the ones I see that I can name.

In one direction the reef trails away into a sandy bottom where the shipwreck starts, and in the other it becomes a wall and the sea a deeper, darker blue.

I swim around the shipwreck looking for a name but cannot make out the letters, only a few numbers. Must have been down here a while. I climb onto the starboard quarter and take a look at what was the helm. Must have been a beauty at one time. I make my way down to the salon. Would have looked nice in its day. Getting a little dark down here, so I turn on my flashlight and it beams onto the galley. A very large grouper glides slowly by me and says, "How's it hanging?" I answered, "great, just great," then continue into the main stateroom, where I stop and stare. What is that? Then as I turn the flashlight directly on a cot, I see a human figure lying down fast asleep. It's Grandmother lying there.

And as I approach, she opens her eyes and says, "Hurry!"

**

Brrrinnngggg, the bell rings and I muffle a scream. Then I see wet spots (drool) all over my test as others pass me and say, "Never tried to take a test while sleeping. Let me know how it works out for you."

Oh crap.

"Mr. Cabrella I cannot wait to grade your paper. I could probably do it from here. Next time I'm writing you up for detention. The only reason I am not today is because your mother has informed the entire staff about a certain situation that may be on your mind. So, you get a free pass this time. Good morning, and try to stay alert or you will be held back for summer school."

"Thank you, Ms. Bleeker."

"Hey guys. What's up D-Dog?" asks Tommy.

"Oh nothing, I just fell asleep during my Greek quiz."

"That's cool, dude. I try to but my teachers won't let me take a snooze."

"Where's Jonny?" I ask.

"Oh, the great actor of the twenty-first century is in the infirmary getting an early start for his debut performance on Friday."

If he only thought in class as much as he thinks about skipping classes, he'd be a multibillionaire in no time. Not sure why he wants to take Friday off.

"Great, I've got to run to calc. Later."

"Hey D, what's up?"

"Nothing, I hope we don't have any more pop quizzes. Who gives pop quizzes one week before school ends?"

"No way, dude. Mr. Calloway is out sick; we got a sub."

"You mean there are others that study calculus on purpose? Man, that sub looks like Hulk Hogan. I am not messing with that."

It's pretty calm morning up until lunch. My life is so boring. I can't wait to grow up and get out of this place. I hate this place. Why is school so boring? I thought I would be much more popular by now. How am I supposed to ask Violet out on a date if I can't find her? The one and only good thing was that lunch was eatable today.

Tommy announces that he told his folks, his entire class was going on a late camping trip.

"They are so lame. I think they believed me. I guess they just want me out of the house, probably for good."

"Has anyone seen Violet today?" I ask.

"Oh dude. I saw her behind the school buses hooking up with Conan. He sure was smiling when he walked back to the cafeteria," Tommy grins.

"Shut up. I'm serious. She wasn't in my class this morning."

"No man, haven't seen that fine-looking thing myself."

I just keep eating and start to tune out my surroundings. *I have one more chance with Violet today, she is in my science class.* "Ciao, gotta run."

I was so early to my science class the teacher looked surprised.

"Good afternoon, Dylan. You're eager today. Anything on your mind?"

"No sir, Mr. Saber, just lost track of time."

"You usually do, son, but it's never in my favor."

As I hurriedly turned to sit down, I almost knocked Violet over. I turned beet red. You know, the worst tasting vegetable in the world—beets.

"Oh crap, I'm sorry. You okay?"

"Yes, Dylan, I'm not made of porcelain you know. How are you doing these days?"

"Great," I reply quickly, a nervous wreck.

"Are you going to swim this afternoon? I sure hope so. I plan on going to the swim meet after school. We need to beat those guys," Violet smiles.

I think my genius self said, "Great, great, just great."

She giggled out loud and said, "Great" as her friends grabbed her and strolled to their seats.

Oh, what a moron I am. Great, that's it, great. That's all I can say, great. I need professional help. Lots of help, real smooth with the ladies, butthead.

The good news is, I sit behind Violet, but the class is full up with some real creeps. Jimmy Johnson is the biggest bully in school along with his gang of disruptive thugs that terrorize the school constantly. He has been bullying me since fifth grade. His dad owns a grocery store in town, and for some reason his gang of thugs always seem to get away with murder.

"Hey D for dung beetle. I hear your bozo friend Mark is throwing a big end of school bash. Did you bring my invitation? I need to know when it is so I can bring my date, Violet."

His gang of thugs begin to laugh.

"Oh, I think that's been canceled. Yep, canceled."

"Riiiigght, water bug. See you at the party. Just look for Violet, she'll be with me."

"Okay class, today we are going to dissect the common house lizard," Mr. Saber explains.

"Anoles, Florida chameleons, Florida green lizards, Cuban anoles. You have no doubt seen them clinging to your shrubbery, climbing your walls, and wolfing down all sorts of bugs and insects around your house. It's Godzilla! No, it's only a green anole, pronounced 'uh-no-lee,' one of Florida's true native lizards. Everyone pick a partner."

My brain kicks into gear, and I begin to tap Violet on the shoulder. As she slowly turns toward me, Jimmy Johnson drops a lizard in the back of her jeans, and you could hear a screeeeeammm all the way to Mars, as she looked directly into my eyes, and pointed towards me, as if I did it.

Before I could answer, Mr. Saber comes over and says, "I knew you were up to something."

"Let's go to detention, Mr. Cabrella. I think detention should do you nicely."

"But I didn't do anything." It was too late.

The entire class was laughing at my expense, and Violet looked at me as if I had the plague. I was so confused, upset, and sad that I just hung my head and shook it back and forth.

All I could say was, "It wasn't me. I'm sorry. It wasn't me."

Well, death by firing squad would have been a better form of punishment. Will she ever speak to me again, or was life over for me? Fifteen years and it's over. Sounds too young to die but you never know when your time will come. Well, if I don't die anytime soon, Mom will kill me. And if she won't, Dad will. I start to think not only will I get grounded and miss the party, I have a swim meet after school. Oh God, take me now. I've lived a full enough life, I think. Some kids never make it to fifteen. Joan of Arc was only nineteen when she died. I feel fortunate. I cannot live another day. This place bites.

"Hello, Mr. Cabrella," the assistant principal, Ms. Harkin, sneers at me. "Sad to see you'll be joining us this afternoon. Please continue onto your next class and we shall see you here at three p.m. If you're late, I will extend it through summer. I mean even a minute late. Do you understand, my lizard-tainted friend?"

"Yes ma'am."

I'm going to kill Jimmy Johnson with my bare hands. Life in prison for murdering Jimmy J. It would be worth it. Well, maybe not. That prison Grandpa was in looked horrendous.

I sit in Spanish class as if I were in a coma. Could barely speak when spoken to, everything is a blur. I know what you're thinking: come on, life will go on. But will it? Love is hard enough to find and now my chance at the only girl I love is dashed, gone in one millisecond of time. Maybe I could turn back time. Yeah, that will work. It worked for Michael J. Fox in *Back to the Future*. All I need to find is a flux capacitor, some plutonium, and a flashy car. No problem. I'm glad that's over. I am full of perfect solutions. Maybe I'll just ask Mom for those things, or I can order them off eBay or Amazon. Or I will be jumping off a bridge. Maybe that would be the better solution.

Briinngggggg. As I depart class with my head about a foot off the ground, I walk towards the detention hall. I cannot be late, so I try to be sure and dodge my friends since they will tie me up and think it's funny if I arrive late to further damage my future. I am not sure why I call them friends. I should think of another name for friends. I'll have two hours to come up with a few names.

Detention class was quite sparse. I could not believe Jimmy Johnson was not also in detention. He was the real culprit. But the more I think about it, the happier I am that Jimmy was not here antagonizing me every minute for two hours. The only good news is it's the best place to study, since no one is allowed to speak. It gets quite boring, so I'll read a few chapters. If they catch you sleeping, they add another day. If you talk, another day. Breathe loud, another day, so it's quiet time for me. Maybe Mom won't find out since she wasn't expecting me after school today due to my swim meet. Oh no, Grandpa mentioned that he may come to my meet. He won't squeal on me if I'm late, but Dad will. Being the swim coach, he might kill me. We swim against Key Largo, last year's county winners.

I feel like a dead man walking. Ha, that's another movie. I'm on a roll. Never saw it but heard of it. The meet starts at four thirty and I get out at five. My opener won't be until five fifteen or so. These meets always run late, but coach wants everyone there at the same time four o'clock sharp or else. Crap, how in the world am I going to get to the meet since I forgot to ask Jonny to come back and give me a ride? I didn't even tell him I was in detention. Great, the only good news is the swim meet was nearby. I could run and get there in fifteen minutes. Oh sure, I always run a couple of quick miles before I enter a marathon swim meet.

Usually my events are later. The better swimmers go last. My best event is the 800-meter freestyle and 200-meter backstroke. But I never had to swim after running like a gazelle before an event. Since it's one of our biggest competitors, not sure Dad will bench me for being late. He may even believe my excuse. Even he wouldn't believe I would do something to upset Violet, at least not on purpose. But he sure knew how to upset Mom, though. Mom some time ago let it slip that Dad was caught taking a night swim in our pool with an assistant swimming coach for another team. I didn't see any in harm in that, but Mom thought swim trunks would have been more appropriate attire.

There is no bell for detention, so as soon as the clock landed on five, I bellowed. "It's time." Ms. Harkin was not impressed and suggested we all stay an extra ten minutes for my outburst. I'm thinking it can't get any worse, that this may be the most horrific day in my life. *Pleeease, somebody shoot me and get it over with now. I hate everything about my boring life.*

I looked at my watch. It's five fifteen. I flew out of there like a bolt of lightning and almost knocked over another student. I looked left and right hoping to see a friendly face and catch a ride. Of course, no one in sight. This day keeps getting better. I start to run, hoping a few short cuts will get me there on time.

I'm not the best runner in the world—that's why I swim, but today I felt great. I had so much on my mind that my legs and breath never tired, as if I was floating on air. As I come across the street corner, my life flashed before my eyes. Jimmy Johnson and his gang of thugs were coming down the street in his huge truck. Now you're thinking they wouldn't hit me, would they. Wrong again. These maniacs are an unknown species of humans and their behavior is *abby-normal* so yes, it is quite conceivable that these species of dung would attempt to run me over. So, I start hoofing it. Now I feel my adrenaline flowing, heart pounding out of my chest, breathing like the oxygen had left the planet. Perfect, Dad won't need to kill me after all, I'll just get run over by a couple of high school punks.

I jump a few bushes to get out of the street, fall down, and scrape my forehead and leg. I try to shake off the pain so I keep moving on, trying to stay off the streets. After I stir up the entire neighborhood dog barking festival, I think I've lost them. I keep on running, and as I turn the next corner, here comes Jonny. I wave my arms like a madman. Finally, he sees me and accelerates at a rapid rate almost too fast to stop in time. He slams on the brakes and skids forward almost running me over. I'm thinking a car is going to run me over, not sure if it's friend or foe.

"Hey dude, gun it. I've got to get to the swim meet at the swim center, yesterday. I'm only two hours late and possibly grounded for life. You may have saved my life."

"You look like crap and you'd better stop bleeding in my car. Grab that rag and wipe your head. It's gross, dude. Why are you so late?" Jonny asks.

"Let me catch my breath and I'll explain in a minute."

I get to the swim meet at five thirty-five. Looking around, I see a full crowd screaming, ranting, yelling at the swimmers in the pool. Oh boy, here I go.

"Hey Tom, how's it going?"

"Where have you been? Coach is looking for you. You missed your first heat and he is not a happy camper. What, did you forget? I'm glad I'm not you," assistant Tom remarks.

Then I hear my name spelled out, which is never good.

"D-Y-L-A-N, get over here," screams Coach.

As I walk over to my torture chamber, I see Grandpa out of the corner of my eye, and he has an odd look on his face. I guess that's the look people get right before they see a lynching.

"Hey Dad. Oh sorry, coach," I say, thinking that would help. It didn't.

In a warm, soothing voice, coach says, "I am so glad you have decided to join us with your almighty presence. Is there anything I can get for you before I club you over the head with a baseball bat, you unbelievable piece of sh——"

He gets cut off by his assistant, Tom.

"Coach, can I see the heat sheet?"

Coach has now turned a burnt red color and is to ready to explode.

"By the way, you look like crap. I would ask where you've been, but I don't care.

Go suit up and I will deal with you later, if you live that long. I might just strangle you in front of all these people, *gooooooo*."

I start to think of how many times I have died today, but I lost count. I put on my suit and join the other swimmers sitting in the corner. Oh no, not today. I see Violet and her mom with my mom, all sitting next to Grandpa. No, it can't be. Mom usually doesn't come since she cannot stand being on the same planet as my dad. What is she doing here? If you think Violet is cute, her mom is awesome. She looks like the perfect Florida blond girl. Flowing blond hair, curves everywhere, and a smile that would stop a train in its tracks.

My mom and Mrs. Samantha Stoner, Violet's mom, are best friends from their school days. According to them, they both dated some or one of the same guys in high school. I get most of this info when Samantha and Mom hook up for some wine cocktails at our house. They always talk a lot and force me to listen. Last time they got together they made me promise not to be an ass to my future wife. I tried to explain to them that I was not yet or ever going to be married, but that didn't stop them. They both giggled and started singing, "Violets are purple, roses are red, I love Violets—weeee." I remember turning beet red and decided it was time to vacate the premises, quickly.

My heat is next and I was already pre-seeded. But as I get ready for my heat, I get a peculiar look from one of the referees staring at my head. He drags me over to the meet director's table and shows them my forehead. Then I figure it out as they DQ'd me for this heat, but said if I could get the bleeding under control, I would be able to swim my next heat.

Blood was coming off my forehead and dripping into my eyes. I didn't feel anything, but saw the blood so I went back to coach, who just grinned like a Cheshire cat and offered no assistance except to see the swim doc and get cleaned up, or I may not swim again in this lifetime.

Great, another failure in front of Violet. I'm thinking, *please someone shoot me.*

Chapter 3

TROADS

N ow, let's move my story across the ocean to somewhere in Africa with my Uncle Tony, who changed his name from Dr. Anthony Cabrella to Dr. Tony Rome, and his good friend Matt Robertson.

"Matt, where is Jamal?" Tony asks.

"He went down the river bank to look for a spot to camp," Matt replies.

"Do you think the natives are correct?" Matt asks.

"Not sure. Jamal is the best guide in this area. I rarely travel this part of Southern Africa. Since we have a limited time here in Namibia, I need an experienced guide. The prime minister only gave me a few days to search, and he was leery at that. He did take some money, which gave us a full week to research. I don't think I was very convincing with all this baggage in tow as to why I am doing research in his country, so let's get to work tonight," Tony explains to Matt.

"Since it took us three days to get here, we only have a few days and nights to explore. The good news is we can work at night for what I seek. The natives will be asleep while we start our search at nightfall. Doubt there is a Starbucks around the bend, so as soon as we make camp, start the caffeine flowing," Tony remarks.

Matt replies, "We passed a McDonald's a couple of miles back. I should have ordered a Big Mac when I had a chance."

"How do you eat that crap? Burger King is the best burger in town."

"Oh, no wonder you like the food around here. Your taste buds have been diagnosed as unfit for human consumption."

"Whatever, check to see if the radio is still working and get the caffeine on tap," Tony smiles.

My Uncle changed his name years ago from Dr. Anthony Roman Cabrella to Dr. Tony Rome, but many refer to him as Tony. He is an archeologist and his only sibling is his sister, Isabella, my mom. He travels all over the world searching for ancient artifacts and his net worth is around ten billion dollars. But most of his money is in valuable relics, not cash.

Tony has been traveling around the world with Matt Robertson for approximately twenty years. Matt is an Ex-Navy Seal, Marine all the way. Tough as nails at six-foot four, two hundred and twenty pounds, and not bad on the eyes per my mom. Matt and Tony are best buds. Kind of like brothers. At least like a brother I've never had but always wanted. They met in Italy when Matt was on his honeymoon and Tony was celebrating his divorce.

Matt and his wife Amy, are both from very wealthy families, and it was funny as to who was treating this particular evening. Tony never ever paid for anything when they first met in Rome. Amy had a unique sense of humor. She would say, "Matt should pay for everything and let me and Anthony save our money. That way when I leave you and marry my new Italian friend Anthony, we will have plenty of money saved up."

Matt's usual response was, "Great, I'll be the best married man who gave up this wench for the sake of Caesar." They all laughed and ordered more vino.

They all became so attached, no one was sure who was comforting whom when the unimaginable happened. Amy died in a tragic car accident. She was four months pregnant. She had just finished teaching her final yoga class for the day. One of her students had asked her if she wouldn't mind helping her with a yoga pose that she couldn't complete properly before her exam next week. Well, it seems the extra fifteen minutes Amy gave her student was her death sentence. As Amy entered the highway, a dump truck lost control and crashed head on into Amy's car. She never saw it coming. The driver had four prior DUIs, but it didn't matter. Amy and her baby were gone in seconds. Unannounced six days after her funeral, Matt showed up at Tony's place in Tuscany, and they have never discussed it since.

Jamal appears from out of nowhere and has found the perfect camping spot.

"It's only another two hundred meters down the river bank," Jamal remarks.

"Perfect, get everyone moving in that direction and set up camp," Tony replies.

As darkness draws nearer, Jamal comes over to Tony's tent and points toward the skies. Tony looks up. *What in the world is that thing flying above? Is it a small jet?* His mind starts to wonder. He hasn't seen anything like that since the kingdom? It was getting to be dusk, so it was hard to see clearly.

Matt, speaking under his breath asked, "Is that a bird? It turned on a dime and it looked as if it was circling."

"Could be a big bird? It's not a plane," Tony responds.

"It looks like a flying lizard. I didn't think we had pterodactyls left in this world but sure does look like one from here. Every kid should have at least one for a pet. I've seen a lot in my sordid life, but I've never seen a living breathing pterodactyl," Matt smiles.

Jamal, with a crazed look, just keeps pointing towards the sky and he says, "That's Tragoon."

Matt says, "Thanks, I feel better."

"Tragoon. And how often do you see it? Do you know where it comes from?" Tony asks.

"Not seen very often. Not sure where it is from," Jamal responds.

"If you know its name, it sounds like you know more that you're telling. We are listening."

"Tragoon has been around before my time. No one knows when it started to appear, but cave drawings suggest many, many years ago. They used to be plentiful in the sky but I seldom see them anymore. It is a very uncommon sighting in the daylight and usually brings with it, bad luck. They used to swoop upon villages and grab humans, or any animals it could find. At one point in time, babies were given up as a sacrifice to spare the villages but that was long ago. Since the babies were so small, these huge beasts needed much more, and then struck upon larger animals such as elephants, rhinos, and zebras for a feast. They hunt at night and can see for miles. Very unusual to see one in the daylight, but darkness is approaching. Something must be wrong for it to be showing itself in the daylight. I feel like we should all turn back at once," Jamal warns.

Tony and Matt did not come all this way to turn around after spotting a flying dinosaur.

Before Jamal could finish, the flying thing called Tragoon just disappeared.

"You seem to know a lot about this creature," Tony remarks.

"It has tormented us for decades but it has not been seen in many years. It's a sign of bad things to come. Bad karma, very bad luck. We must turn back," a concerned Jamal responds.

"Thanks for the heads up. We shall sleep on it," Tony comments, knowing full well that they were not leaving this place until his mission was completed—at least that was his plan.

Jamal reminds Tony and Matt that the natives are getting restless. "We should all leave now. Please reconsider my offer to depart. I am not sure how many men will stay by my side. If I am still here, I will see you at the break of dawn. Good night, and be careful."

Jamal pauses and says, "By the way, Dr. Rome, do you think you will find your miracle cure?"

"I sure hope so. Time is running out."

"Yes, indeed it is. Good night."

Matt adds, "I'd like some sleep myself."

"You slept last night, which should cover you for the rest of the trip. Now quit your whining and get our gear. Meet you back at the tent in half an hour, and bring your Tragoon-slayer sword. I can't wait to taste your coffee," Tony smiles.

"Thanks, I learned how to make it from your ex-wife."

Why did Matt have to bring her up? Tony hasn't thought of Christi in quite a while. They married way too young. They lived a normal life in the outskirts of Santa Fe. But they were in two different places in their lives. She wanted children and Tony wanted to wander around the world, so they compromised. Christi got divorced and Tony started to travel the world, collecting old and unusual artifacts from around the continents.

Tony continues to travel every continent and his least favorite is North America just because the history doesn't go back far enough for his interest. Asia and Europe keep him plenty busy and he's enjoyed every adventure. This one in particular has intrigued him, since it's more personal but it may become dangerous. So that's where Matt comes in.

After years and years, his research finally took a turn in the right direction. It seems that a particular peculiar, bright neon red fish and its odd glowing appearance may be an answer to his prayers. He was indeed intrigued and wanted to learn more about this fellow. He has heard stories about this particular specimen of fish and this may be the place to find his little guppy buddy, according to rumors. But getting any solid info was hard to come by. It finally led him to this far away land. Getting here was not the biggest problem. He's traveled all over the world but just hiring help and obtaining permission was extremely difficult, so hopefully his information is accurate. He felt compelled to lie about his mission and called it an AIDs cure research mission that could only be found in the Orange River. That seemed to calm a few nerves. He still thinks many were not convinced and many decided to decline his offer. But this area is desperate for work so after pleading his case to Jamal, he enlisted some nearby natives.

If Tony does find this particular fish, he's supposed to keep it alive until it can be analyzed. That's why there is so much equipment for an onsite inspection. According to his theory, the fish needs to be examined and items extracted at once before it expires. Hence the huge envoy he's hired. If needed, he will transport it back to Bell in the states. (Bell or Bella is the nickname he gave his sister Isabella). After they spoke, Bell suggested to send it to Boston, Massachusetts. There is a Whole Woods Oceanographic Institution (WWOI) that has the finest equipment they will need for the extraction.

The best fish description one could compare it to is a neon tetra, which is a small slim-bodied tetra species. It is similar in appearance to the cardinal tetra (also named the flame angelfish) with its horizontal stripe that seems to glow, but it is a distinctly different fish.

They can readily be identified, with each fish having a very beautiful red stripe next to an electric blue neon stripe. The difference is that the red stripe on the neon tetra runs only halfway up the body while it runs the full length of the cardinal tetra body. These fish get up to one and half inches or four centimeters. Since they are omnivorous, the neon tetra will generally eat all kinds of small or finely ground foods, live, fresh, or flake. Bloodworms are a treat. To locate such a small fish in this large bay of water, he will need luck on his side.

The team's task tonight was to locate and extract the unknown red neon fish that may or may not be related to the neon tetra. So not only does Tony need to identify a particular fish that he's never seen, but he has one week to find it and transport it back to America.

Should be a breeze. Fish are more his sister's speed, but she could not make this journey so it's up to Tony to solve this mystery and find this little fellow.

"Where the h—? Oh, there you are. Let's get going, Matt. It may be a long night," Tony says.

"I need my beauty sleep," Matt barks.

"We don't have enough time, let's go."

The nights can be extremely dark while hiking through the jungles. Street lights are not an option. Tonight, they are blessed or cursed with a magnificent full moon. You could see a billion stars along with the beautiful moon shining brightly by the river bank, blinding the waterways.

They traveled up and down ravines trying not to stumble while carrying all the equipment they could handle on their backs. Tony still thinks that they are being watched even in the middle of the night. After about two hours, he sees a tiny alcove.

"We will have to swim to the cave entrance. Let's suit up," Tony informs Matt.

They don their dive equipment and head for the cave. As they swim out towards the cave, they could feel little nibbles throughout their bodies. Thank goodness they were wearing wet suits. Not sure what was nibbling at them in the middle of the night in the Orange River, but they didn't want to slow down and ask since piranha, crocs, hippos, tiger fish, and many more are prone to these waters. After a brisk pace, they came upon the cave entrance.

Matt was so close behind Tony he slammed into him.

"Oh sorry," Matt mutters. "I was in a hurry because I thought it best to keep my feet attached to my body. Something was gnawing at my body. Are you sure it was wise to come out after dark?"

"I don't think we have a choice," Tony replies.

They turned on their flashlights and could only hear splashes from unknown creatures jumping into the water, but never really seeing what was making all the noises.

"Okay, now we need to head down the cave a few more paces until we hit a larger waterway that feeds under the Orange River. That's where we can dive again and search for our little friend. I still feel like we're being watched, so be alert. Don't forget our plan if we get separated," Tony says.

"I hear you," Matt replies.

"That may be the waterway just ahead. I'll keep my beam on high and go down first. Hey, turn off your light for a minute," Tony remarks.

Almost immediately flashes of color appeared throughout the cave. Bouncing off the cave walls and the water was a spectacular sight. Sparkles of the rainbow were perforating throughout the caverns. Which rainbow does Tony grab when it hits the water? Before they knew it, both of them were in a mild trance almost hypnotized. Tony shook his head to try and pull himself together and then grabbed Matt. He was also entranced.

"Did you hear anything?" Tony asks.

"Nope, just flashes of light."

"What just happened?"

"Not sure, but it was better than a ride at Disney," Matt smiles.

"Hand me my gear, I'm going in,"

"What for? The show is right in front of us. No reason to jump into a multi-colored whirlpool."

"Wait for me here, I'm going diving." As soon as Tony hit the water, the colors seem to subside and everything was back to calm.

This water was warmer than Tony anticipated. The rainbow displays suddenly stopped, and it was total darkness. Tony turned on his dive light and didn't see one fish. A minute ago, millions of lights. Now nothing. He continues to head toward the cavern walls since some of the neon fish are shy and like to hide in crevices.

All of sudden out of nowhere, something brushes against Tony and it wasn't small. Tony was wondering if Matt saw if it had a fin, and to his surprise, there's Matt right in front of Tony. Grinning like a cat that ate the canary. Tony jabbed Matt's rib as if to say, let's head for that cavern. Once inside the next cavern, Tony takes off his mask and waits for Matt.

"So much for you waiting," Tony quips to Matt.

"I was lonely, plus the lights disappeared and I became bored in the middle of a cave, with this wonderful body of water to swim," Matt replies.

"What about the piranha?"

"I figured since I didn't see any of your body parts float to the top, it was okay to jump in."

"That's comforting and by the way, piranhas eat all your body parts so you wouldn't see any floating. Come on, let's go. We can walk from here," Tony grins.

The cave begins to narrow to the point where Matt can no longer proceed.

"I knew all that pasta would catch up to you. I'll be right back," Tony remarks.

"Oh sure, six four, two hundred pounds is now tubby. I could eat some pasta right now.

"Hey Tubby, don't forget about our separation plan. It looks narrow, I'm leaving my air tank with you," Tony says.

"Sure, no worries. Bring me back some sushi since I doubt there is any pasta around here."

Tony continues walking on and it gets extremely narrow even for him. He see's another pool of water. Tony puts on his dive mask and in he goes. It's almost twenty degrees cooler than the other water. The water was so clear that if there was any sunlight, no need for a flashlight. But in a cave, you always need a light.

Tony sees a trail of a neon light, floating like a cloud of smoke behind a jet plane. He tries to follow as best he can but needs another gasp of air before continuing. He heads back to where Matt is sitting.

"Hey, give me that re-breather? The scuba tank won't fit. I may have seen something. Have the container ready just in case!" Tony yells.

"Right, it's fun around here, I keep hearing voices," Matt responds.

"Great, have a nice chat with the invisible people," Tony laughingly answers.

The probabilities of actually finding and seizing his catch are minimal. Tony gets back into the water and heads straight for the last sighting of the neon strobe light. Sure enough, he sees another or the same one. Not knowing if it's the particular type he's searching for since it's hard to tell under these cave settings, he gets his net ready just in case. Swoosh, swoosh. He keeps missing and almost passes out from all the energy he uses trying to trap these guys. He slams through the water as hard and quickly as possible and smacks his hand against a rock, but cannot believe it. He catches a few little buggers on his sixteenth attempt. Tony is so excited he almost hyperventilates.

Tony gets back and shows Tony his newfound friends.

Matt explodes, "You dragged me half away across the universe for those puny things? Are you sure it's the one you're looking for?"

"No, but it's a start. I grabbed as many as possible, but I think the one I need is the bright red one. I'll keep one or two and you take the rest," Tony said.

"I'm a little beat up. You need to go ahead and keep them secure and in water. Repeat, do not let them get out of water; we need to keep them alive. I am not sure if the enzymes will work if dead. Once you get it back to camp, you can scan them and be a hundred percent sure. Please go quickly. I need a little rest. I'll be right behind you. If we found the correct one, it's most imperative that we get it back to the States, as quickly as possible."

Matt was very hesitant but knew better than to argue and headed back out the cavern. "Okay, I'll get it back to camp and scanned, but I'll be back for you if you're not shortly behind me."

"Great, it's a deal. One more thing—say nothing to anyone, even Jamal."

It was beyond Matt why one tiny fish the size of his pinky toe mattered to anyone, but he knew the mission was important.

After a brief rest, Tony starts back to the campsite and hears something.

"Good evening, Dr. Rome."

Tony looks around and shines his light on a man standing about fifty feet in front of him. Or what looked like a ghost. Definitely an albino of some sort.

Caught a little off guard, Tony answers, "Good evening, Mr.—?"

"Grull will do."

"How can I help you this evening, Grull?"

"Well, it's actually morning and if you would be so kind to hand over your little catch. I may be inclined to let you be on your way. Please obey and be quick about it. I don't have much time. Plus we deplore violence, or at least I do."

"I don't know what you're talking about. I came down here for a little midnight swim. So much cooler down here than out there. I was sweating up a storm and needed a quick dip," Tony smiles.

"Like I said, my disapproval for violence is against my species. But your pain, on the other hand, would be welcomed."

Tony shines his light next to Grull, and now sees two unknown creatures on either side of him. They looked like giant frogs, each the size of a dump truck. This cannot be good. Could they have also found Matt?

"I just wondered off by myself, curious about this region. Plus, I couldn't sleep," Tony says.

"Your friend, Mr. Robertson, has not been found but he will be shortly. Now enough stalling, give me your fish and I'll let you live a little longer. My friends here are very hungry. Troads love the taste of humans. And you will make an excellent breakfast morsel," Grull announces.

"Oh, you mean this cute guy," Tony holds up his catch. "It couldn't feed a minnow. It's a cure for AIDs," Tony proceeds.

Grull looks at it with dismay and Tony turns over the net to let a fish jump out into the water.

"Oops, sorry about that," Tony shrugs.

In a matter of seconds, one of the frog-like creature's tongue grabs the fish before it hits the water. The speed and accuracy of these beasts were on full display. The only good news was the tide was coming in as the water started to rise.

"Now, now, Dr. Rome, no need to be a hero. I am aware of your eagerness to find a back door into the kingdom, but I'm afraid it's not happening," Grull warned.

"Back door to what kingdom? I have no idea what you're talking about," Tony replies.

Grull takes the fish from one of the Troads. "Well it seems you found a lovely neon tetra. Let's hope your friend has the real one. Good day, Dr. Rome. It was a delight to meet you. I hope your stay here was a pleasant one." Then Grull turns away, nods at the giant Troads, and disappears.

Tony realized these Troad things understand English and wonders how long he has before they devour him. Tony starts talking with the hideous creatures, and they look at him as if he may be their next meal.

"Hey, which one will get to have me for breakfast? You both can't, so which one will it be? I'm too small for you both to enjoy!" Tony yells.

At first nothing happens, but the bigger Troad turns to look at its companion. Unsure how long the stare down will last, Tony devises a plan. It's a weak plan, but a plan.

He stands up to show them their next meal but he needed to get to his mask, which was a few paces away. Considering the speed of their tongues, he needed a diversion to get his mask. Swimming without it would be death, so it's either be eaten or drown.

"Look at me, I'm too small for both of you to enjoy, so hurry up and decide which one it will be, while I sit and wait!" Tony taunts.

He takes a few steps toward his equipment and hears a sickening growl, so he decides to stop and sit next to his mask. Tony is ready for the next showdown, and as soon as they turn to look at each other, he grabs his mask and dives toward the water. Something hit his leg, but he pulled away since they both shot out at the same time and possibly got their tongues tied.

Not being able to see a thing, Tony kept swimming as fast as possible, not sure if those Troads were coming in after him. But the cavern was so small they probably wouldn't fit.

Chapter 4

LADYBUG

Not only did we lose the swim meet, I never even got to swim a heat. All I kept saying to myself is, *You're a loser, Dylan. Yep you.* Violet never looked my direction, but I nodded towards Mrs. Stoner, Violet's mom, and lowered my head as I headed for the exit gate.

Grandpa came up beside me and said, "Hey sport, you need a ride?"

"Grandpa, when did you get your license renewed?"

"I didn't, but the car is running like a champ. Come on, you look like you need some cheering up and could use some ice cream. My treat," Grandpa smiles.

"Okay," I say, "let's stop at Gelato's."

We get our gelato and walk over to the beach. It was a beautiful evening sky, just in time to see the sunset.

"I bet you didn't know your Grandma loves gelato. Her favorite is pistachio, sometimes. We would search all over town just for her favorite flavor. I think she changed favorite flavors on purpose just so we could be together longer. She would always leave the house and say to her folks, 'We're just going out for some gelato and I'll be right home.' Her ploy would work, knowing good and well that her flavor would be nonexistent, but she wouldn't leave me until I found her favorite flavor, on that particular day. It could take hours," Grandpa grins.

"I'm confused. Why didn't you say something like, 'Get another flavor, I don't have all day? This is ridiculous.'"

Grandpa says, "Aaaah, you're missing the point, sport. I enjoyed our moments together. I wasn't smart enough to figure out how to be with her for long periods of time, so she would do it all on her own. I would always give her a look and say, 'Whatever thy princess wants.' I think she knew I was in love. I certainly was not sure how to act. We were both so young. Most of the time, we would just talk and talk and walk for hours."

"What did you talk about every day? I've got nothing to say to Violet. Every time I get near her, I freeze up and when I do speak, I say something stupid."

"Well sport, at first I didn't say much either. She did most of the talking and it took me a while before I could get the nerve to ask your grandma out on a date. As far as I was concerned, your grandma was the prettiest girl in town, and I was fairly certain she didn't know I existed. So, I took up the saxophone. Grandma was in the band. That's why I took up to the sax. You never knew how well she could play a musical instrument, and I wasn't very good, which turned out to be in my advantage. She would ask if I ever needed help, that she would be glad to work with me after school. I turned about three shades of purple and I think I said, 'Okay, sure'. She giggled and said, 'How about tomorrow after school?'" Grandpa recalls.

"That's when it all started," Grandpa adds.

"What started?"

"Our dating, sport, but there was one minor problem. Every guy in school wanted to date her, but Bruno, our football captain, had dated her or was still dating her. I wasn't really sure. He was a huge kid who could have crushed me with one hand. I was a bit nervous not knowing the current situation between Elizabeth and Bruno. But I just figured if Liz wanted to see me after school, what harm is that. We were only band members getting together for just a little band practice. A rehearsal in the school lunchroom shouldn't draw attention. No big deal. Just after final period your Grandma comes up to me and says, 'Meet me at my house. You know where I live. It's number six Barca.' I said 'sure' but before I could say anything else, she was gone. It was a small town, so I knew where Barca was located. I was just hoping no one else knew."

My machine gun questioning begins. "Did you go to her house? What about Bruno? Did he find out? What if?"

"Hold on. Slow down, sport, I'm getting to that. I was going to tell my friends about my plans to visit Elizabeth, but thought better of it. The less they know the better," Grandpa blinks.

"I decide to stop off for an espresso to keep my courage up. Slug it down in one gulp, grab my sax, and head out to Elizabeth's house. I keep looking around just to be sure no one was following me but then decided I was just being foolish, and laugh it off. I took a brief walk through the park, a little shortcut. And in hindsight, it was a lousy idea. Guess who was playing football or soccer, as you would say?"

"Who, who, who, Grandpa?"

"Bruno and his friends."

"No way. But he didn't know where you were going, did he?"

"I didn't think so. Why would she tell Bruno? So, I wave and start picking up my pace, and so does he. And I'm dragging my sax and he is in his soccer uniform. Well, he caught up to me rather quickly. I decided it was futile to try and outrun him so I stopped and said, 'Hey, how's practice going? We're going to beat the hell out of Puglia next week, huh."

Bruno says, "If you touch my girl, I will rip your face off and shove it where the sun doesn't shine."

"What are you talking about? I just need some band practice. It's not a date."

"Practice with the nuns. This is your last and only warning," Bruno announces.

"My decision was made in a hurry since Bruno was twice my size and with half the team standing behind him. I turned and went back home," Grandpa hangs his head.

"I don't blame you."

"You might not, but Lizzy was furious the next day. She wouldn't even speak to me. And I couldn't tell her I was a wimp, a coward. What could I say, so I said nothing. And that was the end of that."

"That makes no sense, Grandpa. You married Grandmother."

"Oh right, there is more to the story. Let me think. I can't remember exactly, but about two weeks had passed without much discussion between Liz and me until one day she walks up to me and says, 'You've got one more chance. Meet me at my house after school.' And before I could say whatever it was I was going to say, she bolted, without any hesitation. Now my heart was jumping out of my chest and I didn't know what to do. It pounded so hard I went to the school nurse. I said I was having a heart attack, and she told me that I surely would if I didn't leave her office and get back to class. Such a loving, caring nurse as I remember. I actually did cut myself once and had to see Ms. Strunza. I, that's what we called her and when…"

"Grandpa, stay on track. What happened with Grandmother?"

Grandpa says in a whisper, "I do miss her so and will get her back one day real soon. You'll see. The only thing that got me through prison was true love."

I thought, *She's the reason you got into prison in the first place, you crazy old man*, but didn't say anything out loud.

"Where was I? Oh yeah, well it wasn't a heart attack, but I sure know what one feels like. After calming down a bit I started to think, okay what about Bruno? It's just not fair. All I wanted was to see Lizzy. That's what I called your Grandma back then, Lizzy. I could care less about the saxophone. I would just think about her every waking moment. So, I decided to hell with Bruno. I'm going to see Lizzy after school with or without a broken neck. I stopped by my house just to take one last look at my mom before I headed out. Dad was still at work. I sat on the front stoop thinking about how my life might end at such an early age. Mom comes out and brings me a glass of homemade lemonade and says, 'She's worth it, Son. Don't let anyone stand in your way. No matter what happens, follow your dreams before they disappear. Just do what's right and what your heart tells you to do.'

"How did she know it was a heart issue? I never mentioned Elizabeth once. How did she know? I said, 'Thanks, Mom.' For some reason Moms have some kind of secret radar intelligence. I was ready to tell Lizzy I loved her but decided it wasn't time. I think she had it figured out before I did. All my heart was saying is don't get yourself killed," Grandpa smiles at the memory.

"This sounds familiar, Grandpa. I thought I was dead today over Violet. It must be a Cabrella syndrome. We are related for sure!"

"This time I decided to avoid the park. No reason to rush things, I'll be there soon enough. I get to her street and began to shake uncontrollably. I remember saying to myself to be a man. I told my dad the story the week before, and all he said to me was, 'son, if you don't stand up for what you want, what good are you?' I thought to myself. Thanks, Dad. Thanks for the help. I was hoping you'd go kick Bruno's butt for me, but thanks, I feel better knowing that we've had this talk. He wasn't much of a talker or any help for that matter. I approach number six Barca, I almost had my second heart attack in one day. I forgot my sax. Oh, she's going to think I'm a complete moron. Stupido. She asks me to come over so she can help me with my music lessons, and I appear without my instrument."

"Wait, Grandpa, why couldn't you just run back and grab it? Maybe have your mom drive you back."

"No, sport. We only had one car and Dad had that one, so I begin to turn back when it strikes me. I'll never forget her comment, 'You've got one more chance to meet me at my house after school.' I thought she never mentioned anything about the sax so maybe it'll be okay. If I turned back it would be too late to get back in time, so I had to make a decision."

Grandpa stops and asks, "How was your gelato? Mine is great."

"Really Grandpa, what happened? Please continue. Did you go or turn around?"

"What would you have done, sport?"

"I would have run back home and grabbed my sax."

"Didn't have enough time. I couldn't risk standing her up again. I took a deep breath just to make sure my heart hadn't stopped, and started for her door. I forgot all about Bruno and before I could knock on the door, it swung open. And there she stood in a lovely dress and said, 'It's about time. You ready? Let's go.' Before I could say a word, I hear 'Bye Mom, be back later, going for some gelato with Vincenzo Cabrella.' Through the screen I heard 'Don't be late kids. Vincenzo, I know your mother.' I begin to wonder what was that supposed to mean! A date, oh my, I think, she didn't even ask about my saxophone. Should I tell her?

"I figured out she didn't care. A date, I wasn't prepared for a date. I need prep time. I've never been on an official date before. What do I do? Well, one thing was for sure—this girl knew exactly what to do. Lizzy says, 'How about gelatos at Marciano's on the square?' I said, 'Sure, why not.'

"She did most the talking, but I listened to every word and thought I was in hell a few hours ago. Now I'm in heaven. I remember saying to myself to kiss Mom when I get home. She's talking about her family, where they traveled, and how much she likes to travel. She wants to explore and see the world. I am not sure if anything ever came out of my mouth, but we walked and she talked forever.

I remember thinking she sounds so grown up and I'm such a wimp, what happened to me? I guess girls do mature much quicker, and then I decide right there and then that I'm going to work on that maturity thing. I'll ask Mom, she'll know what to do," Grandpa keeps talking.

"Before I realized it, we were standing in front of Marciano's. We walked for forty-five minutes, and it felt like seconds. Please, Lord, don't let this day end. After looking over the flavors, she asked if they had pistachio. The man behind the counter says no were out. 'Okay, ciao,' she says, 'Let's go. We've got to find pistachio. It's my favorite.' I said, 'Okay, let's go try Gabriel's.' Wow, I said something. We walked another forty minutes to Gabriel's, and she got her favorite. I got lemon ice. She bit into mine as if we had been dating forever. Then we both realized it was getting late, so we decided to head back to her house. As we were walking back, it finally dawned on me that Bruno was out there somewhere. But I didn't dwell on it since we were together, I felt invincible. I think I was glowing when she turned to me and says, 'Would you like to do this again?'

I said yes so fast it was pitiful. 'Great,' she replied and kept on talking until we arrived at her doorstep. This went on for quite a while, Lizzy and I.

"All I could hear was her dad saying in Italian, 'How long does it take to get some damn gelato? *Quanto tempo lo fa per prendere per ottenere un certo gelato maledetto?* Who is that boy? Mama who is that boy?' he repeated loudly.

"She said, 'That's Vincenzo. You've met him a million times.'

'I don't like him around here. What's he want?'

'Oh boy, you forget so soon. Amore, you old fool.' He waved his hand up in the air and headed back to the basement for some more vino.

"Lizzy was always giggling and would kiss me on the cheek. Then one day she whispered, 'I'm going to marry you one day,' and runs back into the house. I am not sure why I was so fortunate to meet such a lovely lady, but the good Lord was looking out for me the day I met your grandma.

"When I got home that night, my mom looked at me and smiled from ear to ear. 'Next time bring her home earlier, young man. Maybe show up with some flowers. She is a beautiful woman, and she doesn't need to be out all hours of the night.'

'Yes ma'am,' I said and glided up to my room. My dad says, 'What's with him?'

'Amore has taken over.'

'Oh crap,' I heard Dad say a little louder than he wanted."

"But Grandpa, you've skipped a few parts. What about Bruno?"

"Well it wasn't long before Bruno found out about my seeing Lizzy. The funny part was she never mentioned Bruno once, so I wasn't sure they were dating anymore or ever. So, one day in school Bruno sees me and tells me I'm a dead man if I see Elizabeth again. I think, I've been seeing her for weeks. I'm not sure what I said, but I just shook my head in the affirmative fashion. Not sure why I did that since I had every intention of seeing Lizzy again and again if she would allow me. But I did not need nor want an altercation with Bruno. It would end badly for me.

"On my next visit to see Lizzy, I do the unthinkable and half-way through the park I hear, 'Hey dead man, come over here.' Do I run or finally face the enemy?"

I yell out, "What did you do, Grandpa!? I would have grabbed a bat to protect myself. Kung fu'd him to death."

"No, sport. I grabbed nothing but stopped and waited for him and his buds to approach. Bruno was standing right in front of me and says, 'Where you going?' All his buddies yell, 'You know where. Elizabeth's house where he is every night.' Bruno looks at me, and says, 'Is that true?'

Not wanting to die, but it came out before I could think what I was saying. 'Yes, I like her a lot.'

"Before I finished my sentence, the next thing I remember is waking up on the ground, blood pouring out of my nose and mouth, and head pounding. No one was in sight, and it was hard to see. I had a headache and blurry vision. I get up and wipe myself off. Not knowing what to do, I head home. I couldn't let Lizzy see me like this—I couldn't even fight for my girl.

"Before I get two steps into the door, I see my mom with her mouth wide open, and she tells me to get into the bathroom. I clean up as best I can, just to stop most of the bleeding. She comes in to clean me up some more, but the bleeding is worse than I thought, so she decides to take me to the clinic. I get nine stiches—six in my lip and three on my forehead. Oh great, Lizzy's never going to want to see me again, and I start to cry. Mom holds me and says, 'You did the right thing. You're my hero.'

'Hero,' I tell her, 'I was a coward. I got clobbered.' When we got back home, Dad was waiting for us at the door. I figured he's going to also punch me, but instead he says, 'This morning you left a boy, this afternoon you come back a man,' and walks me downstairs for some of his homemade vino.

"Mom doesn't say a word and starts to cry," Grandpa recalls.

"Did it hurt, Grandpa?"

"I'm not sure. I don't remember much of it, but I did see a note next to the telephone. It said, *Giuseppe's kid Bruno beat up our boy.* It turns out Mom was not happy and told Dad to fix this. He made a phone call to someone and someone made a call to someone else, and that was that. Mom was always baking this and that, and it turns out one of her biggest bakery fans was Mario Quagliatino's mother. Now Mario was a big shot. He was into import/export business, if you know what I mean."

"No, I don't know what you mean."

"Well, let's just say he was very powerful."

"You mean strong?"

"No, well connected."

"Connected to what?" I ask again.

"Forget it, just listen," Grandpa snorts. "Bruno's father worked for Mario, and after a few phone calls, Bruno never touched me again, nor did he ever come close to me after that day."

"What did Grandmother say when she saw you?"

"She only mentioned it once. The only thing I remember her saying was, 'If you think you look bad now, think about what you're going to look like if you ever leave me, Vincenzo Cabrella.'"

"Grandpa, how do remember so much about Grandmother but can't remember where your car keys are?" I ask bewildered.

"When you're in love, you never forget every waking moment, especially once they are gone."

I was still curious. "How did you know she was the one? How did she know you were the one?"

"I didn't, she did. She said it was the first day I walked into band class and after I agreed to music lessons, she knew then. I had no idea. I just wanted to be with her. How was I to know we were going to be married! And damned if she didn't make me continue my music lessons on the sax. I'm kind of glad she did. I love playing that thing, unless you guys sold it while I was gone?"

"Nope, we didn't sell anything. Mom had your place cleaned up often. But answer me something. How can anyone know after one brief encounter? Come on, Grandpa. I've got to at least sleep with them first. Check 'em out."

"Yeah, okay. How many you sleep with, sport?"

"Well, I can't remember, but it's plenty."

"Sure, I'm sure it's a big number, sport."

Well, wanting to sleep with women counts. "Sure plenty. How do you know who the one and only is forever and ever?" I ask.

"Remember what I said about a woman's radar, sport? Well, it's true. When I was with her nothing else mattered. We went everywhere together. But soon I did all the talking. I was sputtering out stuff so fast we'd get to the gelato shop without her uttering a word. You know, I never had to ask my mom about maturity. I think it found me through Lizzy. Love is not something you search or go on a quest to find. It's more like a butterfly or ladybug that lands on you."

"What are you talking about? I'm going to marry a ladybug?"

"No, no. Your lady will appear one day and you will either know or not."

"Way too complicated for me. I thought it would be easier."

"Well, it was simple for your Grandma Liz. We did everything together, rarely argued. After we married, I had some money saved up for a trip to Venezia. Your Grandma always spoke about Venice and how she couldn't wait to visit. She loved all the animals, plants, stars, you name it. If it was outdoors, she loved it. I couldn't get her out of those damn gondolas. We would ride night and day. My neck was stiff because every second she would say, 'Look at that, look at this and that.'

Finally, I got her out of those gondolas for a little hike in the Dolomite Mountains. We had just finished a nice picnic lunch at Lake Misurina. The locals called it 'the pearl of the Dolomites.' We headed up this magnificent mountain, and about halfway up, my Lizzy sprained her ankle. She said, 'Just leave me and get some help.' We hadn't seen anyone all day, and I wasn't about to leave her anywhere. I scooped her up and carried down that mountain, I never stopped once.

"She just smiled at me and said, 'You're a crazy man, you are. It was a trick to get rid of you, and look at you now. You messed up my plans to run away with a bear.' Once down the mountain, I collapsed. Luckily a ranger guide was at the foot of the mountains and radioed for help. He asked me, 'For how long did you carry your wife? *(Quanto tempo avete trasportato la vostra moglie?)'*

I said, 'About halfway up the Gardena Pass.' He stares at me for about a minute and says, 'The Virgin Mary must have helped. *(La Mary vergine deve aiutare.)*'"

"How far was it, Grandpa?"

"Don't know for sure, probably about fifteen hundred meters or so. I couldn't carry anyone ten feet these days."

"You must miss Grandmother an awful lot, huh?"

"I can't describe to you what's it been like without her," he added, mumbling, "not knowing if she's alive or dead."

"What you say, Grandpa?"

"I said, one day I may have to ask you for some help. You'd do that for me, wouldn't you, sport?"

"You bet I would."

Grandpa looked away and started to wonder if he may have figured out the correct formula by using Grandma's hair to fill in the pillowcase. *She made a wig from her natural hair, thinking one day it may come in handy. While I was in prison, I received some extra fabric from Asia and now I can combine both hair and fabric. Hopefully it will make the perfect pillowcase for my needs.*

Grandpa was lost in thought. I had to get him back on track.

"You know, Mom is always talking about Grandmother, but soon after she mentions Grandmother's name, she starts to cry and she never tells us why. You know where she is, don't you Grandpa? Let's go get her. I'll drive us. I've got my learner's permit, and with an adult in the car we can go get her. Is she close by?" I ask.

I see tears coming down Grandpa's cheek and figure it's best if I shut up, and I hugged him as hard as I could.

He said, "Thanks, I love you, sport.

"We better get back before your mom strings me up. You know she has that Italian temper, must get it from her mother's side."

We both laugh.

"Hey Grandpa, can I drive home? You know I have my learner's permit?"

"Sure, sport, it's all yours. All that talking and memories wore me out. I may take a snooze for the ride home."

"One more thing—you think you could help me with a girl?" I reluctantly ask. As soon as it left my lips, *what was I thinking?* popped into my head.

"Sure, sport, be my pleasure It's been a long time since a wooed a gal, but I still got the moves."

I start to think, *Wooed? What is that? Maybe he'll forget,* as I slowly drive home.

Chapter 5

TOBI

Back in Africa, Tony wasn't sure how long he'd been swimming. His body is aching all over as he hopes he can hold out since he has no idea where he is in relation to the surface or dry land. He tries to focus on his surroundings, but it's so dark that without a flashlight, he would have to survive on instinct. Hoping those giant frogs aren't following behind him, he keeps swimming as fast as possible. His arms and legs are beginning to give out so if he doesn't stop soon, he may drown. But he can't risk being seen again and can't locate the moon, so he keeps swimming hopefully in the correct direction. There are a lot of crocs in these waters. Something brushes against him, and again and again.

Then he hears someone say, "Grab on tight."

Again, he hears it.

Tony starts getting delirious assuming he's about to be eaten by a croc.

"GRAB ON OR YOU WILL DIE!"

That Tony heard, loud and clear. Grab on to what, he wonders.

Immediately Tony reaches in front and feels a fin or a foot or something slimy. *Why not, it's the best advice I've heard all night.* He grabs on and *boom,* away they go. Whatever it is, it's moving much faster than he ever could. They are moving so fast he almost loses his mask. They go down and then up, curve around this and that. He can't see a thing, so he's going on faith. They start heading straight down at some ridiculous speed, and then it stops so fast he smashes his head against it. And off they go again straight up. At this point, he figures he's probably dead, and it's all a dream.

Suddenly they hit the surface with such impact, Tony goes flying into the air, losing his mask and flopping back against the water. His heart is pounding so hard it's about to jump out of his chest. He tries to figure out where he is and how he got there. He sees the shoreline a few yards away, swims to shore, and crashes on dry land.

He awakes just in time to see the sunrise. But that's not all he sees. To his left is a giant crocodile with its mouth wide open as if it's about to chomp down on his head, but it isn't moving. Then he sees why. There is a large arrow sticking out from the back of the croc's head, just behind his eyes. Hoping it's dead he tries to figure out where he is and if Matt made it out alive.

Tony looks up and sees movement from behind the bushes and assumes it's a local tribe that found him and probably killed the croc. One of the tribesman motions for Tony to follow and Tony shakes his head in approval, figuring he has no choice. Most of the natives around here are friendly, but with recent events, who can you trust? As soon as Tony gets to his feet, he passes out. Soon a group of natives carries Tony farther into the jungle.

Tony awakes in a hut of some sort with an older woman trying to feed him. He accepts her eagerly, since he needs to build up his strength to rendezvous with Matt. After a few more mouthfuls, he gets to his feet, and she runs out of the hut. Tony exits right behind her and sees a group of tribesmen waiting, along with a rainbow-painted man who was probably the chief. The chief waves for Tony to come to him.

He begins to speak in a regional dialect that sounds familiar. Luckily it is one that Tony can somewhat understand as the chief wants to know, "Why did you pick such a peculiar place to sleep on the side of a riverbank surrounded by man-eating crocodiles?"

Tony chooses his words wisely, unsure if they are friend or foe, and tells the chief he was, looking for a miracle cure for aids.

He smiles back and says, "Well, did you find your miracle cure?"

"No, but I think it's best if I head back home."

His smile widens as he says, "That will not be so easy. Many are looking for you and your friend. Tragoon has been flying high in the sky during the daylight hours. This means trouble. He has already destroyed your campsite. Only trouble occurs if we see Tragoon in the daylight. You have attracted the worst of sorts and will cause my village much harm. You must leave soon, but I will help you."

Oh crap. How does he know all that? Tony wonders

"Where are we, and can you point me to Walvis Bay?" Tony asks.

"Your friend may be dead. You must leave our country at once. We are near the Namib Desert and I am Chief Namibia. But I will lend you a guide to wherever you need to go. We call him Land Snail."

Tony thanks the chief profusely and comments, "I would prefer a quicker guide. I don't have much time."

The chief just laughs out loud and says, "Good luck" as he hands Tony a small wooden sword. And with that final statement, he rises and disappears before Tony could ask him anymore questions.

Tony returned to the hut for some additional food and drink. While he's finishing up, a male tribesman enters and says in broken English, "I am Land Snail and will take you where you want to go."

He looks lean and fit. Tony shakes his hand and tells him, "I need to get to Walvis Bay as quickly as possible!"

Land Snail leaves and returns with some supplies and off they go. Tony wanted to thank the chief, but no one was to be seen—everyone had just disappeared.

Not sure why they called him Land Snail, since he was gone in a matter of minutes. He just took off like a bolt of lightning. When he came back, Tony asked, "Why is it you're called Land Snail?"

He just smiled and responded, "I am the slowest in our tribe."

Great irony, chief. This guy moves like a cheetah.

What Land Snail does is insane. He runs miles ahead and returns to see if Tony is making it okay, then goes back and forth. He must run ten miles to Tony's one. He is quite clever by keeping them hidden from view, and he knows his way around. Snails are quite extraordinarily diverse, and so is this guy. They are making good time and may be at Walvis Bay by tomorrow morning.

They arrive at a secure location, and Tony thanks Land Snail for all his help.

He looks Tony in the eye and says, "It is not safe, so be very careful and trust no one. Many are looking for you, and the ports are all being watched. Be sure to look high and low when traveling. Goodbye, my friend."

Before Tony could respond, Land Snail was gone in a flash. *He would be a lousy tour guide. The tour would be over in a matter of minutes.*

All of a sudden everything hits Tony like a ton of bricks as he tries to relive the past forty-eight hours, and wonders if he'll ever see Matt again. Matt is a tough son of a gun. You wouldn't know it by his behavior, but he is a tough cookie when he needs to be. He had some special training with the Navy SEALs and the Special Ops boys. He never wants to talk about his duties while in the service, but one could only imagine what he went through.

Tony came upon the place where Matt and he decided to meet if anything went wrong. They agreed to wait only two days for each other, but Tony wouldn't blame Matt if he bolted before that.

Tony sits for a minute before he realizes he's got to get out of this country, and fast. As Tony leans back to relax, he hears a loud noise accompanied with a horrendous smell. Some type of horrible odor up ahead. Tony pulls out his stick sword the chief gave him.

"I don't believe it—Matt, is that you? You smell and look like crap," Tony excitedly grins.

"Thanks, oh buddy, glad you could make it. What, you don't like my rhinoceros poop camouflage? Me either. Where the hell have you been?" Matt smiles.

"Things have been a little tense for me. I can assume for you as well," Tony replies.

"I agree with that statement," Matt exclaims. "I'll wash this rhino poop off on the way. It was the only way to survive when they came looking for me. Whoever and whatever they were."

"Well, to tell you the truth, I haven't had much time to digest what's been happening either, but I think it best if we get out of here, now. Fill me in on the way. The most important thing is, did you get the package off okay?" Tony asks.

"Yes, I think it's safe. Jamal helped me, but he wasn't happy about it. We put your little fish in the special designed crate and sent it off with Tobi."

"Tobi, who is Tobi?"

Matt smiles and says, "An elephant. What, you've never heard about the magic talking elephant, Tobi? That's a first, you don't know something. Jamal spoke to the elephant as if it understood, and off it went with the package strapped to its back. What's so bloody unusual about that? Everything else makes perfect sense. I packed a pitiful specimen of the tiniest neon fish into a large crate for safekeeping. Why would a talking elephant surprise anyone?"

"What about the campsite?" Tony asks.

"Totally ruined. By the time I got back to camp, Tragoon had ransacked the entire area. Most everyone had disappeared."

"Okay, you can fill me in when we stop for the night. I would like a few more details. I can't talk and walk right now, and I'm too tired to do both."

"No problem. I understand. Once we stop, I will be happy to fill you in on some details. I'm just happy to see your smiling mug. Where we headed?"

"Walvis Bay is the nearest port."

Tony turns to Matt and says, "Thanks again for waiting back there."

"No problem. I've always wanted to start my own men's fragrance company. Now I have the secret formula and once I'm back stateside, I'll be rich. I can see it now—*Rhino Poopfume,* for the rugged guy. I can't wait to ride the New York subway with my new rhino odor. I bet the ladies will go crazy."

"Let's park it here. I'm beat up. This should be a good spot to camp for the night. We can easily reach Walvis Bay from here. We'll do the security duty switch. This will be the first time I've been able to relax since I left you back at the cave," Tony says.

It didn't take long to set up camp.

"Matt, why don't you start with your story?"

"Right, well, I got back into the water and followed the line back out of the cave, but something didn't feel right. So, once I got out of the cave, I decided to go farther down the river. I got this eerie feeling I was being followed or watched, so I thought it best to get out on the other side of the river bank just in case someone was waiting for me at the spot we entered. It was morning, and boy was I right. There was a lot of movement, shouting and unknown sounds coming from the campsite. I was thinking maybe I should go and warn you not to come back, but decided to keep to our plan."

"Good thing you did," Tony smiles.

"I lay low on the bank to watch the circus. Then I saw a cloud of smoke coming from our camp's location, so I slowly made my way back to the camp, only to find it in ruins. I wandered around the perimeter of the camp, and wondered how and what destroyed most of our equipment. I did not want to encounter these people, and kept my distance. I kept an eye on the fish to make sure it was still alive. Now, I thought, what am I supposed to do with this little thing? I see Jamal running around barking out orders to the few who remained. I approach Jamal, and all he says is, 'You both must leave at once. Tragoon has destroyed our campsite and may return.'

"I said sure thing, but that Dr. Rome wanted me to get this into one of the crates and pack it for the United State as soon as possible. He told me that will be impossible. And that I must leave at once and never return, for my own safety. I explained we needed to find at least one crate—Dr. Rome was coming back later. He figured you must be dead and offered to help if I left immediately.

"After we rummage around the area, we did find a crate that wasn't damaged too badly. I feel like a complete fool when I show him the tiny fish that is supposed to fit into the giant crate. He doesn't even blink as he places the fish carefully inside the special crate, and we both close it tight.

"Jamal, turns and speaks in some unusual dialect that I did not understand. Next thing I know a native was next to him, and they spoke. Soon the native was off and running. Jamal looks at me and says, 'I have asked him to bring Tobi to me. She will take the crate to the dock for shipping.'

"I start to think, she. What is this Tobi, a weightlifter? It's a giant crate and extremely heavy with all the dry ice packed into it. I can't wait to meet Tobi. Then Jamal says, 'You must leave. We will load crate onto Tobi. All our lives are in danger and you cannot be here. If you find Dr. Rome take him with you. Go now. Goodbye, my friend,'"

Matt keeps the story going. "I tried to argue, but it only made matters worse. I departed but decided to stay nearby to make sure Tobi arrives. After taking refuge in the jungle and making myself scarce, I see an elephant heading towards Jamal. I am close enough to hear some of the conversation between Jamal and Tobi. 'You must take this crate to Walvis Bay. Be careful. Many are looking for this crate, so be quick. Our friend Jani will meet you at the bay. He will unload it for you and get it onto the ship. Stay well, my friend. This may be our last and only attempt to save our—. I couldn't hear the rest," Matt smirks.

"Are you kidding me? What did he say? Where? What?" Tony asks.

"Believe it or not, Tobi shakes her head and thanks him for his loyalty, or something to that affect. I swear, I'm fairly certain she thanked him. Oh, did I forget to mention the fact that Tobi was an elephant? An enormous elephant," Matt grins.

"And you're sure the elephant spoke?" Tony looks skeptically at Matt.

"Well, I didn't see her speak, but no one else was there that I could see. It sure looked like Jamal was speaking directly with her."

"Right, right, then what happened?"

"Damn if that elephant didn't take off like a rocket. I tried to follow her but she lost me, and soon there was a herd of elephants. I couldn't keep up, and so I decided to come back and wait for you. I was sure you'd love this story and would want me to see a shrink right away."

"Not really. It all sounds perfectly normal. While you were listening to an enormous elephant, I was talking to a couple of giant frogs and maybe a fish or two. So no, your story doesn't seem odd. Anything else?" Tony quips, then mumbles, "The kingdom is probably responsible for all this chaos."

"After that episode, I had a few more unusual visitors. While I was working my way to meet you, my internal alarm bell went off again. I could sense something nearby, so I buried myself in some lovely rhino poop. Covered from head to toe and before I knew it, something was almost on top of me, but turned and went the other direction. I wasn't sure what it was since I couldn't move. It wasn't human, but some type of animal. Sniffing around the entire area, growling and snorting sounds. I can't really describe what it looked like. It was right next to me and I've been in the jungles for years. I've seen and heard plenty of animals in my life, but this thing was a hunter—not the usual species. Almost like, *The Predator* movie, I couldn't make it out since I had to stay perfectly still while it was sniffing all around me."

"Coming back to our rendezvous spot, it became clear that nothing was safe. I found myself some more rhino poop and spread it all over my body, then hid in a ditch until you arrived. It was swell. Reminded me of the good times in the military, you know, the same aromas and everything."

After a while Matt didn't hear a sound from Tony except a mild snoring. Tony was fast asleep.

Matt and Tony got to Walvis Bay the next day without any further incident. This bay has been a haven for many sea vessels because of its natural deep-water harbor, protected by the Pelican Point sandpit. It was the only natural harbor of any size along the country's coast. Being rich in plankton and marine life, these waters also drew large numbers of whales, attracting whalers and fishing vessels.

They stay in the background to see what's going on since Tony is sure someone or something is looking for them. Matt hits the ATM and buys a few necessities. They check into a hotel to clean up. Being a whaling town with a huge harbor, shops and rooms are prevalent. They clean up, change clothes, then head for the docks.

Suddenly Matt grabs Tony and says, "Turn left now." Matt's instinct for espionage is superb. They turn onto a small street and stop.

Matt says, "I think those guys were looking for someone, and I bet that someone is us."

"I am not sure they know we are together. We may have an advantage seeing we are two. But I am sure they are looking for individuals fitting our descriptions," Tony replies.

The morning was bustling with activity, probably like every morning. Everybody was running around loading, unloading, barking orders here and there.

"Matt, you see that huge container ship, the Woloza. It's going to the States. Keep an eye on that one. You remember back in 2006, a South African container ship MV Umfolozi was stolen. Namibian government has since expanded security at her docks. It may be in our favor since I am fairly certain it's not the government that's been looking for us."

"Well, you are one walking, talking encyclopedia. Jeopardy is looking for candidates like you," Matt jokes.

While Tony is scanning the entire area looking for anything out of the ordinary, Matt grabs Tony and says, "Look at the Woloza now. It's our crate. They're loading it onto the cargo ship."

"Well, that settles that. We've got to get on that ship. It will not be easy. We may have to buy our way on board, which will be easier than sneaking aboard. At least we know it's safe. But we need a disguise!"

"Great, I've always wanted to be a stowaway on a cargo ship thousands of miles from home. Should be comfy," Matt smiles.

Tony turns to Matt and says, "It's better than rhino dung."

"Wait," Matt barks. "Look."

Someone is pointing at the crate, but they weren't close enough to hear.

"I think I know what they're saying because now they're unloading the crate. It looks like they're loading the crate onto a truck. Tony squints to get a better look.

"Looks like a bunch of ants pouring out of their mound," Matt chuckles.

"We need to follow that truck. You get a car and I'll wait here. I saw a car rental agency next to the hotel. Grab our gear on the way."

Matt takes off, and Tony never take his eyes off the crate. Tony starts to wonder who is running the show down there. Where are they taking that crate? Whoever they are, he needs to find out. Not even sure who the good guys are, or if there are any around here. If Matt isn't back soon, Tony knows he may have to go down to the docks by himself. If he loses sight of that crate, he may never find it again. To get another fish will not be easy since that cave is probably under deep surveillance, of the most unfriendly types. Just as the truck starts to take off, Matt comes flying around the corner in an old beat-up VW Bug.

Matt slows just enough to hear him yell, "Hop in, the meter's running!"

"Any idea where they are heading?" Matt asks Tony.

"No idea, but stay far enough away so they don't recognize us. Even though I doubt they figure anyone would be following." They drive for a while until they see signs:

**

PERMIT REQUIRED.
NAMIB NAUKLUFT PARK

**

"You do know that some of the tallest sand dunes are located in this park.

"No, I didn't, Mr. Science. Tell me more," Matt smiles.

"Okay, you asked for it. 'Namib' means 'open space,' and the Namib Desert gave its name to form Namibia— 'land of open spaces.' The park was established in 1907 when the German Colonial Administration proclaimed the area between the Swakop River and the Kuiseb River a game reserve. The park's present boundaries were established in 1978 by the merging of the Namib Desert Park, the Naukluft Mountain Zebra Park, parts of Diamond Area 1, and some other bits of surrounding government land. The park has some of the most unusual wildlife and nature reserves in the world, and covers an area—," Matt's hand goes up.

"Great, I get it. It's a big park. How we getting into the park?" Matt wonders aloud.

The truck slows down and stops at the park entrance. After a brief encounter with the guard, the truck starts again and leaps forward.

"Alright, here we go. You're on, Dr. Science."

"Okay, put your binoculars around your neck."

Matt and Tony pull up, and the guard slowly comes out and starts shaking his head and finger. Tony decided to get out of the car for this one.

Tony announces, "Hello, we are from the United States bird watching team. I am Dr. Gaines and this is my associate Dr. Jones. I know we missed our turn, but I have limited fuel and thought we could use this entrance. Our team of photographers and equipment will be coming shortly, so it would be greatly appreciated if we could enter here instead of Sesriem."

In broken English the guard says, "This car no good. You need truck. Must turn around."

"We will need photos of locals for our TV and magazines, so if you would be so kind it would be great, you could be on our American TV station. You'll be a celebrity in no time, just like *Slum Dog Millionaire.*"

You could see the guard thinking about it. "I will lose my job."

"Why would you? You've done nothing wrong. Listen, you see my car? I will leave it to you when we're finished. I won't need it anymore and would like you to have it, no charge. Just as a way of thanking you," Tony offers.

"It's not easy to find another job," the guard replies.

"How about a little cash for now, just to hold you over until the camera crew gets here?"

That gets a big grin, as Tony hands him two hundred in twenties. Probably more than he makes in six months. The guard's eyes get wide and he says, "Okay, hurry on through. Stay on the path."

"If you were only this smooth with the ladies," Matt teases.

"Let's get out of here. I am sure there will be other check points. Now, let's go find us a truck. Can't be a lot of traffic on these roads." Tony accelerated into the sandy expanse of the Namib Desert.

Chapter 6

DIAMONDS

Why did I ask Grandpa for help? Maybe Grandpa will forget about me asking him for help with the ladies. Wooed, what is that? And soon I was fast asleep. Mom was not too keen about me riding with Jonny, so I had to take the bus today. Especially since my detention and my last swim meet performance, or nonperformance say I should, I was on lockdown. No way will I get to that party unless I accumulate some huge brownie points. I've been grounded for two weeks. There is only one week left before the end of the year spectacular school party. This couldn't have come at a less inopportune moment. No cell phone was the biggest punishment, along with other details. Mowing, cleaning, fixing, and helping around the clinic. But Mom always relaxed her rules after a few days. She could never stay mad very long, thank goodness. I couldn't risk anything, so I was on my best behavior. Maybe she will relinquish my *"groundedness"* and allow me to go to the big party. Not going to happen. Maybe I'll have to sneak out for that one, but if I get caught, my summer break will be brutal.

Now that Grandpa is back home, Mom will make me do all kinds of errands. But for now, first I have to explain to Violet that I was innocent and beg for her forgiveness, then ask her to the party. I need to clear this mess up. Should be a slam dunk.

"Dylan, your breakfast is ready," Chloe screams through my door.

It was a quiet breakfast since Chloe scampered off to school early and Grandpa was still asleep.

"You do remember that I am going to a conference in Boston and I will be taking Chloe with me?" Mom quizzes me.

"Not really, when are you leaving?"

"Next Friday, I told you thousand times. Do you ever listen to anything I say?" Mom grins.

Holy cow, a beacon glows brightly in my mind. *Party, problem solved. How stupid can I be? This is the miracle I've been asking for.* "Oh, yeah, I remember now."

"What did you and Grandpa do last night?" Mom asks.

"Nothing, we just talked about stuff."

"Yeah, what kind of stuff?"

"Nothing bad. It was all good. We talked about Grandmother, but it must have tired him out."

As soon as it left my lips, I knew it was a mistake to mention Grandmother. What is wrong with me? *I'm dumber, than dumb.*

Her faced turned white as she slowly moved towards me and says in her low, deep death voice, "Dylan, I have tried to explain to you a million, zillion times. Grandpa is getting old, and he cannot withstand a lot of interrogation from you or anyone of us. Please just let him get back to his normal life, and no more discussions about Grandmother or you will live the rest of your life grounded," Mom says emphatically.

"But Mom it wasn't wh—"

"Don't want to hear it. Never again."

"But!"

"Dylan, not one more word from you. I had to listen to your father for twenty minutes about how unstable and irresponsible you are and that I am a—never mind. Just don't test me these days. Listen, you know I love you, and I need you more than ever. You're the man around here, so please act like one," Mom smiles.

"Yes Mom, I'm sorry."

"Okay now, kiss me and eat your breakfast. I've got to go out for a minute while Grandpa's still asleep. Before you leave, stick your head in his room and see if he needs anything."

"Sure thing."

"*Ciao,* honey."

After breakfast I head over to Grandpa's room. He's sitting up in bed looking confused.

"Grandpa, are you okay?"

"Sure, sport, just took me a minute to realize where I was. Thanks, any coffee out there or did you drink it all?"

"Mom left you a full pot."

"By the way, I think I know how to get that girl."

"Great, but I've got to get off to school. We'll talk later."

The dreaded school buses. The fighting and spitting are a real pleasure, but the odors are the worst. And yet sometimes Violet rides it, so maybe it'll be my lucky day. I wonder how many murders have happened on a school bus. I slink back in the most uncomfortable seat and close my eyes.

**

What a nasty morning. Storms and lightening all over the place. I have to get back inside and out of this weather. There's nothing but sand for as far as the eye could see in any direction, not one house or building in sight. Where did this crazy storm come from, anyway?

The weatherman said clear and sunny, zero percent chance of rain. That's the perfect job for me: never right and never wrong and never fired. Oh well, I'll just start walking until I see something. But with all this wind and rain it isn't easy to either see or walk. Man, this is the worst summer storm we've had in years, and it certainly isn't a named hurricane. Might be a funnel cloud. Those things are just as bad. I need to find some cover soon or I'm a goner.

I've never seen so much rain coming down at one time. It must be falling at six inches per minute. But it doesn't seem to affect all this sand. Forget the desert. I might drown standing on this sandy beach. I can read the headline: "Phenom—boy drowns in sand." I can't move or see. Maybe it's best if I dig a hideout in the sand. I start digging as fast as possible until I fall into a hole. It's dark but no more rain. I can't see a thing.

I hear someone say in a female voice, "Hey, do you need help?"

"Who's that?" I say. "I can't see. Where are you?"

"Right in front of you. What are you blind or something?"

"It's dark, I can't see anything? Where am I?"

"You're in our home. I am setting the dinner table, and all of a sudden you appeared in our living room. May I help you?"

"Yes, you can turn on the lights, pleaseee!"

"They are on. What is it you want?"

"Well, for starters, where am I?"

"You're in our home. Are you also deaf?"

"No, smarty pants. I heard you, but I don't understand or like your answer."

"No reason to be upset with me. You're the one that broke into our house. If anyone should be asking the questions it should be me. My mom and dad have not arrived home yet, but they should be here shortly, then maybe you'll be nicer to me when they arrive. Or better yet, I think you should leave before they get here. What do you want?"

"Sorry, I am so very confused since I am not sure how I got here. Where am I again?"

"You're in our home."

"You said that, but I don't know where that is!"

"I'm going to ask you to leave one last time and if you don't, it's trouble."

"I wish you wouldn't ask me anymore. This is a tiring conversation and I do not want any trouble."

"Well, if you don't want any trouble, answer my question. What is it you want?"

"That's your question?"

"Forget it. I can't do this anymore."

"You can't do what anymore?"

"This!"

"This what?"

"You are one tiring little girl. What are you five?"

"No, I'm a two-hundred and twelve."

"You are soooo funny. Please just get me out of here."

"No problem, why didn't you ask? The front door is just in front of you."

"I can't see a thing. Maybe you could help me find the door?"

"Of course, it would be my pleasure. Oh, before you go, I assume you can swim?"

"Yes, very well, thank you."

"Great, just turn around and walk straight. Thank you."

"I hope to never see you again," she says, in a demeaning voice.

Before I could finish my sentence, it just drops off like an elevator shaft without the elevator.

"Oh crap," I start screaming, "HELP."

**

"Everyone off the bus, let's go. We're here. Have a nice day," the bus driver announces.

Oh no, I fell asleep. What a weird dream. As I'm shaking my head, I noticed Violet, sitting across from me?

Violet says, "Good morning, sleepy head. You're not much of a morning person, are you?" she giggles, and leaves.

Before I could say anything, she was gone and off the bus. At least I didn't drool all over her, and she's still speaking to me since the last incident.

Once I get to school, I hook up with Jonny, who says, "Dude, you are one lucky guy. You know Donald McFuller, well he never does anything but play with his video recorder. Well, lucky for you."

"What you rambling on about?" I ask.

"Dude, he's in your chemistry class, right?"

"Yeah, so?"

"Come on, even you're smarter than that. What'd you just wake up? You look sleepy. You've been smoking the funny stuff?"

"No just tell me what's going on?"

"Donald is physically attached to his video recorder machine, and he had it on Violet's fine butt the day you got pinched. It shows Jimmy putting the lizard down her jeans, not you, dude. You're one lucky cat," Jonny smiles.

"Does Violet know?"

"Not sure, but he does want some type of finder's fee for his handy work," Jonny replies.

"By the way I'm going to kill that turkey for taking pictures of Violet's butt. He's a dead man."

"Cool it, man, he's your only salvation. You kill him, you're still in hot water with your gal. By the way, does she even know you're alive? Are you ever going to ask that girl out? All you talk about is Violet this, Violet that. You've got to make your move, dude, or somebody's going to beat you to it. She is one fine filly, and maybe I'll make a move."

"J'man, it would take me all of thirty seconds to wipe you off this planet."

"Calm down, wild man. Just hurry up before some senior snags her up."

"Right, right. What class is Donald in?"

"Not sure, but he always sits in the same place during lunch," Jonny grins.

Lunch couldn't come fast enough. I bolted to the cafeteria, but see no Donald. Great, the one day he goes in hiding. Then I see him carrying his lunch tray. Man, that boy can eat.

"Hey Donald, ole buddy," I smile.

"Yeah, whatever. I know what you want, but it's going to cost you."

"Come on, what for? I'll pay to make a copy."

"I've already made a copy. Do you want to see it?"

"Yeah, for sure." There in front of me on Donald's laptop was Jimmie Johnson dropping a lizard down the backside of my sweet Violet.

"OMG, this is perfect. Thanks, man. Do you have sound?"

"Nope."

"Thanks, this is good stuff."

As I reach for the USB port drive to retrieve the memory stick, Donald smacks my hand and says, "I don't think so. I need some cash to buy some things for Brutus."

"What's a Brutus?"

"It's a Dogo Argento," Jonny says as he pulls out a picture of his dog.

"Okay sure, I'll give you ten bucks towards the Argentina thing."

Donald starts to laugh uncontrollably, "Surely you jest. It's a very rare dog and your ten bucks wouldn't feed it for a day."

"Great then, how much?"

"I don't want money. I want services from your mother."

"Watch it, Donald. I will flatten you if talk about my mother like that again."

"No, you moron, her vet services. I want a free checkup for Brutus."

I think for a minute, knowing that my answer means nothing. "Sure, done, no problem."

Anyway, I know Mom's always helping animals for free. "Now hand over the memory stick."

"Oh, gee just because I'm fat doesn't make me stupid. I want it in writing, on your mom's office stationery."

I start mumbling but know I'll never win. "Okay, but no one see's that tape but me. I get the only copy, you understand?"

"Yeah, I have much better photos of her derriere than this if I wanted to make some real money."

"Donald, you're starting to make me mad."

"Just kidding, cool your jets. Have the note tomorrow and you can have the memory stick. Now can I finish my lunch?" Donald asks.

"Later, see you first thing in the morning in front of the building," I smile.

I've always liked Donald okay. We have been in school together since first grade, and he never has caused me any problems, but I figured one day that recorder of his would. He's not even supposed to have it during school hours. If I tell on him, I'll never get the tape. It's a small town, and there are not a lot of school choices.

After explaining to Jonny the details, he says, "that's one shrewd negotiator."

"Whatever, now I've got to work on Mom. He better come through."

"He will, man. He's about three-hundred pounds and has one friend—a fork."

We both laugh, and I head back towards class as the bell goes *brrinnnnggg*.

You have never seen a nicer kid when I want to be. As soon as school was over, I started for the exit, ready to pamper Mom.

"Good afternoon, Mr. Cabrella. I guess I'll see in a few minutes. You going somewhere?"

"Oh damn, I was just getting my backpack out of my friend's car."

"Excuse me, young man. Language, language."

"Yes ma'am, I'll be right there."

"I know you will," Ms. Harkin hisses.

I can't believe I forgot about detention. If I don't get that letter from Mom, my life's over. Maybe I can skip detention. That's a fate worse than death. Is there any justice in this world? I am in a funk. Nothing ever goes right. I am such a loser. I have such high hopes to be something one day, and it's not going to happen if I keep going to detention. What would it be like to be born with a silver spoon instead of a brick upside the head? As I walk into detention, I think it can't get much worse, but it does. My life is over.

"Hey, useless brat," Jimmy whispers. "Glad you could join us today."

After a few million punches in the back and spit balls in my ear, it's finally over and I get out there so fast I almost knock over Hank, the janitor. "Sorry, Hank, but I'm in a hurry."

Hank says, "You all are. All you kids need to slow down."

I go by the house first, but no one's home. I try the clinic and there they are—Chloe and Grandpa playing with puppies and kittens. The clinic is next to our house.

"Hi Mom."

"Hey darling, any trouble today?"

"Of course not."

"Good, could you help me clean up in here? Gloria had to leave early."

"Sure, Mom, no problem. I am raring to go."

Mom stares and says, "My, my, what is it you want?"

"Well, now that you ask, I need your help with this thing at school."

I begin to explain so quickly, she stops me and says, "Slow down." After I stop my five-minute speech in fifteen seconds, I could hardly breathe.

"Sure, I'll do it. Get me my office pad off my desk."

"You're the best, Mom. I'll love you forever for this." I give her a big kiss.

"Oh, you will, why thank you. I'm glad it's forever now."

When it comes to animals, she never says no. I think she's done more pro bono work than she charges. With a giant smile on my face, I finish my work and head back to my room.

Grandpa says, "Someone's happy. You got that date, didn't you?"

"Nope, but I will tomorrow."

"Well, that's great, sport. You want me to drive you?"

"Maybe Grandpa, I'll let you know."

"Hey Grandpa, can you tell Mom I'm going swimming near the Marquesas Keys?"

"Sure, sport. Have fun. Any girls going to be there?"

"I sure hope so."

I hop on my bike and head out to the fort, as we call it. It is the most awesome place to swim, boat, float, or just snorkel. The water is so perfectly clear blue you almost don't need a mask. When I arrive, Jonny and Tommy are already in the water. Jonny sees me and swims to shore.

"Glad you could make it, King D. You just missed Violet," Jonny remarks.

"Are you nuts? Why didn't you call me?"

"I did, dude. Ten times, no answer."

"Oh yeah, Mom has my cell. I can't stay long since I'm grounded, but she will allow me to keep training."

"Who was she with?" I ask.

"The usual crew of girls." Jonny blows kisses in the air. "I told her about the big party. She said she'd be there."

"Oh great, I was kind of hoping she wouldn't come just in case I couldn't get loose that night. But now I'm a free bird."

"Dude, you're going to let her roam around all night by herself? You're nuts."

"I trust you to watch over her."

"Not me, dude. I'm going to be busy, my man, real busy. If I were you, I'd be there come rain, sleet, or Moms."

"I'll be there. Mom's going out of town, so I think I'm good. Just got to confirm her travel dates, but I'll figure something out. I've got to go for a swim. Later."

Sometimes I train at the school's pool, Jonny's pool, or I swim in the ocean with a mask and snorkel. I can just swim for miles back and forth. Training in the ocean water helps my skin, keeps my mind sharp. As I hit the water, it's a perfect temp, almost too warm but near perfect.

There's nothing more calming then the sound of silence in the water as you swim and glide across the water. I swim for quite a while enjoying the calmness until it's almost black above.

Storms can brew up around here in no time. And I mean brutal storms, and this one looked hazardous. I stop and look around and see no shelter in sight. I sometimes swim away from the shoreline, but this time I drift farther than usual. I figure the next best place is under the water as I head for shore. Thankfully I have my fins on, so it doesn't take me long to get back.

I head down and begin exploring the reefs as I go by. *Wow, these are beautiful.* Soon I forget about the storm. I still have my snorkel, so I never really have to completely surface. I dive back towards the beautiful reef filled with colorful fish and coral. No matter how many times I dive it's always a new experience. It's so beautiful, I think about bringing Violet with me one day. That way I could show her instead of trying to explain.

Wait, what is that shiny thing on the bottom? I go up and take a big gulp of air and swim straight down towards the shiny thing. It looks like a ring of some sort. I reach out but can't quite grasp it. I keep trying with no luck. I struggle to stretch out and I finally grab the shiny object, which looks like a diamond ring. *I'm going to give this to Violet.* My foot gets caught in a nasty coral reef. I cannot get free. I try to get my foot out of the fin with no luck. Great, I'm going to drown with a diamond ring in my hand. Who's going to find me? Forget about the Beatles tune, buy her a diamond ring. I'm dead. I have the diamond ring, forget about buying it. I'll never live to give it to anyone.

I struggle to the point of exhaustion. I can hold my breath for an extremely long time. My record is twenty-one minutes, and I am certain, I can hold it longer, but since I'm hyperventilating, it may be two minutes. I begin to pray to my mom and apologize for every bad thing I've done. *Please don't hate me.* Almost out of breath, I hear something, then I see something.

"Quit moving and stay still, I'll cut you loose," I hear someone say.

"What, who said that?"

"It's only me, Chubby Christina."

"Chubby Christina, who's that? What?"

"I'm just a lonesome crab. Stay still and I'll cut you loose."

I look down and see a crab clipping my swim fin. I start to think I'm not only hallucinating, I'm hearing things. I blink again, slowly open my eyes and I definitely see a crab, clipping its claw over my fin and cutting me loose. Of course, I'm dreaming or dead, so with a smile I thank the crab and swim up to the surface. As I swim away, I could hear, "Be careful, the Mayo twins are out and about." I suddenly realize the storm has drifted away and I am on the surface bobbing up and down.

What just happened? Was that real? I check my right fin and see it's been cut. Not just ripped, but cut with a clean scissor precision.

I am extremely exhausted and wonder if I'll make it to shore. I doubt I'll break any records. I start my stroke. *Oh crap. It can't be. Yep, it's a shark.* And then another one comes swimming by and starts to circle me. I think it's two tiger sharks. They are deadly and not ones to play with. I slow down and come to a complete stop. I thought they usually don't travel in pairs so this doesn't help matters. What in the world are they doing in these waters so close to shore?

From my vantage point these babies look huge. And they seem more hostile as I sit in the water, floating. One comes at me. I already have my snorkel in my hand and whack it on the head. That may have been a mistake. It wasn't very happy, and soon the next one came at me like the speed of light, its mouth open, and I luckily kicked it in the side of its head just in time to keep my legs attached to my body.

I could hear voices. *Oh no, not again.* I think they're talking about me. Then I hear laughter. I couldn't understand what they were saying, but I had an idea they were going to eat me and may be discussing certain body parts. I start to think quickly about how to escape. Mom might know, but not sure if she could get out of this mess. I can't start swimming or they will just eat me whole. I have to keep an eye on them and try to back paddle towards shore.

I can see their fins turn sharply and dive. *Oh crap, it's time.* The giant one disappears first, and I put my head under to see it coming straight at me at full speed. It looks like it's grinning at me. Then I hear, "Hey pal, you're going to be our lunch and there's nothing you can do about it." And you know what? He's right. I take off my mask and use my snorkel as a sword. Whatever that's worth, I really don't have a lot of choices. It comes at me and bites down on my snorkel and mask, crushing it to pieces, but no body parts of mine are missing, yet.

Then the next one, the smaller one only a thousand pounds or so, is a bit smarter. This one decides to come at me from under my legs. All I have to defend myself is a fin and a half. I'm doomed. I should have drowned. It would have been a quicker death. Oh great, I see a third fin coming in so fast I almost choke. I guess the word is out that there is an easy snack floating in the Keys. Come on down, folks, and grab a bite.

I tense up and get ready for the next attack. Before I know it, I get tossed into the air and land on the back of this huge fish. What is going on? A pod of dolphins came out of nowhere and they were taking me away from the sharks. I am holding onto its fin for dear life. I look back in time to see the sharks try to keep up but with no luck, because the sharks were surrounded by countless dolphin fins, and the tiger sharks decide it's time to depart. I guess I made it to land, because I awaken on the shoreline coughing up some water and very much disorientated. I look toward the water and see a pod of dolphins jumping in and out of the water, heading back out to sea. Sitting on the shore for a minute, I try to grasp what just happened.

But before I could analyze my situation, Jonny drives up.

"Hey dude, we've been driving up and down the coast looking for you. Didn't you see the storm? It was wicked. Are you alright, Aqua-man?"

"Yeah, I'm cool. Did you see the sharks?"

"What sharks, dude? I see a drowned rat on the shore. You look like you saw a ghost. Let's get you home. Where's your stuff?"

"The sharks ate everything."

"Cool." Jonny smiles.

All I can think is, I need to get home. I begin to think how to explain my latest experiences. I must have at least a dozen guardian angels watching over me.

"Hey dude, did you see the rainbow? It was like, right over your head. I'm thinking there are leprechauns everywhere, handing out gold. Did you get any gold, dude?" Jonny asks.

I could barely speak, but as I opened my hand and I see a diamond ring. Shining like the sun was a diamond ring.

"Yes, I sure did."

Chapter 7

GRULL

"The fuel gage is busted, so I am not sure how far it will take us," Tony says, as the pair treks through the Namib Desert.

"No problem. I have extra gas cans in the boot. Must be normal procedure around here. Not many gas stations lingering in the desert," Matt replies.

"Hey, I think that's our truck up ahead. Thank goodness there's only one road around here. Even with one road, it's still easy to get lost out here. I think it's slowing down. I'm going to pull over. They are probably stopping for a break."

Tony pulls off the road and they both take out their binoculars to get a better look. The truckers depart the vehicle for a bathroom and smoke break.

"I only see three." Matt focuses the lens. "Two from the cab and one came from the back. It's possible that he's the only one with a gun since he's guarding the crate."

After a brief bathroom break and a few cigarettes, the men are back in the truck.

Matt says, "Easy enough, let's take them out and steal the truck."

"Okay, then what?"

"You're no fun. I guess you'll want to wait and see where they're going, which may be smarter but not as fun."

"We'll eventually need to steal the truck but not sure when and where. We need to call Blinky and get a plane fueled and ready to go. If that truck continues, we're headed right for uranium mines, and there is no way we're getting through those heavily guarded gates," Tony says.

"Why not steal the truck and head for the diamond mines in the area? I have no use for uranium. I could use a few diamonds to hand out. It sure would help in the ladies department," Matt smiles.

"Sure Matt, we'll load up the truck with diamonds. Maybe on our next trip," Tony quips.

"Do you think Blinky stayed put?" Matt asks.

"He probably isn't far away. I told him to wait for us until we are declared dead. He's probably flying from airstrip to airstrip just to stay safe and out of reach," Tony says hopefully and continues. "I'm sure those guys have cell phones. They must be talking with someone, but I doubt there is a signal out here. We'll have to stop them and I may have just the plan."

"No bars on my phone," Matt replies.

"Okay, get down as best you can. Let's try my plan."

Tony accelerates past the truck and goes by waving like a tourist as they glide past them. Matt crouching down, hides as best he can, so as not to be seen. The road is slim but that VW Bug could fit anywhere. Not a lot of room on this supposedly two-lane road but Tony keeps the pedal down, wanting to pass them quickly.

"Okay, phase one worked. We'll try to jump them up ahead with a flat tire," Tony says.

They get far enough ahead for Matt to hide in the sand dunes. As they pretend to have a flat tire, the VW blocks most of the road. The truck is either going to slam into the VW, or stop. The trouble is the unstable ground off the road. They won't want to run off the road and risk getting the truck stuck since they're on a time frame.

Tony starts waving his hands like a crazy person. The truck comes around the bend, and the driver slams on the brakes to avoid a collision. Tony keeps waving his hands after they stop. Their faces show confusion and they look like they are arguing as to what to do next. The passenger gets out and in broken English, tells Tony to "move the car, we are in a hurry."

"Oh, you speak English. Great, old chap. Could you help me with my tire?" Tony says in his best English accent. "I must have driven over something and punctured my tire."

"You must move your car so we can pass. You can fix it on the side of the road."

"Old boy, it's punctured. It would ruin the rim. Maybe if you fellows would help me, that would be grand. I have a spare, thanks so much," Tony flashes a smile.

The passenger yells towards the rear of the truck and out jumps a guard, carrying an Uzi. They both start walking towards the VW Bug, screaming at each other and looking at Tony. As they both start walking towards the front of the VW, Matt jumped out. He disarmed and knocked them both unconscious. The driver was a little slow, so before he had time to get out with his pistol, Matt had already opened the side door and showed him the Uzi. Matt tried to get some info from the truckers, but they all admitted to nothing and insisted they were being paid to deliver the truck to the uranium mines. That's all they knew.

Matt asks, "What time were you supposed to deliver the truck?"

"No later than nine p.m. tonight," one of the guards says. He was looking very scared and not sure what Matt and Tony were going to do with him.

Tony tries to calm them down and tells them they will not be hurt. "Do you know who was picking up the item?" Tony asks.

"No, just a delivery location is all we know. We all have families and need the money. We did not ask a lot of questions and do not care what is in the crate," one of the guards responds.

Matt ties them up and puts them back in the VW with a few jugs of water. The only good news is there was no traffic and the guys would not be found for a while. Matt loosely tied the knots so they could escape in the near future. They shove the VW Bug off the side of the road and take their cell phones, weapons, and truck.

Finally a signal, and they get Blinky's voicemail and leave him a message to meet them at the Sesriem airfield, tonight.

"Please call me back at this number, you useless piece of lard. We need you at the Sesriem airstrip after dark, tonight. Yes, we're both alive but not sure for how long. How about you, any trouble? Call us back ASAP," Matt leaves a message.

"As usual I got his voicemail. I also texted him, so he should follow up shortly. Hopefully, he's still sober. We have to fly tonight."

Blinky's text message beeps: "BITE ME. Will have to look up airstrip location. I am in Cape Town. I'll have more details soon. I'll be there."

"All good. Blinky is alive and well, planning a quick departure. All we have to do is get there in one piece," Matt says.

"Great, it can get pretty hairy out here in the desert. Not a good place to get lost, my friend. If the lions don't eat you, something else will," Tony replies.

Blinky texts again: *Should be at airfield by 8:00 p.m. It's a beauty. I can't bring Lucy. Too small a runway.*

Soon it was another miracle as they drove over a small hill and see an airplane waiting on the tarmac. It was a Twin Otter deHavilland DHC-6, with special gear fittings for landing in all types of elements.

Matt looks at Tony and says, "Something isn't right. I can feel it."

Blinky comes out from the runway smiling and waving like he just swallowed a canary.

"Welcome boys, let's get moving before they change their minds. I loaded them up with cigs, booze, and magazines, so let's get the show on the road."

"Thanks for getting us all squared away," Tony says appreciatively.

"No problem. The flight plan's all set. We will be flying over water. They wouldn't let me fly over land. We've got to pick up Lucy. She is parked in Luanda. I sure miss her," Blinky smiles.

Lucy is Dr. Tony Rome's jet.

"Let's get out of this crazy town, but hold on a minute. I've got to grab our crate," Matt exclaims.

Matt turns and heads for the truck. When he opens the back, he just stands there and stares, saying softly, "Tony, Dr. Rome, um, we've got a visitor."

Tony runs to the back of the truck, stops and says, "Hello Grull, a pleasure to see you this evening."

Grull, smiling says, "You fellows sure are a resourceful bunch. Where are you off to?"

"Well, funny you should ask but you're coming with us. Matt, load up the crate," Tony tells Matt, who is still standing there staring.

"You two know each other. Are there others I don't know about? Lucky for you I'm not the jealous type," Matt smiles.

"Plenty of others. That's one of my friends from the cave. Let's move it, Grull," Tony says.

As everyone enters the plane, Blinky just stares at Grull.

"Let's get out of here. That runway doesn't look too stable," Tony remarks.

"Yeah, it's best you don't look at it," Blinky agrees.

"Well Grull, it looks like you could explain a few things since we'll have a long time to get better acquainted. I hope you're not afraid to fly," Tony says smugly.

Grull responds with a big smile, "I hope you gentlemen are not afraid to fly."

Tony and Matt showed little concern about Grull's comeback.

Tony starts with the questions. "What is it you want with my little fish friend? And what and where are the Troads? Where are you from?"

Matt pours himself and Tony a drink says, "Yeah, by the way, what are Troads?"

"That's what Mr. Grull here will explain," Tony nods.

"I prefer something less alcoholic," Grull remarks as Matt hands him a drink.

"The only question you two should be asking yourselves is if you think they will be looking for me by now. They know you have kidnapped me and will not be happy. So, you should first think about letting me go and you might live to tell about it," Grull warns.

"Who will be looking for you?" Tony asks.

Matt reminds Grull, "Too late pal, we're already in the air and soon to be flying over the Atlantic."

Grull just sits back and grins without saying a word. Matt and Tony just sit back and relax, knowing Grull won't answer any of the questions. Tony falls asleep, and soon Matt is shaking him.

"Wake up, sleeping beauty. We've got company. Not sure what it is, but it's something," Matt grins.

What, is it another plane?" Tony asks.

"It's pitch black out there and Blinky hasn't seen anything, but we both felt it."

"Are we hit, Blinky?"

"No, I checked everything out, but I'm getting an image on radar. We are flying low over the water. Possibly a flock of birds."

"Blinky, take her higher and see if the image follows. Hey Grull, do you have any idea what's going on out there?" Tony asks.

Sure do, it's a friend of mine. Probably been following us and has been waiting until you're farther out over water before he attacks. I asked you nicely to let me go. I do not think he will be happy until I am safe," Grull grins.

"Attack who? What are you talking about?"

Suddenly, a loud bang sound came from the top of the plane.

"What in the world was that?" Matt exclaims.

"Get in the co-pilot seat and help Blinky. I'll stay back here with Grull."

Bam, another loud boom as if the ceiling was falling down. Metal was crumbling and there was a huge indentation on the ceiling.

"Okay Grull, who's your friend?" Tony asks.

Grull smiles and says, "Tragoon."

"Tragoon, that's impossible. Why would that thing be helping you?" Tony asks, bewildered.

"Oh, so you know my friend. He's a very close friend, and he will not stop until I am free, so I suggest you land and let me go, or else," Grull smirks.

Boom, another loud crash.

Matt comes back and says, "We're dropping. Something is pushing us down. Probably a much heavier plane but we can't get a good look."

Tony looks at Matt and in a slow, hesitant voice says, "It's Tragoon, and he wants Grull."

"You must be kidding me. That's insane. Then let's give him to Tragoon," Matt says.

"Good idea, Grull, get up and follow Matt."

"I don't think so," Grull snaps.

Matt looks at Grull and says, "We can do it the easy way or the hard way. Now get up, you albino weasel." Matt takes a hold of Grull as Tony opens the plane door, and Matt tosses Grull out the door.

"Hope you grow some wings," Matt screams.

I hope we did the right thing because now that beast will take us down for sure." Tony says.

Finally, the pounding stopped and everything went quiet.

"Wasn't that fun? Fun times usually occur when Grull is around. He is the fun type."

"Whatever you say, boss. Is that what found you in the cave? Well, you guys have so much in common. I hope you aren't upset about his sudden departure," Matt frowns.

"It may a take a while, but I'll survive."

Blinky announces over the intercom in a calm voice, "You two might want to buckle up. It's going to get a little rough." Knowing that not much gets Blinky too alarmed, they don't hesitate to snap on their seat belts. Within minutes half the planes roof was ripped off and a crash into the ocean was imminent.

Blinky screams out again, "Brace yourself. We're going down."

Wind was coming in and it was not easy holding on, but fortunately they were close to the water after their debut with Tragoon.

Tony yells, "Can you land her?"

"I'm trying," Blinky shouts.

As Tony looks out of the torn roof above the cabin, he could barely make out an object. Sure enough, it was Tragoon and something was on top of him, flying in the moonlight. Tony couldn't believe it, but it looked like Grull was riding that thing like a horse jockey. Grull looked safe and they were doomed.

Little had anyone known that as Grull was being tossed out the door, Tragoon flew under and caught him. Grull was now riding on the back of Tragoon. And this wasn't the first time Grull had ridden on Tragoon.

Blinky is an excellent pilot so if anyone could land this plane, it would be him. The plane can land on water since it's an amphibious aircraft. Luckily the water wings helped slow the brunt of their impact. They slid for what seemed like hours, then the plane flipped over and crawled to a stop. Having a little moonlight helped some. And landing in the Atlantic Ocean in the middle of the night could have been much more catastrophic for all. There was a lot of groaning, but no one was seriously injured. Matt already had the raft opened and on the water. It's not normal to see a huge dragon and someone riding on it, at least not in the twenty-first century. It's just not a common occurrence.

"Bring all the equipment, radio, water you can salvage. It may be a while until we're rescued."

"Hey Doc, what do you want me to do with the crate?" Matt inquires.

"Blinky, help Matt load the crate onto the raft. It may be a bit cozy. I'm sure they'll be back for the crate. I suppose Grull could care less about our well-being."

It is was beautiful moonlit evening, while the boys snuggled up on the South Atlantic Ocean. "Blinky, bring all the booze you can find," Matt adds.

Chapter 8

MAGIK

By the time I got back to my house, I was still a little dazed, but I still had that ring in my hand.

"Hey Dude, maybe I should take you by the emergency room. You look white as a ghost." Jonny looked concerned as he stared at me.

"No worries, man. Mom should be home. She's better than any emergency room. Hey Jonny, thanks again. It was pretty rough out there."

"Anytime, dude. I got to keep you alive for the big party."

"Yeah, for sure, see you later."

"Where have you been?" Mom asks curiously. "Oh my, you look pale. Come here. Are you feeling okay? Chloe, get me my bag."

"Okay Mom, he looks funny."

After briefly passing out, I come to, lying on the couch.

"Well," Mom exclaims, "whatever you've been up to, it's good enough to get you a pass from school. You're staying home tomorrow so you can keep Grandpa company until we move him this weekend. I'm sure he has plenty for you to do."

"But Mom, I need to get to school. It's important."

"Since when did you need to go to school? Not happening. Your heart is racing and your blood pressure is through the roof. Your color is whiter than white, and you are not going anywhere. Do you understand? You really are scaring me that you want to go to school," Mom leers at me.

"Mom, what if I?"

"Not going to happen. Think of it as a long weekend. I'm also calling your father and letting him know that you will not be at practice this weekend. I need you to help move Dad's stuff. Now I'll order some pizza and then you're going to bed."

"Mom, can I run some blood tests?" Chloe asks.

"Not now, Chloe. He needs to rest."

I wolf down the pizza and head to bed. Mom was right—I was beat and could hardly walk down the hall. I call Jonny and beg him to come by the house so he can give Donald the note tomorrow morning.

"Please Jonny, I'll repay you. I promise anything you want, but I cannot leave the house."

"Okay, I'll come by later tonight," Jonny replies with a sigh.

"Great. I'll put it in an envelope with your name on it. Do not lose it or I'll kill you."

"Is your Mom in her nightgown yet?"

"Jonny, not now. Hurry, I'm getting tired, see you soo—"

Before I could finish, I was fast asleep.

Jonny arrives a little later and Chloe answers the door.

"What do you want?" Chloe asks.

"Listen, little Frankenstein, I'm here to see Dylan not you, CC."

"You'll have to wait here. Mom said no visitors."

"Okay, no problem. I'll go see him myself. Thanks anyway."

As Jonny starts walking, Chloe screams, "MOM, MOM, Jonny is here and won't leave."

"Quiet, quiet, you little monster. Oh, hi Isabella. I'm here to pick up something from Dylan," Jonny grins.

"Jonny, it's not Isabella, it's Ms. Cabrella. He's asleep, and I hope he wasn't disturbed by someone yelling in the middle of the night. Go to bed, Chloe. I'll tuck you in, in a minute."

"Sure Ms. C, but Dylan was adamant about taking a note to school for him."

"Okay, wait here. I'll see if he left you a note."

"Sure thing, Isa—I mean Ms. C. By the way, you're looking exceptionally beautiful tonight."

"Jonny, you're a mess. I already feel sorry for your future wife."

Isabella finds a note clutched in Dylan's hand with "Jonny" written on it. "Here you are, Jonny. Have a good night. Dylan will not be at school tomorrow, and do not come by here and take him out for any reason, or I will call your parents. He needs rest. By the way, what happened to him today? He didn't say much at dinner."

"Well, I'm not really sure. He told us that while swimming, a couple of sharks attacked him and he kicked them away. Then he said something about Flipper and a crab saving him. That's all I got until he passed out. Sorry Ms. C, I found him down by the beach, gassed," Jonny shrugs.

"Thanks Jonny. Sorry about the wife comment, but you have to start treating women as humans. Soon you'll be an adult, soon to be dating, and one day you may realize women are not pieces of meat."

"I date now, Ms. C."

"I'm sure you do. Goodnight."

"Good night, Ms."

As she closes the door Jonny, mumbles to himself. "That is one hot Mom, lucky dog."

Morning came quick since I slept like a rock. By the time I woke up it was eleven a.m. I hadn't slept that late in years, and I was still confused, but starving. Grandpa was on the back porch and I went outside to greet him.

"Hey Grandpa."

"Hey sport, how'd you sleep? You've almost slept the entire day. When I was your age I would get up before the sun and start my day. You kids today are pitiful. I bet you're hungry," Grandpa grins.

"Yep, what you got in mind?"

"Well, your mother bought some excellent Italian deli meats along with my favorite, prosciutto. We can make sandwiches and have some of that iced tea in the fridge. How does that sound, sport?"

"Sounds perfect. Let's get to it, I'm starving."

After three sandwiches, I finally say "uncle" and sit down to watch TV.

"You want to help me go through some of my old things? Since I'm moving back to my house this weekend I need to go through this stuff and throw out anything I don't need. I don't really need anything, but let's see what it all is. It's been a long time so it might be fun."

"Okay sure, Grandpa, I'll help."

As we get to the first box, the phone rings. I get up to answer it since we all know Grandpa hates the phone and has never answered one that I can recall. "Hello, hello."

"How are you feeling? I wanted to be home for lunch, but an emergency came up."

"I feel fine, Mom. Grandpa and I made giant sandwiches and we're going through his stuff now."

"Okay, don't lift anything heavy. I'll try to be home early. Love you. Oh, by the way, I gave your note to Jonny last night."

I forgot all about that. What is wrong with me?

"Thanks Mom, later."

Before I can put the phone down it rings again.

I said, "What, Mom?" kind of perturbed.

"Dylan, is that you?"

"Yes."

"Are you feeling better?"

"Yes."

And then it finally hits me. It's Violet on the other end, and I almost pass out again. Then I go into my usual rant. "Sure, fine, fine I'm just fine."

"Well, I am so happy you're feeling better and wanted to let you know that I'm sorry about the other day in class. I thought it was you but it wasn't. Sorry, Jonny showed me the tape."

"Okay, sure, sure. I just thought you ought to know."

"You're so sweet. By the way, do you want to hang out at the party next week?" Violet asks.

Well, luckily, I didn't screw it up. "Sure, let's hang out."

"Okay, sounds like a plan. Hope you feel better soon. I've got to get to class, bye."

"Okay, I'm fine by the way. Thanks." She giggles and hangs up.

Thanks, I said thanks. I need help. Why did I thank her? I am an idiot but what do I care? I have a date with Violet. Holy cow.

I scream, "Grandpa, I did it. I finally did it. Well, she started it, but I didn't screw it up!"

"Slow down, sport. What did you do?"

"I have a date with Violet. Yep, a real date, kind of."

"Good job, sport, and you didn't need any of my help. Maybe I could give you some advice about your date. It's your first one, right?"

"Well, not really. I've been around."

"Sure, sure, but maybe a few tips just to refresh your memory. You need any money?"

"No thanks, Grandpa." Money, where did he get any money?

"You've got to open her door every time she gets in or out."

"What are you crazy? Are you sure? That sounds like an old custom. Dad never opened Mom's door."

"Yeah, where did that get him? Open the car door, sport. That I do know."

"But I'm not picking her up. I'm meeting her out."

"Well, when you do pick her up."

Then I start to think about our date as my blood pressure rises, and I start to get dizzy. Can I go through with it?

"Grandpa, when do I kiss her?"

"Kiss her? Calm down, sport. You're rushing things a bit. Just treat her like a porcelain doll and all will work out."

"But I remember her saying she's not a porcelain doll."

"I wouldn't kiss her on the first date. It's best if you wait unless she kisses you first. You're a gentleman, sport. She'll let you know when it's time to kiss."

"But what if she waits forever to kiss me? That's a long time, Grandpa."

"She won't. If she's going out with you, she's going to want a kiss. I can guarantee you that."

"This is sure complicated. When do I actually take her to bed?"

"Wooo, slow down, sport. I don't think that should be something you need to worry about just yet. You'll have plenty of time for that. Didn't your Dad go over these details?"

"Not really. Mom said Dad wasn't the best role model when it comes to women, and if I had any questions to ask her, but I kinda feel dumb asking Mom about women."

"Well, that's where you're wrong, sport. She knows more than any of us men. She's the best one to ask, not your pals at school. You've got plenty of time, so let's get your mind off it and go through this crap of mine."

"You're not kidding. What is all this junk? Grandpa, what's this thing? Looks like old junk."

"I'm old and you tend to collect stuff. Then before you know it, it's just junk but some of this is pretty cool stuff. Take that thing you're holding in your hand. That's made of gold marble. I gave it to your Grandma Liz many moons ago. I saw it at a flea market and had to have it. It has special qualities. If you hold it up and stare directly into the marble's eye, you can see far into the future. Why don't you try it, sport?"

"Show me, Grandpa. I'm not sure what to do."

"Okay, let's see what she says."

Grandpa holds this giant gold marble up to his eye and squints into the center for a long time. He smiles, frowns, and begins to cry just before his laughter. Then he stops and puts the marble down.

"Well, what'd you see?"

"It won't come true if you tell anyone. You'll have to try it yourself, but I did see some things that may interest you."

"What?"

"Let's just say you're going to have a long and prosperous life."

"Did you see Violet in my future?" I asked inquisitively.

"Like I said, it won't come true, so all you need to know is everything turns out just fine. Only a few minor bumps along the way."

I mumble, "A few bumps, what kind of bumps, you crazy old man? If you can see the future, why not see where Grandmother is and go get her?" But I am not saying that out loud. Mom would shoot me.

"What's this thing, Grandpa?"

"You remember that I used to weave clothing a million years ago? Well, that is a shuttle. My loom is at my house. I'll show you how it works once we set it up at my place. We'll make something. Maybe a nice sweater for your girl."

"Grandpa, what's she going to do with a sweater in Florida?"

"Oh yeah, how about a nice silk blouse?"

"Well, sure maybe. Not sure of her size but it sounds like a plan of some sort."

"That looks like Aladdin's lamp."

"You bet it is."

"Oh sure, let me see that," I smirk. "I know how this works. You rub it real hard a few times, I think." Can't remember, but pretty sure, as I rub and rub and nothing. Maybe I'm not doing it right. I try again. I start rubbing and rubbing really hard, and nothing.

"Grandpa, this lamp is broken. It lost its magic. What's this green thing? It looks like a frisbee."

"Ah, that's an emerald boomerang."

"What's it do?"

"You throw it any direction and it comes right back to you."

"Are you sure?"

"Yes, sport. But take it outside and try it out. It will break a window or two as it comes back to you.

"Where did you get all this cool stuff?"

"I just accumulated items when your grandma and I traveled."

As tears start flowing unexpectedly from Grandpa, I quickly change the subject.

"Cool blade, Grandpa."

"Watch out, sport. That one is extremely dangerous."

"What are you talking about? They're all dangerous. But I know how to hold a knife."

"Not this one, be careful. It never dulls," Grandpa warns.

I pick it up and the sharp end of the blade seems to have disappeared. I put my hand where the blade should be and "OUCH!" I cut myself and drop the knife. "Grandpa, what's up with this thing? It just disappeared. Almost like magic!"

"Well, sport, that's what I call it—Lil Magik, spelled M-a-g-i-k. And you're holding it wrong."

Grandpa grabs it with his large hands. When he grabs it by the handle, the blade again disappears. Now you cannot see the handle nor the blade. It's as if he's making a fist, since everything is invisible.

"Are you still holding it, Grandpa?"

"Indeed, sport. Watch."

Grandpa grabs a book and cuts it in half.

"Holy moly, that thing is awesome. Can I have it?"

"Not yet. All this will be yours one day so hold on, sport. You should see Big Magik. It's a sword that does the same thing."

"I sure would like to see that sword."

"Your Mom has it, stashed away somewhere," Grandpa grins.

"Where did you guys get these Magik blades? And why does Mom have it?"

"Just say it was a gift. I think they're actually called Wasp and Hornet."

"That is so cool. Can I show Jonny?"

"No, sport. Let's keep all this Magik our secret," Grandpa smiles.

"Okay, probably right. That thing in the wrong hands could be really dangerous."

I was a little preoccupied so when I heard *brinnnnggg, brriiinnnng,* I dropped the knife and jumped six feet in the air, then I realized it was only the phone.

"I'll get it." Of course, I'll get it. He won't.

"Hello. Hey Dad."

"How you feeling, Son? We need you for the next meet."

"I'll be there. I'm feeling much better now."

"Good, so I'll see you later today."

"Not today. Mom won't let me leave the house."

"We'll see about that. I was your age. I know how you kids act."

"Sure, Dad, but for now I'm helping Grandpa."

"Okay, watch that old man. He's a nut case, Son. He isn't right in the head."

"Dad, he's fine. He's the only one that listens to me. You never have anytime to talk."

"Yeah well, whatever. See you soon."

"Bye, Dad."

I wanted to ask him a few things but figure he never has much time for me unless it's about a swim meet. He's the real nut case. Yeah, a real role model.

"Hey Grandpa, what's next?" I realize Grandpa's fallen asleep. Oh well, I'll watch a movie. Cool, *300* is on. It looks awesome—blood, guts, and archery. I've always wanted to be a toxophilite.

After a while the phone rings again. What is going on? I'm glad I haven't tried to sleep around here.

"HELLO."

"Well, what's up your bootie?"

"Oh hi, Alex. What does thy princess want? Money, men, Mom, and more money?"

"Funny, genius. I just wanted to remind you guys that I arrive next week."

"No worries, I'll be driving soon."

"Oh no, you're legal now. I'm selling my car and walking from now on."

"Funny. Grandpa will be glad to see you."

"Me too. How's he doing? Any talk about Grandma?"

"No way, Mom has set the rules. Any Grandmother talk and its death. I'm already in hot water, so good luck."

"By the way, what are you doing home today? Playing hooky?" Alex asks.

"Well, not really. Kind of run down. I'm thinking of retiring soon. I've lived a long and hard life so far."

After an outburst of laughter, Alex says, "Whatever, goofy. I'm going to miss the big high school blowout. I am actually attending a real party."

"Good for you. What's a real party?"

"It's a college party, genius. Sorry, I'm not going to make Clancey's house party, I could have helped you with the ladies."

"I don't need any help, by the way," I said proudly. "I even have a date. Well, see you later. Try not to knock out any pilots until you land."

"Later. Love ya, little bro."

"Back at ya, sis."

Alex has a black, red or purple belt with insignias of some sort. She started karate at the age of five, and never looked back. As the story goes, it all started when some girl knocked little five-year-old Alex to the ground because she was talking to some eight-year-old boy. The bigger girl liked this boy and was not too happy about Alex speaking with him, so she decked Alex. Not too long after that, Alex became a bit precocious and was obsessed with karate and soon became a martial arts master.

I remember her tossing everything around the house, which includes me and our dog, and was told she even flung Dad's night-swimming friend, who presumably was naked, and then she kicked Dad in the head. I wish I could have seen that one. My other favorite story was the night her date tried to make a move on her or do something she hadn't asked for. She had to drive him to the emergency room. She really never had a lot of dates after that. She blamed it all on Grandmother's disappearance, but I'm fairly certain that most guys didn't want to end up in the hospital.

You'd never know it to look at her. She's platinum blond, I'm sure with a lot of help from a bottle. She doesn't look or act like a tomboy but get her in a karate competition, and she turns into the *Blade*. I sure don't mess with her. I can still beat her in swimming and archery but that's about it.

She obviously can control her emotions, but who knows how many guys are getting tossed around on her campus. I can only imagine how fast that information runs through these colleges. Watch out for a kung fu, platinum blond, last seen in library. Approach with extreme caution.

It's got to be on every Facebook, Instagram, and Twitter feed. "Girl kicks quarterback's butt, more of the story to follow." No, she loves it in school, and I haven't heard or read of any brutal beatings by a crazed blond in the Missouri area.

She's read every Nancy Drew mystery fifteen times and is enrolled at the University of Missouri at St. Louis. She is probably going for a master's degree. She needs to be the best in whatever she takes on. She always wanted to be a detective, so she settled on criminal law.

She seems to like it, though. We rarely see her, but Mom wanted her home to see Grandpa and have everyone together. I can't wait to pick my school. I'm already thinking Hawaii. Why would anyone not want to go to Hawaii? I'm sure Violet will love Hawaii.

Finally, I get back to my movie, the part where the bodies are getting stacked on top of each other, and I start thinking what it would have been like to be a Spartan warrior. I've always liked swords and archery. What a stud I would be. All the women would be all over me. I'll have to use my sword to fight off the chicks. Before I know it, I'm fast asleep.

**

"Who are you? You must not care much for your life because soon you will meet your maker. Take off that mask and show yourself."

The brief silence is broken. "I will not fight a woman. Please be gone and quit this charade."

"This is no charade. I plan on defeating you here and now."

The Master Swordsman Zavker laughs out loud for all to hear. "Do you hear that, my people? I have been challenged by this salty woman. But I will not fight a weaker foe, so be gone, or you shall die quickly."

"You do not scare me. I want you to release my family or your life will come to an abrupt end."

Master Zavker laughs with the crowd to the point where he falls onto the ground, almost in tears. As he dusts himself off, he is no longer laughing and looks at his female adversary, stroking his long white beard.

"Since your family is imprisoned, it is best they stay there so they can watch you die. If it is a fight you want, it gives me great honor to show everyone your quick extinction." Master Zavker yells out, "Bring me the prisoners that belong to this death wish."

Soon two people in chains are walking towards the arena—Grandmother and me.

"Are you related to this soon to be dead woman?" Master inquires.

"Yes, she is my Granddaughter, and she will prevail. Your rule over us has come to an end. No more of your butchery and death. It is your time to die."

Master snorts and says, "Now I know where she gets her passion. Do you not love this young girl? Why not ask her to depart and live out her final days?"

"If you release them, you shall live to see another day," the girl speaks out.

"What is your name, dead one?" Master asks.

"Just call me Princess. Are you going to release my family?"

The young woman never glances at me or Grandmother.

"Listen to me, little one. I have not decided who to kill first. Would you like to watch them die, or shall I take your life first?"

"You will fight me first and with one last request. Let them go and I will spare your life and depart from this place forever."

"Well, Princess, you've got the final part correct—you shall depart this world forever."

As Grandmother and I struggle with the locked chains, I attempt to kick the guard. But the guard draws a knife and waves it next to my throat. A little drop of blood falls to the ground.

"Enough, enough talk. Choose your weapon, little Princess."

She pulls out her large samurai sword and bows towards Master Zavker.

"At least you have chosen the correct sword and protocol to bow. Many of my foes do not have any decorum. Bring me my sword."

A servant gets off his knees and hands over a giant gleaming sword. Master says out loud to everyone, "Should I cut her in two or three or four pieces? It may be fun to watch her struggle."

The crowd laughs and starts yelling. "Make her suffer. Make her suffer."

The Master looks pleased and bows towards the princess. "Well it sounds like they want a slow death. Sorry for you and your family. Do not worry, I will not kill your family for at least a week. That way they will have much more time to hate and despise me as they observe your body decaying in the sunshine."

Without warning, the Master slices his sword with such speed and force, the princess barely jumps away before he cuts off a large clump of her hair. He catches the hair and brings the bright blond hair up to his nose. "You smell pleasant little one."

Again, Master Zavker brings the sword in a slicing blow, cutting the Princess's arm and drawing blood through her white blouse.

"Soon your lily-white blouse will be a bright red, little one. Maybe you should pick your battles with others that are not great warriors like me because my next blow will not miss its mark. I just wanted to give the crowd some additional entertainment."

In a split second, so swift, no one realized what had just happened, it was over. The head of Master Zavker rolled to the ground.

I looked down and it was the head of my Dad. The princess walked over and freed Grandmother and me.

**

"Wake up, wake up. Hey sport, wake up."

Holy cow, that was me chained to Grandmother, and I think the Princess was Alessandra. What a weird dream.

Grandpa says, "You were jumping and screaming. I thought it best that I wake you up. You okay, sport? You're sweating. Bad dream, huh?"

"Yeah, I guess that movie got to me. I've had some violent dreams recently."

"Can you remember any details?"

"Not really, actually no." I didn't want to tell him that most of my dreams were about Grandmother.

Chapter 9:

PIRATES

Tony, Matt and Blinky float adrift in the middle of the Atlantic Ocean off the coast of Africa.

Blinky begins to sing "Walk on the Water," by Creedence Clearwater Revival.

"Late last night, I went for a walk, down by the river near my home." Then Matt starts in. *"Late last night.* Hey Tony, why don't you join in?"

Tony closes his eyes and tries to tune them out, which is extremely difficult since the only sounds in the middle of the ocean in a small raft are the two sopranos. The beacon on the raft doesn't work. Finally, the liquor and the singing come to an end. They both simultaneously pass out, as a wide smile appears on Tony's face.

They've been floating for a while and have yet to see another seagoing vessel. Soon it will be daylight, maybe a plane will spot them. They are not too far from the coast when Tony spots a shark fin or two swimming past the raft.

"Hey, Tom Jones and Sinatra. Wake up, we've got company," Tony remarks.

Matt opens his eyes and says, "Where are we? I may have fallen asleep."

"Why don't you look for yourself?"

Matt suddenly realizes that the raft is surrounded by sharks. "You think they're hungry? They wouldn't dare attack us on a raft, would they, Doc?"

"On any other occasion I would say they would only attack if we were in the water, but watching their reactions it would appear they may attack while we're floating in this not so sturdy rubber raft. Did you grab any weapons? And no, booze doesn't count," Tony smiles.

Matt wakes up Blinky. "Hey Blinky, you got your pistol?"

Blinky, kind of groggy says, "Yep, never leave home without it."

"You might want to get it ready. We have company," Matt points.

Blinky looks over the sides and says, "Well, I guess my singing brought in an audience. Should I continue with any other songs?"

"I think it's best if we try to keep the sharks calm and not any crazier. I count about six or eight. Never seen that many in a frenzy over a floating raft. Any other weapons we can use?" Tony asks.

Matt suggests, "The oars and his knife and a couple of empty bottles may come in handy. Maybe we can hit them over the head. Could use the flare gun as a last resort."

"Not sure it's a good idea to torment. Let's just see what happens. I'd keep all hands and all feet on board." Tony frowns with growing concern.

"Hey Blinky, why don't you put your head in the water and give us a head count on those sharks? Might help your hangover," Matt jokes.

Blinky's rapid response is, "I don't like sharks, but thanks for the hangover remedy. I've sobered up rather quickly, thanks to the current circumstance."

Suddenly, a fin comes in contact with the raft and tears a portion.

"Well that settles it. Yes, they will attack us while in the raft. Okay guys, let's get in combat mode. I'll take front, Blinky middle, and Matt you take rear. I will let you know when one's heading our way. After it swims past, unload a shot. Blinky, let Matt have your gun, he's a much better shot than either one of us."

"Yeah, sure thing. Don't have any extra ammo, only five rounds are loaded," Blinky admits.

"It may be enough to keep them at bay. Matt, be sure and hit the shark. Once he hits it, we will row away as fast as possible. In theory they should attack the wounded shark, which may give us enough time for them to forget about us." Tony says hopefully. "Okay are you singing nuns ready?"

"Ready," Matt says.

"Ready," Blinky says.

"Okay, I see a big one heading straight for us. Get ready!" Tony yells.

Blinky looked extremely nervous, but most folks don't like sharks, much less when you're at a big disadvantage floating in their pond.

Tony smacks the shark on the fin with an oar hoping to get it off track and a second later, two loud gunshots ring out. "Got 'em," announces Matt.

"That should keep them busy. Let's get rowing while this thing is still floating," Tony says.

But it wasn't long before the sharks were back. "That's odd. You sure you hit that shark?"

"Both shots," Matt replies. "I saw red."

"Well, it seems these boys are still interested in our skins."

"What's next, Doc?" a pale Blinky inquires.

"I'm thinking, I don't think we have many choices," Tony says grimly.

Suddenly, a plane goes roaring overhead. Tony starts waving and Matt shoots off a flare.

As soon as the flare leaves the gun, a shark rips into the side of the raft, and everyone is dumped into the water.

Tony screams out, "Stay close, everyone! Let's all swim towards the crate. Blinky, you get behind me and stay close."

Blinky wasn't a very good swimmer and started to panic. "Matt, can you get to Blinky?"

"Not really, I'm trying to keep these maneaters off us."

While floating, another two shots ring out, then another. "I'm out, let's get on the crate."

Blinky completely panics and starts to paddle away from the group. "Grab him, Matt."

Matt reaches out, but couldn't grab him. Blinky was flailing his arms and screaming. Very unusual for such a calm guy. But moments like this test one's nerves. In a matter of seconds, a giant shark grabs Blinky and cuts him in half. The rest of the sharks are so frenzied for his body they completely leave Tony and Matt alone and go after Blinky. Tony and Matt are speechless, for a moment.

"Can I assume that we're out of back-up ammo?" Tony asks.

"Yep, we've got nothing. Maybe that plane will send some help."

"I sure hope so. It won't be long until those crazed sharks come after us. This crate will not give us much protection."

"I see something starboard," Matt says.

"Okay, which way is starboard on this fine vessel? Oh, I see it. Can't make it out, but it looks to be heading our way. Better get here soon or we'll be the next meal for these chaps." Tony grins.

Matt says, "You won't believe it, but I think I see a pirate's flag flying."

"Are you kidding me? I guess a pirate ship is better than a shark."

"So our choice is fish food or a pirate's booty. Well, we should have a third choice. What kind of game show is this?" Matt asks. "I wonder if those reality shows ever have these situations. Bet not. Let's play it cool. We don't have anything to barter with unless they are after the crate."

"Oh no, you don't think they are looking for this crate, do you?" Tony quips.

"No way, they just want humans to barter with. I'm worth ten bucks, tops."

The ship pulls up beside the floating crate with Matt and Tony sitting on top. There are eight people on deck, and an unknown amount below.

"Hello, our ship had a bad explosion and we are all that's left. Do you mind giving us ride back to shore? We would appreciate your help. It's getting hot and we may be fish food soon," Tony yells out.

One of the pirates replies, "What you say you out here for?"

"Pleasure cruise. Our ship's main cabin caught on fire and exploded overnight. We were lucky to survive," Tony barks.

"Any more of you?"

"No, just the two of us."

Suddenly a burst from a machine gun hit the water. The sharks decide to depart the area.

Tony and Matt climb on board and before they can say anything more, both of them have their hands tied.

"You lucky not eaten by shark. Maybe you better off if shark eat you." They all start laughing.

"Why tie us up? We have nothing and all we want is a ride to shore. We promise you no harm."

They all laugh harder. "You think me dummy. I know who you be. Much money for you, alive or dead. I have to show body, so I don't want smelly dead man on boat. My name is Jayla and for now, you will be our guests." The laughter starts up again.

These guys smell worse than death. Doubt any of them ever used deodorant or have taken a shower recently, Tony thinks before he says, "You must be mistaken, we have nothing."

"You and crate worth lots of money for me and my men."

Tony knew better than to negotiate. If they pay their ransom, they would never leave alive. So, they just sat there. Matt was already in stealth mode.

At least they gave them some water, it tasted like urine, but it was wet and they needed something. Tony's strength was diminishing in this heat.

After a while, the pirates started shouting at each other and pointing towards another vessel. The man with the binoculars kept yelling out, "Boat, US, USA, BIG BOAT!"

Jayla orders, "Speed up our boat, we have trouble. Let's get out of here."

It must have been deployed after the military plane spotted the flare. Hopefully these jokes for pirates don't want to mess with these Navy boys. The oldest pirate is maybe sixteen. A bunch of kids that never listened to their parents. Brats is the word. Matt is ready to fight.

"Matt, I think we're going to have company, and I doubt these boys want to mess with them."

"You two shut up, no talking."

All at once Matt jumps up and kicks one of the boys in the head so hard, he falls overboard. The others start yelling and running around not knowing whether to stop or continue. So, they continue. One hits Matt with a giant club, and he falls to the ground.

Jayla says, "Get these two under deck. They cannot be seen. Hurry."

Matt comes to and sees they are both tied up against a post in the bottom deck.

"Well, I gave it the old college try," Matt shrugs. "I thought they would stop for their bud."

"These kids are ruthless little brat thugs," Tony reminds Matt.

Matt, still a little shaken, says, "I was hoping they would stop and give us more time on deck. Now the Navy boys might not know we are on board."

A small Navy vessel deployed from the huge Navy ship catches them with ease. "They know we are here. I bet they picked up the kid you knocked overboard, and I'm sure he is spilling his guts," Tony whispers.

Eventually a kid comes over and points a machine gun and says, "Quiet, or I shoot you both."

The boat begins to slow and comes to a complete stop.

They hear a bull horn. "Ahoy gentlemen. We mean you know harm. Can we board your vessel?"

"No, we done nothing wrong," was the response.

"Sure, I understand but we have one of your men. He must have fallen overboard. All we want to do is return him to you and in return, you give us your two shipwrecked survivors. I thank you for your help in saving the both of them."

This guy is smooth. He knows he can't really get these guys on any legal matter. They haven't hijacked a ship or killed anyone. These are kids and not very rational. All they want is money.

"We drop off your stranded shipmates. They no longer with us. Put our man in raft," Jayla yells.

"We don't have a raft. We'll just pull up beside you."

"No, no good."

You can hear in his voice Jayla was getting flustered. He wasn't sure what to do. He didn't really care about his shipmate but couldn't outrun the Navy vessel.

"He a good swimmer. Throw him in water and we pick him up."

"No, I don't think that would be appropriate. We're coming portside."

Jayla, knowing he could not outrun the watercraft, was getting irritated.

"We have sick man on board quarantine, cannot board, sickly disease. Very bad Ebola virus."

"I see, but we have a medic on board and he could have a look and heal your sick mate."

"No, no bad. We pick up man on shore. Bye now."

The pirate's engine kicked on and they started to take off.

Matt looks over at Tony and says, "Let the games begin. Should get really interesting quickly."

The kid with the machine gun had already darted back up the stairs.

"What now, Doc?"

"Not sure. Can you get us out of these ropes?"

"Probably, I'm pretty sure what the Navy boys are going to do. It's these little mutants I'm not so sure about. You can tell the love they have for their fellow shipmates."

Then Matt asks suddenly, "Did you hear that? Sounds like a plane just flew overhead and then I heard some gunshots. Oh great, these geniuses are shooting at our military planes. That should get them some brownie points. The only reason they are still alive is we're on board."

"I guess so, but if they hit one of our boys all bets are off."

The engines stop and they're still not on shore. Nightfall is upon them and the chess game begins.

"No one is really paying attention to us. Why don't you try to get loose and see what's up?"

"My thoughts exactly. I'm out of here. Later, buddy. See you back at the ranch." Matt smiles and he's off.

Soon Matt returns. "Well, they aren't the brightest bulbs in the pack. They are all sitting upstairs drinking some swill, and most of them are passed out. The crate is all by itself. I think we could get the crate into the water and start swimming away. Not sure about our shark buddies, but we may have to take the chance."

"I agree. Let's get off this bucket. I am sure the Navy boys are watching us like a hawk, so they may even see us go over board and send someone to pick us up. Let's wait a minute before we go. Maybe more of them will pass out." Tony says.

They quietly make it upstairs and grab the crate without making too much noise, not that anyone could hear them since Matt knocked out any of the remaining crew that were still sober. Soon Tony and Matt are overboard with the crate. After a brief swim, they come in contact with a couple of Navy boys in a little skip. Relieved they climb on board with the crate and thank the boys as the skip heads back to the ship.

Once on board the Navy ship, they both clean up and eat like wolves. As Tony is getting dressed in some borrowed clothes, an ensign comes in and says, "Dr. Tony Rome, sir, the captain would like to see you in his quarters."

"Sure, I'm ready. I'll follow you."

"Thank you, sir."

Tony hears laughter and sees Matt with someone, smoking cigars.

"Dr. Rome, I'm Captain Beauregard. I hope you are feeling full and rested after your adventure at sea. Matt informed me about your plane crash. You were lucky one of our planes spotted your flare and called it in. Sorry about Blinky."

"Hey Tony, you remember my stories about a crazy guy in my training class named Beau? Well here he is, a full-blown captain," Matt smiles.

The intercom kicks on, "Captain, you are needed on deck."

"Right, you boys want to join me? I'm guessing the crew you departed is now awake and not too happy."

They hear Jayla bellow, "We want to get our man back. We board you at once."

"You're kidding me. Are those kids that stupid?" Tony smirks.

"Yes," Matt responds.

"Hello. We dropped off your man during the night. He is no longer on our ship. Have a nice day, gentleman."

"We don't believe you. I board you," Jayla threatens.

As soon as Jayla finished saying "you," one of the pirates threw a handmade grenade at the ship. Luckily it missed the deck and blew up in the water.

Captain Beau looks at Matt and says, "Are they that stupid?"

Matt and Tony in unison replied, "Yes."

"Please do not fire upon us. We are departing and no longer have any engagement with you and your men. Good day."

"We need our man. I'm coming aboard."

"They want the crate back. It's worth a lot of money to those boys. They lost the bounty on us," Tony says.

This time they toss another handmade grenade that landed on the deck. It blows up and burns a small portion of the starboard deck, but the fire was immediately put out.

Matt looks at the captain and says, "Do you need permission from the White House to attack?"

"White House, my tail. Get a shell in the water ASAP. We are under attack. Put a shell in the water, now," the captain orders.

Within seconds, the pirate's ship was obliterated out of the water and it was like there never was a ship or pirates.

Matt says, "Let's go finish those cigars."

"Sounds like a solid plan to me," the captain agrees.

"Well Beau, I guess you got married with all these kid pictures?" Matt asks, glancing at some framed photos.

"Yes sir, I sure am. I married the admiral's daughter. It was almost a shotgun wedding. She dropped our first baby exactly eight months and two weeks to the day. She was actually a couple of weeks pregnant on the altar. And I can tell you the admiral has always known it but has never said anything to me. Now we have four. Every time I go on leave, we tend to go at it. Oh well, she knew what she signed up for.

The kids are awesome. Miss them more than you can imagine. The last one I've only seen once. She's got flaming red hair, just like her mother," Captain smiles.

"How are things going with you?" Beau asks Matt.

"Well, you remember Amy. I miss her every day, but Tony here keeps me plenty busy, so I don't have time to focus on her."

"Are you still traveling the world and hitting on every girl in every port?"

"Not exactly, but we are traveling all around the world. This last adventure is a doozy, and I really can't wait until we get back home. I'm one tired hombre," Matt replies.

Tony interjects. "I have a huge favor to ask of you, Captain."

"Please call me Beau."

Matt says, "Watch it, he's dangerous."

"No problem, I also have a favor to ask you guys," Beau grins.

"Great, would you mind sending that crate out for me? We cannot continue to drag that crate around the countryside. It's too big and cumbersome. I have an address, and all I would need is you to mail it Fed Ex, USPS, or UPS, whichever is easiest for you. Of course, I will pay all the shipping charges. I will leave you all my shipping codes," Tony offers.

"May I ask what it contains?" the captain asks.

"Let's just say it's a rare fish."

Beau looks over at Matt as he is shaking his head in the affirmative.

"It really is a fish," Matt confirms.

"We need to make a few phone calls, is that okay?" Tony asks.

"Sure, no problem."

Matt goes and calls his folks. Tony calls his sister, Isabella.

"Hey sis, what's up?"

"Where have you been? I've been worried sick since I haven't heard from you."

"It's been crazy out here and this is the first chance I've had to call you," Tony interjects.

"Where are you now?" Bella asks.

"I'm on a Navy ship heading for Cape Town. It's a long story. But I'm fairly certain I've apprehended the correct fish. Since I know you're heading up north, I am sending it to you by priority mail to Massachusetts. I will fly up and meet you there ASAP. Once you get the crate, we can extract the potion, then we can go get Mom!"

"Sounds good. When are you heading home?"

"I hope to be home in a few days."

"I would ask what you're doing on a Navy ship, but know better."

"Hey sis, one more thing. Be alert. I have met some unsavory characters on this trip, and I think the kingdom has been looking for the same fish."

"Thanks for the heads up. See you soon. By the way, Dad is home safe and sound. He wants to go and get Mom. He thinks he has the correct formula for the blue pillowcase. It seems Mom's hair can be woven into the blue fabric, and he thinks it will be enough to transport."

"He can't go. It's too dangerous. No telling what has happened since we have been. Tell him we will take care of it."

"I have, but you know how stubborn he is. Be safe, see you soon."

After the phone calls they head back to the captain's mess area. Captain Beau explains that he has no problem sending the package and dropping Tony and Matt off under one circumstance. "You know we still have that kid that fell overboard. When we drop you off, you are taking him with you."

"You mean the kid that I accidentally kicked in the head?" Matt exclaims.

"That would explain the head wound. Yep, the one and the same. I don't need to explain to you that what I did for you guys would not look good, and I can't have a witness on board, even though he has no idea his cohorts are gone. I've chatted with the young man and he's actually quite a nice kid. Has no family and well, you know, tit for tat," Beau smiles.

"Sure, can we meet the young man? By the way, what's his name?" Tony asks.

"He goes by Jake." As the captain gets ready to make an announcement on the vessel's public address system, another man enters and takes Tony and Matt to the young man named Jake.

They find him sitting on a bunk as they enter into his room. He jumps up and salutes, then immediately starts to back into the corner, recognizing Matt.

"Hello Jake, I am Dr. Tony Rome, and this is Matt. We are sorry about what happened back on your boat, but our lives were in danger and well, you know the rest of the story. Your friends never came back for you, did they?"

"Not my friends anymore," Jake says.

"Sure, don't blame you. But we have good news. You're going to be released into our custody. Do you know what that means?" Tony asks.

"No, you hurt me, no," Jake exclaims.

"No one is going to hurt you." Tony looks at Matt.

Matt steps forward. "Sorry about that, I didn't mean to hurt you, I just needed to get away. I won't do that again, okay? Anyway, we are going to need a guide. Can you guide us when we hit shore? We will pay you for your services."

"Okay, where we go," Jake smiles. "How much money?"

"We are going to Cape Town and will pay you each day you work for us."

Jake smiling, asks again, "How much money? I know Cape Town good, take you around. Show fun time. I know Cape Town real good. I grew up there."

"Well, we really don't need fun time but you're hired. See you in the morning." As everyone shakes hands, Jake has a giant grin on his face.

"How about that? He negotiated himself a job, and looked rather proud," Matt remarks.

"I wonder why he never asked about his fellow pirates. But curiously enough, as well as fate, I think he is well aware that his friends are no longer in this world, and he is," Tony remarks.

"All we've got to do is go back through South Africa and get Lucy, and say adios." Lucy is Tony's Gulfstream jet. The G650 is capable of traveling 7,000 nautical miles (8055 miles) at 0.85 Mach or 5,000 nautical miles (5,753 miles) at 0.90 Mach and has a top speed of 0.925 Mach, which makes it the fastest nonmilitary aircraft flying. It can cruise at 51,000 feet, in order to avoid airline traffic congestion and adverse weather. The G650 offers the longest range, largest cabin, and the most advanced cockpit in the Gulfstream fleet. The jet's fastest operating speed is at .925 Mach and approaches the speed of sound (Mach 1).

Lucy is very fast.

Chapter 10

VIOLET

"How are my favorite boys doing today? You feeling better, Dylan?" Mom comes home to find me crunching cookies in the kitchen.

"Feeling much better. Watched a movie and helped Grandpa with some of his stuff."

"Sounds good. You do remember that Chloe and I are leaving for Boston next week, and Alex is coming home for summer break," Mom smiles.

"Of course, I remember, Mom. I listen to every word you say," I reply grinning.

"Yeah, okay. You're not fooling anyone, mister. Don't forget we're moving the rest of Grandpa's stuff back into his home this weekend."

"I know, I know. You know, Mom, I rarely ask you for anything."

"Rarely, you say. Hmm, must be your short-term memory loss. What is it, my love?"

"Well, Grandpa mentioned some magic sword. And I—"

"Nope."

"Let me finish."

"Nope."

"But—"

"Anything else, my love?"

"No, you're so unreasonable."

It was a quiet weekend. I told everyone to stay away and leave me alone. I didn't want any screw ups so I could be as free as a bird next weekend. I was on good behavior detail. Mom could still ground me even if she's out of town. Grandpa was home all week working with his shuttle and loom, making some type of pillowcase. He was constantly working and didn't want to be disturbed. Mom told us to leave him be. I did, until Mom and Chloe left town.

Grandpa's junk was incredible. How does someone collect so much crap? He only showed me a few of his collectibles. Grandpa keeps telling Chloe and I everything is very valuable, and he would never sell it, and he is leaving it all for us kids. Friday couldn't come fast enough. Thank goodness nothing happened the last week of school, which I'm sure put Mom in a good mood.

"Okay Dylan, we will be back early next week. Alex will be here Sunday to help with any chores. Grandpa is beginning to look like his ole self again, so I want you and Alex to watch over him night and day until we return. If you do this, no more time out."

"Don't worry about a thing, Mom. I will be at Grandpa's beck and call."

"Yeah, I'm sure you will."

Chloe starts machine-gunning with the with questions. "What are you going to do while we're gone? Do you have any swim meets I'm going to miss? Do you want to come with us? What are you going to have for dinner? Can you feed all my pets? Are you feeling any better?"

Chloe is asking so many questions, I'm about to strangle her.

"I'll be fine, Chloe. Thanks for asking. I have plenty to do, plus I need to stay here and keep an eye on Grandpa."

I'm hoping Mom isn't about to make me go with them. I'm about to kill Chloe, right here and now. Luckily Brandi starts barking frantically and saves the day. Chloe finally stops talking and hugs me goodbye.

Chloe goes and hugs Brandi and says," Bye-bye, I love you so much."

Brandi is getting so old she can barely move some days.

"Bye, Mom, bye-bye, Chloe, be good."

"I'm always good," Chloe responds.

"I do not want Dad to be alone while I'm gone. I told Dad you were going to spend a few nights with him until Alex comes home. Then you two can spend time with each other until we return. I assume that's not too much to ask, is it?"

"Well, Mom, I really think he can take care of himself."

"I'm sure he can but this is what I want."

"But—"

"But I can ground you and then you're not going to make it to your party."

I almost fall over. How does she know about the party?

I laugh. "What party Mom? I don't know what you're talking about."

"I bet you don't. Well, I'm waiting for your answer."

"Yes ma'am, I would love to spend a few nights with Grandpa."

"That's better. You never know you might just learn something. And be safe tonight. I don't want any midnight calls that you're in any trouble."

"Yes Mom. Thank you."

"Come on, Chloe, put your bag in the car. We've got to go. I don't want to miss our flight. Okay, one more time—when I call, answer the phone. Got it?"

"Yes Mom."

Of course, Mom pops a kiss on my cheek. She is lightning fast. She knows everybody. I must have known she would find out about the party. She takes care of every animal in town and people talk way too much. I make a quick call to Jonny.

"Dude, how did you forget your mom was going to be out of town?"

"How do I know? I've been a little rattled up lately, between detentions, Violet, Grandpa, oh and yeah, a shark attack. I don't know, maybe I haven't been thinking clearly. See you later tonight."

"I'll pick you up around seven p.m." Jonny says.

"Sounds good."

"But dude, you're on your own getting back home, and be ready by seven. I'm not making any promises, so you better have a backup plan for your ride back home.

"Okay, I'll be ready. I don't want anyone messing with Violet before I arrive."

I decide to make a swing by Grandpa's to be sure all is well.

"Hey Grandpa, are you all set? I'll finish up a few things."

"I'm okay, sport. You know I didn't want to be in your way. Staying with you guys was fun, but I felt like a burden, and I like my home. I'm working on this project and I predict it will be finished by this weekend."

Grandpa lives next door. I am working at record pace to help Grandpa so I can finish and get to this rocking party. "Okay Grandpa, I think that does it."

"Yeah, sport, you worked in overdrive. Thanks, I feel better back in my own place. Don't want to be a burden on you kids."

"Hey sport, you want me to drive you to the party?"

My mouth drops. "What party, Grandpa?"

"I wasn't born yesterday, sport. I hear things. I can't see as well but my hearing is still good."

"Well, maybe you can do me a favor, but you can't tell Mom."

"Sure sport, it will be our little secret."

"Since I'm staying here tonight, I may need a ride home but it could be really late. I mean late."

"What's late?"

"Two or three a.m."

"Hmm, that's pretty late. Oh well, I can take a nap and I'll set my alarm."

"Okay, great. I'll call if I need a ride."

What's the difference—he won't answer the phone.

I begin to get a little nervous about the night. I start to think of Violet and feel like I'm going to puke. My head is killing me. Oh great, perfect timing for a migraine. I think it's from lugging all of Grandpa's stuff. Ugh, where is Jonny? He should be here by now.

I hear a car come screeching in the driveway and then a horn honking excessively.

As I walk outside, Jonny yells, "Come on, dude, let's go."

"You're late."

"Sorry, I needed gas and I didn't think you wanted to push the car."

"You got any aspirin?"

"They'll have some aspirin there. We are late."

"Yeah, because of you."

"Did you get the criminal all moved in?" Jonny grins.

"If you're referring to my Grandpa, the answer is yes, moron."

"Holy cow, look at all the cars!" I exclaim. "This party must be rocking and it's still early."

"I told you this was going to be the party of the century."

"I wonder, do you think Violet is here yet?"

"I doubt it. Those girls take decades to get ready."

We find the nearest keg, and I grab a draft. "Hey, who's driving me home if we're both drinking?" I ask Jonny.

"I'm not driving anyone back home tonight, my friend. My parents are out of town, so I don't plan on going anywhere anytime soon."

"But you told me you wouldn't drink and drive."

"I'm not drinking and driving. I'm just drinking. Did you really think I was going to not drink? Who's the moron, now?"

"You're making my headache worse."

"Dude, did you really think I was going to pass up partying just to chauffeur you around for the evening?"

"Now that you say it out loud, it does sound like I was dreaming."

"Oh yeah, dreaming, dream on my friend," Jonny smiles.

The house was packed, and the music blared. I figure I'll worry about a ride home later, but for now I need to get rid of this freaking migraine then find Violet. What a time to get a head knocker.

"Hey dude, watch it," somebody snarled and slammed into the door as I was opening it.

"Sorry, man." The guy looked extremely drunk and I got out of his way. He was huge. I headed back to the keg for another. "Oh hi, Jimmy," I say as I notice he's with his usual thugs.

"Hey butthead. How you get out? Does your mom know you're here? Maybe I should give her a call? You could have brought her with you. You gonna murder anyone here like your *Granddaddy-o?*" Jimmy Johnson taunts.

I'm not in any mood to argue with JJ, so I just let him keep talking. Once he's finished, I ask, "Does anyone have any aspirin?" That in hindsight may have been the stupidest mistake of my life.

Carl says, "Sure do, take two of these."

"I don't think so. What are they?" I ask him suspiciously.

"Oh, they are aspirin, double strength. Bought them yesterday." He taps out two pills from what looked like the original Bayer aspirin box. They looked real enough to me coming out of an original Bayer aspirin box, with a big "B" on it.

Where is Violet, I wonder. She must be here This place is packed to the gills. Well, it wasn't long before I was falling down and slurring my words. I vaguely remember talking about Grandpa's list of collectables with Jimmy Johnson. I think I told him about Lil Magik, and all his other treasures. What was I thinking? I may have mentioned Mom was out of town. Not sure why I was talking, but I was. I couldn't stop yapping about Grandpa's stuff. That was supposed to be a real big secret.

I see Jonny and start screaming, "JONNY, how many girls are you going to make out with tonight?"

"Hey dude, slow down. You're acting like a complete tool," Jonny says. "How much have you had to drink? Slow down. Let's get you something to eat. I saw a ton of barbequed chicken wings in the kitchen."

"I'm fine. Never felt better. My headache's gone, ha." Soon I spot Violet, and I start screaming, "VIOLET! VIOLET!"

"Dude, slow it down. You're lit up pretty good. I think it's best you stay away from her for now. Where have you been?"

"I've been talking to JJ and his buds. They are so nice. VIOLET!"

"Sure they are, are you okay? You sure can't hold your beer. Why don't we just sit here for minute. I'll get you a Coke and some wings." Jonny sets me down.

I start shouting, "I LOVE YOU VIOLET" and take off towards her. She is sitting by the pool with her girlfriends. "Hey baby," I announce to her.

"Baby, who's your baby," someone answers.

"Let's go smooching somewhere."

"Are you crazy? Are you okay?"

"I'm fine, baby. Never felt better." I reply.

"You don't look okay. You're sweating and acting like a wild animal."

"I'm sorry, girls. He's had a rough week and may have gone overboard on the keg," says Jonny as he comes to my rescue.

"He's acting like a fool," one of Violet friends responds. "Get him out of here before he does something stupid, which for him shouldn't take too long."

Thank goodness someone knocked me into the pool before I could get my boxer shorts off. And that's all I remember.

The next thing I know I'm at my Grandpa's house, hugging a toilet bowl. I throw up and wipe off my forehead with a towel, then I head out of the bathroom and see Grandpa sitting on the couch.

"You want something to eat, sport?"

"Yes sir. I don't understand. I only had a few beers, and everything went spinning out of control. I've had more beers than that and never had that type of reaction."

"Are you sure about that, sport? Maybe you're allergic to beer."

"No really, I only had a few. And NO, I'm not allergic to beer."

"Yes, well they all say that."

"How'd I get here?" I tentatively ask.

"Well, let's just say you were driven home safely. It seems the party got way out of control and the police came and shut it down. Captain

Rogers found you passed out on the front yard and tossed you in his car and waited for an ambulance," Grandpa explains.

"Captain who?"

"Your mom's new boyfriend."

"OH NO. That's not good."

"How about I throw a nice giant steak on the stove for you? After some food and a rest, we will talk more about it tomorrow."

"Thanks Grandpa. Are you going to tell Mom?"

"I'm not the one to worry about. I'm sure that captain fellow will fill her in."

"Oh, you're so right. I'm a dead man. The last thing I told Mom was I would be good. At least she didn't get a midnight phone call. Or did she?"

"I didn't call her, that's for sure. I'm scared of her," grandpa smiles.

"Me too."

We both laugh out loud.

As I drag myself into the kitchen, I begin to recall a few details of the party events. Oh no, not Violet. What did I do? It was our date night. I kind of remember a few brief moments and with each memory, I get sick to my stomach. There is no way I drank that much. "Maybe I did have an allergic reaction to the food."

"What you mumbling about, sport?"

"I'm thinking that I'm allergic to something I ate and had some type of reaction."

"Could be, but I doubt it."

"I think I've blown it for good with Violet."

"Don't worry, she'll forgive you."

"How many chances is she going to give me? I'm constantly apologizing to her for something every day. Why would she date anyone that all he does is apologize, daily—no hourly? Ugh, I'm a monster."

I start wolfing down my steak and keep mumbling, out loud and to myself, "I hate my life, I hate my life." My head feels worse. Those pills didn't work. What a minute, Jimmy J's friend Carl supposedly gave me some aspirin, and I'm fairly certain they were not. Those cretins wouldn't, would they? Yes, they would.

"I was drugged Grandpa."

"That would explain a lot. Just tell her that you were drugged."

"I may need some proof."

"You may be in luck. When I went outside to see what all the commotion was, since you were in an ambulance—"

"I was in a what?"

"Ambulance. You were quite messed up, and the only way to get you home was to strap you in, and I think they drew some blood."

"You kidding me, right?"

"I wish I was, sport, but that would explain your unusual behavior."

"When do I get the results?"

"Well, sport, I'm not sure about that."

"Can they just do that without my permission?"

"Not sure about that, sport. I guess he can do whatever he wants. He's the captain of the police force."

I start thinking how I could get those results without opening Pandora's box. Oh my, what a night. I'm never drinking again. I barley finish chewing when I tell Grandpa goodnight and drag myself to bed. Before I could thank Grandpa for letting me stay at his house, I'm sound asleep.

I wake up and see the clock shows three p.m. the next day and my headache is almost completely gone. I crawl out of bed and see Grandpa in the family room.

"How you feeling, sport?" Grandpa asks.

"Actually, better than I thought. I was kind of hoping it was all a nightmare."

But soon I begin to think about yesterday's events, and almost pass out. "Oh no, Violet does hate me. Plus everyone else on this planet. What have I done?"

"Come on, sport, it can't be all that bad. She'll forgive you. May take a while but she will."

"What about the stuff I don't remember? I can't imagine what other foolishness I performed. Most of it is still a blur!"

"Did you ever act this stupid in front Grandmother?"

"Oh sure, sport, lots of times."

"Yeah okay, name one time." I frown.

"I already told you about me showing up for band practice at her house without an instrument."

"Really, you think that compares. Oh, I no longer am fit to be a human on this planet."

"Come on. You're beating yourself up too much. We all do stupid things when we're young."

"We just went over that. No, you didn't—just me. Maybe I have a something on my brain that makes me act like a buffoon."

"Look at the bright side. Your mother hasn't called. If she knew about this she would have called by now."

"Yeah, you may be right. I could be in the clear."

I start to think there may be hope until I realize that's only one hurdle out of a zillion. I was almost in tears. My head was about a foot off the floor from depression. "Grandpa, have you seen my phone?"

"Yeah sport, it's on the kitchen table."

I was afraid to check my messages. Great, someone sent me a video of my late-night performance: *Sincerely JJ, enjoy.* Oh no.

It starts out with me shouting, "I LOVE YOU VIOLET" and me running toward her and her friends. "Hey baby. Baby, who's your baby. Let's go smooching somewhere. Are you crazy? Are you okay? I'm fine baby. You don't look ok. You're sweating and look white as a ghost." In horror I continue screaming while I strip down to my boxer shorts and start dancing around the pool spelling, "V-I-O-L-E-T. I'm in love with V-I-O-L-E-T, Violet. And she loves me." I flinch when I see the moment someone knocked me into the pool before I could get my boxer shorts off.

Then the tape ends, with me swimming in the pool kissing a raft.

"What's a matter, sport?"

"I'm going home for a minute to bury my head in the sand for about an hour. If I'm lucky I won't live. I may have to move to Pluto."

"Come on, sport. You're scaring me. It will be okay. I wish your mom was here to comfort you."

"That's the last person I want to see right now."

"Cheer up, sport. Your mom wanted you to go by the house anyway. You want a ride?"

"No. I've got my bike, I think. I'll see you in a few."

I start walking to the front door and realize Grandpa is holding this bright blue fabric in his hand.

"Is that what you been working on?"

"Yes sir. She's ready for takeoff. When you get back tonight, I'll fill you in," Grandpa grins.

Take off. What's he talking about? Oh, my bike is at home. "I do need a ride. My bike is at my house. I'll ride it back later."

"Okay sport, let me get the keys. Don't forget I'm cooking us a nice Italian dinner feast for the two of us, plus I've got a good story for you. Can you keep a secret?"

"Yeah, of course I can."

"Okay, good. See you back here around six p.m. Keep your chin up. It will all work out."

I depart his car with my head hung low to the ground.

Chapter 11

HARI

I have some time before I return back to Grandpa's for dinner. When I arrive at my house, I am greeted by two giant dogs. This wasn't unusual since we have animals in and out of the house constantly. But they did make me smile. "Hey boys, what's shaking?" Then, I see a note on the kitchen counter. Both tails are wagging a mile a minute. I could have sworn the Rottweiler smiled at me.

**

My dearest Dylan,

I thought you could use some company. I had Gloria drop off this note along with two of my favorite watch dogs. I decided they would be good company for you and Alex. They need to be walked twice daily, and you know where the food is. Brandi will also be happy to have some company. Hari is the male German Shepherd and Teri is the female Rottweiler.

Both are very sweet and extremely smart. They will watch over the house. Just tell them what to do and they will obey. Have fun with Grandpa. Don't forget Alex is coming in Sunday. She has a ride so don't worry. Call if you need me. Hope to be back Thursday evening.

Luv you, be good. Don't try anything stupid. Captain Rogers has volunteered to drive by the house while I'm gone, so behave.

Love you, Mom.

Please feed my fish, guinea pig, turtle and parrot. Love, Chloe.

**

"Oops, sorry Teri, thought you were a boy. My bad." Great, I should be paid for my services.

I could tell Brandi was excited—her tail was wagging more than usual. I sensed she wrote this note before my party performance, or does this mean Captain Rogers didn't tell Mom? She would have mentioned something. I may be out of hot water. But when did she write that note? Hmm, maybe he won't squeal on me.

I take a nice long hot shower. I even thought about taking a sauna in Mom's bathroom but really didn't have any time since I had to feed the two horse dogs and Chloe's critters. After I feed all the critters, I call Grandpa then hang up. What was I thinking? He never answers the phone. I could ring him and get to his house in time to answer my own call.

Briing, briing. I jump. That phone is so loud it could wake the dead.

"Hello."

"Hello, is this Dylan?"

"Yes it is, who is it you want?"

"This is Violet."

"I knew that." My heart is pounding and I'm about to pass out.

"Are you okay?" Violet asks.

"Yes, yes, I'm fine, fine. I am so sorry about the way I acted."

She starts to giggle. "Didn't bother me. I thought your spiderman boxers were very sexy."

"Oh no, I'm fairly certain I was drugged."

"Well, you making out with that raft was very interesting."

Oh my, I thought I was making out with you. "A raft you say?"

"Do you remember anything?"

"Not really."

"How about the guys taking you out of the pool and putting you in a lounge chair? I asked them to, I was afraid you may drown."

"Nope, nothing. I saw a tape, but it ended before that. The only thing I saw was a video tape of my pitiful performance. I remember so little."

"I don't think that counted as a date, do you?" Violet inquires

"Oh, no, no, no." That's all I can say, no. I'm useless.

"Do you want to go out next Friday night? I can come by and pick you up?" Violet asks.

I almost pass out but I said, "Yes, please." Before I did pass out mentally.

"I have a present for you. I hope it gets here in time," Violet says.

"But I didn't buy you anything." *Oh, why did I say that out loud.*

"Don't worry, I don't need a present but would appreciate anything if you do change your mind."

"Oh, yes. I will change my mind. I mean okay. Sure, sure, okay, okay."

"Okay, silly. See you Friday night at seven p.m."

"Sure, sure, thank you."

"Why are you thanking me? You're so funny," she giggles and hangs up.

I start running around the house like a madman. With all three dogs chasing me and barking and howling as if they understood my happiness. I've got to tell Grandpa. Wait a minute, a present. Oh my. What kind of present? I have no idea what to buy her. I start to feel sick again.

I pet all the dogs and they all purr like kittens, very large kittens.

Obey me. Okay, Mom, let see how smart these two are.

"Okay, Hari and Teri, I am leaving now. Watch the house." They both look at me as if they understand and Teri goes to the back door and Hari sits by the front. Brandi just slumps by her water bowl.

Wow, cool dogs, Mom. We always have the coolest pets. I make sure all the doors are locked but didn't see any need to set the alarm. As if someone would be crazy enough to enter while these beasts were on watch. I'd be afraid just looking at them. I look at the clock. It's six fifteen p.m. and I decide I'd better head back to Grandpa's, so I hop on my bike.

"Hey Grandpa, something smells good."

"It's my Italian sausages cooking on the stove that you smell, sport."

"Great, I'm starving. And I have some great news."

"Perfecto, I like good news and I'm also starving. Hey sport, would you mind going to the bar and making me a drink while I turn these sausages?"

"Sure thing, Grandpa. J & B Scotch and soda with a lemon wedge."

I begin making his drink, and I accidently cut my finger while cutting the lemon. "Ouch."

"You okay, sport?"

"Yeah, just a minor cut, only lost a pint of blood. I think I'll live. Now that I have a reason to live again."

"Okay sport, I'm glad you turned your frown upside down. You're much better looking with that smile on your face. What happened?" Grandpa asks curiously.

"I have a date."

"Good for you. With that gal of yours?"

"Yes, Grandpa. Violet is my gal."

"Good job, sport. I knew she would understand."

"Well, kind of. She explained that most of my antics were with a raft, not her."

"A raft you say. Hmm, alright, sounds a bit unusual, but good for you."

"You don't understand, Grandpa. Not sure I do, but she's coming to pick me up Friday night."

"That I understand. Now you're talking."

"I do have one major problem, though."

"What's that, sport?"

"I need to buy her a present."

"Oh, that's easy. What's her favorite color? Her favorite flower? Are her ears pierced? Does she like scarves?"

"Slow down. I can't answer any of those questions. I have no idea."

"Well, sport, if you're going to date a woman, you need to know a little about your gal."

"What are you talking about? I know lots about her."

"Alright, let's hear it."

"She's hot. She's real hot."

"You said that already."

"Oh yeah, she's pretty, oh and smart."

Dinner was spectacular. I could barely move since I stuffed myself. We sit outside on his porch where the view of the water is awesome.

"Well, sport, it's kind of hard to explain. You can't tell your mother or she will have my head on a platter. It's a family secret. Hey, make me another drink and I'll try to explain."

I have been making Grandpa's drinks extra strong. Not sure why, I just have. I try not to cut my hand off this time, which wasn't easy since I was going at warp speed. I'm fairly certain Grandpa's feeling no pain by now.

Grandpa continues, "I'm going to get your Grandma Liz and bring her back home. I hope it won't take too long, but I'm just not sure."

My eyes got as wide as the moon. "Say that again? Where is Grandmother?"

"Do you recollect any of my stories about a place called the kingdom? Well, they weren't just stories. That place is real and I'm going back to get her. I think I figured out a way to go back and get her. I'm just not sure where she might be."

"Grandpa, are you felling okay? I may have made your drinks too strong."

"Now listen sport, this is important."

"Hey Grandpa, why don't I go with you?"

"Because if something were to happen to you, your mother, my daughter, will never forgive me, and I am not willing to take that chance."

"But won't it be easier if we both go?" I plead, thinking I need to be a hero at something soon.

"Possibly, it has been fifteen years and I'm not sure what to expect. I would never forgive myself for putting you in harm's way, but it is such a peaceful place. Almost like one big commune and everyone gets along. Your mother used to love going there because she could take care of all the animals. They loved her and she loved them. It's one big happy family," Grandpa explains.

"Please take me with you. I have nothing here. How do we get there? I need to be back by Friday."

"Remember that blue pillowcase I was holding the other day. Well, I've been weaving some new material with my shuttle, and I think it's ready."

"Ready for what?" I ask.

"That's how you transport back and forth, with the pillowcase. You put your head on the pillowcase and before you know it, you're there. I've been weaving your grandma's hair into the fabric."

"Her hair? Where did you get that?"

"She kept it in a shoebox for wigs and stuff."

"Does Mom know about this pillowcase?"

"Yes and no. Let me finish."

After a long tale, I still don't understand where Grandmother is and I start to believe Grandpa is crazy or drunk. If he knows where she is, why didn't he go get her sooner? But I continue to listen to his stories about large creatures, talking animals, kings and queens, rocks, caverns, waterways, beaches, underwater subways, and such.

"And tonight, I travel there," Grandpa grins.

I've already spoken with a crab. Does that give me any credibility?
"When do you leave?"

"Early tomorrow morning, two a.m. I think the secret is Lizzy's hair. I weaved it into the blue pillowcase. Plus, tonight is the rare super blood blue moon."

"If it won't take long, why don't I go with you? Mom won't be home until Thursday. All I care about is my date Friday night. I could help you find Grandmother. It could be fun. I'm pretty good at those maze games."

"You may be onto something, sport. I could use some help but I, let me think on it."

"Why don't you write Mom a note?"

"Yeah, that may be a good idea. Better if I tell her than you. She'll be mad that you even know about Grandma and the kingdom."

Grandpa scribbles, crosses through, then tosses out the note.

"I'll think of something, sport. Can't think right now. Maybe I should tell her I went to visit a friend and surprise her with her mother?"

"That sounds like a better plan."

"Okay, how about this. Tell your mother that I went out of town to visit Duke. She might believe you since I recently told her that he had the cancer and I wanted to visit him before he expires. Can you do that, sport? I need your help. What do you say, deal?"

"Sure, Grandpa. I can tell her that you went to visit Duke. But I still wish you would take me."

"I can't, sport. It's my job to go get her," Grandpa smiles.

I look at the clock and it's ten eighteen p.m. "I'm tired, Grandpa. Do you mind if I stay here again, tonight?"

"No problem, sport, I'm right behind you. Good night, Dylan. I'll see you soon, but next time I see you I'll have Grandma Liz with me."

"I like the sounds of that. Night, Grandpa. Be careful. I still want to go, so if you change your mind just wake me up."

"Sure, sport."

Poor old man, he's getting delusional. Off to bed I go as I start to wonder if a few things he says are true. Maybe I should go in his place. If he can do it, why can't I? How much trouble can it be? I could even be the hero. This would only make me look good with Violet. Maybe I could buy her a gift while I'm there. He said it would only take a day or two, and Mom is out of town. Why not?

Go back, pick her up, and bring her home. Sounds easy. Not sure why no one has done it earlier. It's destiny that fell right into my lap.

I get up and sneak into Grandpa's room. He's sound asleep. I made those drinks extra strong, so he may sleep until noon. I see this blue pillowcase on the chair along with a backpack. I change his alarm clock to four a.m.

It is a somewhat unusual color blue, but whatever. I take it to my room and lay my head upon it. It feels mighty uncomfortable with all of Grandma's hair sticking out of it. I don't feel a thing. I knew it, he was full of beans. I must still be groggy to believe his wild stories.

**

"Hey, be quiet morons," Jimmy Johnson tells Damien and Carl.

"Dylan was right, there is no security system. I bet the old man is asleep," Damien says.

"Chloroform him just in case. I don't want him waking up while we're cleaning him out," Jimmy reminds them.

"You think Dylan was telling the truth about all his Granddad's stuff?" Carl asks.

"We'll soon find out, now keep quiet."

"Jimmy, Jimmy get over here."

"Why don't you scream my name? No more names, be quiet."

"Better come here."

"Holy cow, what's he doing here?" Jimmy and Damien shine their light onto Dylan.

"We just won the lottery," Jimmy exclaims.

"Look dude, he colored his hair blond as if no one's going to recognize him," Damien says.

"I don't blame him after his keg party fiasco."

"Shut up, you two. This isn't a talk show. Chloroform him, too, and let's take him with us. The cops will probably blame the old man for his disappearance. Grab that pillowcase and fill it with all this junk. If it won't fit, get more pillowcases. I want everything. We will go through it later at my house," Jimmy whispers.

"What's that noise?" Damien asks.

"Sounds like a wolf howling," Carl answers.

"Let's get out of here. You're always hearing wolves." JJ remarks.

They tie up and gag Dylan then heave him into the truck along with the pillowcases full of Grandpa's goodies. They leave with Dylan after dousing Grandpa with a huge amount of chloroform to keep him knocked out.

"Let's go," Jimmy says as they speed away.

Hari is going crazy and can't get out of the house.

"Teri, I need to get out of here and see what's going on at Vincenzo's house."

"But Hari, the house is locked up tight."

Soon Hari jumps through the window and bolts at full speed to Grandpa Vincenzo's house but he doesn't get there in time.

Teri yells out, "Be careful. I'll wait here."

Hari sits on Grandpa's porch and starts howling.

**

The alarm clock sounds, and Grandpa gets up, feeling like he has a hangover. Then he looks around and doesn't see the blue pillowcase. He feels as if he's been punched in the head a few hundred times. What the heck's going on around here? He could have sworn that he brought that pillow to his room. What he can't figure out is why the alarm clock went off at four a.m. instead of two a.m. Plus, the house looks like a tornado tore through it. Grandpa thinks it could be a case for the FBI; they could call it, "The Blue Pillow Case."

What is making all that noise outside?

As Grandpa opens the front door, a giant German Shepard walks in as if it lives here and sits right next to Grandpa. Fortunately, he's been around animals his entire life, otherwise he would've panicked after seeing this huge German Shepherd walk inside the house, as anyone would. He also recognizes that some of Isabella's pets understand everything.

Grandpa sees a dog tag, *Hari.*

"Okay Hari, follow me."

Hari follows Grandpa to Dylan's room. Once Grandpa gets to Dylan's room, he pulls back the covers, and his heart starts racing. He almost falls over when he realizes Dylan is gone. Oh God, he didn't, did he? Maybe his mother came in the middle of the night. Maybe he decided to bike back home. Maybe he couldn't sleep and went for a swim. Why is the house a mess? Where's the blue pillowcase and Grandpa's backpack? Maybe, just maybe, Grandpa's in big trouble.

"Oh, my goodness," Grandpa starts to sob uncontrollably. Hari looks at Grandpa and sits by his feet. Hari looks as upset as Grandpa.

Grandpa needs to calm down and put a plan together. He was obviously robbed, but where is Dylan and the blue pillowcase? Maybe Dylan went home? Maybe he should call Isabella? No, she'll kill him, but she's going to find out eventually.

Maybe not. It's possible Dylan will come back before his mother returns from Boston. Grandpa can't believe this is happening, plus his head is about to explode from all that chloroform. He can't call the police. They will only put him back in jail.

"What do you think, Hari?"

Hari just stares at Grandpa. He decides to a write note for his daughter.

The note says:

**

Dylan and I went to visit Duke. He is in a bad way and I wanted to see him before he expires. You were gone so I thought you wouldn't mind if I spent some time with my grandson, Dylan.

We luv you, be back soon,

DAD.

**

"What do you think Hari? Will she buy it?"

Hari puts his head down and lays his front paws behind his ears as if to say "nope, you're a dead man."

"I think you're right. It's lame but it's all I got. My best bet is to drive to my son's house. Hey Hari, you want to go for a ride?"

Hari looks up at Grandpa and puts his head down and lays his front paws behind his ears again.

"I'll take that as a no," Grandpa grins. He sees Dylan's bike is still on the porch. Grandpa packs a bag and throws it into the back of the car and drives by Isabella's house, just in case Dylan was there. No luck, so he gets on the road before eight a.m.

Chapter 12

ALESSANDRA

*B**rring, briing, brring, brring.* "Come on, Dad, answer the phone!" Isabella calls her father, Vincenzo, one more time.

"Chloe dear, would you pour me another coffee?"

Great, nothing from Dylan either. Doesn't anyone answer their phones anymore?

"That chocolate chip muffin was delicious," Chloe exclaims.

"Hi Alessandra, it's Mom, I know you're probably on your flight, but I wanted to leave you this urgent message. I need a huge favor. Please go check up on Dylan and Grandpa when you land. You know your grandfather will not answer his phone, so do me this favor. Thanks sweetie. Talk later. Love Mom."

Alex's plane is on time and her friend Samantha picks her up. Tami was busy.

"Hey, can we swing by Grandpa's first? Mom needs a favor," Alex asks Sam.

"Sure, no problem. What did he do now?"

"Oh nothing, Mom just wants me to check in on Grandpa and Dylan."

Sam pulls into the driveway. The blinds are still closed with no sign of life.

"Great, they're both still asleep, "Alex remarks.

Alex was about to knock on the door but realized it was unlocked. She assumed Grandpa must be inside with the front door unlocked. Once inside, Alex is greeted by a giant German Shepherd.

"Hello poochie." Hari walks up with his tail wagging. Any other person would be terrified, but after growing up with all kinds of critters, no animal fazes any of the Cabrella children.

Alex sees his collar and says, "Okay Hari, where is everybody?"

As if he understood Alex, Hari just looks up at her and sits on the ground with his paws wrapped around his head.

"Good boy, Hari."

"OMG, it looks like Grandpa has been robbed. Where are they?"

Sam loves on Hari. "He is so cute, but your Grandad is a slob."

Alex walks into the guest room and she sees the sheets, blanket, and drawers thrown all over the floor. Rough sleep, D'man.

"Grandpa where's Dylan?" The master bedroom was also empty and stuff flung all over. "What's going on around here? This place looks like it's been ransacked."

Alex finds the note left behind and starts to read it out loud:

"Dylan and I went to visit Duke. He is in a bad way and I wanted to see him before he expires. You were gone, so I thought you wouldn't mind if I spent some time with my grandson. We luv you, be back soon, DAD."

"Oh great. I've come all this way to visit, and no one is here. Mom and Chloe go to Boston, and Grandpa and Dylan head out. What do I have, the plague? Why visit?" Alex blurts out.

Briiiing. Alex turns and picks up the phone.

"Hello."

"Alex, thank goodness you landed safely. Is everything okay?"

"Not really," Alex replies.

"What does that mean?"

"I'm at Grandpa's, and it looks like he's been robbed. Neither Dylan or Grandpa are here."

"What did you say?" Mom asks with a heavy sigh.

"Grandpa left a note. They both went to visit Uncle Duke."

"Read me the note?"

"Dylan and I went to visit Duke. He is in a bad way and I wanted to see him before he expires. You were gone, so I thought you wouldn't mind if I spent some time with my grandson. We luv you, be back soon, DAD."

"Call Captain Rogers at this number. Tell him where you are, and he'll be right over. Call me when he gets there."

"And Mom, when did Grandpa get a dog?"

"What dog?"

"His name is Hari."

"Hmm, I wonder what he's doing there?"

"I don't know. He was here when I opened the front door. He's real cute."

"He's very protective and smart, so stay close by him. And he has a mate. Her name is Teri. Is she also there with you?"

"I don't see any other dogs."

"Okay, she must be at our house. Don't forget, call me when the captain arrives."

"Okay, Mom."

"Keep those dogs by your side."

"You better call the police and don't touch anything," Sam offers.

"You think the police are going to do anything? Let's look for clues," Alex replies.

"Let's see if that criminology degree you're working on is of any use. You've always wanted to be Nancy Drew. Here's your chance," Sam says.

"Here's *our* chance. Let's make sure no one is still here before we get too far." Before Alex could finish her sentence, Hari starts to walk in front of her and walks into every room just to make sure no one is hiding. The house was empty and looked completely ransacked.

"Who would do this? What did your Grandpa have that anyone wanted, anyway?" Sam asks.

"Good question, let's look for clues." *What's this, a cigarette butt? Grandpa doesn't smoke,* Alex thinks as she grabs a clear baggy and puts the butt inside. "Anything else?"

"Does your Grandpa wear a Grateful Dead bandana?"

"No, nor does Dylan. Put that in another baggy. Good find, detective."

"Thanks, this is fun. Sorry, I guess it's not that much fun knowing you've been robbed," Sam offers.

"Check the trash bags."

Sam finds a few crumpled notes. "Hey Alex, I found these crumpled notes."

"Take those with us. I guess we better call Captain Rogers."

The police arrive and start asking Sam and Alex a million questions.

"No, we didn't touch anything. Called you as soon as we got here," Alex smiles.

Captain Rogers starts, "Okay girls, we will take it from here. If we find out anything, I'll let you know. How's your Mom, anyway? She is the best you know, I—"

"Captain, can I see you a minute?"

"Sure, Tom, what's up?"

"There's blood in the bar area, on a knife on the counter."

"Thanks Tom, bag it up and get it to the lab," the captain remarks.

Darn, Alex thinks, *how did we miss that?*

"You said no one was home at the time of the burglary?" the captain asks again.

"Yes sir, my grandpa and brother went out of town to visit a friend."

"Okay, well we will find the culprits. Nice dog, by the way."

"Oh thanks, it's a present from my Mom," Alex grins.

"We're all done here, Captain."

"Don't forget to tell your mother that Captain Rogers said hello, okay?"

Alex wonders, *why is it all the men fall over for my mother?* She wishes they would do that for her. "Yes, Captain, I'll tell her Rogers is on top of it." Both girl's giggle.

"Good day, ladies."

"Did you hear they found blood? Whose blood was it, do you think?" Sam asks.

"Not sure, but I'm upset we missed it. Well, we have enough clues so let's get thinking."

Alex makes the call. "Hey Mom, how's it going?"

"You tell me?"

"Well, Grandpa was definitely robbed." Dead silence. She thought Mom must've passed out.

"Mom, are you okay?"

"Yes dear, just wish I were home. We're lucky no one was injured since they both were out of town when the robbery occurred. Thank goodness for small miracles. Okay, now you girls go to the house and be sure all the doors are locked. If you head out, turn on the alarm. Not sure if it was an accident or if they were after something specific. So be safe, and do not get in the way of the investigation. I am sure Captain Rogers will take special interest in this case."

"Oh, I bet he will. You promise him a date and he may close this case tomorrow," Alex teases.

"Alex don't be silly. I'm serious, be safe. I know you can protect yourself, but I still can worry. I have an eerie feeling there's something suspicious going on. When you get to the house you should see Teri. She's a Rottweiler, and both Hari and Teri are for protection."

"Protection, Mom. I do love dogs."

"These two are the best. Keep them by your side and do not split them up if possible. Be alert, I love you."

"Mom, we'll be okay. What about Brandi?"

"Brandi would lick someone to death. These dogs are smart and you'll love them. Call if you need me. Love you, dear."

Sam and Alex take Hari to pick up Tami. Tami likes dogs almost as much as Alex.

"I can't believe I missed the robbery scene. He is so cute," Tami remarks.

"That's Hari, Teri is at home," Alex says. "Don't worry, we have plenty of work ahead of us. You didn't miss anything."

Sam and Tami both respond, "As if we haven't grown up with all your animals throughout your childhood. Are you kidding? We love your pets."

The girls get back to the house and Teri is there to greet them all.

"You must be Teri," Alex says as she pets her.

"I feel better already," Tami offers. "Your mom is one smart lady."

The girls hadn't noticed the broken window yet.

"I'm going to make a call. Let's start with Leon."

"Hello Leon, this is Alessandra. Do you mind if I come by? I didn't get home in time for the party, so I just wanted to swing by and say hello."

"Well sure, how about …" Leon says.

"I'll be right there. Thanks, love," Alex hangs up.

"What are you up to now?" Tami asks.

"Let's go visit Leon. It's a good start. He knows most of the scum in this area. Maybe somebody squealed," Alex smirks.

"Go Nancy Drew, you go girl," Sam remarks.

"Should we take the dogs?"

"No, let them watch over the house. We may use them later, though. Okay, Hari and Teri, you guys watch the house. Don't let anyone inside," Alex commands.

Hari was hesitant and seemed like he wanted to go with the girls. He walked up next to Alex and sat on her foot. Teri went to the back door.

"Seems like you made a friend," Sam says. "I guess he's going with us."

"Guess so. I'm not messing with him, come on Hari," Alex comments.

As the girls arrive at Leon's huge house, they ring the front door bell.

Ding dong, dong, dong.

"How big is this house?" Tami asks.

"Not sure, ask Leon. It's huge," Alex replies.

"Oh hi, girl, girls, and the horse," Leon grimaces. "I thought it was just going to be you, but I should have known, so come on in. Take a load off. I don't have much time. Heading out to the Tiki Hut soon. What's up?"

"Let's sit out by the pool. You girls can swim if you like and take the horse with you."

Leon didn't have to say it twice since both Sam and Tami had their suits on and were all ready to jump into the pool. Hari didn't leave Alex's side.

Alex says, "You have such a lovely house. How big is it, anyway? You never really have given me a proper tour."

"Well, okay sure," Leon hesitantly answers. "I'll show you around. Is that horse going to follow us around?"

"His name is Hari and yes, he is. Plus, he obeys my commands."

"I bet he does," Leon grimaces again.

Leon knows full well about Alex's martial arts triumphs. He's not sure why she needs anymore protection.

"Why not make us a drink while we walk around? It's such a big house, I may get thirsty," Alex winks.

"Sure, I'll get us a couple of beers."

After taking a tour of this twelve thousand-square-foot mansion, Alex stops and sits on the pool table with her legs crossed, showing lots of leg. Hari is sitting under the pool table.

"What are you up to, Alessandra? I don't trust you, and I like my nose attached to my face. My girlfriend is coming by, and I'm not sure I can explain why you and your two hot friends are hanging out with me. So, what gives? Don't get me wrong, I'd love to hang with you right now but," Leon holds the thought.

"Okay, you can cool it. I just have one question. I found this in my car, and I forgot who it belonged to. Do you know who's this is?" Alex holds up the bandana.

"Oh, it figures you needed something. I've seen it. Someone was wearing it at the party Saturday night, but I can't remember."

"Well, maybe I can help you remember." Alex kicks up a cue stick and it lands perfectly in her hand like a saber.

"Oh yeah, I think it was a friend of Jonny's. He's your brother's best bud. Why not ask him? Better yet, ask your brother," Leon forces a slight smile.

"Oh, you're so right. Thanks again for the beer."

"But you didn't drink any."

"I wasn't thirsty after all. Let's go, Hari."

Hari pops up on command. Alex thinks, *I'm really loving this dog.*

Leon thinks, *Reminder to self, stay away from that nutcase.*

The girl's next stop is Jonny's house. "You know where it is. This should be a breeze with that horny dog," Alex remarks.

"I think he's kind of cute," Tami smiles.

Samantha adds, "Yeah, if you like the Martian type with octopus arms."

They all laugh out loud as they drive away, and soon they pull up to Jonny's house.

"This won't take long. You all wait in the car," Alex says.

"Don't think so, we're all in this together."

"Okay Hari, you wait for us in the car." Hari just slumps back down in his seat.

After the first ring, Jonny's mom answers the door.

"Hello Mrs. Everette."

"Oh, hi Alessandra. Oh my, is that Samantha?"

"Yes, and Tami."

"Come on in. Well, what can I do for you pretty girls?"

"Thank you, Mrs. Everett. We were looking for Jonny. Do you know where he is today?"

"Let's see, I guess he's not at your house. That's usually where he goes. I'm surprised your poor mother hasn't called me and asked me to come get Jonny. What does he do all day over there? If he's ever a nuisance just call me. Since he got his driver's license, we never see him much. And you know with summer here we may never see him. At least during school I'd see him in the morning then Lord knows when at night. You know his father is always busy. He's never home and I can't control that boy. He's a good kid but needs more discipline.

"Might be my fault I never really stopped him. He's a little spoiled, I guess. Some think so but I think not. He's just a young man and most young men need to run around, stay busy. He never gets into any trouble. Well, once he broke that store front window, but that wasn't really his fault. Who knew a kid his age could throw a rock that far? He paid for it out of his allowance. I remember he worked hard that summer down at the pool center. Cleaning, pretty hard job for a little boy, but he did it and paid off that window repair. Now it's hard to say what he's doing. I do see his grades. They appear to be okay. He never was a straight-A student, but neither was his father at first. I was fairly smart in school, made quite a few A's in my day in school."

"Excuse me, Mrs. Everett, I just remembered I need to let the dogs out for a walk," Alex smiles.

"Oh dear, those dogs need their walks. You know they have to relieve themselves and can only hold so much water. I thi—, come back when you girls have more time. It was fun chatting with you girls."

"Thanks goodbye, bye. Poor kid, now I'm feeling sorry for Jonny. No wonder he's gone all day." Alex waves at Mrs. Everett and turns toward Tami.

"I think she's sweet," Tami remarks.

"He'll surface soon. I have an idea. Let's get back to the house."

As the girls walk back into Alex's house, Hari bolts to greet Teri.

"I'm going to call Jonny. By the way, can someone walk the dogs?" Alex asks.

"We'll each walk one. I don't think one of us could handle both dogs," Sam replies.

Tami and Sam grab their leashes, and both dogs pop up as if they realize a walk is in their future. Those are some trained dogs for sure.

Alex says in her sexy voice, "Hey Jonny, do you know who this is?"

"Nope, but I hope the voice matches your body and by the way, why are you calling from Dylan's house?"

"Why don't you come over to Dylan's house and I'll show you, big boy?"

"Be right over."

Well, that was easy. What a pig he is. Sam and Tami return and both are giggling.

"What's so funny?" Alex wonders.

"Those dogs are the funniest things I've ever seen. I could have sworn they kissed each other. No other dogs would come near them and if one did, Teri would run them off. It was so cute."

Before another word came out of the girls' mouths, both dogs bolt to the front door and start in a low growl. Teeth wore drawn, and both Tami and Sam back up.

"Holy Toledo, those sweet dogs just turned Cujo on us,"

Suddenly the doorbell rings. "Oh, that's Jonny. Jonny is that you?" Alex yells.

"Yep, yours truly."

"Heel, Hari and Teri come here," Alex commands.

Both dogs back off and sit on either side of Alex. This is going to be even easier than she thought.

"Come in."

Jonny opens the door and see's three girls and two giant dogs.

"What's going on around here? Where the horses come from?" Jonny asks.

"They're my watch dogs and pretty good ones at that," Alex smiles.

"Where's Brandi?" Jonny asks.

"Asleep out back."

"Yeah, what a shocker you guys having a watch dog. What's up? Why the voice and where's D'man?"

"First answer my question. No lies, and they will attack on command," Alex reminds him.

"Cool it, sister. What's the question?"

"Who owns this?"

Alex shows the bandana to Jonny, but the dogs stay put.

"That's Damien, Damien Fuller's. Why?"

"Who does he hang out with? Is he a friend of yours?"

"Woo, hold on. I know the dude, but he's no friend of mine. Why don't you ask Dylan?"

"I asked you. Who does he hang out with? Was he at Clanceys?"

"Now what do you think. Who wasn't at Clanceys? Yeah, he and his gang of thugs were there. He's just a lynch man, but the main turkey is Jimmy Johnson, Dylan's favorite bud. Those two don't like each other much. Jimmy's a complete scum. Is D'man still hungover?"

"I know of Jimmy. Thanks, you've been a big help. You can go now. Alex stands up.

"Now hold on there, ladies. There's three of you and one of me. I like my odds. How about a foursome? They do it in golf. Where's Dylan again?"

"Out of town and have a nice day. We're busy."

"I'm not busy, I've got all day and night. Why don't we knock down a few beers, get cozy, start the Jacuzzi? How about it, ladies?" Jonny winks.

Tami and Sam start laughing.

"Yeah, that's it, let's party girls. Come on."

As Jonny moves towards the girls, Alex whispers to Hari. Well that's all it took for Hari to start out in a low growl and start showing teeth. Then Teri walks behind Jonny.

"Okay, no reason to get crazy on me. I'm leaving. You girls missed your chance. Those are some crazy dogs. Later. By the way, watch those thugs. They carry firearms."

Alex commands, "Heel." The dogs relax and Jonny slides by Teri with a grin.

"Alex, we better contact the police. I don't think we should mess with any gun-toting thugs."

"Yeah, I agree," says Sam.

"I'm not worried, we don't need any guns. We have Hari and Teri," Alex smiles.

Chapter 13

CONCUSSION

Captain Rogers places a call to Isabella and tries to explain to her about the home robbery.

"What do mean, blood? How much blood? Who's blood? Where was the blood? Oh my God, I'm heading home," Isabella exclaims.

"Calm down, Isabella. It wasn't much blood, but it was blood. It was on a kitchen knife in the bar area. All I want is to talk with Vincenzo. Do you know where he is?"

"Really Bill, are you trying to tell me that you're accusing my father of some type of murder?"

"Hold on, who said anything about murder! All I asked was where is your father. I just want to have a talk with him."

"Bill, you're lucky I'm not there in person. I'd strangle you myself."

"Calm down. You might get in trouble strangling the captain of the police department."

"Maybe, but I'll have a damn good reason."

"Listen, Isabella, I am sure there is no reason to be alarmed."

"Why can't you wait until I get home? I will only be here a few more days. If you want to see me again, you'll stall your investigation into my father."

"That was a low blow, Isabella. Maybe I should fly up there and see you in person?"

"No, I have Chloe with me. Just delay. He's my father and it's my family, so please, I beg you, stall. I'll sort it all out when I get home."

"Fine, try and track down your father. His history is not the best."

"That was a low blow, Bill."

"Okay, you're right."

"Where did you say your uncle Duke lives?"

"I told you South Carolina, in some nursing home. He moves around a lot, but I have his last known address at home in my address book. Neither one of those nuts will answer the phone. I think they do it on purpose. He'll be back soon—he's got Dylan with him."

"Okay, a few more days. Oh, by the way, I like your new watch dogs. I drove by your house and before I could knock on your front door, I heard a growl that wasn't very friendly."

"Oh yeah, that's my girl. I wanted the kids to have a few special friends with them."

"Yeah, well, she's safe alright. They didn't sound friendly. I'm sure she's okay."

"Don't you worry about her. As long as she is with those dogs, no harm will come to her. Thanks love, you're the best."

What Captain Bill Rogers didn't do before he hung up the phone was tell Isabella everything he knew. He didn't mention the broken window, which was somewhat confusing considering it was broken from the inside. And if her father was heading to South Carolina, why was his last credit card charge in Mobile, Alabama? And the blood on the knife was Dylan's. It matched the blood from Friday night. The captain figures Isabella is in way over her head and needs his help. Her grandfather has caused her enough pain. Her mother's been missing, now her son. Captain needs answers, and quick. Was someone faking a robbery? It may be time to put a nationwide APB on Vincenzo.

"Hey Jacob, get in here. Let's put up a net for Vincenzo Cabrella."

**

"Who Let the Dogs Out" ringtone for Mom starts blaring on Alex's phone.

"Hey Alex, how are things at home?"

"Okay, Mom. How are you holding up? You sound miserable."

"Yes, I wish we were home. How are Hari and Teri?"

"They are awesome. They are the coolest dogs I've ever seen. I think Brandi likes them being around. She seems more energized these days."

"Keep them close by. Hear from anyone yet?"

"No one, Mom. What's going on? I feel like you're not telling me everything."

"Sweetie, I am not sure myself. It's hard to tell from here. The good news is I spoke with your Uncle Tony and he will be coming your way soon. That would be a huge help. Everything is upside down. Just keep your prayers strong. I'm going to make sure nothing happens to my kids." Isabella starts to cry.

"Mom, nothing's going happen to anyone. You'll see, it will all be fine."

"Now Alex, I have to ask you something and you must tell me the truth, no matter if you ever have lied to me in the past. You have to tell me the truth. Do you understand?"

Alex, getting nervous, starts to cry herself. "I don't ever want to lie to you, Mom."

"Calm down, I'm not mad at you, but you have to tell me the truth since I may already know the answer. Did you find any other information, clues, or notes at Grandpa's by any chance?"

Alex starts crying hysterically and Samantha grabs the phone. "Hello Mrs. Cabrella, everything is fine here."

"Great, girls. I appreciate you staying with Alex. She needs you, and I need you both big time."

"We love the dogs—we all feel pretty safe. Here's Alex."

"Hi honey, you okay?"

"Yep, I think so."

"Is there any information that you may have forgotten to tell me?"

Again, Alex starts crying and this time Tami grabs the phone.

"Hi Mrs. Cabrella, not sure what's going on, but Alex is a mess."

"I know, dear. She just remembered something I asked her to do, nothing important."

"Oh okay, I'll tell her."

Alex takes the phone wheezing, "I'm sorry Mom."

"No problem, sweetie. What did you find?"

"A note on the kitchen table. I also found a few notes in the trash, but they didn't make any sense."

"That's okay. Start with the one on the kitchen table."

Alex reads, "Dylan and I went to visit Duke. He is in a bad way and I wanted to see him before he expires. You were gone so I thought you wouldn't mind if I spent some time with my grandson, Dylan. We luv you, be back soon, Dad."

"Perfect, and read me the ones that you found in the trash."

"Well, they don't make any sense so I didn't think it meant anything. It was like he was babbling."

"No worries, sweetie. They probably don't mean anything, but read them anyway."

"Okay, Mom. These I found this one in the trash, and it didn't make any sense and had lines through it."

**

~~Dylan and I are going to visit Duke. You were gone so~~ ~~I thought you wouldn't mind. Luv, Dad. Gone for Dylan, I m~~ ~~sorry will be bring him back. Will bring everyone back. Love~~ ~~Grandpa. Dylan and I went to get Grandma be back soon.~~

**

"Good girl. Thanks dear, you're the best."

"Okay, Mom." Alex starts feeling important again. "Bye Mom, love you."

But Isabella never heard anything else—she had just collapsed.

Alex hangs up and wipes her tears away.

"Well, everything is okay with Mom. I didn't read her all the notes. She wanted all the ones in the trash. I didn't think they were important, but she is okay now. I just felt like I let her down. So now we have to find the thieves for sure," Alex says firmly to Tami and Sam.

Chloe, as cool as a cucumber, grabs the hotel phone and calls the front desk. Then she walks over to Mom's doctor bag and pulls out the equipment to check her pulse and blood pressure. She was about to give her some smelling salts when she heard a knock at the door. Paramedics walk in and see all the equipment on the floor.

"Well, aren't you a little young to be a doctor?"

"Not really, my mother says I am well above average for my age group."

"Is this your Mom?"

"Yes sir."

"What happened?"

"She was on the phone and suddenly passed out. She collapsed, then hit her head on the table."

"Must have been some conversation."

"Probably was—it was with my sister. She usually does that after my talking with my brother but not after talking with Alex, my sister."

"Well that explains it. We're going to take her to the hospital. She may have a concussion. Pack a bag, you're coming with us."

"Oh, I like ambulances," Chloe smiles.

"You say that like you've been in a few?"

"My Mom's a veterinarian, microbiologist, zoologist, and oceanographer, just to name a few. I've ridden in plenty, just never while she was on the stretcher."

"It must have been some phone call for someone with that much experience."

"No, just the normal conversation between a mother and her daughter."

"Let's go," the paramedic says as he wonders how old the kid really is.

"You okay?" he asks.

"Yes sir. By the way, her vitals where okay. She should be fine."

"Turn on that siren and hit it."

Chapter 14

GROCK

*W*hy is my room so dark? Where's that light switch?

"Hey Grandpa, did we have another power outage? Ouch!" I scream out as I trip over something and land on the ground. Crawling on my hands and knees I ram my head into something hard.

Where am I, dang it. "Grandpa, where are you? It's Dylan." We must have had a thunderstorm roll on by. I wonder why the generator didn't kick on. Wherever I touch it's seems so cold, as if I'm in a cave. It's summer and should be hotter than hot outside. As I feel around the room, everything feels smooth and cool and hard as a rock. I must be having another one of my dreams. My knee and head hurt as if it's not a dream, but reality. After crawling from one side of the room and crashing into what felt like a chair, it seems I'm in some type of small cavity. This is so bizarre. Could I be somewhere else? I must be dreaming.

After feeling around the room, I find a box of matches. I strike the first one, and it instantly erupts then immediately goes out. I light another and it stays lit long enough for me to see I'm in a small room but cannot see a door. I light another and see a fireplace. I walk towards the fireplace but don't see any wood, only a rocking chair.

I start talking out loud, "Maybe I'll break up that chair for wood."

Becoming an Eagle Scout was worth the time and effort. I was about to smash up the chair, when I hear a booming voice.

"I wouldn't do that if I were you."

I scream out, "Who said that? Show yourself." Maybe I shouldn't have asked that. "Where are you?"

"Throw a match into the fireplace."

"But there is no wood."

"Trust me, or you will regret it."

I didn't like the sound of that and decided I had nothing to lose. So, I light a match and toss it into the fireplace. In a matter of seconds, a giant fire is blazing. While this illuminated the entire room, I still could not see the person who was speaking. All I could hear was a pleasing purring sound, or moaning. Grandpa had told me about the uniqueness of this world verses our world. Maybe I did transport, and it's not a dream.

"Ooh, that feels so, so good. It's been a long time since someone lit me a fire."

The room is pretty sparse. I can see a rocking chair, some books, empty bottles, plenty of shoes, jackets, goggles, and old-looking blankets. But still no sign of life or a door for that matter.

"Okay, where are you? Please show yourself."

"I am all around you," the voice booms. "Have you not visited with me in the past?"

I start to recall other things Grandpa told me. Many objects and animals can speak. Some you can understand, some you can't, but even the trees and rocks can talk so be kind to everything. They can be your biggest asset. Rocks are very temperamental. Don't ever call one stupid and never argue with one. They can change shapes and hurl themselves in the air. Be kind, and they will return the kindness. Never raise your voice. *Am I dreaming or did I really transport?*

"I have never visited you before."

"Oh, in that case, let me introduce myself. I am Grock, the greatest and maybe the only rock hut in this area and possibly the oldest, but that has not yet been determined. Many of my kind are quite stubborn, but our memories are forever. What is your name?"

"I am Dylan Cabrella."

"Welcome, Dylan Cabrella. I know an Isabella Cabrella, she is so lovely. She used to always light my fire, and we would talk forever and ever. I so do miss our talks. Actually, as I think about it, many Cabrellas have come to visit me."

"You know my mother, Isabella?" I ask excitedly.

"I do, is she coming to visit again? It's been a little over fifteen-plus years since I have spoken with her. She would sit on the rocking chair and rock and rock—we would talk and talk. She was very curious and asked many questions. I so do miss our talks. It is written she will return, to save us all."

"Yep, that's my Mom. She's a talker, alright."

"Is she well?"

"Yes, I think so."

"Is she coming to visit?"

"Not today, but maybe soon."

"I sure look forward to that day. She had the kindest voice and we would talk forever."

"Where am I, if I may ask?"

"You're in my house. Are you lost while in my house?"

"No, no, I wondered where your house is located."

"Rockland."

"What did you mean that she will save us all?"

"It is written that a princess will return and save us all."

"Okay, well, that's not my mom. She's not a princess."

"Are you sure about that?" The voice sounded upset.

"No, not really. I am not sure of anything anymore."

I may have upset this Grock thing. I'd better get out of here. Now I know why Mom asked so many questions. His answers are short and to the point. Great, Rockland. I should have listened more to Grandpa. He spoke of Rockland, but I can't remember. I need to think. What I do remember is how windy Rockland is.

"Is it safe outside?" After I asked, I look and see my watch is now running counterclockwise.

"Of course it is, you're in Rockland. I will alert the others that you have come to save us."

"Oh, I don't think that's why I'm here because I'm not sure what I'm supposed to save you from."

In an extremely unfriendly tone, the voice booms, "Then why are you here?"

"We were told one day a princess would return and save us, and that is today. Isabella told me she would return and save us if needed. Well, it's needed. Our land is being destroyed. Many of my friends and family have been sent to the palace and other locations. Soon there will be no Rockland if we let them continue to destroy our land. My lovely rock hut used to be surrounded by crystal blue water and sandy beaches, but the water has dried up and the sand has all but vanished," Grock declares mournfully.

"Okay, yes, I will save you, but first I need to get back home and get additional help, more forces."

"More forces. Yes, yes, it's a good plan. Get additional help, more forces," Grock bellows.

"I will be back and visit with you soon."

"Please do. I enjoy a nice fire and chat." Grock gleams.

"Um, how do I get out of here? I don't see a door."

"The door is always closed. Isabella always sat in the rocking chair. She was the one that brought me this chair. Why would you want to break it up?"

"No, I love this rocking chair." Maybe, I'll sit in it and it will send me out of this silly dream. I sit on the chair, but nothing happens. I close my eyes and say out loud, "There's no place like Key West, there's no place like Key West. Well, it worked for Dorothy."

"Who's Dorothy? I don't recall her visiting me, and I don't forget names. And why are you going to Key West? The palace is in the Kingdom of Bonita. You can't miss it."

"I will need that doorway now."

"Yes, I keep it closed. Much evil around that would like me destroyed. You will have but a few moments to get through so be quick, but I hope to see you again real soon. Be careful, it sometimes gets very windy outside. You may want to wait until the wind settles down. It may blow you away unless you are strong enough to handle the two hundred-mile-an-hour wind."

"You must be mistaken. You mean twenty, don't you?" I gulp.

"No, I meant what I said. I don't make mistakes. Do not confuse the issue, but you may stay in here where it is safe. Soon everyone will see my smoke if the wind hasn't caused havoc, and there will be questions. I always have time to chat."

I figure it may be best to wait. I do remember Grandpa talking about all the unusual weather conditions here. "May I ask you some more questions?"

"Please do, I enjoy company."

"What is the fastest way to this palace?"

"The subway. It covers this entire land from one end to the other."

"A subway, is it free?"

"Of course, it's free for all. Just show your number and get on."

"Show my number?"

"Yes, you must have a number if you want to ride the subway."

"But I don't have a number!"

"You must have a number. You may be in danger without a number. Everyone has a number. Just show them. Well, you must go now the winds have calmed and people are beginning to talk. My smoke can be seen for miles, and folks will want to know who is visiting my home. Goodbye, Dylan Cabrella. Please visit again soon."

"But I don't have a number. And I have more questions. What people?"

"Don't forget, you have to move quickly. Watch out for the Graeters."

"But …" I never finished my sentence. All of a sudden, a giant seam in the rock was opening along the wall and as I look, the opening was closing as quick as it was opening. I run into the opening, scraping the side, and I hear someone yell, "OUCH" as I fall outside.

It was calm with no wind at all. Grock must have lied about the winds. All I could see were rocks, rocks, and more rocks. All sizes and shapes, and as far as my eyes could see. The sky was a weird gray—I couldn't tell if it was night or day. My watch was not working properly. I looked back at the rock hut. It looked so small and lonely, but it was the only structure standing that I could see. No trees in sight. What an odd-looking place. This is quite a dream. I begin to wonder, where are all the people and the stores? I'm starving. I've been walking for quite a while now and I haven't seen anything but rocks. What did Grandpa say about food, or did he ever mention it? I thought I saw some nut bars in the backpack. In hindsight, I should have brought more food. What day is it, anyway? My watch has gone cuckoo. Do you get hungry in a dream?

What's that up ahead? Looks like rows of corn. That will work. Fresh corn is good cooked or raw. This weather is nuts. Now I'm burning up. It must be at least a hundred degrees out on these rocks. It's not rows of corn, it's mushrooms. All I can see are mushrooms. Shroomland, I think is what Grandpa called this place. I can't remember what he said—do or don't eat the mushrooms. I like them on my pizza. What's the harm? I'm starving. After stuffing my face with delicious tasting mushrooms, I begin to get very, very sleepy.

Is it possible to dream within a dream? That's is the last thing I remember before I fall sound asleep in the middle of a mushroom field.

**

Finally, a decent night's sleep. I have never felt so good. I must have slept for ten straight hours with no interruptions. Ah, I feel so refreshed. What is that noise? I open the front door and a huge wave of water engulfs the house and me with it. Holy cow, I'm going to drown in my own house. I can't move, what is going on? Come on, let's go. Swim time. Shake a leg, get moving.

I look down and see my mother holding my legs. "Mom, let me go, I will drown. Mom what are you doing?"

A giant silver barracuda with shinning rows of teeth goes swimming by. Was that thing grinning at me? Looks like it was laughing at me. Then a hogfish goes by and says, "You better get moving, son." What is happening? As I look down, Mom is gone, and Grandpa is holding my legs. Okay, let me go. This is nuts. What is wrong with this family? A giant Atlantic goliath grouper swims by and says, "Too late, nighty night."

I see a rope dangling in front of me and grab it. It tosses me through the water and into the open air as a dragon swoops down with its claws extended, and I scream myself awake yelling, "NOOOOOOO!"

**

Not sure how long I was asleep. Wow, now I'm having dreams while I'm dreaming. This is out of control. Okay, where am I again? Oh yeah, Shroomland. Maybe it's not a dream. It's time to find that subway station.

I start my journey, and I hear a something rustling behind me. Not sure what it is, so I begin to speed up and hear another sound. That sounded close by. I stop and crouch really low and pull out my pocket knife.

Suddenly someone jumps out and yells, "Stay low and don't move." It was a female's voice, but she moved so quickly I could hardly see her. She turned to look at me and as she was about to speak, a rather large lizard-like creature started coming right for us. She had a sword out and swung it with a precision I've never seen in my life, and the large lizard's head was cut from its body. With one quick swipe, the lizard lay dead a few feet from my feet. Its head was the size of a Volkswagen Beetle. Almost like a large alligator, but no alligator I've ever seen.

She tells me, "Be still, there may be others." I guess she finally decided no one else is attacking. In a split second, she swiftly swings the sword around and stops it within inches from my neck.

"Who may you be in the land of killer lizards with your giant sword in your hand? Is that a toothpick you're holding?"

I'm gasping as the blade is touching my neck and a small sliver of blood is dripping on my shirt.

"I'm Dylan-da, I think."

"Dyland, you think, what are doing here? You don't know your own name."

"My name is Dylan not Dyland. And I'm looking for someone."

"Where did you get that clothing?"

"What's wrong with my clothes?"

"Nothing, you can wear whatever you want while holding your massive knife!"

As I keep looking into her bright blue eyes, I figure she may be a teenager, possibly eighteen. But what's up with the gear? And the purple knit hat. I think my dream is officially over.

"Looking for whom?" she asks.

"My friend who may be lost."

"I'm going to need more information if you want to live, Dyland."

I have no idea who to trust, so I'm was extremely cautious in my response. Her eyes were the brightest, sparkliest blue eyes, almost aqua color, that I have ever seen.

"I was following my girlfriend, and I lost her in the area."

"You brought your girlfriend in these lands, with that tiny weapon? We should look for her body parts. You must not like her anymore, because soon she will surely be dead."

"Of course, I do—did."

"Then why did you bring her here?"

"I didn't. We got lost."

"I have seen no one but you. She is most decidedly dead. You both are lost."

"Yes, that would be true. Can you lower your sword? It's about to cut my head off."

"Why should I trust you? These are very turbulent times, and the king has many spies throughout the land."

"Maybe I have come to help you."

She rolls over laughing loudly. "You and, let me see, no one else. I'll wait here. You'll probably complete your mission in NEVER. You must have a death wish."

"Who are you?" I ask.

"I am Tabitha, daughter of Tabo, and we must get out of here before the mother finds us. That was just a baby I killed."

I gulp. "A baby, you say. That was some big baby. Are there any more?"

"Yes. I cannot take on too many at one time. And since you travel with puny weapons, you will be of no help. I should leave you, but for some reason I feel I must help you. You seem so pitiful and you look familiar. Where is your family?"

"They are at home."

"Where is home located?"

"I, well, it's kind of confusing."

"Try me. Where is your home? It's not a hard question."

"I can't remember."

"Did you hit your head?"

"I think so. I am not sure where I am and where I'm from."

"And don't forget, you can't recall your name. Can you at least walk?"

"Yes, I can walk. I do need to find a subway station."

"Why do you need a subway? Let me see your arm?"

"Why?"

"I could cut it off and then look at it."

"Okay, okay, calm down. Here, see it's my arm."

"Where is your number? Wait a minute." She pulls her sword back to my neck. "You do look familiar. Maybe you're the prince. No one other than royalty has no number. What are you doing here, Prince? Are you spying?"

"I am not the prince? What's with these numbers?"

"It is odd for you to be alone. We need to move now."

"Can you walk?"

"Yes, I told you I can walk."

"Good, then you can run—let's go," Tabitha commands.

"Where are we going?"

"Not safe here, let's go," she demands. "Not only is a mother lizard looking for you, but I have a feeling people are also looking for you, and not the friendly type."

Tabitha starts to run through the mushroom fields.

It was not easy keeping up with her, but I tried my best. We were silent the entire run. Since I had no choice, I kept following. She seems to know what she's doing. Her eyes are stunning, she is cute. Wonder if she has a boyfriend. I'm not normal thinking about how attractive this unknown girl is who almost took my head off. What color is her hair? It's five hundred degrees out here. Why is she wearing a knit hat? I bet she's bald. Maybe a cancer patient?

Where are we going, and how long has she been tracking me?

Chapter 15

JJ

Alex sits in her bedroom trying to figure out her next move.

"Well, what do you think? Should we drive by Jimmy Johnson's house?" she asks.

"Okay Alex, as long as it's a drive by only, right?" Tami replies.

"Of course."

"Should we take one of the dogs with us?" Sam asks.

"Mom suggested, if possible, don't break them apart. It's either both or neither."

Sam and Tami vote for both, and Alex agrees, smiling from ear to ear.

They all pile in the car with Hari and Teri, both trying to hang their heads out the window. It's almost midnight. Alex gives the dogs a sniff of the bandana, not sure what that will do, but it couldn't hurt. Little did anyone know, Hari already knew who robbed Grandpa. As they drive by Jimmy's house, very few lights are on. The main house was no slouch. Jimmy Johnson's dad owns some food stores in the area and is well respected, unlike his thug son. Jimmy lives in the renovated building, what they used to call the slave quarters. Tami remarks that even the slave quarters look rather big. Alex is already driving down the alley to investigate further. Sam and Tami have seen enough and agree they'd rather come back and look around in the daylight.

Alex says. "Just wait for me here. You'll be fine with those two."

Alex starts walking, and Hari starts howling. Even with the windows closed the howling was loud. Alex turns back and decides to take Hari. Teri just sat there and turned towards Hari, as if giving him the okay. He jumped out and ran in front of Alex like he was making sure the area was clear. Alex was certain these dogs were humans in their prior life. Alex realizes it's best just to follow Hari to the back of the house. She looks into a window and couldn't see a thing. She tried another window and, jackpot, there was Jimmy and a few buddies sitting around drinking beers. Hari starts to growl as the back door opens. She can't see who it is, but she could hear someone urinating.

Alex thinks in disgust. *Great, what a pig. Don't you have any bathrooms in that house, you slob?* She couldn't make out a face but suddenly she heard a sound of a small dog barking.

Hari was nowhere to be found. A small dog comes running out the back door heading right for Alex, yelping like crazy. She was busted for sure. She never actually saw it happen, but she could hear the guy yelling "wolf" and could barely make out that Hari has this little dog in his mouth, carrying him like it's a small bone. The dog finally stops barking as Hari dropped it from his mouth, it yelped twice and ran inside. The kid also ran inside, just in time for Alex to head out of there before the rest of the gang came outside looking for a wolf.

"You're drunk. Quit your squealing. Your always crying wolf in the middle of the night. You better shut up and stay inside. You're cut off—no more beer for you anyway. It's getting late. Go home," Jimmy says as he gets up to take a look and sees something running in the alley. "Wolf, whatever. Wasting my time chasing wolves. All I wanted to do is continue looking look through the latest stolen trophies from Dylan's granddad," Jimmy mumbles under his breath.

As soon as Hari and Alex jump in the car, Tami floors it.

"Why are men so disgusting? One of them almost peed on me, it was so gross." Alex explains to the others what happened. "Girls, we have to come back tomorrow night. Good ole Hari, you saved my life." He starts to lick Alex's face. "Let's go home and strategize for later."

**

"Hello Dr. Cabrella, I'm Doctor Moore. How are you feeling this morning? Do you know where you are right now? You have a very special guest waiting for your recovery."

Isabella looks around the room and says, "Not really, where am I?"

"Do you know this little girl?" Chloe approaches.

"Should I?" Isabella asks smiling weakly.

"You're in the Boston Medical Center. You have a mild concussion and some minor head trauma. You may experience some short-term memory loss. I don't think it's permanent, but you will have to stay with us overnight for observations. Is there anyone that can take care of your little girl, Chloe?"

"Hi Mom," Chloe hugs her tightly.

Isabella is still a bit dazed and asks, "What happened? It felt as if someone cracked a bat over my head."

"That's not unusual to feel like you've been beaten with a baseball bat, but you fell and hit your head hard on a glass table. You're lucky the glass didn't crack or it could have been much worse. You did lose a little blood, but everything is showing normal. I just think a little rest and you'll be back to normal real soon. That's enough for now. You need to rest."

"I'm not going anywhere," Chloe announces with authority. "I'm very comfortable on this couch, and the food's not so bad. I'm not leaving my mother's side."

"Okay, her being here will only help. Ring the buzzer if you need anything," Dr. Moore replies.

"Thank you, Dr. Moore," Isabella smiles.

**

Alex's phone starts blaring, "Who Let the Dogs Out, Woof, Woof."

"Morning Mom."

"Hey Alex, it's Chloe."

"What are you doing calling so early? Call me later?"

"Nope, I'm calling you now. Mom is in the hospital and I thought you ought to know."

"Wait! What happened? Is she okay? Why?"

"They think she'll be okay. After she hung up with you, she passed out and hit her head on a glass table. She has a mild concussion and some temporary memory loss, but the doctor thinks she'll be okay after some rest," Chloe informs Alex.

"Oh my God, I'm flying up there."

"No, it won't do much good. She's mostly sleeping and I won't leave her side."

"Now Chloe, I know you think you're an adult, but I'm in charge and I'm coming up on the next flight. What hospital is Mom in?" Alex demands.

"Uncle Tony is heading your way. Mom said you're going to have to help him. It's very important, so you better stay put. We're in Boston Medical Center, room 1809."

"Damn you, Chloe."

"I'm telling Mom you said damn," Chloe screams.

"Okay, keep me updated, and I mean updated. When's Tony arriving?"

"Mom wasn't sure, but she was very adamant about you being home when he got there."

"Great, I'm not going to sit and wait. I'll call him, if you can ever reach him. Kiss Mom for me."

The "Batman" theme rings out on Isabella's phone, and Chloe grabs it.

"Dr. Cabrella's phone, who may I ask is calling?"

"Who's this?"

"You called me, who's this?"

"This is Captain Rogers with the Key West Police Department. May I speak with Isabella, please?"

"Why are you looking for my mother?" Chloe asks.

"Oh crap," the captain mumbles.

"I heard that. I'm telling Mom."

"It's a private police matter with your mo—, I mean Dr. Cabrella. Now may I speak to her, please?"

"Nope, she's not taking any phone calls at this time, goodbye."

"Now hold on young lady. I just want to talk to the good doctor. She asked me to do her a favor, so if you don't mind."

"What favor did she ask you?"

"Aren't you a little young to be so inquisitive?"

"Nope, I'm above average for my age."

"I see, just tell her I couldn't help her and have a nice day."

"Wait a minute, that's not fair. Why can't you help her?"

"Never mind. Goodbye, Chloe."

"Hold on, my Mom's in the hospital."

"What happened?"

Chloe explained what happened and where she was located.

Captain Rogers hangs up and calls his assistant Maggie into his office. He asks her to find out when the next flight to Boston, Massachusetts is and book him on it.

"Yes sir. You going to save that woman?" Maggie smiles.

"How many times have I told you to quit listening to my phone calls?"

"I promised your mother on her death bed that I would look out for you, and I like that Isabella woman, so you be nice."

"I am being nice, just book the ticket. I'm going home to pack," captain replies.

"What about that APB?"

"Hold onto to it for a few more days."

"Will do. I'll throw it away if you'd like."

The captain ponders silently, *Vincenzo what are you doing in Houston, Texas? Are you heading for the border?*

"Maggie, one more thing—call border patrol in El Paso, Texas. Ask them to be on alert for a Vincenzo Cabrella. Have them contact me if he shows up."

"Sure thing, Captain."

**

Alex got up early, and takes Hari and Teri for a walk.

She didn't see any need for the leash, so she let them roam on their own. Those two acted like an old married couple, funniest thing. If a dog would sniff Teri, Hari would growl and vice versa.

Her cell phone vibrates and it displays a restricted number. "Hello."

"Hello Alex, do you know who this is? I bet you don't. It's been a while."

"Not sure."

"It's your Uncle Tony. How are you, dear?"

"Oh my, I was just about to call you. Are you at the airport?"

"No, not yet. I'm still trying to get there. What's going on? Your mom is usually fairly calm and cool, but she was rather upset the other day."

"Well, I'm not sure what's going on myself. But you won't believe what's happened recently."

"Go ahead and try me. I'd like to hear everything," Tony replies.

"Not sure where to start, so here goes."

Alex begins to explain Mom's visit to Boston and her current condition. Also, about Grandpa and Dylan slipping out of town to visit Duke, about the break in, and anything else she could remember.

Tony just listened and said, "It sounds like quite a variety of events unfolding. I'll be there soon. Just wait and don't do anything rash. I'll handle those thugs when I get there."

Alex gets an attitude and tells Tony, "Just go visit mom. I've got it under control."

"I'm sure your Mom's in good hands. If the doctors can't cure her, Chloe will," Tony says jokingly. "Be careful and I'll keep you informed as to my arrival. I'll bring Matt with me."

"Well, that's a different story. I wouldn't mind seeing him again," Alex gleams.

"Okay then, it's settled. You stay put and we'll be there soon. Ciao."

"Goodbye, Uncle."

Alex begins to think even though Uncle Tony has been a bit of an odd duck, he's consistently kind to her. *Not sure what he can do better than me, whatever. Men. Well, I'm not waiting for him or any other man. But I would like to see Matt.*

Tomorrow night couldn't come quickly enough for Alex. She had a plan.

"Okay girls, everyone ready?" Alex asks.

"I think so," Tami and Sam replied in unison.

Alex's plan was to break up Jimmy Johnson's bunch of hoodlums, so she starts by calling his gang members. *Briing, briing, briing,* "Yello."

"Hey Jimmy, this is Susie. You and your buddies ought to come down to the Red Barn. I'm here with a few of my girlfriends just looking for a good time."

"Sure, who's this again?"

"Susie, we met at Clancey's party. Did you forget me already?"

"No babe, I'll never forget you. We'll be there, wait for us."

Samantha hangs up and said, "He's coming. I wish it was that easy all the time, especially with the good ones."

"Okay Tami, you're up."

Brring, brring, "yo."

"Hello, is this Damien?"

"Yeah, what do you want?"

"You said you'd buy me drink if I ever called. Well, I'm calling you now."

"What the hell you talking about, lady?"

"I'm at the Tiki Hut and I'm thirsty."

"I don't care if you're dying. I'm not buying no drink. How'd you get my number?"

Tami starts to get flustered. "My girlfriend met you the other night."

"Who's your friend?"

"Angie Dickerson," was the first name that came to Tami.

"Yeah, sounds familiar. What's your name?"

"Traylor, I mean Taylor."

"Oh, I like trailer trash better." Damien begins to laugh. "How about you buy me a drink?"

"Okay, sure, meet you later. I'll find you. Bye."

Who would date that creature? Tami shrugs at the thought.

The plan was to break up the gang and to call Alex when they arrived at the bar. Alex figured Jimmy wouldn't allow anyone to be at his house without him. This way he couldn't keep a count on how many beers they drank, and these are high school boys. No one knew how many grades they were left behind. Alex brought Teri, and Hari went with Tami. Alex pulls into the alley and stops the car. The dogs looked okay with the split up since they got to play outside most of the day so they would be ready for some late-night espionage.

Tami kept asking about the commands. "Just say it and he'll know what you mean. Don't worry," was Alex's answer.

Alex's cell phone rings, and it's Sam.

"Hey Alex, he's here all by himself. He's not going to be very happy since there's not a lot going on in here tonight."

"Okay, you may have to stall him. I need some time."

"Okay, but if he touches me, I'm kicking him you know where."

"Go get 'em, girl," Alex laughs.

As soon as Alex hangs up, Tami calls.

"The creature has just arrived. He looks like he's alone. There are plenty of folks inside to keep him busy. Hari hasn't left my side."

"Good, call me when he leaves. I'm heading in," Alex says.

Teri jumps out and starts up the alley. Alex kiddingly asks Teri, "How do we get inside?" Teri starts sniffing around like she understands, then she stops in front of a planter and starts to wag her tail. Alex picks up the planter, sees a key, and decides the dogs aren't normal.

The key opens the back door. She returns it under the planter, and Teri runs into the house. She starts running around, up and down the house checking rooms for whatever, and then she stops. Teri starts a low growl and soon someone is at the front door. Alex hits the floor. Someone starts banging at the front door. Finally, the knocking stops.

Carl is at JJ's house and calls him when no one answers the door.

"Hey JJ, I'm at your house, dude. Where are you?"

"I'm at this lame bar. I'm leaving soon. Meet you at my pad."

"I'm not waiting outside until you get here. Where is that spare key?"

"It's around back under the back-door planter. Don't drink all my beer, or I'll clobber you."

"I brought plenty, dude," Carl replies.

Teri is still alert and the knocking stops. Alex continues checking the rooms with her flashlight. All she can think about is taking a hot bath when she returns home after roaming through Jimmy's stuff.

Alex stops and sees someone tied up and gagged on the floor. It looked like Dylan but with blond hair. Alex unties the dazed looking Dylan.

"These people should be under the jail," Alex says she when starts untying Dylan and takes the gag out.

"Thanks!"

"No problem, let's get out of here," Alex says.

"Absolutely."

"Is that Grandpa's stuff? Pigs," Alex blurts out and asks Dylan to help her put some of the stuff inside this blue pillowcase.

The back door pushes open and Teri starts growling at someone. Carl, one of JJ's buddies just came inside, and Teri's about to pounce.

Bang, bang, two gunshots reverberate like a cannon in the middle of the night.

"Holy smokes, let's get out of here." Alex grabs Dylan, and he looks at her very confused, but he follows. As they approach the back door, Alex sees Carl lying on the floor whimpering with Teri on top of him. Teri is growling, and Carl is begging for his life. Dylan and Alex run past Carl.

Teri slowly jumps off Carl, who looks comatose. Poor Teri limps gingerly back to the car but doesn't make it. She collapses. Alex suddenly realizes Teri's been shot and tells Dylan to pick her up and put her in the back. Blood is all over Dylan's shirt.

Alex calls Gloria, mom's veterinarian assistant, to help with Teri since she has been shot and most likely needs surgical treatment.

"You okay, Dylan? You look wasted." Alex asks.

"They had me drugged the entire time. I'm still a bit confused, but I'm not Dylan, I'm Prince Mako."

"Okay prince, you sound dazed. Let's get you home and cleaned up, those pigs."

When Jimmy (JJ) comes back home, he finds Carl on the floor shaking uncontrollably, and he has wet himself.

"Where's my stuff?" JJ asks.

Carl tries to describe the events, and Jimmy wasn't happy.

"I have been robbed. Did you see who it was?"

Carl, not wanting to say it was a girl says, "Nope. She ran out before I could get a good look."

"She, you telling me a girl beat you up and made you pee on yourself?"

"No, well maybe. She had a big bad dog with her, a huge Rottweiler."

"She took my stuff, and I guess she grabbed Dylan too."

"Yep, he left with her."

"And you didn't recognize her or the dog?"

"Nope, nothing."

"What good are you?"

"It was dark man, and this dog was huge."

"Huge dog, you say. Not a wolf this time. Get up and clean my floor, you moron!" Jimmy starts to think a huge dog could only be a Cabrella pet. *How did they know I took their stuff?*

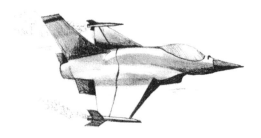

Chapter 16

LUCY

Matt puts Beau in a big bear hug and thanks him again, as they gather on the ship's deck. "You saved our butts, big time."

Tony shakes Beau's hand, "I can't thank you enough for everything you've done for us. I think the admiral is a lucky guy to have you as his son-in-law."

Finally, Jake shakes his hand and says, "You good, Captain. Wish you are on our side."

Beau smiles and responds, "I am, I think." He salutes as they all depart his ship.

"Okay big man, it's your show. What's the quickest way to Luanda?" Matt asks.

"No problem, I grew up in Luanda."

"I thought you grew up in Cape Town?" A confused Tony asks.

"Sure, I grow up all over. You see. Follow me, work hard for the money."

"See, Tony? We have a world traveler helping us."

"Okay, we need taxi to airport."

"Okay boss, I get taxi, stay here."

"Ambitious little fellow," Matt says. Soon Jake shows up with a cab, smiling broadly.

"Cab here, boss. Come on, we go."

Tony tries to explain to Jake that they no longer need his services and hands him fifty US dollars, from the money the captain loaned them.

"No boss, I go with you. I have nobody here. I work for you."

"But we're heading back to the States. You can't come with us," Tony says.

"Sure, I hide in back. I have no one. No trouble. You my friends. Please, boss, don't leave me alone," he pleads as he clings to Matt's leg.

"Oh well, I guess he's ours for a minute. Let's get going," Tony sighs.

After a few phone calls, Tony books seats on an Air Namibia flight to Luanda. It wasn't long until everyone was sound asleep en route.

"Come in Condo number 1, come in, this Condor number 4," a voice crackles over a remote console through the Namibian airwaves. "Thought you would be interested in that one Dr. Anthony Rome and one Mathew Robertson have boarded a flight from Cape Town to Luanda. It arrives at fifteen hundred. They already departed Windhoek, and they will have a brief layover in Lubango."

"Did they check any luggage?" asks Condor number 1.

"None that showed up, sir."

"Thank you, Condor number 4. You will be amply rewarded for this information. Come in Condor number 2."

"Yes sir, Condor number 2 reporting."

"Our friends have surfaced. Not sure how many lives they have left, but apprehend them in Lubango and any cargo they have on board."

"No problem, sir. Will be there shortly."

Tony, Matt and Jake's flight lands in Lubango, and Jake is sleeping like a baby.

Tony informs Matt that he is going to get some food because he knows Matt is always hungry. Matt responds with a thumbs up and confirms that he is still hungry, even after he eats.

"Better yet, I'm going with you. You never buy enough food. I'm a growing boy," Matt smiles. "Maybe I'll splurge and get Jake a candy bar."

As Tony and Matt enter the small airport center, a man walks towards them and says, "Good afternoon, Dr. Rome. We've been expecting you."

"Well, nice to see you to but we have a plane to catch. A real pleasure to see you again. We've—"

"You're going nowhere." Four heavily armed guards walk up to Matt and Tony.

Matt knows when he's out numbered, so he didn't try anything.

"Move another inch, please. They already have orders to shoot."

A man comes running back and says, "No crate on board, sir."

"I assumed not. Bind them both and put them in the van. Bring them to the campsite."

"There is no reason to keep you two alive since the crate is no longer in your possession, but if you are smart, which I think you are, you will tell me where it is. Let's go."

Jake is now awake and watching from the airplane steps. He watches as Tony and Matt are being taken away. Jake is now trying to decide how he plans on following everyone. His new friends need his help. Stealing was not a problem for Jake, so he finds a car, hot-wires it, and turns onto the highway, not far behind the caravan carrying Tony and Matt.

When the van finally comes to a stop, Tony asks, "Where are we?"

One of the guards says, "Huambo, the last place you will see on Earth."

"At least we're heading in the right direction," Matt says.

"Quiet, both of you, no one speak. One more word and you die. We're here, get out."

"I hope it was a safe journey, Dr. Rome. You can call me Condor number 2. I know how you like the water, and since the Cuanza River has extremely friendly crocs, I picked this perfect spot for you two to die. It's a slow and painful death, very brutal to watch, but these boys do enjoy it so. My friends here were hopeful you wouldn't tell me where the crate is, and if that's the case, it's crocodile food for you both. Unless you tell me where it is, then they will make it swift—a bullet between the eyes. Well, Doctor, if you would, please?"

"I doubt your boys over there are that accurate," Matt taunts.

"Maybe not, so it's two bullets in the head. I don't care."

Tony speaks as loud as possible to get the guard's attentions. "May I ask you a question, Condor number 2? Why do you want this crate? It's a cure for AIDS and this country is so overwhelmed with that horrible disease, I thought you would be happy to help these poor families."

Well, that got their attention, alright.

One guard says, "Why you not want cure AIDS? My sister and brother die of it."

"Shut up and keep your guns on these liars. Do you see anything that will cure AIDS? He is a lying dog. Now shut up, or you will not get paid."

Even louder this time, Tony starts yelling, "This crate has been sent back to the States to my laboratory so my team of expert doctors can convert the specimen into the desired AIDS cure. Once I extract this special serum, I can cure this horrible and debilitating disease. If we die, so does the cure. Why did your government give me special permission to look for this cure? You know the government never allows anyone into their country and travel around to pick and send samples back to America."

Condor number 2 is now shifting in his chair. The guards are talking and mumbling between themselves about how much pain and suffering AIDS has caused their friends and families.

"Okay everyone, calm down. He is just trying to trick you. He is a lying devil." Condor number 2 realizes he has no weapon of his own, and that these guards would flip sides on a dime. "I'll pay you double. Take them to the river."

"See, he wants to pay you to keep you quiet about this cure. You four could be saviors of your country. Heroes for saving your race from extinction. You can never bring back those that have suffered in the past, but you can help the future generations."

It wasn't clear if they understood what Tony was saying, but they were suddenly looking at Condor number 2 as if he was now the devil. Tony starts to feel sorry for these guys, wishing he did have a cure for that disease. Maybe after this ordeal he'll spend time on finding a cure for this worldwide epidemic.

Condor number 2 is starting to sweat and gets up from his chair. "Okay, enough talk. Take them to the river."

The guards do not move but instead turn their rifles on Condor number 2. "You fools. He is lying and making fools of you all."

Out of the bushes comes Jake, who begins to talk in a native language which neither Matt nor Tony could understand or translate. Then Jake walks over and unties them both.

All four guards nod their heads in agreement, wave goodbye, and take off in the van.

"See, boss, I find you. We friends, okay?"

"Sure, Jake, we friends." Then Matt grabs and squeezes him.

Matt wants to know what they should do with Condor number 2. Tony suggests they tie him up and put him in the trunk. "What did you say to the guards?" Tony asks Jake.

"I tell them you saved my mother from the AIDS, and you best doctor around."

"You little con-man, you're okay by me," Tony smiles.

"We friends, okay."

"Okay, we friends."

Then they hear, "Come in Condor number 2, come in." Tony looks at Matt. "You heard his voice. Try to duplicate. We need some time." Matt picks up the phone. "This is Condor number 2."

"Anything you have to tell me?"

"No sir, they wouldn't talk. I threw them in the river as croc food."

"Yes, I figured they wouldn't. They will make good crocodile food. Go back to your base. We'll make a visit to his family. Condor number 1, over and out."

"That's not good," Matt says. "We've got to get rid of this guy."

"Matt, I can't kill a man just like that."

"I can. You heard what he said. Your family is in jeopardy."

"Hey Jake, any way to get to the coast from here?"

"Yes boss, train."

The car Jake stole is out of gas, so Matt puts Condor number 2 in the trunk.

"The heat will probably kill him," Tony says.

"Possibly, but we should ask him who Condor number 1 is."

"He doesn't know. I'm sure they've never met face to face."

Jake takes Matt and Tony to the Bengula Railway tracks.

Jake says, "We can jump on here. We always jump trains. It's easy. You see, boss."

After a minor wait, a train is rambling down the tracks. Tony starts to think, *That puppy better slow down. There is no way I can jump that train.* "Where's Jake?"

Jake returns huffing and out of breath. They both look down the tracks and see Jake had dragged a large limb across the tracks.

"The train have to stop, boss. Happen all the time."

"Well, we've hired the slickest one of the bunch," Matt remarks.

They all climb on and join a couple of other natives sitting in the open train car full of straw. As the train slows again, others jump on board. Why buy a ticket? They arrive at Lobito without any further delays. Jake suggests they jump off early, otherwise trouble.

"Okay, now you're in for a real test. We need to rent a helicopter," Tony says.

"Okay boss, never been in *hellichopper*."

"Hey Matt, go ask around which one of these oil rig boys wants to take us for a ride up the coast."

Jake and Tony wait in the shop across the street. "You hungry, Jake?"

"Yes boss, always hungry."

"Good, you sound just like, forget it. Let's go."

Matt arrives at the diner.

"Here, I ordered for you."

"Thanks boss," Matt smiles.

"See he boss," Jake says.

"He sure is, Jake. He boss alright," Matt grins at Tony.

The entire ride Jake was staring out the window, speechless for once.

They finally arrive at the airport where Lucy is parked.

Jake asks, "What now boss?"

"You know, Jake, you've been a great help. Here's a hundred American dollars. Be safe and enjoy yourself. Don't get into any more trouble," Tony smiles.

"No, I go with you, boss."

Tony looks over at Matt and says, "You handle this, okay? I don't have time for this. He's a great kid, but we can't be smuggling any South African kids across the seas. Here, call me on this number when all's clear. I purchased us a couple of cell phones while you were hiring a copter."

Tony heads toward town and Matt starts to talk with Jake. Tony's phone starts ringing. It's Matt.

"Hey Tony, Lucy's is ready to go. I handed out all kinds of goodies, so I think we're all set. The liquor was a big hit. I've got a flight plan to Santa Fe, so come on down."

"Where's the kid?"

"Gone home, I guess."

Matt shuts the door and they are rolling down the runway in a matter of minutes. Matt's takes the pilot's seat and Tony sits in the co-pilot's seat. Matt is an excellent pilot, much better than Tony.

"This was the best investment you ever made, Doc."

"Thanks Matt, I'm glad you approve of my eighty-million-dollar purchase."

"No problem, it almost handles better than that Italian chick, Sophia, in Naples," Matt smiles.

Matt put Lucy, Tony's Gulfstream G650, on cruise control. After a shower and a change of clothes, they are ready for a much-deserved rest.

"Well Tony, we survived another mission, toast."

"I guess so. I'm not really happy about my family threat and Blinky, but I feel much better we're heading home," Tony answers.

"Me too, boss." Jake climbs out of a side compartment.

Tony looks at Matt, who has nothing to say except, "We can't turn around now."

"No boss, we friends, okay."

"Go clean up. There should be some clothes that fit you. You look like Blinky's size," Tony sighs.

Other than the usual stop for fuel, plus a customs examination, it was a very quiet flight. It wasn't too difficult to get Jake past customs since Tony made a few calls prior to their landing. It doesn't hurt to know the right people, but he still had a suspicious feeling someone or something was following them.

They land and jump into Tony's jeep and head to Tony's Santa Fe house.

"It's been a while since I've been here. I sure do miss these beautiful mountains," Matt remarks.

Jake's mouth hangs open as they pull up to this huge house set against the mountains. "Boss, how many people live here? I be okay stay here."

Matt laughs and says, "You think you'll be okay staying here, do you. Smart kid we got here."

"Yeah, real darn smart."

They pull into Tony's eight-car garage. Tony sees another vehicle that wasn't his own. *What are you up to, you crazy old man?* "We've got company."

Matt hops out and says, "Is that who's I think it is?"

"Yes, it's him. Who else do you know drives a 1970 Cadillac Convertible Coupe Deville, with Florida plates?"

Tony hugs his dad.

"Who dat, boss?" Jake wants to know.

"Well Jake, let me introduce you to the man that started all this mess, say hello to Mr. Boss's dad, the infamous Mr. Vincenzo Cabrella." Then Matt gives him a giant hug.

Tony's housekeeper Angelina let Vincenzo Cabrella inside.

"This can't be good news, for you to have driven all the way from Florida. Remind me to reprimand Angelina for letting vagrant's inside. What's going on, Dad?"

"You know I love that car, and since I've been a little confined as of late, I just needed to stretch my legs."

"I bet. Where's Dylan?"

"Later Son, later, I'm starving. How about you Jake, you hungry?"

"Me always hungry, boss Dad."

After a great meal, it was time for the adults to have a little chat, so Tony shows Jake to his room.

"Not sleepy, boss, can't I stay up?"

"Not this time, good night. We've got a long day planned, so you'll need plenty of rest."

"Okay boss, sleep now."

Tony tells Matt and his father that he will be with them soon and to start the after-dinner cognac and cigars—he has to make a quick call.

"No problem," Matt says. "Mine's already lit."

Brring, brring, "Hello."

"Hey Alex, it's Uncle Tony, were alre …"

But before he could finish, Alex says, "No worries, I took care of everything."

"Alex dear, what are you talking about?"

Tony decided not to tell her Grandpa is with him, at least not just yet.

"You know you're not the only adventurer in the family. I am a Cabrella, you know."

"Yes you sure are, dear, just like your mother but prettier. So, tell me what the good news is? I assume it's good news by the sound of your voice."

"Guess who's sleeping at home right now?" Alex asks gleefully.

"Your mother's home from the hospital. That's great news."

"Nope, wrong. Guess again?"

"Listen sweetie, I don't have all day so please tell me."

"Okay, party pooper. Dylan is home sleeping in his room."

"Dylan is back home you say," Tony says hesitantly.

"Yep, I found him. Well, let me explain."

Alex begins to tell Tony all about the discovery of Dylan, the shooting, the stolen items. When she finally finishes, she says, "What do you think now, huh? Pretty good, no great."

"Have you told your mother yet?"

"Nope, she's still in hospital a bit confused, so I told Chloe to call me as soon as Mom is feeling better."

"That is great news. I hope the dog pulls through. Too bad sis isn't there for her, but her assistant is awesome so I'm sure she'll pull through. Listen, you need to be careful. Those guys might come after you, so be alert."

"I can take care of myself," Alex exclaims.

"I'm well aware of that. Just be careful and keep Hari by your side at all times, okay?"

"I don't need Hari anymore. Everything's okay now."

"Listen sweetie, just for me or at least until I get there, then we'll talk about it. It's only for another day or two. And it sounds as if you like Hari enough so just appease your old uncle, could you? It would make me feel better. I can't handle worrying about my two favorite ladies."

"Yeah, he is a great dog. He's pretty down about Teri, so he might like being around. Okay, good deal. Are you coming down tomorrow, and where are you anyway?"

"I'm in Santa Fe getting some R and R. I need a little rest, so I'll probably see you in a couple of days. I'll be with Matt, remember?"

"You must be kidding. How can a girl forget that hunk!"

"Okay, whatever, we'll see you soon."

"Everything okay?" Matt inquires. "You look like you've seen a ghost."

"I think so, I'm not real sure. Hey Dad, when did you last see Dylan?"

"He spent the night. I went to bed and when I awoke, he was gone and I figured he left. The place was a mess."

"Alex says he's sleeping in his bed right now. Snug as a bug," Tony says.

"Awesome, Son, that's great news. I wasn't sure where he'd gone to, but now we know. Wow, what a relief. I don't think I could have broken the news to your sister, if anything happened to that boy. I wasn't really happy with myself for letting him get away, but now everything is fine. Make me another, my good man."

"It's about time we had some good news. Salute," Vincenzo toasts.

"Hey Dad, did you pay cash for gas or any purchases on the way, or did you charge everything?"

"I charged everything, Son. Why?"

"No reason, just curious."

Shortly everyone was sound asleep.

Chapter 17

GAYLOK

I arrive at what looks like a village of some sort. I nearly pass out
from exhaustion trying to keep up with Tabitha. She prompts
me to sit. Once seated inside she serves something that looks like
seaweed but tastes amazingly good. Probably since I'm so hungry.
"Dyland, wait here."

"My name is Dy—, forget it, okay."

I start wondering what in the world has happened to me in past
twenty-four hours. The last thing I remember, I was lying down to go
to sleep at Grandpa's. I awaken in a rock house in the middle of a rock
garden, could be on Mars for all I know. I'm not on Earth, at least
from what I can tell. And I'm certain I'm no longer dreaming. I can't
believe I begged Grandpa to take me with him, now look at me. I'm
not real bright! I grab my backpack, or rather Grandpa's, just to verify
its contents and look for some more food. Plenty of packs of gum,
two Swiss Army Knives, compass, googles, headlamp, reading glasses,
water pistols, roll of toilet paper, rope, tape measure, roll of twenty-
dollar bills, four bright rubber balls, picture of Grandma and Mom,
two rolls of duct tape, and nature bars. I didn't see the nature bars the
first time I went through the backpack. I consume those instantly.

Now I'm ready. What good is all this crap? I can see the Swiss Army
Knives possibly coming in handy, unless it's a giant lizard. Why did
Tabitha laugh at me as she left? After going through my stuff, I look out
and see some faces staring at me. Some human, some unknown. Tabitha
walks back in and looks at all my belongings I dumped on the floor.

"What's that stuff for?" she asks.

"I don't know. I guess I was packing for an adventure of some kind." Then I ask her, "What are those things looking at me through the window?"

"Which ones? Many are shy but very friendly, and some can become fierce if agitated. The good news is we don't usually see any Graeters around here. Do not upset the Graeters, or they will eat you. But don't worry—most of the inhabitants are very kind," Tabitha admits.

"Okay, I understand don't upset the Graeters. Better yet, be nice to everyone, got it."

Something huge is now looking at me. Tabitha jumps up and runs outside, and for some reason I follow her. This thing just stares at me while Tabitha is hugging it. It looks like a real dragon. I jump back a bit startled and grab for my Swiss Army Knife. Is it possible? I don't remember Grandpa mentioning anything about dragons.

"What are you going to do with that?" Tabitha laughs. "Pup, meet Dyland."

Pup says, "How do you do, Dyland? What are you planning to do with that, attack me?"

I can't talk. I may be in shock. *What in the world is that thing? Plus, it can talk and it looks like a dragon. It's going to eat me after they fatten me up.* Finally, my lips start moving.

"What he, he, he can talk?"

"Of course, she can, can't you? And by the way he's a SHE, and her name is Pup. I wouldn't call her a he if I were you."

"Well yes, I believe you. But where I come from, the animals don't speak."

Oops, maybe I wasn't supposed to let her know that I am not from here, but I have a feeling she already knows that.

"What kind of primitive place doesn't allow the animals to speak?" she asks angrily. "Where are you from and how did you get here?"

Just as Tabitha finishes her sentence, some guy comes walking in.

"Hello, my name is Gaylok, friend and protector-watcher of Tabitha. Not that she needs much watching these days now that she is all grown up. Welcome to Rockland."

I'm thinking Tabitha doesn't need much protection from what I saw.

"Hello, I am Dylan."

"Just Dylan," Gaylok says.

"Yes Dylan, Dylan the Swimmer," I mumble, not knowing what to say.

"Welcome to our humble village. If you are a friend of Tabitha's, you are a friend of mine."

Pup staring at Dylan says," Doesn't he look like someone, you know, imperial?"

"Indeed, he could pass for Prince Mako. It's remarkable the resemblance. Are you his brother?" Gaylok asks.

"I don't think so. I don't know a Prince Mako. Maybe one day I'll meet him."

"It's best you never meet him. If the king thinks he has a twin it could be fatal for you. Twins are outlawed in his kingdom."

"Whatever does that mean, outlawed?" I ask.

"A decree came out that twins are forbidden in the kingdom. If twins, or anything resembling one another, are to be born, one or both or more must be killed."

"Well, that sounds a little harsh."

"Indeed, but everything is harsh these days. What are you doing this far from the palace? Are you sure you're not the prince? You not only look like the prince, but you wear a timepiece."

Now we're getting somewhere. I would make a great prince.

"Well no, but maybe I should be."

Then Gaylok grabs my arm and turns it over. "No number, either. You look like the prince, have no number, and wear a time piece. If you are not the prince prove otherwise."

I'm not sure what to tell these folks, but I doubt they can be fooled. "I'm from out of town, just visiting. I am not this prince. If I was this prince fellow, wouldn't I have guardians nearby?"

"That's what disturbs me," Gaylok smiles. "We shall see. I am still not convinced. Your hair is a different color. Maybe you are trying to disguise yourself?"

"No, I've always had black hair. I am looking for someone."

I can hear grumbling and noises coming from outside.

"Dylan the Swimmer, you would not last one day on your own, plus you have no number. How do you plan to travel?"

I begin to think—Grandpa never told me anything about a number. "What's up with a number?" I ask curiously.

"Everyone at birth is assigned a specific number, and it is tattooed on your arm. Anyone human that is. So, without a number, you're on your own."

"I don't have a number."

"That's impossible, unless. Everyone has a number except the royal family. How else do they know how much food, clothing, and housing everyone needs?"

"Who's they?" I ask.

"They are the Kingdom of Bonita. The king and his men."

"Listen, all I was looking for was the subway, so I will be on my way now."

"How do you expect to get on the subway?" asks Gaylok.

"I have money."

Gaylok burst out laughing. "Now you sound like a prince, but money is of no use here. No one has money."

"Okay, this is crazy town. How do you pay for things?"

"The kingdom provides us with everything. At least it used to. Now it's, well, let's just say things have changed and not for the better. You showing up at this time is very disturbing and complex."

I begin to wonder what I've gotten myself into. These people are nuts. Just then someone or something comes in and whispers into Gaylok's ear and departs.

"Okay, Dylan the Swimmer, we need to keep you out of sight for now," Gaylok proclaims.

Gaylok, sensing I was getting nervous, says, "Don't worry, you will be safe here if you prove not to be the prince or a traitor. But for now, we need to keep you hidden."

Tabitha says, "We can hide him with the Graeters."

"Oh no. You told me they eat people."

"They do if you upset them, so don't upset them," Tabitha smiles.

I think the food was drugged because before I could answer, I fell fast asleep.

Gaylok says, "Bring Bruden to me." Bruden is a large black bear, and Gaylok asks Bruden to bring Dylan the Swimmer to his house. "He is too exposed here. I will be with you shortly. I am not sure who or where he is from, but somehow I feel he may be of importance to us down the road. Try not to be seen. I think many are looking for him. I need more information."

Bruden picks Dylan up like a toothpick and carts him away.

I was awakened by a something that sounded like a loud bullhorn. It was being blasted all over the place. I shake my head and see Tabitha sitting across the room. "What is that noise?"

"What, you don't know what that is?"

"No, I do not."

"Maybe you are from another land. Everyone knows what that is. Follow me, I'll show you."

I'm about to ask another question when we go outside. As far as the eye can see is a line of people, animals, creatures big and small, some I recognize and others I did not. Everyone was lined up like they were ready for battle.

I whisper to Tabitha, "What in the world is going on? Are they going into battle? Where did all these people and creatures come from?"

"No, come on, no one misses yoga class."

"What yoga? What are you talking about? My sister does yoga, not me. And I don't recall her telling me about animals in her classes."

But I don't think she heard me. The bullhorn stopped and everyone was singing and swaying, this way and that. I see a giant giraffe that looks like it's instructing the entire massive crowd. I wish I had my camera because no one is ever going to believe this. So far, no one is going to believe anything I have seen. I could only watch and stare since everyone else was participating. I just sit back and try to get my thoughts together.

What is my next move? I need to get to this palace place. They will have answers. Am I a prisoner? Do I need to escape? How long would I last without their help? This place is much different than back home. I haven't seen one Seven-Eleven nor a gas station, not even a single car for that matter. To top it off, not even one Starbucks. Next, I hear swooshing sound and heavy breathing. The entire landscape was full with everyone doing yoga. I'm guessing twenty thousand. A mix of animal and human, but they all seem to know what they are doing. After about an hour or so, Tabitha comes back.

"You look refreshed," I remark.

"You don't. You should have participated. It would have calmed your nerves."

"You're probably right but I have a lot of questions."

"So do I."

"How come I don't see any grocery stores? Or cars, or gas stations, or streets, or houses, or buildings, malls, McDonald's or the sun, or a Starbucks?"

"We are far out in the countryside, not a lot of activity out here. As you get closer to the palace, you will see many sights."

"Is Gaylok your dad? If not, where are your mom and dad? Are they still married? Do you have a boyfriend?"

"One question at a time, please. My parents passed away when I was very young," Tabitha replies.

"You are still very young, and I am very sorry about that."

"Where are your parents?"

"They are divorced." I reply.

"We have rules about that."

"Rules about marriage? Are you married?"

"No. Why did you ask about marriage?"

"I was just wondering how it works."

"What a silly question."

"Is it really? I was just curious."

"Well, it's fairly simple," Tabitha tries to explain. "You can marry anyone you like and the high priest or priestess marries you."

"So, you can marry anyone?"

"Of course, you can. Why, can't you where you're from?"

"Well, it's yes and no."

"Why not?"

"We just passed a law that says gays can marry each other."

"What's gays? Are you gays?"

"I'm not gay?"

"What are gays?"

"Simply put, it means guys like guys and girls like girls."

"Well, what's wrong with that? What does that mean?"

"Oh nothing, I was just saying I'm not gay. I like girls." I grin.

"Good for you. I like both."

"Well, that's fine for you. Then you're into a threesome."

"Now, what are you talking about?"

"I don't know, I'm not comfortable talking about any of this."

"Well, you started it."

"I know, I know. I'm sorry, but I am a bit curious, seeing how you all just get along with each other and have so many friends."

"Why, don't you have friends?"

"Yes, but not five million, *gillion* friends. I have about three or four close friends."

"Why so few?"

"I don't know, not enough time maybe." I respond.

"We have plenty of time. Maybe it's you?"

"It's not me, people like me."

"Then why do you only have three or four friends?"

"You know, we do things differently where I'm from."

"I can see that. You have no friends, only gays can marry, and—"

"No, no, I didn't say that. I said gays can now marry. We could always marry."

"That seems so primitive. I can marry anyone and anything I like, well at least if approved by Gaylok, but we do have one strict rule— you can only marry twice. If you break it off or get divorced after the second marriage you will be thrown into the pit, which really means you shall be killed. It seems a lot of second marriages work out just fine. Tabitha smiles and continues.

"You are also encouraged to marry within your species. Some species have strict rules about marrying within your species. Humans have to marry within their species. Take for instance a Kondo. They should marry within their own. I mean who else could marry a Kondo other than another Kondo? They are at least fifty feet tall. Some species should marry within their own, it just makes sense. Who could a Kondo marry if not another Kondo? But now that I think about it, I don't think Kondos have a strict rule."

"I can see why that would cause concern. Otherwise it could be crazy," I reply sarcastically.

"Oh, that's crazy but where you're from is not. Whatever." Tabitha starts to get annoyed.

"My parents were married for twenty years before they died."

"Oh, I'm sorry about that. Mine hate each other."

"I miss mine every day. But Gaylok takes care of me now. He is very wise, and let's just say he has many friends."

I was curious to see her hair color. Her eyes are an awesome sparkling bright blue. "Do you ever take your hat off?"

"That's a ridiculous question. Of course I do."

I finally ask, "Am I a prisoner?"

At that exact moment, Gaylok walks in with a big smile and alongside him is a large black bear.

"Prisoner, you ask. Yes and no. You can leave whenever you wish, but you will probably not last very long," Gaylok answers.

"What does that mean?"

"You would be killed instantly."

"So, I am a prisoner. Why not kill me now?"

"I didn't say I would kill you but others would."

"First, we do not know why you look so much like the prince, why you are here, why you carry pictures, plus many other unanswered questions. There is a battle, a struggle going on, and I am unsure which side of the struggle you are on."

"I am on your side," I reply.

"That is a wise answer. I didn't expect anything else, but can you be trusted is the real question?"

"Of course I can be trusted."

Smiling, Tabitha interjects, "He does have three or four friends."

"Well, that does change the landscape. You're free to go. It would devastate our village if your three or four friends attacked us."

"Okay, okay, I'll stay put, but I need to get to the palace."

"No, no, no, that is the last place you need to be. If you are telling the truth and you are not the prince, the king will have you killed on the spot. Twins are outlawed, and either one or both twins can be killed at any time. Since the prince will not be killed, one can assume you will be. So, I don't think you want to risk being seen by the king, or better yet the kind-hearted queen. She would gut you faster than the king's men. I do have one question that you could answer. Who is this?" Then Gaylok hands me a picture of Grandmother.

"That is my Grandmother," I quickly respond, feeling proud that I knew the answer. "Is she here?"

"I am asking the questions. When did you last see her?" Gaylok asks.

"I have never met her face to face. She has been missing since the day I was born."

"And how old are you?"

"I am sixteen, well soon to be."

"Interesting, very interesting. Can I assume you are not aware that she is Socreen, the queen's handmaiden who works in the palace?"

"What!" I scream. "You have to take me to her at once. That is why I am here, to take her home."

"This is getting very fascinating. You could be the prince's twin, but yet you don't know him. And your grandmother looks like the queen's handmaiden, Socreen, but you're not so sure. Why am I beginning to disbelieve everything you are telling me, plus now I think you're a spy? And a lousy one at that."

With that, the huge black bear Bruden starts into a low growl and shows large amounts of teeth. I may be dead in seconds. "I swear, I don't know what's going on, but I am no spy. I don't even know where I am. What kind of spy is that? Certainly not a very good James Bond-type for sure."

"I do not know what a James Bond-type is, but you're starting to get on my nerves."

"Don't you watch TV or go to the movies?" I ask.

"What is that?"

"TV, cable, MTV, internet, reality shows just to name a few."

"No, we have no such thing. We only have national broadcasts from the palace."

"Well, aren't you bored all day without the internet?"

"No. Why are you here? Maybe we should take you to the palace, probably a reward out for you."

"I am here to take Grandmother, or Socreen as you call her, back home. Since you know where she is, I can leave you."

"Back home where?"

I figure, what can it hurt. "Back to Key West, Florida."

"Key West, Florida. And where is that located? I am not familiar with that area."

"It's as far south as you can go." It really is south of everything, I begin to think.

"South, you say. We shall see."

"Who is this?" Gaylok shows me another picture.

"Oh, that's my mom. She doesn't know I'm here."

"Your mother. Can you tell me where she is?"

"She's in Boston."

"And where is Boston?"

"It's in Massachusetts."

"Another place I have never heard of. Are you sure you're not from the concrete country—upper land?"

"No, I don't think so."

"Thank you, I will talk to the elders and get back to you at once. If I were you, I'd just relax until we decide what to do next."

"But I need to see Socreen, or whatever you call her."

"So you have said, but until we decide, your future is to stay here for now. You are very fortunate to be accompanied by one of my greatest warriors, Tabitha and her trusty sidekick, Pup."

Chapter 18

KING

The king of the kingdom is extremely disturbed. His son is missing and heads are about to roll.

"Good morning, sire. We've had a breach in Sector 37, late last night."

"Why was I not alerted sooner?" the king demands.

Crate trembling says, "I did not want to disturb your highness at that time of night until I discovered the issue, which is most likely a malfunction. I had to be sure there was a breach, sire. Ever since the rebels destroyed all of the equipment, it has been difficult to locate if and where there is a breach."

"Was the breach at the same time my son was to be transported?"

"Yes, I believe so, your highness," Crate replies shakily.

"Then why did you allow my son to be transported?"

"It happened simultaneously, my lord."

"Where was the breach?"

"We think it was Rockland sire, Sector 37."

"Think, does anybody know anything around here? Find out for sure and get back to me at once. If anyone harms my boy, it will be death to them and their family. Go."

"Yes sire, at once." A trembling Crate bows and takes off running. Crate is the king's most faithful and head servant. Many report to Crate, and now he is yelling at everyone to get him answers.

"Good morning, my dear. How was your sleep?" the king asks the queen.

"Not well," the queen responds in her usual agitated voice, "since your screaming awakened me. What has happened now?"

"We may have had a security breach in Sector 37?"

"Well, find out what has happened. Has my son left for his journey?"

"Yes, Prince Mako left early this morning."

"Was he traveling near Sector 37?"

"No, my queen, he was not supposed to be near Sector 37, so I can assure you no harm has come to him."

"You can assure me of nothing. If anyone has harmed my son, I will personally take their heads off."

"Crate is looking into the matter. I should have an answer soon."

"You continue to be too soft with your people. If I were you, I would have cut off his head or thrown him into the pit and replaced him with someone who knows what they are doing. You surround yourself with incompetency. You are weak."

"No dear, it's called diplomacy. If I cut off everyone's head as you prefer, there would be no one left to work. Please, calm yourself and go back to sleep. We shall talk later, my dear."

"I cannot sleep until I know my son is alive and well."

"Yes, my queen. I will alert you as soon as the information arrives."

The queen stomps off, growling to herself, "My day will come when I will take over and the peasants will shake in my presence." She considers speeding up her secret plans. The queen turns down the deep hall and screams, "Socreen get in here at once. I may be heading out this morning. Be quick."

As the queen departs, the king starts mumbling to himself, "I hope that witch of a wife has not turned my only son against me."

Crate returns to the king and begins to explain what happened. "It seems the prince was transported into Sector 37 by mistake. The transporter coordinates were set for California, but for some reason it may have sent the prince into Sector 37, Rockland. The tech has been reprimanded."

"Reprimanded? For that mistake, kill him," the king commands.

"Yes, my lord. We are trying to figure out the mix-up. That sector has been shut down for years. All transports have been shut down."

"You are aware that the prince is traveling with a small contingency against my wishes, but the queen thought it best. I need answers at once. Where is my son?" the king screams. "Did that small contingency get transported with the prince?"

"Sire, I am working on all that information and will have an answer soon. It was certainly a malfunction. The Rockland transporter was destroyed long ago."

Crate was not about to tell the king that the small contingency traveling with the prince was never transported. At least not yet. The malfunction happened while the prince was being transported.

"You do know that the rebels are constantly trying to overtake my throne, so if I don't have an answer soon, you will pay for this travesty. Find my son, NOW."

"Yes sire, at once."

Crate is now running from the king's quarters knocking over anything or anyone in his path.

It turns out the San Francisco coordinates are 37.7749 N, 122.4134 W. And only the first two digits were entered before they encountered a disturbance, which turned out to be Dylan being transported to Grock in Rockland via the blue pillowcase.

The king is very solemn but understands that all the recent events in his kingdom have created unrest and turmoil. This land of his, the Kingdom of Bonita is named after its beauty but times have changed, and not for the better. Previous kings, which include his father, would walk out among the people and be cheered all across the land, loved by all. But that was eons ago.

The current king can recall being at his father's side and people shouting and chanting throughout the night, "long live the king." Business was flourishing and crime was at an all-time low. The queen was also very generous and kept her king (husband) humble at all times. She loved helping everyone, always reading to the children and allowing kids to run around the palace and play hide-and-seek. Plenty of laughter was in the air.

The palace has its own transportation system. The royal subway system runs throughout the land, through mountains, under lakes and rivers. Travelers could see fish swimming by. Back then the kingdom had an abundance of water, but now it hasn't rained in over five hundred days. And now it is unsafe for the current king to even walk outside without hundreds of escorts. There are many who would like to crush him and his entire way of life.

Committees have become a nuisance and since all the animals can speak, it's impossible to imagine how many committees are out there.

Everyone has suggestions, and it can get pretty monotonous at times. For instance, one grievance was about skipping rocks, and the previous king had to make a judgment. The question arose that it wasn't fair if someone decided to skip or throw the smaller or younger rocks against the water and watch them skip. Many parents were upset since it took so long for their loved ones to come back to shore. They wanted signs posted on all the beaches:

**

DO NOT THROW ROCKS.

**

The current king remembers as a child, he could care less about rock issues, but the actual king was very concerned about this issue. His answer was that each rock should consider it an honor to be skipped, and the rock that skipped the furthest would be allowed to have the beach named after that rock for the week. The current king rarely sits in on the grievance committees. He thinks they are a waste of time.

Many are trying to take over the kingdom, including the king's bride, the queen. Even the king thinks his queen killed his first wife but does not and has not been able to get the proof. And yet she has become extremely powerful and evil. Putting so much trust in the queen may have been the downfall of the king as well as his kingdom.

The queen was extremely agitated this morning as she started recalling some of her recent accomplishments. She reminds herself that she is the only one around that gets anything done. Who else makes the workers work harder and faster? It was her good works that increased the size of the palace and keeps it running smoothly. If not for her kindness this place would collapse. Who does the king think he is talking to? Who was it that got the people to work extra hours per day? While the queen was getting dressed for the day, Socreen was also wondering who breached Sector 37.

The queen screeches, "Socreen, get back in here. Hurry up, you old hag."

"Yes, my queen."

"Bring Trigon to my chambers at once. Hurry."

Socreen knows this cannot be good. Trigon is extremely evil and is usually called upon for dark deeds. She must get in touch with Carolyn, since trouble must be coming this way. Her mind raced back to the question of who came through Sector 37?

"Hello, my queen, you have requested my presence. I am at your service," Trigon bows. Trigon is an enormous dragon and very faithful to the queen. She does most of the queen's dirty work.

"Yes Trigon, how nice of you to come at such short notice. I do need your help, but complete secrecy is required or it will be trouble for us all. This mission before you cannot fail, and I trust you and only you to accomplish my wishes."

"Yes my queen, I will not fail you."

"You are my most faithful and greatest warrior."

The queen remembers Trigon's last mission was a success, killing the king's first wife.

"This is a mission that needs planning, precision timing, and complete secrecy."

"What is it you need, my queen?"

The queen looks around to be sure there is no one nearby. Not even Socreen, who she trusts little.

The queen starts,"The prince has started his adventure but may not have left the kingdom. I have talked the king into allowing the prince to travel with a small contingency, and he has succumbed to my wishes. I think he is in Sector 37, Rockland. The transporter is acting up, so I am not a hundred percent sure. The king is weak and knows nothing. But if he is in Sector 37, you need to get to him first. I need the prince to have an accident and it has to look like the Trefars are the culprits. If we can blame the Trefars for the prince's downfall, the king will finally come to his senses and wipe them out for good. That area is unsafe, plus the Trefars cannot be trusted.

"Can you do this for me? And once I am in charge you will be by my side."

"I can, but Sector 37 is in Rockland, not anywhere near the Trefars," Trigon remarks.

"I am aware of that but as I said, make it look like a Trefars attack. I don't care how you do it, just so as we can blame the Trefars. They have been known to attack anywhere. T is getting stronger and stronger. He must be stopped," the queen smiles.

"When do you want this to take place? I will see to it that the prince has a quick death."

"I don't care. Quick, slow, or painful—just get rid of him. After his demise, I will eventually purge the king and have my place as master of all. I am sick of his laziness, but that is for another day. Do it at once, before the king sends his men to bring him back to the palace."

This made Trigon's smile widen. "Yes, my queen."

"If the king suspects I had anything to do with the prince's death, I will deny it and I will tell him I discovered your plans to kill the prince. So do not make any mistakes. I shall get his location to you at once."

"Yes, my queen, your wishes are my pleasure," Trigon grins.

"Thank you, Trigon. Do not tell anyone of this, not even your brother."

"My brother Tragoon has yet to return from his last mission. He is also getting weak. I will tell no one, and soon the crown will be on your head, my queen."

"You are too kind, Trigon. Please be safe, and may success be in your immediate future."

"Both our futures."

They both laugh out loud.

Crate, the king's assistant has returned with information for the king.

"Your majesty, Crate is here to see you."

"Send him in," the king commands. "I have been waiting for him and he has two minutes to spare."

"Good day, your majesty," Crate exclaims. "I think we have found the prince. There have been some unusual events happening in Rockland, and word is it's the prince. As far as the transporter goes I—."

"You think. Stop thinking and listen," as the king holds up his hand. "I need your assistance. I also know he is traveling alone thanks to the tech's blunder."

"Yes sire, what it is you wish?"

The king whispers, "I would like someone to follow the prince. He wanted to have some freedom, so let him. But be sure to protect him from any foul play. He was so excited and very anxious about this journey, so let him have a longer leash for a few days. But I want him followed by a ghost. He must not know he's being followed. Let him have his brief moments of freedom. But make sure no harm comes to him, or I will blame you. I don't want to delay this mission. I want daily reports of his progress. He was supposed to go to California, but with any luck this will satisfy his desire to visit the concrete country. Do you understand?"

The king ponders to himself as to why he ever allowed the prince to go without a team of warriors. The king said nothing to the queen about a spying on the prince.

Crate suggests, "I will put Grande on the job."

"He knows Grande too well. How about his son Grando?"

"Oh sire, you are wise. I will see to it at once."

**

Kaptuk is a wise two-hundred-year-old cheetah, who is in charge and trains all of the recruits for the king's guards.

"Grando, what are you doing? Quit chasing that butterfly and listen to me," Kaptuk says.

"Why do we always have to work? Why can't we play sometimes? All the other recruits play all day. Why is it that I have to always work?" Grando whines.

And as Grando goes off chasing a butterfly, Kaptuk just shakes his head. How will he ever train this youngster if he never listens?

"You must complete your lessons or your father will have my head on a platter. Now, would you like that, would you?" Kaptuk asks Grando.

"Well, if you put it that way, sure, why not," Grando replies.

"Not funny, little one. Now let's get back to work. Or I will summon your father, Grande, and you know the outcome of that conversation."

"Please take me to Lake Demise," Grando begs Kaptuk.

Kaptuk recalls the lake and its perils. The lake is appropriately called Lake Demise. This man-made lake is the main source of all the water for the kingdom, and the king added plenty of creepy monsters to protect it. Its depth is unknown and it's always very dark. Only unwise and foolish people ever come near the lake. Few that approach the area have survived its grip. Countless have died, before even touching the pitch-black waters. Creatures large and small live in and about the lake, and no one dare enter unless they are a simpleton or do not know of its dangers. When approaching the lake, no one would ever know it's cursed since everything surrounding it used to be so exquisite.

Everything surrounding Lake Demise is so lovely, it's a shame. Wonderful waterfalls are there no longer and a few giant trees overlook the lake. But the beauty is misleading, for no one is for sure what is in the lake itself. Unknown sounds are constantly coming from the lake. Screeches and screams can be heard day and night. Since it is so difficult to determine if it's day or night, it's best never to visit.

Since the king controls the lake and all its inhabitants, many think the king does many experiments at the lake since no one dare enter. It is his own private experimental laboratory.

Kaptuk explains to Grando, "You should never enter the lake. It is very dangerous by the lake, and your skills need plenty of work. Maybe if you ever attempt to listen and learn, we will visit the lake, possibly next year."

"My father has seen the lake many times and has lived, so I too, shall visit and become a great warrior," Grando replies, then takes off running.

"Grando, get back here and try that again. How many times do I have to tell you, always be still and stay low. Patience is your ally. Rely on your instincts. You leap too early to surprise your opponent. You cannot rush into an attack. Stay calm and wait for your prey to come to you. Never show yourself too soon—there may be others nearby. Survey the entire arena before you make your move." Kaptuk's tone is instructive.

"But Kaptuk, I am quicker and larger than anyone else. Why should I go through these useless assignments? My father says one day I will be a leader of many, and I think now I may be ready. These classes are boring," Grando moans.

"Little one, one day you will lead many, but you are just too young and stubborn to understand that you need additional training before you will be ready to lead." The little one that Kaptuk refers to is Grando, a twenty-foot saber-toothed tiger, son of the great Grande.

Kaptuk has been summoned to the palace and informs the class that Shai will take over the lessons for the day. Kaptuk is escorted to the royal subway. Kaptuk arrives at the king's palace, wary indeed. Nothing good ever comes from being summoned to the king's audience.

"Wait here, the king will see you soon."

Kaptuk, attempts to relax as he lies next to one of the luxurious chairs in the king's outer office. The palace surroundings are full of gold and silver with sparkling diamonds everywhere. The palace itself is made of diamond and gold, indestructible from outside threats. Kaptuk considers it a waste of fortune with so many starving. In the past everyone was fulfilled with plenty of food and jewels, but times have changed. No one is allowed to have any jewels, as everything is the property of the king. The queen has certainly made her mark on his reign.

"The king will see you now."

Kaptuk bows and walks into the king's main study. It was so bright that it almost blinded him. Nothing is that bright in all the land. He has not been in the king's palace in a long time, which suits him fine. Kaptuk has no reason to ever visit the palace and prefers it that way since nothing good ever comes from visiting the palace.

"Good afternoon, your highness. I am glad—"

"Get up, Kaptuk. It is I who should be thankful for all your hard work. We do not see much of you these days. You must make it a habit to come visit more often. I miss my old friend," the king remarks.

"Yes sire, I shall try."

"How is your training with my new recruits coming along? I need strong warriors to protect our land."

"All is well, your highness. We have plenty of recruits finishing the training program and ready for battle, your majesty."

"Good to hear, but I need to borrow one of your students for some reconnaissance work; is okay by you?"

Before Kaptuk could respond, Grande glides into the room.

"Hello Kaptuk," he says with a giant grin, "how is my son Grando doing? The king needs his services."

Kaptuk, a little alarmed, just smiled and waited for his next orders knowing full well that arguing with Grande would be pointless. "Yes Grande, what services could Grando provide?"

The king interrupts and says, "I have a mission for him. It's a minor mission but of great importance to me."

"Certainly, your highness, whatever you command."

"Thank you, Kaptuk, you are a great leader. I will let Grande fill you in on the details. I have some other issues to attend to. Thank you for coming."

Kaptuk bowed as the king departed and asks himself what choice does he have. Kaptuk also trained Grande, who was one of his best students and now the most feared warrior in the land.

"The king was being kind when he suggested it was a minor mission. There is no such thing as a minor mission, and you will not fail the King!" Grande says to Kaptuk.

Kaptuk wonders what is this great assignment. Kaptuk is fairly certain that his own son's death was caused by Grande, but keeps it to himself, or he also would be killed.

"The king would like the prince to be followed, but secretly. Grando cannot be seen by the prince, and report all his daily activities back to me," Grande grins.

"Where is the prince now?" Kaptuk asks.

"He was last seen in Sector 37. I am awaiting his exact location as we speak, but in the meantime, I would like you to alert Grando of this mission. He starts at once. That information should be enough for a skilled warrior to find his trail. He is to follow as a shadow and to make sure no harm comes to the prince."

Kaptuk, starts to say, "I do not think th—"

"I do not care what you think." Grande walks up to Kaptuk with a huge smirk, showing all his teeth. "Just follow your orders. If he fails, I will blame you and only you. Goodbye, old friend."

Kaptuk just stands there with Grande staring him in the face. It's a little intimidating to have a thirty-foot saber-toothed tiger gritting his teeth and staring down at you. Grande never was really warm to his son Grando. He was a runt of the litter and always getting into trouble. Maybe he wanted Grando to fail.

Grande never really cared for Kaptuk. He was a great instructor and a close friend of the king's father, but Grande never forgave Kaptuk for making fun of him in class one day.

"Certainly Grande, I await your next command and he will not fail," Kaptuk responds and walks out of the palace.

Kaptuk worries that Grando is not ready for this mission. They seem very disturbed in the palace today, and he starts to wonder what the prince is up to. It's possible his radical mother, the queen herself, is planning a takeover with him leading the charge.

**

Grando thinks Shai is much easier and understanding than that old fool Kaptuk, plus she is very cute.

Shai announces to the class, "Split into groups of two. Cato and Grando, Calif and Zetha. Everyone should know the drill. You all have one hour to hide and capture the other team's post. Be safe and be wise."

"Now, that's what I'm talking about," Grando says to himself.

Cato and Grando take off. And all Grando can talk about is Lake Demise, but Cato is not falling for it. Cato wants to go into Rockland. They only have a short time to capture the opponent's post.

"You are such a wimp," Grando whispers. "Rockland is boring!"

"No, I'm just wise. You're a twit. You always want to go to Lake Demise."

"Oh boy, you are so lame."

"I may be lame but I will live another day. Why don't you ever take this stuff seriously?"

"I do. The rebels are getting out of control, and soon we will be in a battle."

"Who told you so? Don't tell me, your father, Grande."

"Yes, my father says, if we don't rid the kingdom of these rebels, all will be lost."

"Yeah, well, if we rid the kingdom of all the rebels, who will be left to do the king's bidding?"

"You may be right. My father doesn't understand that the people are just upset with the everyday needs put on them from the royals." Grando remarks.

"Don't start with the rebellious attitude. If Kaptuk or your father heard you now, you would be in big trouble. Now focus and quit complaining."

"I'm not complaining, just trying to figure out why everyone is in such an uproar."

"Let's quit talking and get going. Maybe on our way to Rockland we will come across a few rebels and take off their heads. That will be fun." Cato smiles.

"Oh yeah, lots of fun, slicing off heads. Sounds like a thrill."

Watching a huge snow leopard and twenty-foot saber-toothed tiger take off at full speed is quite a sight to behold.

Chapter 19

BLUE PILLOWCASE

Tony and Matt awake rested in Santa Fe and convene in the kitchen.

"Morning, Matt. Thanks for the coffee—it tastes good," Tony remarks. "I know you didn't make it. Is anyone else up?"

"No not yet, but wait until you see this."

Matt starts flipping through the TV channels and stops on the CNN station. "CNN has a couple of eye witnesses that said they saw an unusually large flying object off the coast of California. It was described as a new-world pterodactyl. No pictures have been released to us at this time."

"Could it be our buddy, Tragoon?" Matt wonders out loud.

"Yes, probably. I hate to speculate, but I would say we haven't seen the last of that creature."

"I've got this nasty feeling there's a lot of things you haven't told me," Matt exclaims. "Now would be a good time."

Tony smiles and says, "How right you are, my friend. I think you should get a quick synopsis."

Matt says with a laugh, "Great, boss."

"Okay Matt, here goes. Get comfortable and I'll try to explain the unexplainable. You recall my stories about another world or kingdom is what it's actually called. Well, it seems the pearly gates have reopened."

"Pearly gates, what in the blue moon is that?"

"Funny you picked the color blue. I'm not a hundred percent sure myself, but I'll fill you in on what I do know."

"At this point, I'll take whatever I can get."

"No questions until I'm through or I'll never be able to finish my story. It's going to sound outlandish, unique, impossible, and just downright insane."

"Everything we've ever done has been all those things, so don't worry. I'm a big boy, just start your story."

Tony begins his story. "Okay, it all started hundreds of years ago. My great, great, great grandfather purchased a piece of fabric in ancient Italy. The fabric was a very unique color blue, almost purple, and it stood out from any other color in those days. It also turns out that fabric had mystical powers, but no one knew it at that time. I think the seller may have known, but who knows the real story. At least I don't think my great grandfather at the time knew what powers it possessed—he just purchased it for its beauty and thought his wife would like its vibrant tint and unique coloration. As time went by, the fabric began to shrink and so my great, great grandmother, who wanted to keep the fabric intact, decided to knit some other unknown fabric to this unique piece of blue fabric and made it into a beautiful blue pillowcase. For years it sat in the corner of the room, and then one day my great grandfather fell asleep on this blue pillowcase and he disappeared.

"It turns out, when he put his head upon the pillow, he was actually transported into another land called the Kingdom of Bonita. The blue pillowcase has been handed down from generation to generation along with the stories, and any helpful information passed along with it. Being transported into another land or world is quite the experience. The stories were very helpful to those that did transport. But the fabric kept shrinking, and as time went on, it was more difficult to locate additional fabric and interweave it to keep it intact. Today, this special fabric has depleted and the powers of transporting slowly faded away."

Matt interrupts, "Did you ever transport?"

"Not yet, let me finish. Yes, I have been many times, and I never understood how the transference worked. And this disturbed me greatly. What happens if we transport into this land and cannot return? No one knew if or when the powers would deplete, or if the magic would stop. But it happened while my mother was in the kingdom. I constantly reminded Isabella about the danger and begged her not to continue until I could find something to stabilize the situation. This blue pillowcase was not attached to anything, no machine or pod. It made no sense to transport into another land just by laying your head on this mystical pillowcase. I needed some kind of concrete evidence on how it worked just in case the system failed. And then that day arrived, and my mother is paying the price."

"So that's where she is."

"No questions or comments please, but yes," Tony admits.

"I have been to this kingdom many times but have not been able to return in fifteen-plus years. Knowing that Mom was left behind and not knowing if she is dead or alive has taken its toll on my family. No one has been able to get back and rescue her. Before the magical powers stopped working, Isabella was going back and forth more than she should have—she loved it there. It was paradise. Plus, she got to help all the animals. And since all the animals could speak, she was thrilled. Not all could be understood, but many spoke fluent English. This was very enticing for my veterinarian sister."

"That would explain Tobi," Matt interjects.

"Yes, indeed. When I heard you describe a talking elephant, it got my attention. Isabella was like a hero to them. As one would say, she is the Good Witch of the South."

Matt asks quickly, "So Grull, Tragoon, and Troads are part of your past?"

"Yes, my friend, they are. But I didn't meet any of them on my past visits. Times must have changed because everyone and everything I've met were very courteous and friendly. This latest bunch not so much. But it has been fifteen years since my last visit. A lot can happen in that amount of time. It's a fragile world they live in with a king and a queen. They have an entirely different lifestyle than we do in our world." Tony saw no reason at this time to divulge the fact this is how he obtained most of his wealth, since the kingdom is full of diamonds and jewels.

"I have given you a shortened version, and I have reason to believe Dylan is in the kingdom. But since Alex said he's home, I'm a bit confused. Dad was fairly certain he figured out the correct ingredient needed and was all set to go get Mom. But somehow Dylan found out about the pillowcase and tried to go himself. Dad hasn't told me, but I'm also guessing he told Dylan about the magical pillowcase, and

Dylan took it upon himself to go instead. I don't know but I need to speak with Dylan as soon as he is awake. Alex is going to call me once he is up. That's why I'm heading to Key West, ASAP." Tony leaned back, lost in thought.

"Wow, so where is this magic blue pillowcase now?" Matt asks.

"Good question. Dad left it at home back in Key West. Not sure why, but I think he panicked, so it's another reason to get to Key West. The other piece of the puzzle is that strange fish we found. I think its neon strip can be extracted to a drinkable formula that will allow transportation to the kingdom. That may have been confirmed when I found Grull waiting for me. He must have figured it out as well or knew all along. Once Isabella extracts it to a drinkable formula, we were going to find Mom and bring her home. But now it's a mess. I have been trying to get answers from many people. That's why I travel around so much, but I usually get stares along with inadequate answers. Sorry I didn't fill you in sooner. Just thought you would think all this was insanity, and I would need some mental help from a highly paid professional."

"You know, Doc, I only have a billion questions. Do you think your mom's still alive?"

"Dad does, but I'm not so sure. Now that I've seen a few creatures, it may be getting a little messy over there, and since no one has been back in fifteen years, who knows. Isabella and Mom were the last to visit. Bella got out but Mom didn't. The whole situation has been driving Bella crazy so when this opportunity presented itself, I jumped on it."

"Do you have any idea where the kingdom is located? Mars, the Moon, or is it its own planet?"

"My best guess it's under our feet. In think it's down under and I don't mean Australia."

"Why don't we start digging?" Matt suggests, half joking.

"The Earth's core is approximately 3,959 miles from the surface. Where do we start, and how deep?"

"Okay, okay, I get it, Mr. Science. Never mind," Matt smiles. "Then how would you get back from this kingdom? Did you take this pillowcase with you?"

"Yes, if one was to lie down on the pillowcase, anyone touching, holding hands, a string, rope, or a belt, they would all be transported together. We always traveled with the pillowcase.

At first, we lost a few pets in the process. Sleeping on a lap or jumping on someone's chest could get them transported."

"Well, let's go get this blue pillowcase and take care of business," Matt grins.

"That's my plan. I need to talk with Alex and Dad."

"I'll ask Angelina to move in for a while. She can cook and clean for Dad."

"He'll like that. Maybe I can stay for a few days."

Not what I had in mind, good buddy." Tony glares at Matt.

"I'd like to visit my folks for a few days. I can meet you later in the week, if that's okay by you?" Matt asks.

"Sure. I'll drop you off on the way to Key West."

"I'll take a commercial flight to San Francisco and drive out to Antioch. You need to get to Key West sooner than later. What about Jake?"

"How about you take him to see your folks?"

"Oh great, how will I explain that one? Not that it would matter since Mom would love him."

Tony starts to think it's time he had chat with Dad, father and son. With the son doing the questioning.

"Morning Dad. How did you sleep?"

"Like a rock, Son. That's some comfortable bed. Just a bit comfier than my last bed. I could get used to staying in a place like this."

"Good thing, because you're going to have to stay here for a few days. At least until I get things under control in Florida."

"Well, it sure wouldn't be a bad thing," Vincenzo replies.

"Dad, I need you to go over again what happened back home. How is it that Dylan knew about the blue pillowcase? Be honest with me, Dad, I don't have time for the usual runaround."

"Well, Son, you know I love that boy, and I may have been talking about my adventures, and I may have mentioned something about the pillowcase. But I never asked him to take my place."

"You mean, bragging," Tony smiles.

"Son, I may have talked more than I should. But he's home safe and sound, so what's the problem?"

"No problem, Dad. Just wanted to hear it from you. And you left the pillowcase behind?"

"Yeah, that was a mistake but I didn't see it. So, who's going to get your mother?"

"I'm working on that. That's why I'm heading to Key West."

"You think she's okay, don't you, Son?"

"Yeah Dad, I think she's fine."

"You know I'll never rest in peace if anything has happened to my gal."

"I know, Dad. I'll get her back home, you'll see."

And soon Vincenzo is crying on Tony's shoulder.

"Hey Dad, to sweeten the offer for you to stay put, as if you have a choice, Angelina will stay and hang out with you for a few days. She is awesome, so be nice."

"I'm always nice, Son. I like the sounds of that." As he wipes his tears away.

"Great, she went shopping and should be back before noon, but Matt, Jake, and I have to take off soon. I left you my cell number. Call if anything happens or something unusual occurs. I don't want to alarm you but there may be people looking for you, so stay close to the house. Everything you need is here, so there is no need to go out. If you do need something, tell Angelina and she will get it. There are limits so don't ask for a new sports car or anything too extravagant."

"Darn, Son, you're no fun. Hey, with Dylan turning up, they should cancel the APB on me."

"It's not the law I'm worried about. Just do as I ask for once. I will call you with any updates. Just let me know if you see anything out of the ordinary, okay?"

"Okay, sure, whatever. Hey Son, why not keep Jake here with me? He could be my guardian."

"You know, Dad, that's a great idea." Jake walks into the room rubbing his eyes.

"Morning boss, I can sleep forever in that room. Very nice and soft."

"Good, because you're staying here. Matt and I have to leave."

"Oh no, boss, I go with you."

"Not this time. You have to watch over my dad while were gone. He's going to need someone with a lot of experience to watch over him. Be sure he's safe. Matt and I will be back in a few days, to get you both," Tony explains.

"I'm not sure, boss. How I know you come back?"

"What do think, I would leave behind my own father? This is an important job. He needs a guardian. Tell him, Matt."

"Oh yeah, boss needs your help to watch over Papa. Don't let anyone near him, especially a girl named Angelina."

"What Angel?"

"You forgot her already?"

"Oh, that Angelina, the girl that lives here, right boss?"

"Thanks Matt. Listen guys, she's a good friend of mine. She has agreed to help you guys out while I'm gone. I'll text her to let her know that Jake will be staying and he will also be her bodyguard."

"Oh, that sounds good. I stay watch over Angelina and Papa. Okay boss."

"Does this job pay any money?"

"Yeah, room, board, and food."

"Hey Son, call me as soon as you get some information about Mom?"

"Will do. We've got to go, be careful." Tony hugs his dad. "Now Jake, you make sure everyone is safe. I'll be back as soon as possible."

Matt and Jake shake hands, and Matt grabs Vincenzo in a bear hug.

While driving to the airport, Matt says to Tony, "You think they'll be okay back there?"

"Sure, I wouldn't have left them if I thought they were in any danger. I actually feel like they're much safer staying there than being with either of us. I've asked Torch to fly with me. I'm going to need an experienced pilot since I'm dropping you off."

"Are you trying to make me feel bad? I promised Mom, and I don't want to disappoint her, but Torch? Ha. I could visit my folks later. I don't trust him, Tony."

"He's over that, besides, do you know a better pilot?"

"You've got a good point—he is an excellent pilot but I still don't trust him.

"What's your plan?"

"I'm going to drop you off. Head to Key West. Pick up Alessandra and Dylan and off to Boston to pick up Isabella and Chloe then head back home to the Keys."

"What about the crate and the pillowcase?" Matt asks.

"I'm picking up both the pillowcase and the crate."

"Is it wise for your entire family to be on one airplane?" Matt asks.

"I may rethink that part of my plan."

"Remember, if Tragoon finds you, then you and everyone else are goners."

"That's a great point. I will see how it goes. I think you and your family should be fine."

"If I get far away from you and your family, I should be fine," Matt starts laughing.

"Do you think Isabella is going to let you go get your mom all by yourself?"

"No, I've been thinking about that. That's where you come in."

"Slow down, buddy. What am I supposed to say to her? She can kick my butt up and down the street," Matt admits.

"I'll have plenty of time to think of something. But I can't lose anyone else. I'm expendable—she has young kids and a thriving business. I may need you come back, just in case we have visitors."

"If you do get back to this kingdom, how long do you anticipate it will take you to find your Mom?"

"Good question. My plan is three days. I hope to be making contact with some old friends. One thing is for sure, everybody knows everybody's business. It's hard to keep secrets around there. So many eyes and ears and since everything can speak, word travels fast. Someone will know where Elizabeth is," Tony sighs.

Tony reminds Matt, "It's best if you keep this to yourself."

"No worries, not sure I believe it myself. Don't need to visit the looney bin this early in my life. Who's going to believe me anyway? It will be our little secret."

When they get to the airport, Tony heads for his plane and Matt heads for his. Nothing else needed to be said.

"Hey Torch, let's get this thing in the air. I need to be in Key West yesterday.

"Will do, Doc."

Chapter 20

CAPTAIN

Captain Bill Rogers is about to step into the elevator as his cell phone rings. He looks and see it's Maggie calling.

"Hey Maggie, what's up?"

"Hey Captain, where are you?"

"None of your business, what's up?"

"Are you visiting that sweet girl?"

"Maggie, what is it?"

"Okay, okay, good news. Dylan Cabrella is fine and sleeping at home."

"Are you sure?"

"Sure am."

"Did you see him yourself?"

"Well no, I didn't, but Alessandra Cabrella called and said he was at home sleeping in his bed."

"Maggie, you've got to confirm that info. Get someone over to the house this morning and confirm that he is home. I am not telling Ms. Cabrella anything until you have seen him with your own eyes."

"Why would his own family lie about a thing like that?"

"Maggie, send a squad car over there ASAP. I'm go..g into an el.. ator a.. w.ll pro...ly loos. ..u."

"Captain, captain, oh well. I understand your in an elevator. I'll send someone." Maggie ends the call and says to herself, "Don't get your pantics out of sorts. You think he'd be happy that all is well with that family. They have the worst of luck." She forgot to tell him she canceled that APB on Vincenzo Cabrella. But why should he mind? They found their grandson, and it's all one big happy family. Whatever happened to their Grandmother Elizabeth? Maggie wonders.

Maggie calls Jacob (Car 73), an officer in the Key West Police Department.

"Car 73, what is your location? Come in, Jacob. The captain needs a favor, come in."

"Yes, Maggie, what is it?"

"You need to go by the Cabrella's and check in on them."

"Check in on them. What for?" Jacob asks.

"Just see if everything is okay."

"Why, what happened now?"

"Nothing, the captain wants you go by to make sure everyone is safe and secure, specially Dylan."

"Isn't the captain out of town?"

"Yep, he's up in Boston visiting Ms. Cabrella."

"I'm not going to do his little personal love duties just because he's having a fight with his little girlfriend."

Maggie laughs. "You'd better watch it—he likes that nice woman."

"Well, what am I supposed to do? Knock on the door and tell the kids, 'I just wanted to let you know that while my captain is sleeping with your mom, I want to make sure everything is okay here.' Is that what you want?"

Maggie, rolling over with laughter, says, "You'd better hope no one else is on this frequency or the captain will have your head. Be a little more supportive, the family was just robbed. Do a little detective work for once?"

"I've got more important things to tend to, but I'll drive by and see if anything looks unusual."

"Okay, sounds good—over and out," Maggie announces.

Jacob goes back to his fishing pole and shakes his head. He's not a babysitter. And that girl Alessandra is a menace to society. He has a scar from when she kicked him in the head. If the captain wants to date that woman that's his problem, crazy man.

**

Sam and Tami awaken at Alex's house.

Sam yawns, "Morning Alex, how's Teri doing?"

"I think she's going to be okay, but I wish Mom were here. Gloria called Dr. Donald, who is an expert vet for these types of wounds. He arrived a few hours ago and I think she's stabilized. But Hari doesn't look so good—he looks very depressed. Didn't know dogs could be so unhappy and sad."

Hari is at the front door, growling before the doorbell rings.

Alex yells, "I'll get it."

"Well hello, Jacob. What brings you over by our neck of the woods?"

"I don't want any trouble. I'm here on official business. Is Dylan home?"

Alex looks at Jacob and says, "Yes, he's sleeping."

"Can you wake him up so I can see for myself?"

"Do I need to kick you in the head again. What kind of question is that, Barney Fife?"

"I'm just doing my job. Anyone else here to confirm that he is here?"

"Sure, detective." Alex screams, "Sam and Tami, need you at the front door."

"How have you been, Officer Jacob? You married yet?" Alex asks.

"Listen, I'm sorry about our—." He abruptly stops as Sam and Tami come into the front foyer.

"Hey J," Tami says.

"Hey. I just need to confirm that Dylan is home."

"Are you investigating the kidnapping case?" Tami asks.

"I can't tell you. It's official business. Well, have you seen Dylan?"

"I sure did, why do you ask?"

"Ditto," Sam says."

"How did he look?"

"Pretty darn good," Sam blushes.

"Okay thanks, that's all I need for now."

"Bye ladies," Jacob says as he's walking back to his patrol car.

Alex yells out, "Drop by anytime." They all start to giggle.

"Maggie, this is Car 73 reporting."

"Yes, Jacob what's going on?"

"I just left the Cabrella residence, and all is well. Dylan is alive and well."

"That's just dandy. I'm sure the captain will be happy to hear the good news. How did he look?"

With a slight delay, Jacob replies, "He looked darn good."

**

"My Girl," starts playing on Isabella's phone. Chloe answers, recognizing the ringtone for Alex.

"Hey Chloe, how's Mom doing?"

"Okay, I guess. She seems more alert this morning. She had a visitor this morning and that seemed to have lifted her spirits."

"What visitor."

"Oh, it was Captain Rogers from back home. You know they date off and on, mainly on."

"Yeah, I met him—he's a handsome one."

"He wanted me to leave the room, but I wasn't leaving Mom's side. He told her that Dylan was home. That sure did bring a smile to her face. He brought up Grandpa, and she got angry with him. Her blood pressure went up so high the nurses almost kicked him out, so he stopped talking about him. She asked the captain to do her a favor. That's when she made me leave the room. I'm not sure what she asked him, but he left in a hurry."

"What favor did she want?"

"I don't know. She wouldn't tell me."

"Damn."

"I'm telling Mom you cursed."

"Okay, calm down. Try to get Mom to tell you what she asked him?"

"I'll try, but she's changed a little since she's been here. She talks in her sleep and looks at me as if she doesn't know me. Keeps mumbling about stuff. I'm a little scared," Chloe admits nervously.

"Oh, poor thing. I'm sorry, I sometimes forget how young you really are but you're doing a great job, and Mom is lucky to have you near her side. I am sure you being there is helping her recover."

"I'm not sure if I can do this alone." Chloe is now openly crying into the phone.

"Okay, sweetie. Listen, Uncle Tony is flying in today. Tony, Dylan, and I will fly up to Boston and bring you guy's home. Didn't you say the doctor said she's almost back to normal?"

"Okay," she sniffles into the phone. "Her memory is almost completely returned. The doctor said she did extremely well in her test this morning and she's getting better every day, so she might be released soon, possibly tomorrow. I can't wait for her to be out of here and back home."

"Listen, sweetie. I will be in touch. Call me anytime and I will let you know when Uncle Tony gets here. Tell Mom he's coming—that will brighten her day. Okay, sweetie, you hang in there. You're the best sister anyone could ask for," Alex reminds Chloe.

As soon as Alex hangs up, she wants to book a flight to Boston ASAP.

"Shouldn't you wait until your uncle gets here? And he has his own plane," Sam remarks.

"You're right, but I'm telling him we're going to Boston and getting Mom back home. Hey guys, I didn't sleep much last night. Do you guys mind going home and I'll call you after my nap? Dylan's still sleeping, and I bet he sleeps 'til three or even later. I need some more rest myself."

"Okay, but call us if you need anything."

**

Captain Bill Rogers arrives at the Boston Scientific Lab front desk. Isabella has sent him to pick up the crate. He can't figure out why the crate wasn't sent to Key West in the first place. He's beginning to wonder about the decision-making process in her family.

"Good afternoon, I'm Captain Bill Rogers, and I was instructed to meet Dr. Granger."

The front desk manager is gleaming at the sight of the tall and handsome Captain Rogers with a huge smile.

"Have a seat and I will ring her, Captain."

After calling Dr. Ashley Granger, Kelly rings her friend in the office. Whispering into the phone, Kelly tells her coworker that she may want to come by her desk, and hurry.

"Hello Captain Rogers, I'm Doctor Granger. I was expecting Dr. Cabrella, but I've heard she's been delayed. Follow me."

"You just missed him," Kelly informed her coworker.

"No, I didn't, Dr. Granger just yelled at me for almost knocking over the poor man as I ran into him in the hallway. I almost knocked them both over." They mutually started giggling.

"I wish you had called me before making the trip, but the crate is still in customs. I didn't tell Dr. Cabrella because I selfishly wanted her here for another reason, and she never would have agreed to come otherwise," Dr. Granger explains.

"Are you telling me the package that she urgently needs is not here?" a dejected Captain Rogers asks.

"Yes, that's what I'm telling you."

"Then, may I ask where it is?"

"We tracked it down and it's stuck in customs."

"Great, I'll go down and get it out."

"Well, it's not that easy."

"Why not?" the captain starts getting a little perturbed.

"Well, it's in the port of Gloucester customs," Dr. Granger sheepishly replies.

"Okay, thanks. Is it possible for you to give me the exact location of this shipment so I can be on my way?"

"Sure, sorry, I know you're a little upset. Tell Dr. Cabrella hello for me."

"I will. Could you just get me the info, please?" the captain asks as he makes a call.

"Hey Maggie, did someone go by the house and confirm what I already told Ms. Cabrella?"

"Yep."

"Dammit, Maggie, I'm not really happy right now. Did you, or didn't you?"

"Jacob went by and said all is well. Dylan is snug as a bug."

"So he saw him?"

"Yes sir, everything is fine."

**

A call came in as Chloe was picking up the phone.

"Mom, it's Uncle Tony," Chloe says as she hands the phone to Isabella and heads for the bathroom.

"Hey bro, how you doing? I know Dylan is at home with Alex. And I asked Captain Rogers to pick up the crate for us."

"That's probably a good idea. Everyone is looking for that crate. I didn't want to alarm you. You're just now recovering from head trauma."

"Tony, who's everyone? Tell me what's going on," Isabella practically screams into the phone.

"Let's just say I've confirmed that what's in the crate could be the secret formula we're looking for. I had some visitors from the kingdom while searching for our neon fish."

"And these visitors were not friendly?"

"Not in the least," Tony replies.

Isabella asks, "Did you ask Dad why he bolted in the middle of the night?"

"Yes, he panicked when he found Dylan missing."

"So, what's so unusual about that? I never know where Dylan is half the time. He's always on the move. Didn't he think he could have gone home?"

"It seems Dad's been telling Dylan about his kingdom adventures, and he was concerned."

"Why is Dad talking to Dylan about the kingdom? And concerned about what?" Isabella asks eagerly.

"Dad said he's fairly certain the blue pillowcase is back in working order and it was missing, so he thought Dylan and the pillowcase— Bell, you there? Isabella?? Bell you there?"

Dylan is the last thing she remembers.

"Oh, my!" Chloe exclaims as she grabs the phone.

"Hello, Uncle Tony. What did you tell Mom? She just passed out again."

"Oh nothing sugar. She's just upset about the robbery. Everything is fine. Make sure no one bothers her and she gets lots of rest."

"Don't worry, I'm on it. Plus, Captain Rogers is also in town watching over Mom."

"That's great. Between the two of you she'll be well in no time. I'm glad he's there watching over my two favorite girls. Chloe, your mom wanted you to try and get in touch with Alex."

"I just spoke with her. She went down for a nap."

"Great news. I'll call you with an update once I get to Key West."

"Okay, Uncle Tony. See you soon. Love you."

"Me too, sugar. Love you."

Captain Rogers's "Batman" ringtone starts ringing, and Chloe answers.

"Hello Chloe, how's your mom doing?" Captain Rogers asks.

"Well, she was doing great until a few minutes ago."

"What happened?"

"I'm not a hundred percent sure but she was talking to Uncle Tony and all of a sudden, she passed out again. The doctor is examining her now."

"Did she hit her head?"

"Nope, she just collapsed back into the bed right after Uncle Tony called."

"Did she say anything?"

"I only heard her say something about Dylan and boom, she hit the bed. You know Tony's coming up here to take us home in his private plane. I've never been in it but Mom says it's awesome, like riding on a cloud. If you need a ride, I bet he wouldn't mind taking you with us."

"Might take you up on that, but I have something to do for your mother first. It sounds like it's the only way to travel. I'll be back at the hospital later this evening."

"Oh, can I help you? You know I am very advanced for my age. Mother says I'll be a vet in no time."

"I know Chloe, you're doing great job, but it's a quick trip and I'll be back soon. Could you give me your Uncle Tony's phone number?"

"Sure, you can ask him for a ride. It will be fun."

Captain Rogers departs while dialing his phone. Captain is not too sure about Tony's stability. He's always off on some safari or Egyptian artifact hunt, like a freewheeling bird, half nut case. He sure doesn't stay in one place long, and the captain usually worries about those folks who can't stay still. Probably not a fisherman, either. Now where is that customs office?

"Hello, Tony here."

"Oh yes, hi. I'm Bill Rogers a friend of your sister's and—"

"Sure, Captain, what can I do for you? I am so pleased you're up in Boston with my two favorite girls. It makes me feel much more at ease."

"Well, I'm not exactly in Boston right now. I'm heading for Gloucester. It's something Isabella asked me to do. I'm going to pick up your crate for her, for you."

Tony was a bit confused as to why it was in Gloucester, but kept it to himself.

"If I may ask, what's in the crate?" the captain asks.

"It's a tropical endangered fish."

"A what?"

"A fish. You do know what a fish is, don't you, Bill?"

"I don't need a smart ass right now. I'm flying all over the place for a damn fish. Can't you come up with a better story than that?"

"Sure, but then I would be lying."

"Okay, well, I just flew from Key West to Boston to pick up a fish. You do know we have little fishes in Florida. I could have saved you the one I caught last week. Cutest little bugger."

"Right, take my word for it—this is a very rare and special species."

"Hey Bill, can you hold on a minute? I have to take this call. Better yet, I'll call you back."

Chapter 21

#126

Gaylok begins to explain to Tabitha that the elders have decided to take Dylan to the Trefars. It may be dangerous journey.

"Tabitha, I entrust you to take Dylan the Swimmer to the Trefars. Many are searching for him and the journey may be perilous in these times. There is already a lot of activity in the area that may be caused by his appearance. As usual our biggest threat is from the king. The elders have come to the conclusion Dylan is not the prince, but their similarities are startling. The Trefars will transform him. I do not want to tell you anymore just in case you're captured and possibly tortured."

Gaylok continues as Tabitha listens intently. "It is imperative that you get Dylan the Swimmer to the Trefars unharmed and with extreme secrecy. I think it's best if you travel with a small group to avoid suspicion. Take Pup, and choose any two of our best warriors and leave at once. Do not delay. Stay away from the subway. Avoid any confrontation with others. Keep him well hidden. Once you're inside the Trefars compound you will be safe, and T will take over from there. When you are ready you should return home. I would have preferred others to take this mission, but I know you would disapprove. You know I love you very much, as if you were my own daughter. Be safe. It is very dangerous these days. Make sure T sees these pictures."

Tabitha says, "Don't worry yourself, Gaylok. I will not fail you." Tabitha hugs Gaylok tightly.

Gaylok assumes the Trefars will transform Dylan the Swimmer into the current prince. They'll dye and cut his hair, plus place any markings on his body as needed, then teach him the correct body language and speech, to turn him into a mirror image of the prince. Gaylok is still confused as to why Dylan is carrying pictures of Socreen and Princess Xandra.

On the way to the Trefars, Tabitha makes a fatal mistake of allowing Dylan into one of the kingdom's grocery store.

"Tabitha, I am so thirsty."

"We all are. Quit complaining, Dylan the Swimmer."

"Can we stop for a Coke?" I ask.

"A what?"

"A Pepsi then?"

"What are you talking about?"

"I'm thirsty. Don't you have any grocery stores?"

"Yes, we have stores, but you're not coming in with me," Tabitha sternly replies.

"Why not? I never been inside your stores. I'll just take a Gatorade."

"I have no idea what you are talking about," Tabitha sighs.

"Okay, then take me inside with you."

"That would be a mistake."

"How about a Red Bull?"

"You want a red bull. Why?"

"They're delicious and I need energy."

"A red bull gives you energy? Have you seen a red bull?"

"Yes indeed. I drink them often."

"You're tiring me out." Tabitha asks, "Pup, what do you think?"

"He seems very eager about the whole experience, why not. It may silence him for a minute. I could use the peace and quiet," Pup answers.

"You need to wait outside," Tabitha tells me.

"No way, I want to see what a grocery store looks like. Please," I plead.

"This is a bad idea, but I don't want to hear you whining any more. You've been whining ever since we left. If this will keep you quiet, I'll do anything. I've never heard someone complain so much at one time. Just do as you're told. Keep your hood up and eyes down. I think it's best if you're not seen by anyone. Don't touch anything, and stay close. Do not talk to anyone and keep your mouth shut. Got it, Dylan the Swimmer?"

"Okay, okay, no problem."

"I see 126. What does 126 mean?"

"That's not being quiet. It's store number 126," Tabitha replies. "Now keep quiet."

Only Tabitha and I go in while Pup and the others stay outside. The place is so bright I can hardly see. It's as if they want you out of there as soon as possible. We walk in and I see two armed guards with giant swords, each looked about eight feet tall. I later learned they are the palace guards and they watch over all the stores. One looks our way and I forget and stare. Tabitha kicks me in the leg and says look down. The guard didn't respond but keeps watching us just to be sure. You would have to be out of your mind to rob this place. Tabitha fills the basket with bread, veggies, fruits, nuts, and some other crap I didn't recognize. Actually, most of the stuff I didn't recognize.

"Where is the cereal aisle?" I ask Tabitha.

"Shut up, don't know what you talking about."

"You know Captain Crunch. Frosted Flakes."

"Oh my, this was a mistake. Keep quiet, I'm almost done. Then I'm going to frost your flakes."

"Fine," I mumble.

It was so bright I had to keep my eyes down, and as I was walking with my head down, I bumped into another patron. Big mistake. Whatever it was that I bumped into wasn't happy. It wasn't human and it started screaming at me, which now got the guard's attention.

"Watch it, stickman," I hear someone say.

I say "sorry" and keep walking. Well, that wasn't enough to calm it down.

This thing was still upset. "What is your problem?" it says.

"I'm sorry," I replied again.

"You should be sorry, stickman. Let me see you. Take that hood off. What are you doing in here anyway? Can't you see I am shopping and don't want to be disturbed?"

Oh no, Tabitha sees that I bumped into a Graeter and now she is trying to calm it down, but with no luck. Graeters are rarely happy to begin with plus very aggressive, dangerous, and just downright mean and ugly. Tabitha is looking at me as if to say "do not take that hood off and get out of here ASAP." I head for the exit, but the guard stops me.

"What's going on back there?" the guard asks me.

"I accidently ran into someone but I apologized."

"It doesn't sound like he accepted your apology—he still sounds upset. Maybe you should pay for all his gum?"

"Yes, of course. I will pay for all his gum."

"Good, go to the scanner and pay. Quit arguing with me."

Tabitha runs to the front with her arm out almost screaming, "I'll pay for it."

"No, he should pay," the guard points to me.

"No, no, it's my treat. I started it," Tabitha insists.

Now the Graeter hearing this is getting more and more upset.

"She shouldn't pay, he should." It grabs me by my arm and holds me up. Graeters are very strong. I am now dangling in the air. The Graeter is still making a crazy racket as only a Graeter can.

Tabitha looks around the corner and sees the other Graeter taking full advantage of the situation, cramming packs of gum in her mouth. Graeters love gum—they chew it all day long. It's the only thing they eat, breakfast, lunch, and dinner. It keeps them calm, so everyone gives gum to a Graeter if there's trouble. It usually works, but you never know. Graeters usually travel in pairs. And this store must have a lot of Graeters since two rows were designated just for gum. Some of the gum comes in rows of sixty-inch lengths with all different flavors. At the end of the row was a UPC checkout, so you could eat it in the store. But when this Graeter finally used up all her money, she suddenly turned angry. So now we have two upset Graeters in one store. Not a good picture. Graeters have a UPC code on their hand.

Tabitha pulled something what looked like a fire alarm, but it is really a sprinkler system, and nothing happens. As it turns out, it's not for fires but for Graeters. Graeters are afraid of water and when it rains, they are nowhere to be found. Since it hasn't rained in over five hundred days, most of the sprinkler systems were completely dry. The male Graeter sees his mate getting angry and drops me like a rock. This time he starts to run towards Tabitha.

Tabitha yells, "Pull out your water gun, and squirt her with it."

As I fall to the ground, I accidently step on someone's tail. "Excuse me, sir."

"She's a female, not a male. Hurry before she eats you." Tabitha screams. "Pull out your water gun and squirt her. Now!"

I start fumbling with my backpack, grab the water pistol, and start squirting the female Graeter. This stops her in her tracks and she runs to her mate. The male Graeter now turns and heads back for me.

He grabs me before I can squirt him. I drop the water pistol and my hoodie comes off my head. One of the guards is watching all this and see's my face.

"Unhand him now," he tells the Graeter.

Graeters are crazy, but not crazy enough to start a fight with the king's guards. He drops me on the floor and walks out the front door with his crying mate following close behind.

"Sorry, your highness. I did not recognize you. What are you doing here?"

Before I could respond, Pup opens the front door and yanks me out so fast I couldn't answer.

Tabitha finishes paying for all the food and gum the Graeters ate. "Again, I am very sorry."

The guard is watching her very carefully and asks, "Was that who I think it is?"

Tabitha starts to laugh and says, "We make fun of him all the time about that. Of course not." She runs out the door.

The one guard that saw the whole event says to the other. "Hey, I'm off in fifteen minutes and haven't been home in weeks, so I'm not about to write up a report. That will take another day. What about you?"

"I'm with you. Why would you write up a report? Those Graeters are troublemakers. Did you even get their names?"

"No, I didn't. Did you see that guy's face? He looked just like the prince."

"Then in that case I would not write up any report. Anyway, what would he be doing out here all by himself with that young girl and no other guardians?"

"You're right. Help me pick up this mess and let's act as if nothing happened. I'm not sure how to write up a report anyway. But he sure did look like the prince," the guard mumbles to himself.

Now I realize why so much gum and water pistols were packed in Grandpa's backpack. I later find out this meant Tabitha may not have food for herself later in the week. She spent all of her weekly rations because of me. You can only purchase food once a week, which is calculated by each one's UPC code. That's why everyone has a code tattooed on their arm at birth.

When we depart, I see a blinking big "G" in red with a line going through it. Someone forgot to turn on the sign. The sign is faulty. In every store there is a sign. It's a bright neon red glowing G, and when a Graeter is inside, the G has a line through it, which means a Graeter is inside—beware. Most people refrain from shopping until they leave, but the light wasn't on when we arrived. Otherwise Tabitha said we would never have gone inside.

"Well, that was fun," I say kiddingly.

"Are you a complete moron? You know you just proved you're not royalty by any means. You're a whole new kind of stupid. Pick a fight with a Graeter, are you insane? You do know that food was supposed to last me, or us, a few days. Thanks, Dy-land the Swimmer. Or is it Dy-land the Dimwitted. You were lucky they were young guards and weren't sure who you were. If they stopped and questioned you, that was it, we were all dead. How am I going to explain why I am with you? I was crazy to let you inside," Tabitha moans. "Why does Gaylok think you will mature? And I left without filling my water pouch."

I begin to think it's safer outside than inside, even with all these strange-looking creatures. "I am sorry about all that trouble, I caused."

Tabitha is still upset. "Are you nuts? If those guards weren't getting off soon, we'd be off to the palace in chains."

"Great, I want to go to the palace anyway."

"Not in chains you don't. The penalty for disturbing a palace store is either death or hard labor for a minimum of two hundred days."

"Wow, that sounds pretty severe."

"That's why nobody fights in the stores. Or steals. Or makes any disturbance of any kind. I cannot tell you again how fortunate we are, so let's get going and get as far away, as fast as we can."

"Okay, but you know I want to go to the palace."

"You are so not ready for the palace—you have no idea," Tabitha shakes her head.

"I said I was sorry."

"I heard you. Let's get going so we can camp for the evening. I've had enough for one day."

"I'll fly ahead to make sure our path is safe," Pup announces.

"Thanks Pup. I'm real close to jumping on and flying away from this moron."

"It will be fine. He just proved to us he's definitely not the prince."

"That's for sure, possibly a Prince of Fools."

Pup takes off, and I later learned a few tidbits about Graeters. Graeters only travel in pairs, male and female—very rarely will you see a Graeter alone. They are considered loners because you never see more than two together and they don't like to get wet. They love this weather since it hasn't rained in over five hundred days. Most of them have a huge mouth and big feet. They cannot run very fast with such large feet, but they can dig for miles. Their nickname is "Excavators." Their only source of food is gum. They eat nothing else unless mad, then they will try to eat you. No bladder or bowel functions. The only way they dispose of their gum or anything else is by puking. It's disgusting. They have their own *puke-atoriam.*

Graeters cannot reproduce. They have no sexual organs. The only way to distinguish a male from a female is the female has a tail. If you lined up ten male Graeters, you could not tell them apart. Graeters are not hatched from eggs nor born from a womb but from a tree—one-of-a-kind tree called a *graper gum tree.* Kind of crazy, but when a leaf falls from the tree and it hits the ground within the canopy of the tree, a baby Graeter is made. If a leaf falls and is blown out of the canopy, it is just a normal leaf and doesn't form into a Graeter.

There is only one tree, and it is under the watch and control of the king. That's why every Graeter works for the king. They can dig quicker and better than any bulldozer. Legend has it that the Graeters had almost gone extinct. When a leaf would fall and turn into a baby Graeter, other Graeters would eat them. They basically ate their own species into extinction. They are not nurturing or loving since no one takes the time to nurture. They chew and eat more gum in a week than most people do in a lifetime.

Story is told, that one day a Trefars was riding past the "tree of life." That's what they now call, the *graper gum tree,* the "tree of life." This Trefars picked up a baby Graeter and brought it back to the village. He nurtured and raised the Graeter as if it was one of his own. The other thing is Graeters are extremely loyal. If you can gain their trust, they will die for you. The Trefars that nurtured and raised his own Graeter was supposedly the great T. A distinct rumor is that T's Graeter has been imbedded into the palace workforce since the king would have no idea who the spy could possibly be.

Pup reappears and says, "I found a good spot for us to camp."

We finally stop for the evening to make camp. The noises I heard were quite unique. I had no idea who or what was making all the noise. The stars were out bright and blinking. Odd, it seemed like the stars were so close I could touch them.

I need to make it up to Tabitha. I can't have her thinking I'm a moron of some sort. I'm beginning to think she is the prettiest girl in the world. How soon I forgot about Violet, I must not be human.

"He is young, very naive and after you explained what transpired today inside the store, I am beginning to believe our new friend Dylan is from the concrete country," Pup whispers as he and Tabitha glance at Dylan nearby.

"I think you are correct. Nobody from here would act like that."

"Just give him some time. I feel his heart is in the right place."

"Yeah, it replaced his brain," Tabitha shakes her head.

"You need to calm down," Pup sighs and looks again in Dylan's direction.

"You are right. I'll never make it to the Trefars. Sorry, Pup, I am just so upset."

"Why don't you go talk with him?"

"You are so wise for someone so young."

Tabitha walks over to where I was settling down for the evening.

"May I join you?" Tabitha asks.

"Of course, please do. Again, I am so sorry. It will never happen again, I promise."

"Okay, I accept your apology."

"Thank you," I smiled a little.

I don't want her to think I'm even more of a moron, but I have to ask.

"Why are all those stars blinking and moving so often?"

"We have no stars. Those are giant fireflies."

"Wow, that is magnificent."

"Yes, it is exquisite."

"What are all those sounds?"

"Which ones?"

"Are you kidding me? I—"

Then a loud horn sounds and I jump forty feet in the air. "Holy smokes, what was that?"

"Shift change. It sounds twice a day for shift changes at the palace."

"Why didn't I hear it before this?"

"Gaylok had all the sound systems in Rockland destroyed. I am beginning to believe you when you say you're not from here."

"Is it that obvious?"

"Yes. Tell me about your world," Tabitha asks curiously

I wasn't sure at first what to tell her about "my world" as she calls it. But I figured it didn't matter since it's obvious I'm not from here. "What would you like to know?"

"What do you do every day? Explain to me what an average day is like for Dylan the Swimmer?"

"Well, let me see." I start to think maybe I should embellish some things so she will think I'm real important. "I get up and then go to school."

"School, what trade are you studying?"

This one threw me for a loop. I panicked and said, "Veterinarian."

"Wow, good for you. That's a great and noble profession. We need more animal doctors here. When we get back to my village, would you possibly take a look at some of my friends, they could use your expertise?"

"Oh, sure, be my pleasure." What a dummy. Why did I tell her I'm a veterinarian?

"Should I call you doctor?"

"Oh, no, no, no. I haven't graduated yet. Still learning, lots and lots every day. Just Dylan will be fine. I have much to learn."

"Okay, but you may prefer doctor, since it sounds like you will be one day soon. Maybe you can look at Pup's front leg, it's sore."

I need to change the subject, I'm drowning here. "What is it you do all day? Enough about me," I finally blurt out.

"My parents worked for the palace and each were excellent farmers. I have a small plot of land that I still work and grow some vegetables. In the morning I tend to my garden, and by afternoon I practice with the sword and hone my warrior skills," Tabitha explains.

"Could you train me how to be a great swordsman?"

"I am taking you to the greatest warriors in the kingdom, the Trefars. They are far superior than I, ask them to train you."

"Okay, cool. I don't know what a Trefars is."

"I'll try to explain. Trefars have their own village, where all of them live. They're self-sufficient in providing their own food and labor. In battle the speed and agility of a Trefars is unsurpassed. It's also hard to persuade a Trefars once their mind is made up."

"So, they're a stubborn bunch of folks?"

"That's one way to put it. It's better if you make your own decision."

"I will let you know after I meet with them."

"I doubt our paths will ever cross again," Tabitha replies, suddenly serious.

I didn't like the sound of that. "What do you mean, that our paths will never cross again? Where are you going? I like you." Oops, I shouldn't have said that out loud.

"You will eventually go to the palace, and I try to avoid that place."

"Why not come with me?"

"That's not up to me."

"I will tell them they will have to let you come with me."

Tabitha falls over in laughter. "I don't think you'll be telling the Trefars anything. It's you that will be doing the listening. Now get some sleep. We have a long journey ahead of us."

"Aren't we going to stop at a hotel or something? I would love a Big Mac right about now."

"It's going to be something, alright. Your tent is all set up. Good night, Dylan the Swimmer or should I say doctor. Maybe we can find you a big mac tomorrow?"

"Good night. Are we safe out here?"

"Pup is on watch, good night."

I close one of my eyes. It's going to be hard to sleep with one eye open. Sleeping outside was not something I usually did back home. I begin to think as I drift off that it can't be safe out here. What are those noises, and where are they coming from?

Chapter 22

PRINCE

Prince Mako wakes up to an empty house in Key West, Florida. He thinks it's all been a dream and he's back in the palace. He starts calling out for his valet, Jelab.

"Jelab, Jelab, bring me my robe and some food." Then the prince starts yelling, "Is anyone here? Hello!" Maybe it's not a dream.

This room was definitely not the prince's chamber. There are pictures of scantily clad women plastered all over the walls. The prince no doubt would like to meet a few of those girls, but for now he has work to do. That is only a distraction. He does wonder if the person living here knows these girls. What he doesn't realize is he is in Dylan's bedroom in Key West.

The prince tries to recall the current events that caused all this confusion. He was getting ready to be transported to the coordinates in San Francisco. What happened was, he transported to someone's house and got clobbered over the head. Then he was tied up and drugged. Someone takes him from that dwelling to another dwelling. He was kept drugged and tied up until his supposed sister, which is odd since he's the only child, rescues him from that dwelling and places him in this dwelling. What is the meaning of all this?

He has no idea what's going on and is pretty sure these people are all crazy. He certainly doubts he transported to the correct coordinates. He has a rare headache and is hungry, but he is no longer tied up. And he's not sure why people are referring to him as Dylan. That's probably why he was tied up—wrong identity. Where is everybody? Wait until the king hears about this blunder. What happened back at the palace? Do the king and queen know where he is? The prince starts wandering around his current location to try and figure out where he is.

He sees this huge dog with a name tag. "Hey Hari, where am I?" the prince asks. Hari just looks at him with no response. Then he recalled Socreen had told him the animals in this land cannot speak. Too bad he would probably be able to tell him a lot.

"Good boy," as he pets Hari.

He walks around the empty dwelling and starts opening cabinets, drawers, and then suddenly he stops and stares at all the photos on the wall. One photo is of a young girl, older girl, boy, and an older woman. The boy looks exactly like the prince but with dark black hair. There are photos everywhere and one in particular got his attention. The lady in the picture looks like a younger Socreen. He's confused as to what this is all about and wonders why they have pictures of Socreen and him as a youngster, or at least someone that looks like him. Who are these people? He needs answers. The king never mentioned this would be part of his travels.

The next item that needed to be addressed was the prince's hunger level. There must be food in this place somewhere. He locates an ice box/refrigerator, and finds something to eat. In the kingdom, the prince and most every inhabitant only eats plants and vegetables. There is no meat to be consumed except by a dragon, and they eat anything they want.

The container he chooses to eat says "meatballs." It tasted unique and didn't sit well. He starts vomiting and wonders if it is the same ingredient in something called a burger. If so, that would explain why he was so sick after eating something from Burger King, his captors would feed him. His father would like to know there are kings other than him. He finds an address and maps then soon figures out he is in a place called Florida, not California. Now, how far is California from Florida?

Well, isn't this a dilemma. How in the world is the prince going to get to California from Florida? It is too far to swim or run. He needed some type of transportation. He has no money, which his father explained was needed in this land or as the king calls "the concrete country" and its habitants "concrete dwellers."

Socreen is from this country, and he is trying to recall all of her experiences. Travel by plane, car, or train. Subways do not run the length of the land like it does in his kingdom. Socreen said a plane was the quickest transportation for long distances, but he is in need of money. He wasn't planning on this turn of events.

Maybe there is some money hidden in this dwelling. He starts to rummage through all the rooms looking for money and throwing stuff everywhere. Now it looks as if the place has been robbed, but he finally finds a large amount of cash in the back shelf of someone's room.

He sees another picture of some woman kissing Socreen on the cheek, a ton of animal pictures with the same woman, and more pictures of his look-alike. He should get out of here before someone finds him rummaging through the dwelling. Where is that young lady that saved him? Whoever lives here does have a nice dwelling with an excellent view. Nothing like the palace, but it overlooks a large amount of water and exploding sunshine in the bright blue sky above.

Suddenly he hears a noise coming from within the house and wonders what that annoying noise is. *Bringgg, bringgg, bringgg, bringgg.* Sounds like an alarm. Where is it coming from? He finally locates the source, the telephone, and he just stares at it as it continues to make this horrible noise. Finally, the noise stops, but now he hears a voice talking yet sees no one—only some type of talking machine.

"Alex, Dylan, pick up the phone, it's Uncle Tony. Hello, anyone home? I'm heading your way. I'll come by the house and pick you guys up. Call me as soon as possible. You have my cell number."

Someone named Uncle Tony is heading toward the house. It took the prince a few minutes, but he finally figured out how to turn on the water and take a bath. Primitive people, where are the large bathing tubs? He sure does miss his Jelab.

He needs to change clothes since his original garments are full of blood from that dog, Teri. He is not accustomed to picking out his own outfits, so this may be fun for him. Jelab would be proud.

He sees no smocks or dressing garments but does find a pair of Levi Strauss and some shorts. Since the prince has never worn a pair of shorts, he chooses those. It's a perfect fit. He looks into a mirror and sees his reflection wearing khaki shorts and a blue button-down dress shirt. He is pleased but feels naked. Shorts are nonexistent in the kingdom. All his clothes for this trip were supposed to be waiting for him upon his arrival. Where is his entourage along with his new clothes? The king, his father, may have beaten some folks, but he can't imagine what his mother has done to the people in charge of his transport.

In one of the drawers he finds an ID that says "Dylan Cabrella." The picture looks just like him, and he figures he could use this for confirmation if anyone asks. What's next? The prince is trying to recall everything Socreen told him. He needs an airplane, and airplanes are located in airports. Thank goodness she told him stories about her land and he listened, otherwise he wouldn't know what to do. He needs transportation to the airport and figures that an automobile is nearby.

He starts opening every door until he finds a room with automobiles. He chooses a silver Audi convertible. The top was down and it looked righteous. Luckily, the king let him practice driving a car at the palace. Socreen showed him how to drive. No one else knew how. They don't have cars in the kingdom, but the king did.

His practicing came in handy. It was indeed needed because now he would be driving in this land of concrete dwellers. He starts pushing every button and suddenly the doors behind the cars start to open. How does this thing start? This is ridiculous. What the prince didn't realize was it was a push-button start. Socreen didn't have these when she was in the States.

He locates a booklet in a compartment and begins reading until he realizes it's a push-button start. There is no place for the key. Must be a new device. The engine starts, and a wide smile appears on the prince's face.

The prince departs with cash, Dylan's ID, bottled water, and a few bags of something called pretzels. He can be Dylan for a while. He puts on a pair of dark glasses and a hat with an "M" and a dolphin on it, still confused as to why he looks just like this Dylan character. He types in "airport" into the GPS, and Miami and Key West airports pull up. The sun is shining in a beautiful blue sky—something that doesn't exist in the kingdom. He could get used to this. Socreen was correct when she spoke of how beautiful it is.

He chooses Miami's airport, not sure why, but it turned out it was the best choice since it was a longer drive. It's nice to be so liberated without everyone falling all over him. He may never go back. So it's on to California or at least the Miami airport. He assumes his mother is taking someone's head off for this debacle and hopes it's not father's head.

He turns on the music box almost full blast, top down, grinning from ear to ear and starts down the road without any adult supervision. Thank goodness Socreen had been thorough with her stories, and he had listened to everything she told him about this land. The king was right, there is a lot of concrete around here.

The drive to Miami was semi-uneventful, even though it was his first time officially driving with others on a road. Back in the palace he was the only one driving, so the only accidents were him crashing into the wall. It's much more difficult driving with others around. It seems the prince likes to drive fast, enjoying the speed. Luckily, he never got pulled over for speeding.

The highway is full of large and small automobiles, reckless bicycles, plus giant fast-moving vehicles. They are so big, he almost stopped when one was near, but he just kept driving. The reckless bicycles were motorcycles, and the giant fast-moving vehicles are eighteen-wheelers.

As the prince gets close to the Miami airport, automobiles are everywhere. He pulls into a parking lot with a board across it and a piece a paper comes out. He finally pulls the paper, but someone behind him kept making a noise—honking a horn. He parks and walks inside the terminal.

Once inside, he sees someone holding a sign that says "Carmine."

The prince asks, "Where do I go for flights to California, San Francisco, please?"

"Dude, you are in the wrong terminal. This here is international. You need to go to the local terminal."

"Thanks. He gets on a subway tram to the local terminal and sees an information booth. He walks up and asks, "How do I get to California?"

The lady looks at him as if he has a disease. "Where do you want to go?"

"San Francisco, please?"

"Let me see your ticket."

"I don't have a ticket. Do I need a ticket?"

"Okay. Are you by yourself?"

"Yes, I am."

"Where is your mother?"

"She's running late. I'm supposed to meet her."

"Oh, okay child. Well, you go to the American counter, and you can buy your ticket from them. They will tell you what terminal you will need." The lady turned and pointed in the direction of the counter.

"Thanks."

The American counter is crazy. He hopes they know what they are doing. People running all over the place, kids screaming. Just complete turmoil. Who's in charge of this place? He's convinced if he gets to California it will be a miracle.

"Next. Hello young man, how can I help you?"

"I need your next flight to San Francisco, California please."

"Are you traveling by yourself?"

"Yes, I am. I'm meeting my mother there. She left earlier to visit our sick grandmother."

"How old are you?"

"Fifteen, almost sixteen," he smiles.

"Oh dear, well let's see. You seem very sophisticated for a fifteen-year-old. I have a seventeen-year-old at home, and he doesn't do anything. There is a flight departing in sixty-five minutes, but I doubt you can get there in time."

"Oh, I can. I'm very fast. I really need to be on that flight or my mother will just die."

"What about your return flight?"

"We are driving back. Don't need a return—just one way."

"Okay, young man. You have any luggage?"

"No, my mom has it all."

"I need to see some ID if possible. Oh, I see you have a birthday coming up. Happy birthday. That will be three hundred and twenty-five dollars."

The prince pulls out all his cash and places it on the counter.

"Oh my, you're paying in cash. That's a lot of money for a young man to be carrying around. You best be careful around here. There are a lot of pickpockets."

"Yes, I will be." Before she could tell him the gate number, he grabs the ticket and takes off running. "Thank you," he yells back.

The TSA security area line looks about a half mile long. This doesn't look right. No way, he'll never make it. He starts crying and passes everyone saying he lost his mom. Socreen said to use the sad mom story anytime you're in a bind. "I need to get on that flight," he starts whining and most everyone moves over. Finally, he gets to TSA security guard, who looks disgusted and upset.

"Ticket and ID please."

He looks suspiciously at the ID and then looks at the prince. It seems like it's taking forever. He scribbles on the ticket and mumbled something.

The prince goes through a scanner machine that most likely showed him naked. Not sure what they are looking for. They finish scanning him and point.

"Final boarding for flight number 2-8-3 to San Francisco."

"Here I am, ready to go," he yells, out of breath from running.

"Are you all by yourself?"

"Yes, I am."

"Okay, welcome aboard. You're lucky it's half empty, so you can probably pick your seat."

"Thank you." This nice lady shows him the assigned seat, and he slumps down with a sigh of relief. This would be the prince's first airplane ride so he wanted to look out the window. It was exciting, even though it was somewhat of a nuisance. Some guy sits next to him, so he gets up and asks the nice lady after she was ordering people around if he could change seats.

"Sure, honey. After we take off, I will find you an empty row."

"Thank you." Right before takeoff, the nice lady comes by and says, "Follow me. Here's a row all by yourself."

The prince is looking out the window and can't believe what he sees. It's beautiful with a huge body of water, beaches, houses, and a beautiful landscape. His face is glued to the window.

**

Matt is calling Tony with some important news from the San Francisco airport.

"Hey Matt, what's up? You've called me twice, which usually means trouble."

"Well, you may want to sit down, but guess who I'm following right now?"

Tony replies, "A cute blond in a mini skirt."

"Not even close, Doc. It's your nephew, Dylan. I yelled out his name, and he never winced. Then, I almost ran right into him and said "Dylan" but he looked right through me as if he didn't know me. So I decided to follow him. We're walking through the San Francisco airport. I thought he had black hair. I guess all those beach boys have blond hair. I could swear it's him."

"Are you sure it's him?"

"Yes sir, fairly certain, Doc. What's he doing here? It's been a while, but you know I never forget a face. Hold on, Doc, he's stopping at the Hertz car rental counter. Looks like they are arguing about something. Looks like Hertz won't rent him a car. I think you have to be twenty-one. Not sure what his ID says. I'm on the move. Looks like he's heading for the Budget rental car. I guess he figures he may have better luck with them. That didn't work out so well, either.

"Doesn't look like anyone is willing to loan him a car. Now it looks as if he is walking through the parking lot looking into cars as if he's going to steal one. What's going on? When did your nephew get into the car stealing business?"

"It's a family trait. Matt, it may not be Dylan."

"Yeah, you could be right, but he sure does look exactly like him. I'm not usually wrong about these things. I'm going to keep following and see where it leads."

"Alright, keep me updated? I'm heading to Key West now."

"Will do. Mom's going to kill me. Could you call her and tell her I'll be a little late?"

"No problem, Matt. Be careful."

What are you up to, young man? Matt wonders.

The prince starts walking through the parking lot, and is looking around. A car pulls in, then he walks over to the driver, who looked in his late sixties. Matt can no longer see the driver, but he does see who he thinks is Dylan driving this guy's car out of the lot. Matt doesn't have time to rent a car, so he jumps in the taxi line and hands the lady in front of the line a fifty for her kindness in allowing him to take the next cab. Matt tells the cabbie to follow that car. Matt sits back and calls Tony.

"Hey Tony, I'm in a cab following our friend. Your sweet nephew just knocked out a guy and stole his car. Not sure where we're going, but I'll let you know when we stop."

"Really. Hey Matt, be safe. This doesn't sound like Dylan."

Matt begins to wonder why Dylan is heading toward the middle of nowhere.

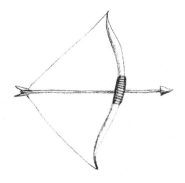

Chapter 23

TREFARS

"Good morning, Dylan," Tabitha remarks as I wake up in what looks like the middle of the desert. I slept okay since I didn't have any crazy dreams that I recall.

"Morning, I guess. It's still dark, what time is it? Are you sure it's morning?"

"It's morning and we have to move."

"What about breakfast?"

"Here's your breakfast." Tabitha throws me something.

"What is this?"

"Your breakfast. Hurry up or you'll have to eat while on the move."

Now I know why everyone is so fit—no one eats around here. I'm almost done chewing and off we go. I'm afraid to say anything as it may make Tabitha angry at me again, so I keep quiet and trudge onward. We finally arrive at the outskirts of the Trefars.

"Hey Tabitha, are we there yet?" I ask.

"Yes, be alert, we have arrived and they see us, but you won't see them, so don't do anything stupid. If that's possible."

"I told you a thousand times, I am sorry about the store. It was an accident," I remind her.

"I know, but accidents will get us all killed around here and that isn't on my schedule for today. Are you sure you're a doctor?"

"Pup, why don't you fly ahead and alert them we have arrived."

"Okay, will do, even though they know we are here," Pup says to Tabitha as she takes off.

Tabitha looks me straight in the eye and begins. "These people are not jokesters, and they will kill you without blinking. So, Dylan the Swimmer, soon to be doctor, let me explain to you again, how things work here. The Trefars are very private people. If they tell you to do something, do it. Eat what they feed you. Do not complain. Do not depart. Do not whine. Do not—"

"But I need—"

"No, listen to me. They do not care about what you need or want. They will train you for their needs, not yours. If you are fortunate, they will make a warrior out of you. But remember, you will never be at their skill level, so listen and do as you're told."

"Why are you bringing me here if I need to get the palace and by the way, they may kill me?"

Tabitha starts shaking her head. "Have you not heard anything I just explained to you?"

"Are you going to stay here with me?" I ask.

"Yes, I plan on staying. I always like to hone up on my warrior skills, and this is the place to do it. So just calm down."

"Calm down, that's easy for you to say. They don't want to kill you."

Tabitha impatiently repeats, "They don't want to kill you, unless you disobey them."

This sounds like being at home except Mom wouldn't kill me, she would just punish me. Well, she may kill me if she finds out I left Key West and I'm here. Oh boy, what have I gotten myself into? Before I could finish my thoughts, my entire body was surrounded by arrows.

Tabitha says, "We're here. Stay still."

"I couldn't move if I wanted to. I could have been killed."

Laughing out loud, Tabitha says, "If they wanted us dead, we would be. Now keep quiet."

Within seconds a small, strange-looking elfish guy comes out and says, "Hello Tabitha."

"Hello Cranky," Tabitha replies. "I apologize in advance for my friend here."

Cranky, now that's a name. "Are these your arrows?" I ask. And before I get an answer, the arrows begin to melt away.

Cranky looks at me then just shakes his head and says, "Follow me."

I grab Tabitha and whisper, "What's that?"

"That's Cranky, guardian of the west gate," she replies.

"Is he a Trefars?"

"No, he's a turtle, dimwit. Keep quiet and keep up."

I'm pretty sure this is going to suck. I was beginning to like Tabitha more than I should. I had yet to see her without her hat off. In fact, she never takes the darn thing off. I wonder what color her hair is. She must be bald or something. Falling for someone would be nuts. I don't even know where I am, and what I'm supposed to do.

Igagbee, a Trefars warrior has been assigned to me, which means I am with him every waking moment. I ask him a ton of questions, but he always replies that T will answer all my questions.

"For now, I will to train you," Igagbee assures.

"Train me for what, a battle possibly?"

I like Igagbee, so I try not to hound him too much with my all my questions and curiosity. I want to become a warrior, but they seem to be preparing me to be more refined. That alone is a joke for sure. Igagbee trained me a little in hand-to-hand combat. I was mainly being groomed to be more eloquent, walk and talk and act just like the prince guy. I was being groomed to impersonate the prince. I was getting perturbed because I wanted to learn how to be a warrior fighter, but they had other ideas. Talk of going to the palace was squashed.

Trefars are like well-oiled machines. Each Trefars makes their own weapons along with their own specific notches, niches that are designated on every arrow and weapon per each maker. You can trace every weapon and arrow back to its origin. They make all their own bows, arrows, spears, swords, knives, and every other weapon. The skill of a Trefars warrior is unsurpassed. Trefars are the best archers on the planet. They can pull twenty arrows out of their quivers in seconds, and fire. And they never miss their mark, and I mean never.

You could throw ten dimes in the air and they would all have been hit by arrows. It's an amazing thing to watch. Each Trefars is assigned an elephant. They are together at birth until death. I'm not sure if the Trefars pick the elephant or the elephant picks the Trefars, but it seems to work. This isn't the best part, though—they ride on these huge elephants. It's like they are one and it's kind of funny since Trefars are not very big. The tallest Trefars ever documented is three-feet-eight inches.

Since the Trefars are amazing archers, I wanted them to show me how to become an ace archer while riding an elephant, which by the way does not look easy. The elephants are not as steady as a horse, but the Trefars still don't miss a shot. I haven't been allowed to ride an elephant yet, but maybe soon. The Trefars bounce from elephant to elephant while firing arrows along with changing colors. More about that later. It's like a circus act. Crazy stuff, watching them train is a sight.

They were the first inhabitants in this land, and the king cannot get rid of them. Many have tried and many have died. So, for now the palace just lets them be. No matter what has been tried, they cannot win, so the king has given up. But will the queen ever give up?

The Trefars feeds trees to the elephants. The elephants tell them which tree to cut down, they cut it, and then the Trefars plant another. It's their own ecosystem. A perfect union between man and animal.

I have never worked so hard in my life. I figured if I did all my grooming crap, they would teach me how to fight. Not so much. They are stubborn people. I still haven't met T, the head of the Trefars. My food looks funny, but tastes okay. I have not had any headaches or stomachaches or crazy dreams. I do miss Mom's cooking. I keep thinking about home and what Mom is doing. I almost forgot about Violet, which I thought was impossible. Could I possibly get used to this life? I miss Tabitha though. What's wrong with me?

The only thing Trefars can't do is swim. They wanted me to swim but since the nearby lake was dried up, I couldn't show them. The only area to swim was Lake Demise, and that was off limits. I explained to them that swimming was my specialty, but I am not sure if they believed me since my other skills were less than stellar. They told me the prince was an excellent swimmer. So am I, was my comeback.

Daily yoga has been fun to watch. The elephants doing yoga, if I only had a camera. I don't miss my phone. Kind of don't want it anymore.

"Hey Igagbee, why is Lake Demise off limits?"

"You would be eaten before you jumped into the lake," was Igagbee's only response.

My training begins to get more intense. Igagbee is only teaching me skills that the prince himself excels in, and nothing more. I'm fairly certain the Trefars are now convinced that I am not the prince but a dead ringer, look-alike—a twin maybe. I constantly complain that I want to learn more, but Igagbee refuses to take the time to train me. Igagbee has been summoned to T.

"I think he will be ready soon," Igagbee tells his superior, T.

"We have to be a hundred percent sure he is ready. Have you told him, that he may have to kill the king?"

"No, I haven't. I thought it best if he heard it from you."

"I have a backup plan just in case he does not complete his task. We will not know until the occasion. Speed up your training and get him ready. I want his movements in the palace to be smooth and natural."

"He has been asking to see you."

"Soon, my good friend, soon."

"Yes sir," Igagbee responds and departs.

T is confident that he only needs to get the prince into the palace. If the prince does kill the king, then few will be alarmed. But if a Trefars attacks, revenge would be imminent. Sons have been killing fathers/kings for years. Once the king falls, most of the royal guards change loyalties instantly. The best part is that it isn't his real father, so it may be somewhat easier. But striking a blow for death is harder than one realizes, so he shall see. T will have Tic in place. The palace continues to attack the forest and tries to burn the Trefars out, but they have resisted. T is more worried about the queen. If the Trefars fall, the entire kingdom will be under the king's rule, and everything will be controlled by the palace. T doubts the king can take the Trefars without some additional outside help.

I haven't thought about Violet at all. It's not normal that I just fall for anyone, but Tabitha is pretty in her own athletic way. How is it I look so much like this prince? What would it be like to be a real prince? That would be so cool. Ordering people around, nobody talking back. Sounds like fun to me. Order girls to go out with you. Hmm, better ask Igagbee that one, and not Tabitha. She strikes me as the jealous type. What if this prince guy comes back while I'm in the palace? All this thinking caused me to doze off and dream vividly again.

**

Wow, this place is awesome.

"Oh sire, your bath is drawn."

"Thank you, I have had a rough day and need a nice hot bath."

"You certainly do, sire. The king would like to see you after your bath, so I have laid out your garments."

"Thank you, servant man." I don't know his name, I'm dead for sure.

"Yes sire."

The tub is the size of a small swimming pool. As am about to disrobe,

I see Violet in the corner of the tub grinning.

"Come on in. You don't need your suit. I don't have one."

"What's happening. Are you naked?"

"Yep, come on in. The water temperature is perfect. Let me bathe you."

"Gulp, aaahh, okay," I mutter, as I disrobe and jump in quickly so she can't see me naked.

"What's wrong with you? We do this every night. Quit being such a baby."

"I'm feeling shy tonight for some reason."

"That is so cute. Come here next to me."

"Okay," I say and swim up closer. I see her face change to Tabitha as she holds a giant sword and starts to swipe it at my head.

I start screaming, "NOOOOOOO!"

**

"Wake up, my prince. You're screaming in your sleep." I hear as Igagbee is shaking me awake. Igagbee now only refers to me as Prince Mako, and I figure it's useless to argue at this point.

"Hello Prince Mako, have you been practicing while I was away? Looks like you've been daydreaming as far as I can tell."

"Oh sure, I was working hard. Just dozed off for a minute."

"Why do I doubt you?" Igagbee smiles. "We have to ramp up our training since our mission will start soon. Daydreaming is not part of our training."

"That's what I'm talking about. Did you tell T, I would like to see him?"

"You don't tell T anything, but I did inform him that you would like to visit with him."

"What did he say?"

"Soon."

"Soon, what does that mean, s—"

Before I finished my sentence, Igagbee jumps up and throws himself in front of me. I heard nothing, but Igagbee did and he blocked an incoming arrow. He deflected it from hitting me, but it caught Igagbee in the hand. The Trefars have excellent hearing with their long pointy ears. He heard the arrow coming but a second too late for his own sake. Now the arrow was protruding through his hand.

Alarms were sounded and the place turned into an organized dance class, with people running here and there. I was whisked off so fast, I'm not sure what carried me away.

Once in place, I asked, "Where is Igagbee, and will he be alright?"

No one answered as people were running in and out of the hut. As I begin to rise, someone knocked me back down and says, "Stay put."

"I demand to know if Igagbee is alright."

"You will be told of the extent of his injuries once an assessment has been completed," an unknown Trefars replies. And he didn't sound very happy.

"I want to know now." I demanded.

Then every Trefars near me jumps to attention as someone walks in. One stays in place, the others depart.

"Well, well, how is the prince today?"

"Who might you be?" I ask.

"Oh sorry, excuse my rudeness. I am T, a minuscule part of this clan."

The Trefars guard smiles broadly and says, "Bow when T enters the room, you fool."

"It's okay," T tells the guard.

"Are you okay?"

"I am fine. I want to know about Igagbee." I reply sheepishly.

"It does not look good for Igagbee's hand but we have found the assassin, and he will be thoroughly interrogated. It seems the arrow he used was poisonous so the damage to Igagbee may be irreversible, but he is in the best of care."

"Too bad my mother isn't here—she would know what to do. I have come to really like Igagbee and consider him a good friend."

"He also refers to you as a good friend. Who is your mother?"

"She is the greatest veterinarian doctor in the world."

"Yes, indeed she would be of great help. I was informed that you were following in her footsteps."

"Yes and no. I'm not fully trained." Oh no, Tabitha told him.

"I see. Well, I have decided to implement my plan in two days. I feel you and all our lives are in danger and it's best we get you back to the palace, Prince Mako."

"Do you think I am ready?"

"Do you?"

"I think so. I must do it for Igagbee."

"You must not think so, you must be a hundred percent certain. It must be done for the kingdom to survive. Igagbee told me you are ready, so you have two days. But enough talk, get some rest and we will talk more later. Good night." T turns but before he departs says, "Oh, one more thing, you are not allowed to leave these quarters until further notice."

I was about to say something but figured it would be useless, plus I was too tired to argue with this guy. Another amazing thing the Trefars do is change colors like chameleons. Not sure when or how, but they can. While resting, I get a visit from Igagbee. He is bright green. I almost burst into tears when I see his left hand missing.

"I am so sorry to have caused you this injury. I feel like it's entirely my fault."

"No, it was all my fault. If I'd been alert and had not let my guard down for one second, no one would have succeeded in this assault. They used a Trefars arrow so it would go undetected, and that was most unusual. The arrow was poisonous, which means it would have killed you. All I lost was my hand—it had to be amputated to save my life," Igagbee says with a big grin on his face.

"You're extremely happy considering you just lost your hand."

"I will become a legend—everyone will remember me as the one who protected and saved the future king. I will be a real hero, and for centuries people will talk about the great and courageous Igagbee. Legends and lore will be written about me. You haven't been with us long enough to know we love legends, and in our minds, we are constantly thinking about ways of saving the kingdom or saving T or saving someone. And mine came true. This is so glorious, I am sure an occasion will be in my honor one day."

"Are you not sad about your hand?"

"Not at all. I was doing my duty and saved you. What's a hand? I have another. I am still alive and well, and so are you. I did my job even though I was a bit slow."

Wow, I think, these people are amazing, I would be very, very upset. I cannot comprehend his enthusiasm, but this is a whole new world for me.

"Well, that's great, I guess. I leave in two days."

"Yes, I know, you have been visited by the great T."

"Am I ready?"

"Yes, more than ready. T will give you more details. Be brave my friend, until we meet again."

And in a flash, he was gone.

The next morning, I was brought to T's house. It's very small in stature and doesn't look like royalty lives here.

"I spoke with Igagbee, but I am very confused."

"About what?"

"Why isn't Igagbee upset?"

T explains, "That is the life of us Trefars. We are happy to help those in need and see a greater purpose in others than our own life. For instance, we care more for our elephants than we care for our own lives."

"I cannot comprehend this way of thinking. It's like a high priest or pastor."

"Sure, you can put it like that."

"Why are you building what looks like a moat around your people? Is that to keep me in?"

T starts to laugh. "You are a jokester. No, I am preparing for the day the rains return."

"I was told it hasn't rained in five hundred days." Then I ask, "Is Tabitha okay?"

"Let me tell you a story about a little girl. One day this little girl was working in the field with her father and she found an odd-shaped, unusual colored rock. She asked her father if she could keep the rock and he said, 'You found it, it's yours. What are you going to do with such a big rock?' 'I will take it everywhere I go,' she told him. So, she put the rock in her pull wagon and covered it with a blanket. She never left it alone. It was by her side night and day. She would sing to it and talk to it as if it were a real person. And one day the rock started to move. This little girl wasn't frightened, but delighted it moved. She told her parents about it moving and they wanted to see her prize rock. It turned out the rock wasn't a rock, but an egg. Extremely rare to find a dragon's egg. Her parents were afraid that the dragon parents would come back and be upset, and that she should place the rock back. She didn't understand that she had to give back her prize rock. She had cared for this rock and it had been by her side every minute for many days. She was very sad, so she decided to depart from her family and hide deep in the forest.

"Soon after she left, a tragedy occurred and both her parents perished. At the same time, her egg hatched. It was a beautiful dragon. She named her Pup. And they have never been apart," T smiles as he finished the story.

"Hey, you're talking about Tabitha."

"I would not worry about Tabitha, but only those that confront her. She is safer than anyone with Pup at her side. But lying to a dragon or its companion could be fatal. Did you know that a dragon can read your thoughts?"

"No, I didn't."

"Let's have a smoke, doctor," T says as someone instantly appears with a tray.

Trefars smoke a lot, not cigarettes, cigars, or marijuana, but some type of herb—not sure what it is. They told me but I still don't know. I tried to smoke at home once and I got sick. Being a swimmer, I didn't think smoking was a good thing, but I was not about to tell T no.

"Sure," I say as we both light up and T starts asking me some questions. But I can see T changing colors like a rainbow. Trefars change colors like we change stations on a TV. The ancient ones can change into multi-colors, but most Trefars can only change into a single color. T is beginning to look like a rainbow.

"What is your name?"

"Trick question, Prince Mako," I respond, kind of dizzy feeling.

"What am I smoking?" I ask T.

"Where are you from?"

By now I am on cloud nine.

"Key West, Florida."

"Why are you here?"

"To take my grandmother back home."

"Socreen?"

"Yes, Socreen. At least that's what you guys call her. What is this stuff? It's awesome."

"It's damiana leaf and peyote."

"How did you get here?"

"I am not sure about that."

"Who is your mother?"

"Mom, her name is Isabella Cabrella. I miss Tabitha," was the last thing I remember saying. I must have passed out.

T stops the inquisition and leaves the room.

"Take him to Tara. She will get the rest of the information I need," T commands.

Tara is T's mother. She is purportedly over four hundred years old, and quite wise. She is well protected and it is told she can see the future. I'm barely aware when a Trefars places me on an elephant and transports me to Tara, who is very old and feeble. Her voice is so low it's hard to understand her.

"Lay him down on the floor next to me," Tara says softly.

"Thank you, Tank. Ah, let me see your future, young man."

I am still knocked out but semi-conscious. Tara lays her hands on my face and closes her eyes. She holds my face for a few minutes, which felt like days. When she is finished, she opens her eyes and asks Tank to bring me back to my cabin and have T come visit her.

Tara begins to tell T what she saw. "He is the one we have been waiting for. The kingdom will become at peace once more after Dylan the Swimmer is placed on the throne."

"Thank you, Tara. I had a feeling about this one, and he will be ready."

"Be careful, Son. The queen will not be as easily fooled as the king."

T discovers that the intruder used a Trefars arrow, and that is why it was not detected. Every night Trefars are supposed to account for their weapons. The assassin was sent by the queen. *It is time.*

Chapter 24

NEON

T he actual prince finally arrives at his destination in San Francisco. Proud of his driving expertise and perseverance. He sees the sign that confirms he is at the correct location:

**

WELCOME TO TRIPOLEE (EEE)
EMERALD ENVIRONMENTAL ENTERPRISE
WE ARE GREENER THAN GREEN WE ARE EMERALD

DO NOT ENTER
PRIVATE PROPERTY
NO TRESPASSING
WE PROSECUTE TRESPASSERS

**

A small sign says, Welcome To The Greenest Of Green. Environmental, Ecological And Conservation Is All We Do. We Care For All And All We Care For Is Your Future.

Thanks again for the talking directional gadget as the prince arrives at the rendezvous point. The GPS worked perfectly. He still can't believe he found his way to San Francisco. The king would be proud of his traveling skills. He punched in an eight-digit code, and the gate slowly opened. Just the sight of Grull alone would scare them. If the transporters were working properly, this project would have been completed long ago.

Another gate is locked as he gets out and punches in the code. The prince recalls why he is here, in this concrete country. A door opens, and there was Grull.

"Welcome, your highness. We have been expecting you, and I am happy you have arrived. It seems you have been missing for a short while. Where have you been? Is everything okay?"

"No, everything is not okay. I was sent to some place called Florida by mistake. It's far from here and whoever is responsible should be reprimanded." The prince decides to keep the confusing family photos to himself.

"Yes, I am sorry, your highness. The person responsible will be taken care of. If I had known where you were, I would have picked you up myself. No one was sure where you were sent. The transporters have been an issue, but we have another alternative thanks to a good friend of mine," Grull laughs.

"I took an American Airlines flight. It was very interesting to see everything below. Lots of open land and water everywhere. Now fill me in on your progress."

"Yes indeed, your highness. Let me get you up to date."

It looks like an abandoned project that ran out of resources, but in reality, it's a fully functional and ongoing project. No one was in sight, but he knew they started work when it was well into the darkness of night. This was a highly sensitive mission. Most of the workers only come out at night since their appearance may scare the people living in the surrounding area.

Grull begins to explain how the project is progressing. "I have the final piece of the puzzle and my crew is working on the potion as we speak. The final piece was a neon fish, which a friend of mine found and crated for me. Let's just say it fell into my hands. Once the potion is made, workers can transport back and forth from the kingdom to this concrete country. Since the transporters are down, this potion will be a perfect remedy. By the way, you were followed, but I am taking care of the matter."

The prince replies, "Driving around here is difficult enough, so trying to go unnoticed was low on my priority list. Being transported to Florida was an unfortunate interruption."

Grull senses the prince's irritation. "Yes, your highness. Now that you are in safe hands, I have it all under control," Grull remarks. "It is much safer to make the *Megontrolite* here, then to transport it. Transporting it would be an issue so I had to make everything here. The plan is perfect, and no one will suspect foul play. These people are very gullible."

Grull is making liquid *Megontrolite*. It is so powerful that it makes a stick of dynamite seem like a firecracker, and it leaves no trace. Just a cupful could do extensive damage to the palace. It's what Grull's men are using on the Andreas Fault, to make it look like an earthquake.

Grull reminds the prince that, "There will be a few causalities but it is needed for our survival, your highness."

"Yes indeed," the prince replies. "My kingdom needs water and with this detonation much needed water will pour into my kingdom. The trickledown effect could also wipe out some of the kingdom's enemies, mainly the Trefars, which would be an added benefit. Collateral damage is what my father calls it. The Trefars can't swim. This will get the kingdom's water supplies back to normal. It has not rained in over five hundred days and all will be lost without more water. The palace's water supply is indeed in jeopardy. No one will suspect it was done on purpose, but all the blame will be put on every American and their toys."

"You will be considered a hero back home, your highness. It's a perfect plan."

The prince begins to think about all the local people that will perish, but cannot worry too much. The kingdom needs this water. So, the rebels and the Trefars die. *They're always attacking our way of life, never doing as they are told. We know what is best for them. Why don't they listen? Everyone answers to my father, the king.* As his mind continues to wonder, he begins to reflect on the pictures of this Dylan guy and why he looks just like him. He pulls out the picture of the Socreen look-alike. Why does she look like Socreen? Why is that? Who are these people? He cannot wait to see Socreen and tell her about this family and show her the picture. He wonders if that is why the king has outlawed twins. Too much confusion.

"Prince, we have to depart and get you cleaned up. We have plenty of events planned that command your attendance," Grull smiles.

"You must tell my father that I have safely arrived."

"Yes, my prince. Flobak will accompany you back to your hotel. I have to take care of a few things here."

**

"Hey Torch, smooth landing. I'll text you when I'm ready to fly out. It will likely be tomorrow morning," Tony says as his plane lands in Key West.

"Okay, Doc. I'm sure I can find a few things to do while in this part of the world. This is my kind of place."

Tony jumps in a cab and heads to his sister's house. He keeps calling, but no one answers their phones. Where are they? He doesn't have time to hunt them down. These kids are all usually attached to their phones. Where are they?

As Tony approaches the front door, he hears some growling. Isabella did warn him that she has added a guard dog or two. Growing up he wasn't afraid of any animals, so the growling was of no concern. Tony opens the front door, and sees Brandi and a giant German Shepherd, who he recognizes as Hari.

"Is that you, Hari? You look great, my friend. What's up? I come all the way across town and no one is here. Where is everybody, Hari?"

Hari and Teri could always speak but they never did in front of some people.

"I have some good news and some real bad news," Hari finally replies.

"Start with the good."

"The good news is Teri is slowly healing with no major harm to any vital body parts."

"That is great news. I'm ready for part two. I presume that's why you're here, to keep these kids safe."

"Yeah, well, while I was visiting Teri that is when everything went sideways, but I have a theory."

"I'm listening," Tony adds with a big smile. "Give me your best guess."

Stalling, Hari says, "It's been a while my friend."

"It sure has, too long. Where are Alex and Dylan? I don't have a lot of time."

As they walk from room to room, Tony notices that everything is on the floor—clothes thrown all over, drawers opened. It looks as if someone was looking for something, or the place was robbed.

"Looks like she was robbed. I'm waiting, Hari, since I am fairly certain Dylan doesn't wear a shirt like this." Tony holds up the prince's smock, covered in blood.

"That blood is Teri's," Hari remarks, grimacing.

"That's not comforting, I'm waiting, Hari."

"I'm fairly certain Alex is in the kingdom along with Dylan."

"Are you telling me they both went? But how?"

"They both used the blue pillowcase."

Tony is unaware that Isabella instructed Hari to hide the blue pillowcase.

"Keep going," Tony sighs.

"The bad news is they both went at separate times and are all alone."

"Are you saying they both went to the kingdom by themselves?"

"Yes, same place, different day."

"Then who turned this place upside down? Is this part of the robbery?"

"Prince Mako, or Michael as he's also known, did this."

"Prince who?" Tony asks.

"Prince Mako, from the kingdom. He looks just like Dylan but has blond hair. They could be twins."

"Repeat that?" Tony looks at Hari in confused way.

"It seems Dylan has a twin and he was here," Hari grins.

"Are you kidding me? Where is this twin?"

"Not sure about that, but I think he's in San Francisco."

That would explain the look-alike in San Francisco, Tony thinks.

"I really dread making a call to Bella. Hey Hari, you want to talk with Isabella?"

"No way, pal, she's all yours."

Tony made the dreaded phone call to Isabella, prompting "*Yellow Submarine*" to ring out on the other end in Boston.

"Hello, Chloe here."

"Hey sugar, it's Uncle Tony."

"Oh hi, you coming to pick us up? Mom's doing great and we are ready to go back home."

"Yep, coming your way tomorrow, first thing in the morning."

"Is your mother available? Yes sir, hold on."

"Hey Bella, how you feeling?"

"Much better. They are either ready to release me or kill me. I'm not the best patient, as you know."

"That I do know. I bet they wanted to get rid of you three days ago," Tony smirks as they both chuckle.

"Where are you?" Isabella asks.

"I'm sitting in your den, with two of your favorites."

"Excellent, I knew you would save the day. How are my little ones?"

"Hari and Brandi are great."

"Oh gre—, what did you say? Where are my kids?"

"Well, that's a good question. I don't know and neither does Hari."

"What do you mean, not there? Where are they? What is going on down there? Find Alessandra and Dylan and come get us, now."

"Okay, will do. See you tomorrow."

"Call me when you find them? Alex can't be far. Call her friends. They will know—they don't leave each other's side. All their phone numbers are on the fridge. Samantha and Tami will know where Alex is, and Dylan is probably with Jonny."

Tony didn't want to alarm her at this point. He decided to wait and tell her the real story face to face.

"Will do, I'm on it. Hey, one more thing. Did your friend get my package?" Tony asks.

"Not sure, he should be back any time now."

"Thanks."

"How's Dad?"

"He's fine. Feels kind of bad about Dylan, but he is much better now. I didn't tell him too much, no need to upset him. He's being well taken care of in Santa Fe."

"I bet he is. I've been to your little hideaway fortress, it's heavenly."

"You are welcome anytime, little sister. See you in the morning."

"Thanks, big bro, later."

Tony's first call was to Matt. No answer.

Second call to Torch. "Get her ready to leave in the morning around eight a.m. We're heading to Boston."

"You got it," Torch replies.

Third call to Samantha.

"Hello."

"Is this Samantha?"

"Yes, it is. Who's this?"

"My name is Tony Rome and I—"

"Oh yeah, hi Uncle Tony. What can I do for you?"

"Is Alessandra with you?"

"No, she's at home sleeping."

"Were you with Alessandra when she found Dylan?"

"Oh, it was so exciting."

"Can you give me every detail?"

Samantha tells Tony everything she knew. And when she finally finished, Tony asked, "So you never actually saw Dylan?"

"Nope, just heard that he colored his hair blond."

"Thank you, dear. One more question?"

"Sure."

"Do you think Tami is with Alessandra?"

"No, silly, Tami is with me?"

"When are you getting into town?"

"Any minute now. Thanks again."

Tony hangs up and wearily glances in Hari's direction. "Hari, you may be right. Alex nor Dylan is here, and my sister is going to blow a gasket."

Chapter 25

GRANDO

Grando and Cato hear the horn blast, which means return to base at once.

"See, all that bickering about Lake Demise lost us valuable time," Cato complains. "I wonder if Kaptuk returned from the palace with some news for us."

"I hope we are going into battle," Grando says.

"I don't mind being prepared, but I would prefer to never go into a real battle. Times are upside down, but I would not be surprised if a war has erupted."

"Who would be crazy enough to take on the king's men?" Grando asks.

"The rebels have been mobilizing and getting bolder. I heard they sabotaged a subway train last week. Not just any subway, it was a royal subway," Cato exclaims.

"My father never tells me anything. He is so loyal, all he ever talks about is how great the king is, how great the palace is, and how lucky I am to be part of the royal warriors, blah, blah, blah. I am sick of the palace and the royals," Grando groans.

"You better watch yourself saying things like that. You could be beaten or even killed for saying such things. Come on, let's hurry or we will be late," Cato reminds Grando.

Grando dreams that one day people will see what a great warrior he is. Meanwhile, all the young warriors gather around Kaptuk and await his announcement.

"Welcome back, everyone. I hope your class was satisfactory. I apologize for cutting today's lesson short," Kaptuk remarks. "Thank you all for your participations. Our next class will be announced at a later date.

All the students start asking, "Well, what's the news? Why are all further classes canceled? Are we at war with the rebels?"

"You will know in due time. Do not get ahead of yourselves."

Knowing that it is useless trying to get anything out of Kaptuk, everyone departs.

"Grando, can I see you for a moment?" Kaptuk asks.

"Yes, of course."

Grando fears Kaptuk may have heard what he said about the king. *How does he hear everything I say? I'm dead for sure.*

"Grando, I know you all talk among yourselves, but I have a special assignment for you. You cannot tell anyone about this mission. It comes directly from the king himself."

"So, the king knows about me?" Grando grins excitedly as he fantasizes again. *It's about time someone recognizes my greatness.*

"Yes, the king has given you a secret mission with Grande's approval, I might add. It is very special and you must be very secretive."

Grando's mind is swimming with thoughts. He is going to lead the warriors to battle. He may be the king's new special assistant. He will be honored as the greatest warrior ever. He is the fastest warrior in the kingdom, of course the best of the best.

"Grando, quit your daydreaming and listen. This is important." It is not a simple assignment, even though you are going to think it is, so listen carefully and do as you are told. If captured, who knows what they will do to you."

"Captured? Me never. Who could capture me? I am the fastest, the greatest ever—"

"Listen, don't speak. Listen and pay attention. Stay focused, listen," an annoyed Kaptuk remarks.

"You are to locate the prince and follow him. He was last seen in Rockland. You are not to be seen by anyone. And you are not to make contact with the prince. Plus, you are to report your findings daily by messenger back to me. Do you understand?"

"Not really."

"All you have to do is follow the prince and report his movements."

"Well that's not exciting. Can't I—"

"Are you listening to me? No, NO, and triple NO! Just follow the prince and report his daily movements. Got it?"

"Bu—"

"NOOOOO!" Seeing that Kaptuk was about to explode, Grando acquiesced.

"Okay, okay, I understand, I'm going."

"He was last seen in Rockland, Sector 37. Go at once and tell no one." Kaptuk explains.

Grando takes off and starts to wonder why such an easy task was given to such a noble warrior as himself. He sees all the caves and thinks about wiping out all the unsuspecting rebels hidden in those caves. He'll be a hero in no time.

**

Alessandra did transport and she is very confused. It has been many years since she has visited the kingdom. She used to visit with her mother when she was much younger and had begun to think all of her visits were a dream of some sort until now.

"Hello, is anyone out there. Where am I?" She can't see a thing. The last thing she remembers was that she lay down for a nap in her bedroom and awoke somewhere else. "Hello, probably a dream. Ouch!" She stubs her toe and falls. "Ouch, that hurt. Hello, hello!" she keeps screaming.

In a booming voice a response comes back, "HELLO. How are you?"

"Not too good. Can you turn on the lights? I can't see a thing."

"Who are you?"

"Who are you?"

"I asked first, and you are in my house."

"What? What house? There must be some mistake. I was taking a nap in my own house. How did I get here? Are you in my dream?"

"Why are you here?"

"Listen, I don't feel comfortable talking in the dark to someone I can't see. Can you please turn on the lights? I'm getting scared."

"Oh, I'm so sorry. Just light a match and throw it into the fireplace."

"Umm, I don't have a have a match or a flashlight, so maybe a little help would be nice?"

"Who are you? Why are you here?"

"Not the help I was looking for. Do you have a match?" Alex asks again.

"Of, course I do. I love fires, it keeps me warm."

"Can I borrow one, please? You're starting to annoy me. Show yourself."

"How do you think I feel? You arrived unannounced and broke into my home."

"I am so sorry, but I didn't mean to. It was a complete accident. Match, please."

"The matches are next to the fireplace."

"Oh thanks, that helps even though I can't see anything."

Alex feels around and finds a box of matches, lights one, and throws it into the fireplace.

Poof, a huge fire is roaring in minutes.

"Aaaah," the booming voice is now making a purring sound. "That is nice, thank you."

Alex looks around and still sees no one. "Where are you? I can't see you."

"I can see you. Have we have met in the past?"

"Well, I can't see you. And I doubt I have ever been here."

"You're staring right at me."

"Okay, sure I am. Wait a minute. I have been here—it's been years."

"What is your name?"

"Alessandra Cabrella."

"Oh my, you have returned. Did you bring Isabella?"

"If you're talking about my mother, no, she is not with me. You know my mother?"

"Of course, I remember everyone that passes through my house. It's too bad she has not returned. It is written she will return one day and save us all."

Okay, this is a dream for sure. Alex is sure she's dreaming and suddenly realizes she's in a cave of some sort. Then she spots the only furniture in the room—a single rocking chair.

"Did you kidnap me?" Alex asks.

"I am Grock, the greatest and possibly the only rock hut in this area and possibly the oldest, but that has not yet been determined. Many of my kind are quite stubborn but our memories are forever."

Alex sees a lot of shoes, boots, jackets, helmets, empty bottle, and blankets. She had visited when she was very young but thought it was a dream. It was so long ago, and she was traveling with Mom and Grandma.

"It is a pleasure to meet you, Mister Grock."

"Oh thank you, the pleasure is all mine. I'm not a mister. I'm just Grock."

"Oh okay, Grock it is."

"I like my talks with your family. I miss my talks with Isabella very much and had a great talk with a Dylan Cabrella the other day."

"What did you say?"

"I like my talks with your family. I miss my talks with Isabella very much and had a great talk with a Dylan Cabrella the other day."

"Are you saying my brother just came through here?"

"If you say so. He said his name was Dylan Cabrella. He was very nice. We had a lovely chat."

"Do you know where he is now?"

"He's either with the rebels or the Trefars."

"The rebels. Oh, that doesn't sound good."

"Ahh, both are very nice. It's the king's men you want to avoid."

"Okay, thanks for the tip. Where do I find these rebels?"

"Oh, I wouldn't worry. They will find you. They already know you're here. My smoke has alerted them."

"Well then, thank you again. You're very nice, Grock." Loud purring sounds filled the hut.

"Would it be okay if I borrowed a pair of shoes and a jacket? I seem to have left mine behind."

"Pick out anything you wish. Isabella brought me most of everything you see. She knows I love shoes. But you will have to repay me with another pair."

"As soon as possible I will drop off a brand-new pair of shiny shoes just for you. Better yet, two pairs. Is there a particular color you prefer?"

"Aaahh, that would be sooooo nice. Surprise me with any color you wish. It has been a long time since someone brought me a pair of shoes. Isabella Cabrella was the last one who brought me gifts. I'll never forget all her kindness."

Alex wonders what in the world is Grock, going to do with all these shoes? So many different styles, sizes, shapes, high heels, stilettos, sneakers, boots, sandals, plus many more.

"Well, it's been fun but I must go now and find my little brother. I don't see a door, so what am I supposed to do? How do I get out?" Alex asks.

"Don't you remember?"

"No, I was possibly four years old the last time I was here."

"But you just got here. Can't we talk a little longer?"

"Okay, sure, but I need to find my brother."

**

Grando leaves Kaptuk and picks up a scent as soon as he arrives in Rockland. He's convinced the prince must have visited Grock, the infamous rock hut. Grando hears a noise and tries to hide for cover. After realizing there is no cover, he just freezes still. He could see someone with short blond hair coming out from the rock hut. Could be the prince. The scent is remarkably similar.

There are no hiding spots around the barren rock hut, especially for an enormous twenty-foot tiger. Well, so much for being a secret. Grando is spotted, and Alex screams. Seeing a saber-toothed tiger in wide open space would make anyone scream, much less a huge twenty-foot tiger.

Alex slowly turns and starts to bang on the rock hut trying to get back inside, but with no luck. Soon she starts yelling, "Grock, let me in. Grock, help." Alex bends down to pick up a rock.

"Ouch!" she hears the rock shriek, drops it, and faints.

"Oh my," Grando remarks. "Hopefully she's alright. Just the sight of me puts fear in their hearts, and she is clearly not the prince." Grando throws her on his back and scampers off into a giant cave.

Alex finally comes to from fainting and jumps up as she sees this giant tiger sitting across from her. "Stay away, nice kitty," Alex remarks.

Grando asks her, "Who are you talking to? If I wanted to eat you, I would have. What are you jabbering about?"

"You can talk?" Alex asks curiously.

"Why yes, can't you, little one?"

"Yes, I'm just not accustomed to speaking with ah, ah, tigers."

"Sounds like a personal problem. You passed out and I carried you here. You should be more appreciative—we are in hostile territory. Giant lizards live around here. They will not bother me, but you would make a nice morsel for them." Grando smiles at the thought.

"Well then, I should thank you, I guess."

"What is your name?"

"Alessandra Cabrella, and yours?"

"You should know my name. It's Grando. I am a great warrior on a secret mi—, I mean the greatest warrior ever in this land."

"Where are we, anyway?" Alex responds.

"Shroomland, just outside Rockland."

"Shroomland, what is that?"

"You asked, I told you. Shroomland. Are you always this confused?"

"No, I'm usually very alert."

"Well, you sound confused to me. Most alert people don't pass out that easily. Are you part of the rebels?"

"No. I'm just here looking for my brother. Are you a rebel? What are you doing out here?"

"Well, I'm not supposed to say anything, but let's just say I'm on an important mission."

"Good for you." Alex grins at Grando.

"Isn't it though? I'm one of the greatest warriors in this land, so you'll be safe on my watch."

"What is your mission?"

"I can't say, it's a secret."

"Okay, well good luck with your secret mission. Would you like to help me find my little brother?"

"It depends, but I guess we could travel together for a while."

Thinking to herself, Alex was pleased, that she befriended a giant saber-tooth tiger. It could only help her.

"My friends call me Alex."

"Okay Alex, but I am on a mission, so I may to have depart before we find your little brother. I am on a very important mission and hopefully soon I will pick up a scent of my target."

"Maybe it's my brother?"

"I doubt it unless your brother is the prince." Then Grando laughs out loud.

"I don't think so, maybe the prince of dummies." Alex joins in on the laughter.

"Is there an IHOP, Whole Foods, or juice bar nearby?" Alex feels famished.

"I have no idea what you are talking about."

"Food, don't you eat food?"

"Yes, when I'm hungry," Grando grins.

"Well, I'm hungry. Is there a mall nearby?"

"A what?"

"Okay, it's not my favorite, but let's just go to Starbucks. You must have one of those—they're everywhere."

"A what buck?"

"Quit kidding with me. I'm hungry and when I get hungry, I get angry if I don't eat. *Hangry eyes*, they call me. Food court, possibly?"

"I have no idea what you are talking about." Grando is getting annoyed. "You know it will be night soon. You should rest."

"But I need food ASAP." Alex grumbles.

"It's too dangerous to travel at night. In the morning I'll bring you some food."

"Okay, but it's been dark all day. How can you tell if it's night or day?"

"I am a great warrior. I know everything."

"Is it dangerous for you? I mean, who would attack someone as big as yourself?" Alex is thinking that if they are crazy enough to attack him, then she's in big trouble, so maybe she should stay put until daylight.

"Oh, you are too kind, but there are many evil creatures much larger than I," Grando replies.

"Are you kidding me?"

"Nope, but stay close. I will protect you."

"Thank you. You're so cute and kind."

"Aaahhh, thanks."

"Where are you from?" Grando asks. "I know you're not from here. Must be from the north. Your questions are very unusual."

"I'm from Florida. I didn't have time to eat before I left."

"Where is that? Never heard of that land?"

"It's on the ocean, way down south," Alex points down.

"Oh, the ocean, huh. My father, Grande, told me stories about all the waters that used to be part of this land. But everything has dried up. I would love to see an ocean one day."

"Well, maybe I'll show you. My mom would love you. She is the best vet in the world."

"Vet?"

"Veterinarian."

"Oh, an animal doctor. She sounds nice. I'd like to meet her. We need more of those around here. The king doesn't care when you get injured, he just summons up another to replace us."

"Are you part of the king's men?" Alex asks, concerned.

"Of course, I am. What did you think I was, a rebel? I'm a powerful warrior for the king. Probably the best and greatest warrior he has."

"Sure, I understand." Remembering what Grock told her, Alex gets suspicious.

Grando grins as his own suspicions creep in. "May I see your arm, please?"

"No, why?"

"Would you rather me pull your arm off then check?"

"Well, you leave me no choice. Why do you want to see it?"

"I just do." Grando is getting annoyed again. "You're too big to be a Trefars."

"Now you're calling me fat!"

"I didn't say that, you did."

"You do know that women are sensitive about those type of comments."

"Not really. Seems silly to me."

"Well, try not to call me big in the future?"

"Why are so hung up about being big?"

"I don't know, I just am."

"All I said is, you're too big to be a Trefars."

"There you go again."

"Calm down. You are much taller than three feet, aren't you?"

"Now you're picking on my height?"

"What are talking about?" Grando shrugs.

"You just said I was not much taller than three feet, and big and fat."

"Wow, you do have an imagination. Does everyone from Florida have such an imagination? Why are you getting so upset?" Grando asks.

"I feel like you're making fun of me."

"Do you even know what a Trefars is?"

"No, not really."

"Then calm down. Most are no bigger than three feet tall, so that is all I was saying. You are a tiring little girl. Let's start over. Let me see your arm, please?"

"Here, see. What is it you're looking for? I have no tattoos. My mother would not allow any. Took me a while to convince her to get my ears pierced. She is so old fashioned."

"Hmm, you have no marks. You're a rebel for sure. Only rebels try to remove their marks at birth. Never seen a rebel without a weapon, though."

"I am no rebel."

"Well, where is your ID?"

"I left it at home."

"What are you talking about? You cannot leave your ID at home since it is tattooed on your arm. Did you leave your arm at home?

Everyone is supposed to have a number. How else is the palace going to count and keep up with their subjects? Since you are a rebel, I cannot be your friend."

"Why not? I told you I am not, and what if I am? What do you care?"

"The rebels are destroying this land. The king is our only hope. My father tells me that the king is going to make everything right again. And purging the rebels will be his first task."

"By purging, you mean killing?" Alex asks loudly.

"Well, yes if you're against the king's wishes," Grando answers defiantly.

"I don't even know who this king is, but I don't like him already."

"You best not say that in my presence."

"I am starving. Is there a fast-food place nearby? I'll eat anything at this point."

Grando's patience runs out as he swats at Alex. She screams, jumps out of the way, and kicks his paw. Grando, caught off guard, isn't prepared for Alex's speed and quickness.

"You are very quick, little one. Who taught you these skills?"

"I have been training for years."

As Grando strikes again, this time he gets kicked in the head.

"Okay, that is enough playtime. My next attack will be—"

Before they knew it, they were both surrounded. Their screaming at each other may not have helped. A warrior jumps in front and finds out the hard way how quick Alex is as she kicks him to the ground. Another jumps in and finds the same fate. Grando grabs another pair and throws them both. Then several arrows land next to Alex 's feet, shot from a young woman. Alex and Grando's brawl ends abruptly.

"That is enough. Stop, or the next one will be at your head," the young woman yells out.

They both look up and see at least a hundred people with arrows pointed at them, along with a bunch of animals.

Grando is sure he's dead, his mission compromised. "Fighting with you caused me to get captured," Grando yells at Alex.

"Ditto!" Alex replies angrily.

"The rebels have us surrounded. Are you happy now?"

"Not really."

"Okay, you two follow me and keep quiet."

Alex whispers to Grando, "See, I told you I'm not a rebel, you donkey. And I'm still hungry."

Chapter 26

DYNAMITE

An attendant at the San Francisco airport walks up to a car in the Hertz rental aisle and notices the driver is fast asleep. He also noticed notices that it isn't a Hertz rental car, so he calls his supervisor over. A discussion ensues, and they both decide the driver is either asleep or passed out, drunk. The attendants conclude the driver was flying back to his wife and had a few too many. After a few knocks on the driver's door with no success, the supervisor decides to look in the trunk. The driver still wasn't budging. The trunk release was in the glove box and luckily the passenger door was unlocked. They disengage the trunk and look inside expecting luggage, but found something else. What they weren't expecting was a load of dynamite. The supervisor immediately calls the head of airport security, and reinforcements race to the scene.

Matt opens his eyes. Sirens are blaring as he is surrounded by policeman, fireman, firetrucks, ambulances, swat teams, FBI, dogs—you name it, they were there. Matt tries to recall what happened. Soon he hears a voice from a bullhorn, "Hands on your head and step out of the vehicle, slowly."

Matt's head is about to explode as he struggles to remember how he got here. And who's car is this? It may be the stolen car the prince took from the airport. He figures he must've been drugged, but is confused as to why he is surrounded by so many policemen.

"Sir, you're going to have step out of the vehicle and put your hands on your head. I want to see your hands at all times."

The ringing in his ear from the megaphone almost knocked him out of the car. Surveying the situation, Matt decided he best not play with these boys, especially in his current state and considering how serious they look. *Is all this attention for me, or did someone call in a bomb threat? I haven't seen this much artillery since I left the service.*

"Okay, here I come, be cool," Matt replies carefully.

The driver's side door was already open and as soon as he steps out of the car, he is tackled by six swat team members. Though he didn't fight back, he still got his lip cut, arm bruised, face scraped, left ear bloodied, then he was handcuffed. Before Matt could say anything, they tossed him into the back of a van. What in the world is these guys problem he wonders, as he tries to figure out where he had been and why he blacked out? It wasn't a dream since blood was dripping on his boots. Dylan, that little rat. He was following Dylan and pulled up to a large gate, got out of the cab, and then it all went blank. What did that sign say? Matt's head is throbbing.

"You're not taking him. He's ours. We found him on airport property and we're booking him right here. He's coming with us. When you get your paperwork done, bring it to me, and then I'll decide what to do, but for now he's mine. I'm going to interrogate this lowdown scumbag myself. I've read how you boys interrogate."

"Great, well, I'm coming with you," the FBI agent insists.

"Sure, come on along and see how it is done."

"Captain Jones, we searched the suspect and he was clean. No wallet, no ID, no phone, nothing. Clean as a whistle."

"Did he give you his name?"

"No sir, he hasn't said a word."

"Okay, get some help and put him in the holding cell downstairs. He's a big son of a gun."

"Yes sir, he is."

"Hey, see if those SWAT boys are done with all those explosives. I'd like to open this airport back up, ASAP. Damn mayor is screaming his head off."

They grab Matt and escort him out of the van. Soon he's sitting in a cell underneath the San Francisco airport tarmac.

**

Captain Rogers is still trying to pick up the crate from customs.

"Hello, I'm Captain Rogers to pick up package number 287654389097380T. The shipper confirmed with you guys about me picking it up."

Agent Jack responds, "Just a minute, sir. I'll be right back, please wait."

"Is there an issue?" Captain asks.

"No sir, I just have to check something. I'll be back in a few."

"Okay, thanks. Do you need any help? I can go with you."

"Oh. No sir. Only official state employees behind this line. You have to stand behind the green line. This is a confidential and secure area. I'm sure you're high and mighty where you come from, but around here I am in charge and know what's best. Been working here for thirty-eight years."

"Okay, great, just the package would be fine."

"Yes sir."

"Dave, what are you saying?"

"I'm saying while you were on one of your ten breaks, someone came in and claimed the package. He had ID."

"Let's see who signed for it then."

"Tony Rome, it says here. That's the name labeled on the package."

"Then who is this fellow, Jack?"

"I don't know, I'll go back and ask. But he's a tall fellow and he's not going to be happy. Maybe you should come with me. He's some kind of captain."

Dave replies, "Oh no, I don't need any trouble. He's all yours."

"Well, just be ready. I may need your assistance."

"Someone already signed out for the package. It was the same person, who the package was addressed to. He had ID," Jack informs the captain.

"Are you saying that Tony Rome signed for the package?" Captain Rogers asks, very frustrated at this point.

"I'm not saying it, you did. But yes sir, that's the guy."

"When did he sign for it?"

"Listen, that is privileged information so—"

"Listen to me, little man, if I have to come across that counter it's not going to be pretty."

"Alright, alright, he signed for it about twenty minutes ago. You might be able to catch him. It's a big package."

"Okay, where's your loading dock?"

"Behind this building on Post Street."

Captain takes off in a hurry.

"Dave, that was a close one. I think he was going to clobber me."

Jack mumbles, "They don't pay me enough for this aggravation."

Captain starts swearing under his breath. Why didn't Isabella tell her brother, I was in town picking up his *package?*

Captain decides to call Tony himself.

"Is this Tony Rome, it's Bill Rogers?"

"Sure is. So Bill, what's up with our patient?"

"She's doing fine, but that's not why I'm calling. I didn't want to disturb Isabella, but are you in Boston by any chance?"

"No sir, on my way. Why do you ask?"

"Not sure how to put this. When I got to the customs office in Gloucester to pick up your package, they tell me you already signed for it."

"That's impossible. I'm not even in the state yet."

"Well, they said Tony Rome signed for it. He had ID."

"That's not good news at all. Do not tell Isabella! I bet they have a camera in there. Maybe you can get the tape and see if we can ID this fellow."

"Great idea, this should be fun. I scared that little man to death. May have to again."

"Good luck, I have complete faith in you. I'll be there soon."

Tony's phone is ringing, showing an anonymous number.

"Hello, Tony Rome here."

"It's Matt, I'm in a soothing hot tub and wanted to give you a call."

"Hey big boy, what happened to you? I've been trying to reach you."

"Not sure where to start other than you're my only phone call."

"Oh no, what happened? This day keeps getting better and better every minute."

"I don't have much time so I'll explain quickly. I was following Dylan to a location in San Francisco, and the next thing I know is, I'm drugged, and in a car at the airport full of explosives."

"What in the world is going on over there?"

"Good question, but whatever it is isn't good."

"Can you find the place you last saw Dylan?" Tony asks.

"I think so, but not anytime soon. May need some bail," Matt says.

"Alright, stay put. I will send you one of my best attorneys. One more element, someone signed out our packing crate from Namibia."

"Stay put. You're so funny. Where do you think I'm going? Just get me out of here."

"Sorry you're in a mess because of me."

"No worries, I've been in worse spots," Matt laughs. "Oh, would you call my folks. You were my only call."

"Will do, I'm calling them right now."

After a quick call to Matts folks, Tony calls Isabella.

Tony's "*Yellow Submarine*" ringtone rings out.

"Hey babe," Isabella answers.

"Hello sis, you're sounding much better. How you felling?"

"Not bad, ready to get out of here and get back home."

"I hear you. Listen, I can't find Alex or Dylan so I'm heading your way. I will be there soon."

"Okay, works for me. I'm not too worried about Alex. She's probably with Tami and Sam. Those three are inseparable."

"Possibly, but there's a lot of weird stuff going on."

"What else is going on?"

"I wanted to wait and tell you in person. No reason to alarm you. You need a lot of rest."

"Tony, tell me what you know, or else. I'd rather have the information now so I can digest it."

"Okay, well I hope you're sitting down."

"I am, plus Chloe is not here. Start talking, old man."

"Who you calling old man?"

Tony explains the missing crate and that Matt was arrested with a trunk full of explosives. "That's enough to keep you busy for now. Dwell on that and give me your thoughts when I get there."

"Holy moly, do you think it is the kingdom?"

"Yes, I do. See you soon."

**

Tony arrives in Boston and heads directly to his sister's hospital room.

"Hey sis, nice room. You getting discharged today?"

Chloe runs and jumps into the outstretched arms of her uncle.

"Hey Uncle Tony, I am so glad to see you. Are we going to ride in your plane? Please, please."

"Of course, I came up here to steal my girls and take them home. We'll make a break for it."

"Yeah," Chloe shrieks.

The nurse comes in with Isabella's final papers.

"Good news, you've been discharged. I'll get you a wheelchair."

"You guys have been awesome, and I will be writing a letter to the president of this fine establishment." Isabella knows how important it is to show appreciation for people who take care of you.

"Where's your captain friend?" Tony asks.

"Not sure, he has been on this wild goose chase trying to track down your package. I think he was looking at the tapes trying to figure out who signed for it."

"Okay, let's give him a call to see if he needs any help."

"Hey Rogers, how's it going?" Tony asks.

"Well, it's slow going. You in Boston yet?"

"Yes sir, taking my girls home. On our way to the airport. You need any help or a ride home?"

"I may take you up on that ride. What time you leaving?" Rogers asks.

"Let's meet up at Logan around three thirty p.m."

"Great, I'll be there. I have a picture of the culprit, but he's not hitting any data banks. He must be clean. I'll bring the picture with me, and I'll do some more searching at my home computer. I have a friend with the feds that can help."

"I have a few friends myself," Tony adds.

Chapter 27

CAGED

Alex and Grando are taken back to the rebel's hangout in Rockland. Suddenly a bad storm brews up and it gets wicked cold and windy. This quick weather change is not unusual, but Alex is shivering and has to get under Grando for warmth.

Grando mumbles to himself, "Now you like me," since they put Grando and Alex in the same cage. Alex stays close to Grando not only for warmth but possibly for security. She doesn't know who to trust.

"Now what?" Alex asks Grando.

"That's a good question, Alex, my ex-friend."

"What are they going to do with us?"

"I have a feeling they are watching us to see how we interact. Soon, if not already, they will confirm who I am, but the next issue is who are you? I am not yet convinced, so we shall see if you can convince the rebels."

"I have not hidden who I am."

"Yeah well, that doesn't help matters, does it?"

"What will they do once they realize who you are?"

"I most likely will be a bargaining tool. Trades are made all the time. Once the rebels capture a palace member, they usually bargain for the release of another imprisoned rebel. There is usually a trade. I am a powerful leader, so I am sure they will be making a trade soon and I'll be on my way."

"And if they don't realize how powerful you are, then what?" Alex asks, shaking from the chill.

"I am not worried. Well, somewhat worried, but once my father finds out I have been captured, everyone will be in danger. My father is the king's head bodyguard and will not let any harm come to me."

"For both our sake let's hope you are right," Alex quips.

Gaylok tells the guard to bring the girl to him and Alex is promptly brought in.

"Be careful, sir. She is very quick to kick. She knocked out four of my guards. She must be highly trained in combat, sir."

"Hello, young lady. This is a very informal meeting, and all I want is the truth so do not be alarmed. We are quite civilized here, no need for violence. What is your name?" Gaylok asks.

"Alessandra Cabrella, and I'm starving, freezing, and thirsty. Can I please have something to eat and drink?"

"Certainly." Gaylok gestures for someone to bring some food and drink.

"What are you doing traveling with a palace guard, some would say a thug or killer, named Grando? His father is Grande, the king's head bodyguard, a cutthroat killer who despises us and calls us rebels, just because we don't agree with the king."

"I did not know he was a killer. He found me. I was looking for someone and there he was." Alex replies.

"And you became instant friends with this thug?"

"Well, I wouldn't say friends, more like traveling companions."

"Traveling companions, traveling where?"

"I'm not really sure." Alex knew that answer wouldn't be well received.

"Let me get this straight—you are not sure where you're going and who you are traveling with, but you are searching for someone. I have heard you are well trained in hand to hand combat. Did I miss anything?"

"Yes I am, but I am not here to harm anyone. I am just lost looking for my friend."

"Could your friend be a Dylan Cabrella?"

"How do you know him? Have you seen him?"

"I have seen him and I gather you both are lost?"

"Can you take me to him? Is he also a prisoner here?"

"Who said you were a prisoner?"

"Well, I am in a cage," Alex says as she rolls her eyes.

"Yes, that was for your own safety."

"So, for my own safety you caged me up with a giant saber-toothed killer tiger. Really, well that seems odd to me."

"What seems odd to me is to find a brother and a sister both lost, looking for each other in the wilderness without any weapons for survival. It was as if you were transported here without you knowing it."

Alex put on her best poker face and didn't say a word.

"Listen, I do not want to harm anyone. I am just here to take my brother and grandmother back home. I do not want to get in the middle of your local issues."

"I appreciate your honesty. Now you have included your grandmother. But these are trying times and you have shown up in an inopportune moment in time. Do you know Prince Mako?"

"I have never heard of a Prince Mako. Believe it or not, I do not know any princes personally. Not that I wouldn't mind knowing a prince, possibly marrying one, but no, never heard of him."

"That seems odd that someone traveling this land does not know the name Prince Mako."

"I am from out of town."

"Ahh, that would explain it. What town are you from?"

"Florida, Key West to be exact."

"Where is that located?"

"It's south of everything."

"Is there anyone else that is missing from your family?"

"Not that I am aware of."

Gaylok pulls out the picture of Socreen and asks Alex if she knows her.

"I do indeed, that's my grandmother. Is she also a prisoner here?"

"No, she works for the queen. And I am sure she cannot be trusted, and you tell me you're related to her and are traveling with a king's thug."

"I didn't know she worked for the queen. Where is this queen?"

"She's lives in the palace, and I doubt you will be able to visit anytime soon."

"Why not?"

"Let's just say the queen would rather cut off your head than give you an audience with her. But she may be amused that you are Socreen's grandchild."

"You never answered me as to where Dylan is now."

"He is with the Trefars."

"The what? Is that a place, person, or thing?"

"Trefars are the finest warriors in the kingdom."

"Why would he be with them?"

"Next time you see him you should ask."

"Does this mean I'm free to go?"

"I have heard enough. Take her back to Grando. Let the two traveling companions hang out some more."

"No, I do not want to go back into that cage. I want to find my brother and grandmother."

"In due time, my dear, but for now I must think."

Hearing that, Alex lunged a kick straight at Gaylok's head, but he was much quicker than she would have ever expected. He easily blocks her and knocks her to the ground as she screams in pain.

"Goodbye, Alessandra Cabrella. We shall speak again."

"Okay, but I want to see my family, soon."

After she departs, Gaylok has a change of clothes brought to the cage. Grando is sitting there and doesn't move when the cage is opened.

"Turn around. I need to change clothes." Alex demands.

"Change, I don't care."

"But I don't want you looking at me while I change."

"You're starting to sound like royalty What did you find out." Grando mumbles.

"I learned you are a trained killer, and I am lucky to be alive. And they also know your name, Grando. I hear your dad is a swell guy."

"That's it. You found out my name. I already told you my name. Wow, you are a great interrogator."

"Hey, I was in no position to interrogate anyone. I was the one being interrogated. What is a Trefars?"

"Why do you ask?"

"That's where they took my brother."

"Good luck, I'm not going anywhere near those people. You are on your own."

"Why, what's wrong with them?"

"For starters, they hate the king and anyone that has anything to do with the king. Do I need to explain any further?"

"Why would they take him to the Trefars if they are so mean?"

"I don't know. Ask them. Your brother's chances of survival are minimal."

"You don't know my brother. He's so annoying they will want him to go sooner than later."

"If he annoys a Trefars, his life expectancy is zero point zero."

"At least I found out where my grandmother is."

"Good for you."

"You should be happy she works for your queen."

"The queen, really. What's her name?" Grando inquisitively asks.

"Sosheen, I think."

"Socreen."

"Yes, that's it," Alex smiles.

"She's your grandmother?"

"Yes."

"Why didn't you tell me your family works for the royals?"

"I wasn't sure where she was."

"That changes things. They'll be negotiating both our releases. They will not want to upset the king. Who did you meet with, and did you happen to ask when they are letting us out of here?"

"Someone named Gaylok."

"Gaylok, he is the head of the rebels in Rockland. I am afraid you and I aren't going anywhere anytime soon."

"But if he is the head guy then he should know I am not a rebel."

"I don't think he's concerned if you're a rebel, but he may think you and your brother are spies."

"Why don't you tell them I am not a spy?"

"He hasn't asked me and I doubt he will."

"Well he doesn't sound very civilized to me."

"Civilized is the last thing these people are, so you better realize that quickly and help me devise a plan to get us out of this cage."

"Now you're talking. What can I do to help?" Alex asks.

"Let me make sure I have all the details before we make a break for it. Your brother is a spy and your grandmother works for the queen. How do you fit into this puzzle?"

"I told you a thousand times. I didn't know my grandmother worked for the queen or that my brother Dylan is here, and it's unconceivable that he's a spy."

"Are you sure you're all related? Sounds like the left hand doesn't know what the right hand is doing."

"Don't start quoting Confucius on me."

"Confusing on you. You're confusing me. Typical w—"

"Don't say it. Do not dare say it. I know you're going to say 'woman.' You're a chauvinistic male."

"Say what? What are you raving about now?"

"I know what you're about to say."

"Wow, you are a handful. All I was going to say was a typical waste of my time talking with you. Is that what you thought I was going to say? You're the confusion, not me."

"Confucius was a great Chinese philosopher. Probably one of the greatest. You should follow his philosophy."

"I have my own philosophy. It's called, how to stay alive."

"That's not a philosophy. That's a way of life for you."

"Call it what you want."

They both fell fast asleep. Alex passed out on top of Grando since all their food was drugged.

**

Dylan wakes up and for a minute isn't sure where he is. At first, I'm not real sure where I am when I wake up. That was some strong stuff T and I smoked. I don't remember much of our conversation. I hope I didn't say too much.

"Hello Igagbee, how are your hands?" I ask.

"Hands. You seem to forget I only have one. But it is fine, thank you."

"Oh, I am so sorry. I didn't mean, well you know what I meant. I was told we are almost finished and soon I'll be heading to the palace."

"Yes, as we discussed, you are indeed ready."

"Hey Igagbee, why do you think I look so much like this Prince Mako guy?"

"Not sure. Did you ask T?"

"No, I failed to bring that up."

"Why didn't you ask him?"

"I forgot. Not sure what we talked about. Before I knew it, I was comatose after smoking some high potency pot or something."

"I have to get you ready to go. When addressing the king, show me how?"

"Really can't you show me more fighting techniques? It seems like I may need those skills just in case I'm found out to be a fraud."

"If you're found out to be a fraud, no fighting technique is going to help you because you will be dead."

"That doesn't sound good. I thought you said I was ready. Okay, but as a friend, what are my chances of surviving this mission?"

"One hundred percent success. T never fails."

I'm not worried about T failing, I'm more worried about me failing.

"Let's try a king greeting." Igagbee commands.

"Good morning, my king. I hope your day is splendid," I practice with a bow.

"Very good, and bowing makes it even better."

"Now show me the queen?"

"Good morning, Mother? How did you sleep?"

"No, no, how was your sleep?"

"Oh yes. How was your sleep, Mother?"

"Very good. After breakfast we will go directly to the archery stadium."

Now that's what I'm talking about.

We arrive at the stadium, and Igagbee directs me to take an arrow out of the quiver as someone releases the target. On command a clay-like bird is seen flying by, and I am supposed to hit the target with a single arrow. The target is moving at a quick pace, so I quickly nock my arrow and draw back and take aim. The bowstring is at full capacity and I let the arrow fly. Within seconds the target is hit and is falling to the ground. Dang, even I was impressed.

"Excellent shot, my prince." Igagbee is very pleased, and smiles approvingly at me.

While I was training at the archery stadium, word came back that Rockland was attacked. Rumor is they are looking for the prince. Seems the battle was over quickly with almost complete devastation. Without the Trefars help, the rebels in Rockland didn't have a chance.

Tabitha announces she is leaving at once. Before I could say goodbye, she was gone. She jumped on Pup and took off like a rocket. I had wondered why we just didn't fly here but it turns out only Tabitha can ride Pup. Or least that's what I was told.

Will I ever see her again?

Chapter 28

ROCKLAND

Grando and Alex are still stuck in the cage during the Rockland battle.

"Who is it attacking Gaylok and all these people?" Alex asks Grando.

"Those are the king's guards."

"Why haven't they released you? Aren't you part of the king's guard?"

"That's a good question. Let me get their attention. Maybe they don't see us caged up?"

"I don't think they can miss us. You're bigger than a house."

Alex slides under Grando scared for her life. Arrows and spears are flying everywhere. Both are still a little dazed from the drugs.

"Don't worry, little one, they will not harm me. I'm close to the king himself. Hey you, let me out of here. I am Grando, son of Grande," Grando yells at one of the guards.

Alex was hiding so well, they didn't even notice her.

"Hey you, are you not listening? Are you deaf? I am Grando, son of Grande. Get me out of here, NOW." Grando lowers his voice into his best whisper directed toward Alex. "See I have their attention. I should be set free soon."

At that the guard turns and yells to others for help. Seven of the king's guards raise their arrows and spears and throw them toward Grando.

"Wait, what are you doing? I'm Grando one of the king's guards."

Shooting a caged animal is cruel enough but this was just an outright slaughter. Grando was not only protecting Alex but trying to defend himself from the onslaught of arrows. Finally, the arrows stop and Grando falls. It didn't take long to take Grando down while he was caged.

Alex screams as one of the guards cautiously opens the cage. Alex kicks him in the head and he drops instantly. She's a bit outraged and crazed at this point. Another guard laughs as he approaches Alex, and she drops him in seconds. The next guard is much smarter and pulls back his bow, telling her to come out with her hands up or he will shoot to kill.

"Okay, okay," she says to the guard. As he gets close, she kicks him in the side of the head. Soon another four have her surrounded and throw her into another cage. Alex could see Gaylok running around bellowing orders, taking on two and three guards at a time. Before long he was easily overtaken. It was like a massacre—Gaylok and Grando were left to perish. The king had sent over one hundred thousand troops. The Rockland rebels, without the Trefars, could not defend such an attack.

The king's lead guard, Commander Tazer, tells his lieutenant "Fall out. Let's go. We are finished here, and so are they. Back to the palace at once."

"Commander Tazer, we have not found any sign of the prince, but we have taken a few prisoners. One of them was caged with Grando and we thought it was going to be the prince, but it was not. It was a young female. Shall we kill her?"

"No, take her with us. She may be of use. Maybe she knows where the prince is? I will catch up. I want to look around."

Commander Tazer finds a barely alive Gaylok and starts with his own interrogation. The only question is the prince's whereabouts. Since Gaylok has no idea, he is unaided and clings to life. Grando was left behind in the cage to an inevitable death.

Alex is thrown into another cage and is beyond frustrated. She wants to know where they are taking everyone. And sitting next to her is a young boy, who looks stoic and fearless.

"Where are they taking us?" Alex asks him.

"Back to the palace. Most of us will become workers, others will be put in the dungeon."

"Why would they put me in dungeon? I have done nothing wrong," Alex says to her fellow prisoner.

"You will have your chance to explain your situation to the king."

"What is your name?" Alex asks.

"Tinker."

"Yours?"

"I'm Alessandra Cabrella."

"That's a pretty name."

"Thank you. I like Tinker."

"Where are your parents?"

"They are dead. I saw them fall in Rockland."

"I'm so sorry. How old are you?"

"I'm nine." Tinker puffs up his chest.

"I can see you're a very brave and strong young man."

"Thank you, Alessandra Cabrella."

"And smart."

"Yes. My mom taught me everything about the royals just in case something happened to her."

"Sounds like your mom was a very smart lady."

"Yes ma'am, she was the best." Tinker starts to cry.

Alex holds little Tinker by her side and brushes his hair with her hands.

After a brief cry, Tinker looks at Alex and says, "I've never seen you in the village before. Are you the reason we were attacked?"

"Of course not. At least I hope not."

"But why were you caged?"

That question took Alex by surprise. "It was a case of mistaken identity. Once I meet with the king it will be resolved. Why, has someone said something?"

"There was talk that you were a spy for the king but were captured in time."

"I am not a spy. I've never met this king."

Alex is getting frustrated that she is even having this conversation with a nine-year-old. But if he thinks this, what might the others be thinking? Alex starts to recall all the events that had taken place since she arrived in this new land. Most of the time she has been caged. She looks out across the horizon and can see barren land. Caves, rocks, and hills—it looks like the western part of the USA but without any roads or houses. All the streams and waterways look dried up. There is no sun in the sky, but every now and then a strange-looking bird flies overhead.

**

Tabitha and Pup survey the situation from the air and they cannot believe the devastation. It looks like a king's squadron was heading back to the palace. The damage didn't look promising for finding survivors. And if anyone did survive, they were probably taken back to the palace.

Tabitha's biggest concern is Gaylok. She is relieved to locate him still alive, but he looks half dead.

Tabitha says, "I am so sorry I was not here to protect you," while holding Gaylok's head. "Why attack now?"

"It seems they have lost the prince," a smiling Gaylok replies.

"Well, that explains why T wants Dylan the Swimmer to impersonate the prince," Tabitha remarks.

"Yes, he is wiser than most."

"Is there anything I can get you to make you more comfortable?"

"Just seeing you again was my only desire. Thank you for coming," Gaylok mumbles.

"I wish we could have arrived sooner. I have sent Pup to find any survivors."

She promises Gaylok that she and Pup will take revenge. This disturbs Gaylok as he would prefer her to wait for T, who will surely have a response.

Tabitha finds Pup wandering the village, which is completely destroyed, but Pup did find something interesting and shows Tabitha. They both stop in front of the giant cage and see a giant saber-toothed tiger lying still.

"Is he dead?" Tabitha asks Pup.

"No, but close to it."

"Who is it?"

"It's Grando, son of Grande."

"Why would he be in this cage and not be released by the king's guards? I bet Grande will not be happy about this."

"Grando was caged with a young girl who they took as a prisoner."

"How did a young girl survive in this cage with that beast?"

"You haven't asked what her name is?" Pup grins.

"Okay, what is her name?"

"Alessandra Cabrella," Pup replies.

"Why does that name sound familiar?"

"She is the sister of Dylan the Swimmer."

"My oh my, this is getting interesting. Who are these Cabrella's, and why all of a sudden are they appearing? We should alert T at once."

Pup takes off to inform T.

Tabitha stays behind, doubting that a second attack is coming from the king since the village was completely destroyed. She just hopes Gus wasn't a part of this. Gus is Tabitha's secret boyfriend. Once Pup departs, Tabitha heads back to stay close by Gaylok.

Chapter 29

SOCREEN

S ocreen (otherwise known as Grandmother or Elizabeth Cabrella), one of the queen's handmaidens, begins to wonder if her savior has returned. Whoever came through Sector 37 has not been caught, which in itself is a minor miracle. Socreen is trying to recall how long she has been in this awful place, watching and caring for this monster, who calls herself queen. If she could only tell the real story, but she cannot since the queen would slay everyone that Socreen loves.

Socreen has made a few special friends in this place but her favorite is Siena. Siena, also a handmaiden for the queen and is young, beautiful, kind, sweet, and full of life. Socreen, on the other hand, is getting old and feeble. They work side by side, two handmaidens at the queen's beck and call every minute of every day.

Siena has lived in the palace almost her entire life. Both her parents passed when she was very young and being the only child, she showed up at the palace doors all by herself at five years old. And in a rare weak moment, little Siena was allowed into the palace and started a friendship with the prince. Siena is only a year older than the prince. She was five and the prince was four. The prince and Siena grew up playing together, and Socreen essentially raised them both. One night she confided in Socreen that she was in love with the prince. Socreen told her to keep it between themselves. Many co-workers in the palace likewise care and watch over Siena.

Socreen watches the queen run around, yelling orders, and screaming. Not that this is any different from any other day, but something has her in complete turmoil. She wonders if her Michael, Prince Mako, has caused the queen's current misery. He was supposed to be transported to America, but it seems something went wrong. She tutored the prince with as much information as she could about her country. Their lands are completely different so she wanted him to be educated. But why would he be sent to Sector 37, Rockland?

It seems she's been in this place for a hundred years, but it's actually been sixteen years since Isabella, her daughter, and she were visiting the kingdom. One big problem is that Elizabeth was stuck behind, and prays Isabella got away safely.

Isabella just loved this land. She enjoyed speaking with the animals, being a veterinarian and all. Years ago, this place used to be extremely beautiful and everyone was so nice. Now it seems upside down, as Socreen is getting older and misses her man, Vincenzo.

Life here has changed dramatically, and not for the better. Everyone blames the changes on the king's new bride, an evil woman at best. The king's first wife died suddenly and some quietly accuse his new bride of murder, but dare not speak it out loud. The king has been consumed with his new, wicked bride, and everyone has suffered for her madness.

Socreen plugs along and prays her knight in shining armor will one day take her away from here. They'd better hurry—this place is getting more and more dangerous every waking moment. She is not allowed out of the palace, so she knows little about the outside world these days. She did hear that since all of the lakes have dried up, the king has worked out a plan to acquire additional water. That's why the prince was sent back to America.

Socreen begins to dwell on the current world she lives in called the kingdom. This land used to be called the Land of Lakes, but now everyone calls it the Kingdom of Bonita. With no significant rainfall, this land has all but dried up. In its prime it was so unique and beautiful. There is no sun, but they have four moons. Each moon rotates in any direction at any given time, which means one can be up while the other three are down. Or all four are up or all four down with no consistency, so you never know if it's day or night. The royals like it that way as it keeps all their subjects completely confused most of the time.

Rumor has it that these moons have fought among each other and that is why the rotation changes so often. A local story is that in the beginning there was only one moon, named Lightner. During King Primis's reign as the first king, he lost his wife, Queen Tafnut, to the creature Lantern. King Primis cursed the moon, the land, and all its inhabitants. Shortly afterwards a second moon was overhead. He named the second moon Queenie, after his deceased wife, Queen Tafnut. But at the time no one realized that she was a great sorcerer who always wanted to be in charge of the weather, so many think she may have gotten her wish.

Soon after, both moons were competing, fighting, arguing, and causing huge disruptions to the climate until they finally came to terms. They decided to split the kingdom in half. Queenie took one half and Lightner took over the other half. But eventually Queenie got greedy and decided to shade a little more than her half, and thinking Lightner would not know the difference, she kept creeping into his area. But in reality Lightner was getting very annoyed and upset.

Lightner was an extremely kind moon to give Queenie half of the kingdom since it was all his to begin with, but he got so furious that he split himself in two. This may sound like old folklore, but how can anyone dispute it. Are there four moons anywhere in one land?

Some have said that Queenie and Lightner were a married couple. The local story also explains the additional two moons, which are said to be their offspring's. They had one boy, Moonie, and one girl, Moonbeam. Moonbeam never leaves her father's side, and Moonie is always next to his mother. The four moons are never together anymore. There is no rhyme or reason to the patterns of the moon.

One could actually climb the tallest mountain in the kingdom and almost touch a moon, but it is prohibited by the king. Some have tried and suffered a horrible death for their foolishness.

All four moons can speak in a dialect unknown to most. Only T understands moon lingo, and can point out which moon is which.

It hasn't rained in the kingdom in over five hundred days, and yet the windstorms can be wicked. Even though there is no sun, the moons control the weather, and it's extremely unpredictable. Lightner and Moonbeam control hot, cold, and wind. Queenie and Moonie control cold and wind. Supposedly it will only rain if Lightner and Queenie reunite.

The past and current kings have employed some rather large creatures for their dirty work. Some of the tallest creatures work for the king and are called Kondos, which is a fitting name, since they are the size of a condominium.

Kondos answer to no one else but the king, and now the queen. They never before would listen or take orders from the queen, but now they do, and it's not a good thing. These creatures are quite large, and very loyal. Kondos range from twenty to ninety feet tall. Most are meaner than hornets and do not like anyone, with the exception of royalty. When Socreen first saw a Kondo, she screamed so loud she became comatose, and started to shake.

Graeters are another unique creature to the kingdom. They are like bulldozers. Their nickname is "Excavators," they can dig for miles. They have huge mouths and carry the dirt and sand in their mouths as they dig. Big in stature and stubborn, they love to argue, hate water, and love gum.

There is a secret room in the main palace that houses artifacts, and books from the upper land or concrete world. The kingdom has no electronic gadgets or any of the conveniences back home in the States. No fast food, no cell phones, no malls, no banks, no credit cards, no money, no cars, no planes, no TV, no computers, no medical facilities, no pharmacies, are just a few differences.

So, Socreen is stuck here in the kingdom until someone comes to rescue her. Her closest friend is the lovely Siena but she has made another friend from the outside world—a beautiful butterfly. She is very colorful and stunning, a lovely black and white with a red stripe. She is an 88 butterfly, and her name is Carolyn. Carolyn flies into Socreen's room and is Socreen's main communication with the outside world beyond these palace walls.

"Hello Carolyn, any news today, my precious?" Socreen asks.

"Yes indeed, Socreen. It seems Sector 37 has been penetrated and many think it is the lost prince. No one is for sure if the prince is in Sector 37, but there has been another to come through that sector. She has been undetected by the king, and I have her name."

"Oh my, what's her name?"

Socreen is so excited, it has to be Isabella. She has returned to save her.

"She goes by the name of Alessandra Cabrella," Carolyn answers.

Socreen is stunned when hearing the name of her granddaughter for the first time in over fifteen years.

"Are you sure about this?" Socreen asks.

"Yes, Socreen. The prince cannot be located and this is causing quite a stir. Is everything okay, Socreen?"

Tears are flowing down Socreen's cheeks. Then she hears, "get in here now you old hag, hurry," as the queen starts screaming.

"Yes, my dear Carolyn, everything will be fine. Thank you so much. You are a lifesaver. Get away before you are seen."

"I will keep you updated as best as possible. It's getting dangerous everywhere. I'm afraid a war is ready to break out."

"Yes, my queen, what is you need?" Socreen replies while running into her quarters.

"I have a meeting with Trigon, and I want to look my best so get my new gown out, and hurry. You're getting slower and slower. What good are you to me if the prince is not found, you old slug!"

Siena announces that Trigon is here to see the queen.

"Trigon, thank you for taking the time to see your lowly queen."

"It is I who should thank you, your highness," Trigon responds.

The queen claps her hands, and tells everyone to leave her and Trigon at once. It is usually not a good thing when Trigon is around. She is an enormous dragon and very faithful to the queen. She does all the queen's dirty work.

"It seems my earlier plan didn't work. If you fail me again, I will have your head on a platter, my lovely Trigon." Then the queen leans over and whispers to Trigon. "Let's try this again. I need the prince to have an accident and it has to look like the Trefars are the culprits. Those Trefars are pesky little vermin. We have had this discussion, and yet you failed me."

"Yes, my queen. I am sorry, but the first time a pesky Trefars stopped me."

"Well, try, try again."

"Yes, my queen."

"If I can get rid of the prince before his birthday party, it will make it easier for my plans to progress. Any word from your brother, Tragoon?"

"No, my queen."

"He's worthless! Now go and do not return until you succeed."

"Yes, my queen." Trigon departs.

Chapter 30

ACCIDENT

Torch informs everyone that it should be a smooth flight back to Key West. Tony, Isabella, Chloe, and Captain Rogers all sit back while enjoying the luxurious flight home in Tony's plane, Lucy. Isabella and Tony never really had a free moment to talk with Chloe clinging onto every word, plus Captain Rogers was on board. Not much was said, and everyone was so tired it wasn't long before everyone was asleep. After a smooth landing, Captain and Tony have a brief conversation about the missing package and the picture of the individual signing for the crate, and agree to stay in contact.

"Hey Bella, I've got to fuel up and head out to see Matt. He's in a bind and this may be another piece of the puzzle," Tony explains to Isabella.

"Okay, let me know what you find out. I'm going home to see if I can find any other clues."

"Clues for what, Mom?" Chloe asks.

"Clues about the break-in, sweetie."

Isabella yells back Torch to thank him for the flight home. Torch and Tony are fueling up to head back to San Francisco. Tony is suspicious as to why Isabella is taking all this extremely well.

Isabella and Chloe walk into their Key West home and both immediately wonder where Alex and Dylan are. Chloe was so excited to see Hari and Teri, that they almost licked her to death.

"Mom, these are the best dogs ever," Chloe smiles while hugging Hari.

Teri was still limping, and with all that excitement she got winded quickly and lay back down.

"Watch out with Teri. She still has stiches," Isabella reminds Chloe who cries out giggling, as Hari tackles her to the floor. The house looks like they have been robbed with stuff thrown all over the place. The broken window must have been their way in.

"Hari, come to my room, please."

Hari jumps off Chloe and runs into Isabella's room.

"Okay Hari, where did you hide it?" Isabella asks.

"I hid it from Tony. Here it is." Hari drags the pillowcase into Isabella's room.

"What is that all over this? It looks like hair."

"It's Elizabeth's hair."

"That's it, he used her hair. Oh my goodness, that was the missing piece, Mother's hair. Dad figured it out and didn't tell anyone."

Human hair was woven into the blue material to round out the blue pillowcase.

"Hari, did it work?"

"It worked, alright. Alex used it," Hari tells Isabella.

"Okay. What about Dylan?"

"Not sure, but chances are good he also used it. I couldn't get out of your house quick enough to check on Dylan, so it was me that busted your window."

"That's okay, I understand."

"One more detail you should know. Somebody who looked just like Dylan was here. Alex brought him home thinking he was Dylan, but it wasn't. By the time he awoke, Alex had taken a nap on the blue pillowcase, and she transported."

"So where is this look alike?" Isabella asks.

"He took one of your cars to the airport and flew to San Francisco. I confirmed this when I spoke with Tony. He was very kind and wanted me to talk but I wasn't saying anything."

"You think he was from the kingdom?"

"Yes, I do. He could be Dylan's twin brother. The resemblance was uncanny. He was some type of prince."

"I better call Tony and confirm something with him. Thanks, Hari."

"Are you okay? You look flushed?"

"I'll be okay, it's just been a rough couple of days."

Hari just nods and heads back to play with Chloe.

Tony hears Isabella's ringtone, "*Well, you don't know what we can find, why don't you come with me little girl, on a magic carpet ride.*"

"What's up, Sis?" Tony answers.

"Hari just confirmed that the guy in San Francisco was probably Michael and not Dylan."

"Matt was right then. Are you okay?" Tony asks, concerned.

"Tony, you know what this means? He's alive and you have to bring him to me."

"I know, Sis. I'm on it. Now I've got to find him. Should be no problem in a small city like San Francisco."

"With Matt at your side, I have complete faith in you two."

"Thanks, Sis, I hear you. Now stay put and I will be contacting you soon."

"Sure thing, talk later, bro."

Isabella had no intention of staying put. She started to admire her dads handywork on the blue pillowcase. What a thing of beauty! All she has to do is come up with a plan to tell Chloe why she was leaving and when she will return. This should be interesting. Isabella decides to call Gloria, her assistant.

"Hey Gloria, I have to go back out of town unexpectedly. Can you come over tomorrow and watch over Chloe until I get back? Take her to the office with you and she'll be fine."

"Oh, no problem. She helps a lot around here—it will be my pleasure."

"Thanks, Gloria, I should return in a few days. You can both hang out either at your place or here, whatever works."

"Sounds good. Teri is making a slow but excellent recovery," Gloria informs her.

"I can see that. Great work. Thanks again for all your help while I was down and out."

Isabella is thinking about telling Captain Rogers about her car but is sure he will ask too many questions. Then Isabella hears Chloe shouting out.

"Mom, you better get over here!"

"What is it, dear?"

"Look, it's strange. All the glass from the broken window is on the outside. It was as if someone was trying to get out."

"Oh my, that is strange. Maybe the burglar put a suction cup on the window and pulled it out. You know they cut the panes now and reach in. Maybe it broke the entire glass."

"That's probably how the burglar got inside," Chloe suggests.

"You're probably right. I'll call Captain Rogers and let him know. Thanks, luv."

When Chloe leaves the room, Hari walks in and again apologizes for the broken window.

"I heard something coming from Vincenzo's house and had to check it out."

"I understand. It's getting repaired."

"I didn't get there in time." Hari hangs his head.

"It's okay, I'm going to take care of everything," Isabella assures Hari.

Isabella has decided that she must depart at once and she is taking Hari with her. Teri needs time to heal, otherwise she would take them both. This way Teri can watch over Chloe. Isabella is determined to find Dylan, Alessandra, and her Mother. It seems everyone is there except her. And this has turned into a fiasco. Hari barks and runs out of the room as Chloe enters.

"Mom, why haven't Dylan and Alex come home yet? I don't understand."

"Sweetie, they're probably enjoying this beautiful evening. Don't worry. It's getting late, young lady, so off to bed." Isabella kisses Chloe's forehead.

"Okay Mom, see you in the morning. I hope Alex is home when I get up."

"I'm sure she will be."

Isabella has Hari and Teri in her room, trying to explain the plan to them.

"Teri, at midnight, Hari and I will go. I have everything packed, and we will make this an evacuation plan. Once we get there and get some intel, we can go from there. Who knows if they're together or not? Alex and Dylan could be. They probably haven't wandered far from Grock. Not sure about Mom. Let's just hope they're all safe and secure."

"It doesn't sound like much of a plan," Hari responds.

"She doesn't have much to go on, so leave her alone. You should have never let Alex go by herself to begin with, so hush," Teri remarks.

Hari hangs his head, "sorry."

"It's alright. I know it's rudimentary, but I don't know where they are and it's not like going to the mall to pick someone up. I will need a lot of help and that's why I'm bringing Hari. I would bring you to Teri, but you're still healing and I doubt you're ready for any type of conflict. I know you hate to be apart but I really need Hari by my side. And this way you can keep an eye on Chloe."

"I wouldn't see it any other way. I'll watch over Chloe and you guys take care of business. I need a break from this droopy guy. He has that gloomy look on his face every day. I'm going to be fine," Teri replies.

"It's been so long since I've visited the kingdom, it's hard for me to recall what I need to pack. I hope I haven't forgotten anything? Let's all meet in my room at eleven thirty tonight."

Hari bolts out of the room and returns with Lil Magik in his mouth. He drops it in front of Isabella.

"Oh yeah, I'll need that. Thanks, I'm somewhat flustered, I almost forgot. Hopefully Big Magik is still with Grock," Isabella smiles.

For some reason, Chloe couldn't sleep and wakes up around eleven fifty p.m. after hearing sounds coming from her mom's room. She decides to investigate, since she is confident one of the voices she hears is Alex.

"How does this sound, guys? I'm going to leave a note for Bill, otherwise he will start snooping around," Isabella says and then reads the note out loud.

"Hey Bill, driving to Miami to take the kids on a little diving trip. I promised them I would, and since I was down and out, I owe them. If urgent leave me a message, and I will call you back, cell service unknown. I'm sorry I didn't tell you on the plane but wasn't sure if taking Chloe or not. PS: You know us women change our minds a million times per day, luv Bella."

"At least that would put the car in the correct location," Isabella reminds Hari and Teri.

Teri suggests, "Take out the 'I'll call you back' sentence. Just put in cell service unreliable.'"

"Sounds good, thanks, Teri."

All Chloe can think about is seeing her older sister Alex as she runs toward Mom's bedroom door.

"Okay, ready, grab the rope and let's go," Isabella comments.

Teri turns and is about to say something since she can sense someone coming, but it is too late. Teri tried to move toward the bedroom door just as Chloe burst into the room screaming, "Alex, I miss you," and Chloe suddenly stops and grabs the end of the rope, thinking it was a game of some sort.

Teri stands there in disbelief, thinking she should have stopped her.

**

"Oh Chloe, what are you doing here?" a sad Isabella remarks.

"Sorry Mom, I heard voices and I thought it was Alex. Where are we?"

EPILOGUE

My entire family is now in the kingdom. My mother, Isabella (Princess Xandra), my grandmother (Elizabeth, Socreen), my older sister, (Alessandra, Alex), and my younger sister (Chloe), who transported with mom. All I have to do is find everyone and get them back home to Key West, Florida. The Trefars are grooming me into Prince Mako, and any day I will make my appearance before the king and queen.

There is a vast difference between the kingdom and back home. In the kingdom there is no money, no TV, no fast-food, no malls, no cell phones, no internet, no video games, no cigarettes, no soft drinks, no bottled water, no McDonalds, no Starbucks, no automobiles and no airplanes, just to name a few differences. Electrical gadgets are nonexistent. The only mass transportation is the subway.

The time is present—day but the kingdom seems like the medieval period. No clocks, or watches, just unique horn blasts to alert you as to what is happening next. No guns or cannons or explosives. All combat is hand-to-hand or bow and arrow.

The weather changes constantly. No sun and stars but since the four moons move around so much, a storm can brew any second and last for months, days, or minutes. Usually, the only time the weather will be calm is when the moons are asleep. Many storms can rival any Category 5 hurricane. Since stormy season is ongoing, no one knows when a storm will hit. There are no news stations forecasting the weather, so everyone must be prepared at all times. Same goes for the beautiful weather—it is quite radiant.

At birth, everyone gets a UPC code imprinted or tattooed on their arm for identification. It is mandatory. The only ones that don't have UPC codes are the royal family, most animals, and the Trefars. If caught without one, it could be grounds for death. As part of your UPC code, everyone has an assigned day to visit the doctor. You can only visit the doctor on that day. Everything is run by the UPC code from purchasing items to annual physicals. There are no emergency rooms or clinics. All visits are preplanned, so if by chance you're sick before or after your assigned visit, you're just plain out of luck.

Good news is that almost every village has their own medical personnel. They use natural herbs. There are no pills, like Tylenol, or any antibiotics. That's why Mom is so popular. The main medical clinic is in the palace, and it's for the royal family plus any current personnel that work closely with the royals.

All factories are run by the king. The factories provide materials for the palace, food, clothing, and a few other items. Every factory has a medical clinic for newborns, so they can place the UPC codes. Most of the inhabitants work for the king, so it's convenient to bring all their children to the factory for daycare if needed.

Schools are located in every factory from daycare to adulthood. Someone is considered to have reached adulthood when they become sixteen. What most of the schools teach is how to become a factory worker or a store employee. They teach folks to be employees of the king, and that's it. Not a lot of expanded learning.

No magazines, no newspapers, or books to read outside of school. Everything is supplied at the school. If you are caught stealing a book, it's death.

Animals are used instead of machines. For example, Graeters are used for digging and excavating. Kondos are for taking care of tall spaces. There is much more but so far this is what I have learned or figured out on my own.

Yoga is very popular. The entire kingdom comes to a complete halt and everyone is allowed to participate in a yoga session, including human and nonhuman.

Alex found grandmother first but has been imprisoned and will not be much help. Now, how does she escape the dungeon and grab grandmother and transport back home? While imprisoned, she will have plenty of time to think of a plan. But what she doesn't realize is someone from her past has surfaced. Alex had visited the kingdom with her mother when she was young, and played with others that lived there. One friend that has never forgotten her is now grown up and is one of the palace guards.

Isabella's brother, Dr. Tony Rome, is still back in the States trying to figure out how to transport into the kingdom. Tony changed his name many years ago from Cabrella to Rome. Tony and his friend and confidante Matt are found by the huge male dragon, Tragoon, and their fate is unknown. It doesn't look good for those two best friends.

The queen is getting more and more agitated while seeking additional power. She must rid of the king and prince so she can become ruler over the kingdom. Why she needs more power is beyond comprehension, but it is causing trouble for all the inhabitants. Trigon, the sister of Tragoon, is loyal to the queen and does all her dirty work for her.

Prince Mako has arrived in the States and is enjoying America much more than his beloved kingdom. He may never return home. He has freedom, which is a luxury that was not available to him while in the kingdom. He and Grull have started the process to detonate an explosive in the States. This is going to cause quite an uproar.

**

Does Dylan, Alex, or Isabella get their entire family home safely? Will all the Cabrella's endure? Will Grandpa ever see his wife again? Does Gaylok or Grando survive? Is Dylan going to fool all the council members in the palace? Does the real prince re-appear in the kingdom as Dylan is trying to convince his father, the king and his mother, the wicked queen, that he is Prince Mako?

These answers and more are in the second novel,
The Blue Pillow Case in the Kingdom.

CAST OF CHARACTERS

Alessandra Cabrella (Alex, 21-year-old daughter of Isabella)
Amy (Matt's wife)
Angelina (housekeeper)
Ashley Granger, Dr. (Boston Scientific Lab)
Beauregard (Beau, Captain of Navy ship)
Bleeker, Ms. (high school teacher)
Blinky (airplane pilot)
Bradley (attorney)
Brandi (Labrador)
Bruden (bear)
Bruno (Italian bully)
Brutus (Dogo Argentino)
Caitlin (T's elephant)
Calloway, Mr. (high school teacher)
Calif (king's guard apprentice)
Captain Rogers (Key West police chief)
Captain Jones (airport police chief)
Carl (school bully)
Carolyn (88 butterfly)
Cato (snow leopard, king's guard apprentice)
Chloe Cabrella (10-year-old daughter of Isabella)
Christi (Tony's ex-wife)
Christina (crab)
Cranky (Trefars, guardian of the west gate)
Crate (king's assistant)
Damien (school bully)
Dave (customs agent)
Donald McFuller (classmate of Dylan)
Dr. Donald (veterinarian specialist)
Duke (Vincenzo's friend)
Dylan Michael Cabrella (15-year-old son of Isabella)
Elizabeth Cabrella (Socreen, Liz, Lizzy, Vincenzo's wife, mother of
   Isabella)
Everette, Mrs. (Jonny's mother)
Flobak (Prince Mako's American chaperon)
Gaylok (rebel leader)

Ginger (German Shepherd)

Gloria (veterinarian assistant)

Grande (30-foot saber-toothed tiger, father of Grando)

Grando (20-foot saber-toothed tiger, son of Grande, king's guard
     apprentice)

Grock (rock hut)

Grull (bright white hairless albino)

Hank (high school janitor)

Hari (German Shepherd)

Harkin (assistant principal)

Igagbee (Trefars, Dylan's handler)

Isabella Cabrella (Bell, Bella, Princess Xandra, veterinarian; mother of
     Dylan, Chloe, and Alessandra; Vincenzo and Elizabeth's daughter)

Jack (customs agent)

Jacob (Key West policeman)

Jake (pirate)

Jamal (jungle guide)

Jani (jungle guide)

Jayla (pirate)

Jelab (prince's valet)

JJ (Jimmy Johnson, school bully)

Jonny Everette (Dylan's best friend)

Kaptuk (200-year-old cheetah, King's Guard master instructor)

Kelly (receptionist)

King Primis (first king of the kingdom)

Lantern (creature in the kingdom)

Lightner (moon)

Leon (friend of Alessandra)

Maggie (Key West police department assistant)

Mark Clancey (high school student)

Mario Quagliatino (Italian big shot)

Master Zavker (swordsman)

Matt Robertson (Mathew, Tony Rome's associate)

Mayo Twins (tiger sharks)

Moonbeam (3rd moon)

Moonie (4th moon)

Moore, Dr. (Boston hospital MD)

Paul (prison guard)

Prince Mako (Michael)

Puddin (20-foot female Kondo)
Pup (young female dragon, Tabitha's companion)
Queen Tafnut (first queen of the kingdom)
Queenie (2nd moon)
Sam (Samantha, friend of Alessandra and Tami)
Samantha Stoner (Violet's mom)
Shai (teaching assistant for king's guard apprentice's)
Siena (queen's handmaiden)
Socreen (Elizabeth Cabrella)
Sophiabee (Trefars, mother of Igagbee)
Strunza, Ms. (Italian nurse)
T (Trefars leader)
Tabitha (Pup's companion)
Tami (friend of Alessandra and Sam)
Tank (Trefars)
Tara (T's mother, 400-year-old Trefars)
Taylor (high school student)
Tazer (commander of king's guards)
Teri (Rottweiler)
Tinker (young man from Rockland)
Tobi (elephant)
Tom (assistant swim coach)
Tommy McFuller (high school student)
Tony Rome, Dr. (Anthony, archaeologist; Isabella's older brother;
    Vincenzo and Elizabeth's son)
Torch (airplane pilot)
Tragoon (adult male dragon, Trigon's brother)
Trigon (adult female dragon, Tragoon's sister)
Troads (froglike creatures)
Vincenzo Cabrella (Elizabeth's husband, grandpa)
Violet (Dylan's love interest and schoolmate)
Wally (prison guard)
Zetha (king's guard apprentice)

ABOUT THE AUTHOR

The mystical and enchanting Tennessee mountains of his childhood home inspired Roger Lawrence Quay to write fantasy novels. The author delights in sharing his storytelling with young adult and adult readers alike. Roger enjoys life with his wife and best friend, Carol, at their oak-arbored retreat in Mandarin, Florida. Learn more at OneIronPress.com. Email comments and questions to RLQ@OneIronPress.com.

The Blue Pillow Case is the first novel in a trilogy series, followed by *The Blue Pillow Case in the Kingdom* and *The Blue Pillow Case Is Closed*. Available from your favorite retailer and through OneIronPress.com.

Made in the USA
Coppell, TX
11 June 2021